WEST BY RAIL

A Brother's Wish

BOOK 2
HOME ON THE RANGE SERIES

Rosie Bosse lives and writes on a ranch in northeast Kansas with her best friend and husband of many years. Her books intertwine history with fiction as she creates stories of the Old West. She believes the sign of a good book is one that pulls you in and holds you until the end. May this second novel in her Home on the Range series be one of those books.

WEST BY RAIL

A Brother's Wish

Rosie Bosse

**POST ROCK
PUBLISHING**

ISBN: Soft Cover – 978-1-958227-33-6
ISBN: eBook – 978-1-958227-30-5
Revised Second Edition
First printed 2020, Revised Second Edition published March 2024

POST ROCK
PUBLISHING

Post Rock Publishing
17055 Day Rd.
Onaga, KS 66521

www.rosiebosse.com

I dedicate this book to our soldiers, those fighting men and women who give so much to make our lives better, and who often carry scars no one can see.

Courage

Courage is such a little word for all it really holds,
The strength to do what's truly right, and you often stand alone.

It is pride in what you stand for—a belief in what is right,
That truth is truth despite the cost, that it will rise above the fight.

It's easy to just smile and nod or even turn away,
And when the tide turns, pat the backs of those whose efforts paved the way.

But those who hammer out the roads and shade it with their valor,
Those are the folks I want to know—the ones who proudly fly their colors.

Rosie Bosse

Prologue

West by Rail, A Brother's Wish is the second novel in my Home on the Range series. It begins where *North to Cheyenne, The Long Road Home* ended. As in the first novel, most of the characters are fictional. However, I did intertwine interesting people from the past into the storyline. With some characters, I created a personality for them based on their true stories. In other cases, the personality is fictional.

This story takes place in 1870, during the beef boom in Wyoming Territory.

Wyoming, Where Cattle Ruled

As people moved west, the beef industry grew. These newcomers, who included settlers and soldiers, increased the demand for beef. The expanding rail system allowed fresh meat to be shipped longer distances safely. The Civil War, with the necessity to feed large numbers of soldiers, encouraged the centralization of the beef-packing industry.

In Texas, the exodus of young men to aid in the war effort meant fewer cowboys to manage the large herds. In addition, the Union control of the Mississippi River cut off the Texas beef supply to the Confederate Army. These two things resulted in a glut of longhorn cattle in Texas.

By 1865, the end of the Civil War, a longhorn in Texas sold for $2 to $6 per head while the same three-year-old steer with just a little more meat on it would bring $86 in the East.

When the Union Pacific Railroad decided to run its rails through Cheyenne instead of Denver, the demand for beef increased even more. The extermination of the buffalo also opened more grassland and forced the Indians to be more reliant on government beef. The cattle industry was lucrative, and investors swarmed to capitalize on the profits.

Unfortunately, as the value of cattle increased, cattle rustling became more prevalent. However, with a growing population, conflicts between cattlemen and rustlers were increasingly settled in a court of law instead of with a rope and a sturdy tree.

Cost of Land

Plantations in Georgia after the Civil war were selling for $50 to $100 per acre. These amounts were based on location and improvements. Improvements included anything attached to the ground that made the daily operation of the plantation run smoother. This meant fences and buildings added value. Many of the southern plantations were now barren land as much of the South had been decimated when the warring armies fought back and forth over the fields. In addition, General Sherman's "scorched earth" policy targeted civilian infrastructure as well as military installations. That policy disrupted the Confederacy's economy and wrecked their transportation system. It did help break the back of the South and contributed to its surrender. However, the repercussions lasted much longer as the South fought to rebuild in a devastated economy.

Land in the West was much cheaper than in the East, even after the war. While I did not find an exact amount that land was selling for around Cheyenne in 1870, I estimated it to be $7 to $8 per acre. $12 was certainly too high.

Barney Ford, Ex-Slave and Entrepreneur

The Ford Restaurant in Cheyenne, owned and operated by Barney Ford, burned in 1870. Cheyenne was only three years old, and the massive fire destroyed two city blocks. Ford was one of the few business owners who had fire insurance, and he rebuilt the Ford House quickly. He then sold it in 1871 and turned his attention toward the growing city of Denver. His send-off parade and writeup in the local paper when he left Cheyenne showed how much he was loved and respected by the community.

I continued Barney Ford's friendship with the fictional Rankin family in this book. I did take liberty with Mr. Ford's personality based on the articles I read about him.

Barney Ford was an incredible man with a tenacious spirit. During his lifetime, he became one of the wealthiest men in the West.

A Westward Flow of People

Many of the soldiers who fought in the Civil War migrated west. Some were ramblers who followed the wind while others were seeking a new life. The West called to the free spirits of those seeking adventure, opportunity, and open spaces. Doctors and surgeons were part of that migration.

Outlaws and thieves followed the movement west as well. They sought to get rich off the backs of the emigrants. The West provided them with new opportunities and many places to hide.

The flow of people from the East to the West increased at the end of the Civil War, and rail transportation aided that movement even more.

New Words to Describe Migration

Noah Webster published his first dictionary, *An American Dictionary of the English Language*, in 1828. He included his newly invented words, immigrate and emigrate.

In 1806, he took the word migrate with all its variations and gave his new words, immigrate and emigrate, specific meaning through an extensive study of word origins. The United States was a young country, and the strong policy beliefs Webster held as well as his own historical experiences affected his results.

Webster made space, time, and purpose fundamental parts of his definitions. His definition of immigrate was "to remove into a country" while his definition of emigrate was "to remove from place to place."

You will see both immigrants and emigrants mentioned here. Immigrants were people who came to the United States from another country seeking a better life. Emigrants were citizens who were established in this country but uprooted their families to seek a new life further west. These definitions have become blurred over time, but Noah Webster's 1800s definition is what I am following in this story.

Rails West

The First Transcontinental Railroad was completed on May 10, 1869. It was originally known as the Pacific Railroad and later as the Overland Route. It ran west from Council Bluffs, Iowa to Promontory Summit in Utah Territory. It was met by the rails running east from the Oakland Long Wharf on San Francisco Bay in California.

The Transcontinental Railroad changed travel across the country as it took what was once a two-month trip from coast to coast and reduced it to a week. One thousand, nine hundred seven miles of continuous rail were laid in six years. It was built by multiple rail companies.

The Western Pacific Railroad Company built 132 miles of track from the western terminus at Alameda, California to Sacramento. That stretch of rail was finished six months after the railroad opened for through traffic between Sacramento and Omaha.

The Central Pacific Railroad constructed 690 miles of track eastward from Sacramento, California to Promontory Summit, Utah Territory.

The Union Pacific Railroad built 1085 miles of track from the eastern terminus at Council Bluffs near Omaha, Nebraska west to meet the Central Pacific at Promontory Summit.

These combined lines of track linked the San Francisco Bay at Sacramento, California with the existing eastern railroad network at Omaha, Nebraska. It did much not only for commerce and trade, but also opened large parts of the West to settlers. However, the actual rail route between Omaha and the Eastern terminus of the Pacific Railroad at Council Bluffs, Iowa—across the Missouri River—was not finished until a railroad bridge was constructed. The bridge was finished on March 25, 1873. Prior to that time, transfers were made by a ferry operated by the Council Bluffs and Nebraska Ferry Company.

The Denver Pacific Railway between Denver and Cheyenne opened on June 23 of 1870. This route breathed new life into the floundering city of Denver. It also opened the beef market between the two cities and decreased the weight loss that was often associated with long and strenuous cattle drives.

Other rail companies rushed to build additional routes. By December of 1881, two more transcontinental railroads were completed including one that ran to Denver. This new line allowed passengers to embark on the East coast and disembark on the West coast without being ferried across the Missouri River. Instead, it connected the eastern rail network via the Hannibal Bridge across the Missouri River at Kansas City.

Those who built the Union Pacific section of the Transcontinental Railroad were mainly Civil War army veterans and Irish immigrants.

Most of the engineers hired during the building were also ex-army men who had learned their trade during the war.

The Central Pacific Railroad faced a labor shortage as the West was more sparsely settled. It hired many Cantonese laborers from China. They built the lines over and through the Sierra Nevada Mountains and east across what would become Nevada and northern Utah.

Fare for the one-week trip from New York to San Francisco ranged from $65 in an "emigrant" or third-class bench seat to $136 for first class in a Pullman sleeping car.

The third-class bench seats were by far the least comfortable and the most crowded. These cars accommodated those who could not afford either the second- or first-class cars.

Second-class accommodation focused more on function and less on aesthetics. Those seats were usually wooden with reclining backs and minimal furnishings. A wider range of travelers rode in second-class cars. The cost was $110 for the one-week trip.

First-class fare gave the travelers better-quality accommodations as well as an increased level of security and respectability. These cars were usually outfitted with upholstered chairs, curtains, and a carpeted interior. They were designed to include the comforts of home for those who could afford the luxuries. They also exuded a clearer social and economic distinction from the other two rail options.

The placement of the cars on a train offered distinct levels of comfort as well as safety. The cars closest to the engine were more likely to catch fire, derail, and take in more smoke resulting in poorer air quality than those located toward the rear of the train. Baggage, mail, and emigrant cars were placed at the front of the train. They were called head-end cars. First-class, dining, and sleeping cars were usually located closer to the rear of the train.

In this book, I estimated the fare charges from Columbus, Georgia to Cheyenne, Wyoming Territory as I did not find exact cost amounts for that route.

For Sale: Railroad Land

To allow the rail companies to raise additional capital, Congress granted the railroads not only a 400-foot right-of-way corridor, but they were also *given* alternate sections of government-owned lands. The 6,400-acre-per-mile plot ran ten miles on both sides of the tracks.

The rail companies received the odd-numbered sections while the government retained the even-numbered sections. This formed a checkerboard pattern. The railroad then sold bonds based on the value of the land. Some land was sold directly to settlers which vastly increased the settlement of the West.

The Homestead Acts passed between 1861 and 1863 granted applicants 160-acre parcels of land with the requirement that he or she must "improve" the land. This stipulation was enforced differently based on the location, but it usually included breaking the sod, building some kind of shelter, and bringing in water through a well or by irrigation. If the rail companies failed to sell the land granted to them within three years, it reverted to the government at a value of $1.25 per acre which was the prevailing government price for homesteads. In addition, if the bonds were not completely repaid, all remaining railroad property, including trains and tracks, became the property of the United States government. Of course, the legislation lacked adequate oversight as well as accountability, and corruption was rampant.

Identification of Civil War Casualties

During the Civil War, there was no organized method of identification. Soldiers were justly concerned that their bodies would not be identified after a battle. Some soldiers pinned or sewed their names to the inside of their clothing while others scratched their names into the soft lead of their belt buckles.

In 1862, John Kennedy of New York offered a proposal to the Secretary of War to manufacture and supply all Union soldiers with a name disc. His offer was declined. However, other manufacturers soon began to produce "Soldiers' Pins" for private sale. The discs were engraved with the soldier's name, unit, and even battle information.

Soldiers in the field were often not aware of this new method of identification available to them. They rarely had access to current reading material let alone advertisements.

The sutlers—the civilian merchants who followed the armies to their encampments, selling goods to the soldiers—began to offer identification disks in their mobile tent stores. One side of the disc was engraved with the soldier's name. The disc sometimes included his unit and hometown as well. The other side had a variety of design options from Abraham Lincoln or George Washington to an eagle or a shield. A hole punched in the tag allowed it to be attached to a string or cord to be worn around the neck. Later, the Union Army did offer a military identification tag to its soldiers.

Few of the Confederate soldiers carried any military identification. The Confederate Army lacked funding to even feed and support its troops so unless a soldier could afford to purchase one himself, professional identification methods were not used. Most Confederate soldiers were unable to afford them.

Unfortunately, those who identified the bodies of the fallen did not always recognize the discs for their importance. The dead were usually identified by the papers or letters they were carrying. That often led to misidentification of bodies.

It is estimated that five percent of the dead from both the North and the South buried in national cemeteries remain unidentified while that number increases to forty percent when all Civil War dead are included.

Civil War Tombstones

Union tombstones were rounded on top while Confederate stones were pointed. According to some of the Confederate records of the time, this was done so that the "damn Yankees can't sit on our heads." I loved this bit of trivia and added it to this story. I was able to confirm its accuracy after speaking to someone who toured Arlington Cemetery.

The CSA on a Confederate tombstone stands for Confederate States of America. The cross at the top is the Southern Cross of Honor indicating that the soldier buried there died with honor.

North vs South

Over the years, there has been much discussion about the Civil War including the rights and wrongs of this terrible conflict. Most soldiers were very loyal to whichever side they fought for although their reasons for fighting were often different.

Individual Confederate soldiers were more likely to fight for independence or state's rights than for retaining slavery. Slaves were expensive so the average Southern family would not have been able to afford one. While racism *was* rampant, it was not limited to Southern sympathizers. Many Yankees also believed that the Black man was a lesser being.

In an ironic twist, after some slaves acquired their freedom and became successful, they purchased slaves of their own. I saw this when I toured an old mansion in New Orleans, Louisianna several years ago and was told the history of the ex-slave owner.

Many of the generals and high-ranking officers from both sides attended West Point and were in classes together. They found it difficult to fight men with whom they were friends. In addition, they had the same training which made the battle strategies even more difficult.

The Civil War was called the War for Southern Independence by the South. It was a very divisive war because in both the North and the South, it pitted brothers and neighbors against each other. I tried to show that conflict through interactions between Paul and his father even though both were fictional characters.

The Gold Room Saloon

The Gold Room Saloon was built in 1867 and was one of the first two saloons to operate in Cheyenne. It was a two-story structure quickly built with wood transported from Omaha, Nebraska. Construction materials were brought to Cheyenne by bull teams since no rail was yet completed. By 1872, it was called the Bella Union Variety Gold Room, and was known throughout the West as the "classiest of the classy." The building that housed the variety hall and saloon was located at 310 16th Street, and Doc Holliday once worked as a card dealer there.

Court was usually held in one of the larger saloons. All the saloons vied for that opportunity as it meant lots of extra business. Trials were also a form of entertainment. Some of the early lawyers even had their own following.

Judge William T. Jones

Judge William T. Jones was a judge in Cheyenne's early years. He began to practice law in 1865 and was appointed justice of the Wyoming Territorial Supreme Court in 1869. At the age of twenty-seven, he was considered young for a judge, but he was described as "entirely cool and impartial on the bench."

The personality I gave Judge Jones is completely from my imagination. However, from that quoted statement, I like to think he was just a little like the judge in this book.

Colonel Grenville Mellen Dodge

Colonel Grenville Dodge was a Union Army officer during the Civil War. He was also a pioneering figure in military intelligence, serving as Ulysses S. Grant's intelligence officer. He created such a highly effective intelligence-gathering network that the identities of his 100-plus agents remain a mystery today. In May of 1866, he resigned from the military and became the Union Pacific's chief engineer. He is considered a leading figure in the construction of the Transcontinental Railroad.

Dodge was instrumental in making Cheyenne part of that railroad not only because of her location between Omaha and California, but because of the grade and slope of the land as well. The easier the proposed route was to cross, the faster it was to lay the rails.

In this story, Bandy is a fictional character. However, I enjoyed tying him to Colonel Dodge as part of Dodge's Civil War intelligence team.

Wyoming: First Territory to Have Women Serve on a Jury

Wyoming became a territory on July 25, 1868. March 7, 1870, was the first time in the *world* that women served on a formal jury. The passage of the Suffrage Act by the Wyoming Territorial Assembly in 1869 gave women the right to vote and hold office. Wyoming Territory was noticeably short on women. In fact, there were six adult men to every woman in 1869. This, of course, resulted in very few children. The legislators hoped the good publicity they would receive from such legislation would draw settlers, including more women, into the territory.

Women served on juries in Wyoming Territory from 1870 through 1871 until a different judge decided the Suffrage Act did not apply to juries. With one exception, women did not serve on juries again until Wyoming law was changed in 1949, seventy-eight years later.

Wyoming became the forty-fourth state in the United States when President Benjamin Harrison signed Wyoming's statehood bill on March 27, 1890.

Thank you for choosing to read my novels. May this story catch you within the first few pages and hold you until the end. Enjoy the history I wound through it as well.

Rosie Bosse, Author
Living and Writing on a Ranch in the Middle of Nowhere
rosiebosse.com

Rocking R Ranch
South of Cheyenne,
Wyoming Territory
June 1870

CHAPTER 1

LIFE ON THE ROCKING R

MOLLY PUSHED THE CURLY, BROWN HAIR BACK FROM her sleeping baby's forehead. At nearly two years old, Paul Broken Knife Rankin was a beautiful little boy. His bottomless blue eyes like his mother's drew people in, and his grin was infectious. Molly's heart swelled with love. Then her stomach tightened. She remembered her father's reaction when he found she was with child. Her attack and rape at the hands of Quantrill's Raiders had been traumatic. She shuddered.

"What would have become of me had Lance not been on that riverboat?" she whispered to herself.

Her attack happened a little over two years ago, and with Lance's help, she was beginning to heal. Lance now wanted her to contact her father and invite him for a visit. Molly frowned slightly and shook her head. She dabbed her eyes with her apron and took a deep breath.

"I miss you, Father, but I'm not sure I can do that."

Lance. Molly smiled at the thought of him. *God truly blessed me when He brought Lance into my life.*

The smile wrinkles were deeper around her husband's eyes since he had become a father, but he was still the ornery, good-looking cowboy she had first met. It was hard for Molly to believe how much her life had changed in such a short time.

She touched her stomach where a new life was once again growing. She was going to tell Lance when he arrived home today, and she knew he would be excited. Stepping back from the crib, Molly pushed a strand of hair behind her ear. As the sun's rays touched her, the gold in her red hair shone. She smiled contentedly.

"My life is not what I had once imagined it would become, but it is everything I could have wanted," she whispered softly as she looked down again at the sleeping little boy.

Sammy came rushing into the house. "Ma, can I go fishin' with my grandpappies? They found a new water hole!"

Molly looked down at Sammy's earnest face. The little boy became Molly and Lance's son when his family was killed. They had taken him in on their long, cross-country trip to Cheyenne. *All our lives certainly changed on that trip,* she thought as she wiped a smudge of dirt off Sammy's face.

"Are your chores done?" Molly asked as she kissed his ruddy cheek. "You know your father is counting on you to keep an eye on things here while he's gone."

"Yeah, the chickens are fed, an' I slopped that ol' pig. I'm a gonna call him Bacon 'cause that's what Pa says he'll be soon enough!"

"You have fun, but you tell your grandpappies to have you home by dinner." Molly smiled and tousled Sammy's blond hair. "And tell your Grandpa Badger to have Granny Martha come over this afternoon so we can make bear sign."

Sammy grinned and nodded excitedly as he raced out of the house shouting, "Barley, you an' me git to eat those little cakes with holes in 'em today! Ma calls 'em bear sign. Pa says that's cause if ya leave the hole out, they look a lot like a pile of bear poop. I ain't never seen bear poop but I sure like 'em.

"Now don't ya jump around. Hold still while I climb up on ya."

Molly watched Sammy run toward his pony.

Whenever anyone asked Sammy how old he was, he always said, "Almost five!" Of course, he had been saying that for the two years he had been their son.

Sammy was three years old when Lance and Badger rescued him. Outlaws had attacked the little homestead in Kansas where he had lived with his parents and older sister. His sister survived that attack and her kidnapping, but she died on the trip to Cheyenne. That was when Lance and Molly asked Sammy if he would like to be their son.

Molly was always a little worried about Sammy riding Barleycorn, but Lance said an "almost" five-year-old boy should have his own pony.

Barleycorn was a little brown Shetland. He was a wonderful little pony around small kids, but he loved to crow-hop if older kids tried to ride him. Molly watched with a mixture of fear and pride as Sammy led Barleycorn close to a bucket he had turned upside down. After three jumps, the little boy finally made it on. The Shetland started off at a rough trot and Sammy dug his heels in to hang on. Lance told Sammy he had to learn to ride bareback before he could have a saddle of his own.

"Grandpappy, I can go! Let's get a movin'! We're a burnin' daylight!" Sammy hollered as he bounced on the little pony.

Old Man McNary had his horse saddled. The wooden fishing poles he had made leaned against the corral fence. His eyes glinted with pleasure at the sight of Sammy. Molly often told Sammy he shouldn't bother his grandpappy so much, but Old Man McNary didn't mind.

His cabin was less than a quarter mile away, and he was enjoying his quiet life since he sold the ranch to Lance. *Well, not so quiet.* Old Man McNary grinned as he thought of how often the two little boys appeared at his house, sometimes on Barleycorn and sometimes walking. He blessed the day Lance had ridden in as well as the day his young foreman brought his new wife home.

Two grandsons and it has barely been two years. He grinned to himself. "No, life just doesn't get any better than this." he murmured as he waved at Sammy.

Sadie moved to stand beside Molly, and she smiled at her friend. Together, they watched from the doorway as Sammy and his grandpappy left the yard. Sammy gave the two women a big wave, and Molly blew him a kiss. She hoped he remembered to pass her message for Martha on to Badger.

Molly smiled at the thought of her good friend. Their ornery neighbor to the south, Badger McCune, swept Martha off her feet in Manhattan, Kansas, two years ago at a church box supper when he passed through on his way to Cheyenne. Martha was not quite as old as Badger but was a very settled widow and had no intentions of ever marrying again. Badger rattled her placid life and proposed the day after he met her. They married in Julesburg and never again would Martha's life be boring. Even Mule, Badger's temperamental mule and longtime companion, loved Martha. Sammy considered Badger his grandpappy, and Martha stepped into the role of grandmother easily. Children delighted her. She had no children with her first husband and loved being part of Badger's "family."

The scent of baked pastry filled the air and Molly rushed into the house to take her pies out of the oven "My pies! I hope they didn't burn!"

Sadie already had them out and they were sitting on the table to cool.

Molly hugged her friend. "Sadie, I am so glad we found you in Julesburg," she whispered.

Sadie was working as a washerwoman in Julesburg, Colorado, when the Rankins passed through there two years ago. met. Molly was horrified by the rawness of Sadie's hands and arms from the lye in the soap she used as well as by the way she was being treated. Molly had invited Sadie to go with them to Cheyenne. Now in just a few months, there was going to be a wedding on the Rocking R. Sadie was marrying Slim, Lance's best friend and foreman.

"I am so going to miss all your help, and just having you here. You are like a sister to me." Both women had tears in their eyes as Sadie hugged her friend back.

When Molly told Lance how she hated to see Sadie leave, he laughed. "Now, Molly, you know they are only going to move to the other side of the ranch!" Still, the house would be quiet without Sadie's quick laugh and friendly conversation.

Sadie caused quite a stir with the cowboys when she arrived at the ranch with Lance and Molly. All the cowhands on the Rocking R, as well as every other bachelor within one hundred miles tried to court her. Slim had to work hard but he finally won.

Molly laughed softly as she thought about their courtship. *Slim had Sadie's heart from the first day she met him, but she didn't want to appear too eager. She said she remembered my warnings about Slim and how he was a notorious ladies' man.*

Women were scarce around Cheyenne in 1868, and beautiful ones who could cook were even more rare. Slim put his womanizing aside when he met Sadie. He became a one-woman man, and they were a happy couple. Now their new house was going up. It was going to be a busy and exciting fall.

Lance and Slim had worked together as top hands on the Rocking R Ranch. Even after Old Man McNary made Lance foremen, Slim wasn't jealous, and the two men remained friends. When Lance bought the ranch from Old Man McNary, he made Slim his foreman.

Now, as a wedding gift, Lance and Molly were giving Slim five hundred acres of land that connected to the little spread Slim just bought. Slim and Sadie did not know this yet, and Molly couldn't wait to tell them.

CHAPTER 2

BLOOD ON THE SADDLE

MOLLY LOOKED OUT THE WINDOW AGAIN. *LANCE should be home anytime.* He had shipped ten train cars of cattle last week on the newly completed Denver Pacific Railway. Their cattle were some of the first to be shipped to the growing town of Denver on the new railroad, and both were pleased.

When they received the contract, Lance was excited. "Molly, we can ship beef on a regular basis from Cheyenne by train! Why, we can ship three times a year, maybe even more often. Denver is growing, and shipping beef by rail is faster and safer than driving a herd down there."

Molly agreed. Still, Lance had been gone for a week and she was ready for him to come home. She looked up at the sound of horses on the lane and rushed to the window, smiling expectantly. Her heart thudded heavily in her chest when she realized the riders were strangers.

The six men appeared to be rough and were looking around as they rode up. Molly picked up her rifle and stepped toward the closed door.

Lance told her to always keep the pistol loaded and never to answer the door without both guns. Molly was an excellent shot. However, Lance wasn't around, and she was nervous.

The men began to water their horses, and Molly heard one say, "Cap, I don't think anyone's around. How's 'bout we just go on in that house an' see what we can find?"

Molly's heart turned over as the name "Cap" churned up a memory long forgotten. The seven men in the group who attacked her in Georgia were dead. However, she now remembered one they called Cap.

He was the first to take her. He had the men blindfold her before he began. The rape was violent, and Cap didn't talk. He rode away to look for meat while the rest of the men took turns at her.

Molly's face went white as she whispered to herself, "There were eight! I only remembered seven but there were eight. He escaped and now he is here!"

Another man in the group began to protest.

"We come here lookin' fer a ridin' job. We don't want no truck with harmin' women."

Molly peered through the small hole in the door and watched the men.

Cap shifted his rifle to cover the man who had protested. He said something Molly couldn't hear. Two other men moved closer to the man who had protested. They backed their horses up and sat quietly with their hands on the horns of their saddles.

Sadie grabbed the shotgun. It had two barrels but wouldn't do much damage at a distance.

"Sadie," Molly whispered, "stand back where they can't see you. Don't shoot until one of them is rushing the house. And only use one barrel. We may need the second one."

Sadie's brown eyes were huge, and her face was pale. She nodded her head and eased to the left of the door frame.

Molly opened the door and stepped into the opening. The men outside looked startled. The one they called Cap looked hard at her and then grinned.

"Well, little missy, we meet again!" he exclaimed mockingly.

Molly pointed the rifle at him. She was terrified, but now her anger was going icy cold. She knew she would do whatever was necessary to protect Sadie, Paul, and herself. As she looked over his head, she saw Lance's mustang. It was being led by one of the men, and there was blood on the saddle. Molly's heart turned over and she gasped.

Just then, two men charged the house. Sadie stepped into the doorway beside Molly and fired both barrels of the shotgun. The kick from the gun knocked her back into the house.

Molly's head was calm. Even though her heart was pounding, her hands were steady. She fired at Cap, but his horse reared at the sound of the shotgun blast. The bullet meant for Cap took the horse in the head. The animal fell backwards and went down, pinning Cap's right leg and thigh underneath its body.

The two men Sadie shot were down, and neither was moving.

Sadie gasped at the pain in her shoulder, but she reloaded as fast as she could and rushed forward to stand beside Molly. The three remaining riders appeared to be stunned and stared at the downed men without moving.

Molly was terrified but her mind was clear. She shot again at Cap. This time, she aimed for the leg that wasn't pinned. He screamed as the bullet shattered his knee cap.

She calmly swept the rifle around to cover the remaining men.

"Drop your guns," Molly ordered. Sadie aimed her shotgun at the three remaining outlaws as well. The three stared, shifting their eyes from the dead men on the ground to the two women standing in the doorway and back again. The violence and death had been so sudden and unexpected that they seemed unsure of what to do.

Sadie stepped closer to the group. Her shotgun was steady, and she moved the barrel slightly.

The man on the left screamed, "Don't shoot! I'm outta this deal!"

As he dropped his guns, Molly moved her rifle to the man on the far right and Sadie shifted the shotgun to cover the man in the middle.

The man who had dropped his guns had his hands in the air and was trying to move his horse away from the other two.

"Hicks! Joe! Drop yore weapons! These gals are crazy!"

Cap was trying to pull his rifle from the boot. Molly turned her gun on him again. This time, she shot the arm pulling on the rifle. Cap fell back, bleeding and screaming.

Hicks and Joe dropped their guns.

"Get down and stick your faces in the ground," Molly ordered quietly. "Put your hands in front of you. Sadie, keep that shotgun on them."

Then she moved towards Cap as she gestured toward Lance's mustang.

"Where is the man whose mustang you have?"

Cap was moaning and refused to answer so Molly pointed the rifle at the one called Joe and repeated her question.

Joe's eyes were huge as he stared at the screaming Cap.

Molly pulled the trigger and grazed Joe's shoulder with a bullet.

"He's dead!" Joe screamed. "Cap shot 'im in the back, an' he went down. Cap must a knowed yore man was a carryin' money 'cause he took his money belt. Then he rolled 'im down a bank an' pushed dirt over 'im.

"Yore man ain't a comin' back. Have mercy, lady! We're ridin' with these fellers but we ain't backshooters! That was all Cap!"

Molly began to tremble as the meaning of what she had just heard began to penetrate her mind.

Just then, Badger came rushing into the yard. He held Ol' Betsy, his buffalo gun, and was riding Mule. When he saw that Molly and Sadie were all right, the fear went out of his eyes. However, the fury remained.

"Ladies," Badger stated quietly, "You'ins go on back in that thar house. 'Ol Mule an' me'll take 'er from here."

Molly began to shake. She dropped the rifle.

"Lance?" she gasped.

Badger's eyes became harder.

"Lance be in a bad way, Molly. I'll take you'ins ta git 'im soon as I clean up here."

Paul was crying and the women turned toward the house. As Sadie helped Molly inside, they heard Badger ask, "Now which one a ya coyotes shot my boy in the back?"

As the men shouted and pointed at the groaning Cap, Badger growled, "Now I'm a gonna tie ya fellers up, an' if'n that boy a mine dies, I'm a gonna turn Mule loost onto all a you'ins."

Badger tied each of the men to a corral post. He left Cap on the ground still under the dead horse. Badger bent down beside him.

"Looks ta me like you'ins is a bleedin' out. I think I'm a gonna let that happen." Cap groaned and tried to pull on Badger's shirt.

"Please. Just get me out from under this horse!"

Badger could hear crying from in the house and his blue eyes looked like flint rock.

"Hep ya? You'ins tried to kill my boy, an' hurt my girl!" Badger spat and walked into the house.

Molly's breath caught in her throat as she sobbed, "There were eight, Badger! Cap was there!"

Sadie stared at Molly in confusion, but Badger understood. His eyes glinted and became hard again. He spun on his heel and headed back outside.

Badger whistled for Mule. He tied a rope to the dead horse and backed Mule until the horse was off Cap's leg. Then he grabbed Cap by the collar and drug him towards the creek.

"Come on, Mule," Badger growled. "You'ins an' me's got us a job ta do."

CHAPTER 3

A Trial on the Rocking R

MOLLY SAW HORSES ON THE LANE. OLD MAN MCNARY was leading a horse, and Lance was tied to the saddle. He had bled heavily and was now unconscious. Sammy's horse was beside Lance's mount. Sammy's eyes were huge and frightened. Even Barleycorn was subdued.

Molly rushed outside. Tears were streaming down her face, and her hands covered her mouth as her shoulders shook.

Old Man McNary looked hard at her as he grated, "We need to get him inside, Molly, and then I'll ride for a doctor. He's in bad shape."

As they lifted Lance off the horse, Molly sobbed and held his hand. "Lance, stay with us. Don't you give up!"

The men carefully laid Lance on the bed, and Old Man McNary rushed off to Cheyenne to find a doctor.

Sadie already had water heating. She could barely use her right arm. She tentatively looked inside her dress at her shoulder. A huge bruise was beginning to show, and she quietly pulled her dress up.

Tears were streaming down Molly's face as she opened Lance's shirt to bathe the wound.

Sadie touched Molly's shoulder and then hugged her friend.

"I'll take the boys to Martha's," she whispered. Wincing, Sadie lifted Paul and took Sammy by the hand. "Let's go see your Granny Martha, shall we?"

Badger hitched the team, and Sadie headed across the ranch to Badger's spread.

Molly cleaned Lance's wounds. He had been shot in the back and then at close range in the chest. However, there were no bubbles coming out of his mouth. As she held Lance's hand and talked to him, Molly wondered if the bullets could have passed through without doing terrible damage. *Please, Lord, let Lance live.* Her breath caught in her throat as she whispered, "We need a miracle. Two bullets and so much blood."

Badger arrived with a concoction of plants. He began to make poultices to put on Lance's wounds.

Lance was trying to talk but he was out of his head. His eyes looked feverish. He tossed around in his bed, and it was difficult for Badger to keep the poultices on his wounds. Molly tried to hold him still.

Lance's eyes finally locked on her. He grinned.

"Say, you sure look like my Molly. She is the best-looking gal I have ever seen!" He tried to lean forward as he whispered, "But I don't think she would like it much if she saw you hanging on me like this!"

A sob caught in Molly's throat as she whispered, "Oh, Lance."

Lance frowned. "Where is Molly? I need to find her and keep her safe! Where are my boys? Has anyone seen my boys? I can't find them!"

Molly sponged his head and talked softly to him. Lance continued to talk out of his head, sometimes muttering and sometimes shouting. He tried to pull the poultices off and get out of bed.

"Let me up! My family is in danger! I need to get home!"

Finally, the doctor arrived. Old Man McNary had found a surgeon, one that was familiar with bullet wounds. Even though he looked young, the doctor had been an army surgeon during the War Between the States, and he had much experience treating chest wounds.

After examining Lance, he determined the bullet from the chest shot had gone completely through. However, the slug shot from behind was lodged in Lance's chest. The doctor gave Lance some laudanum to quiet him and make him sleep. He could see the trajectory of the bullet and wanted to perform surgery immediately. The doctor's voice was quiet as he spoke.

"That bullet must come out. I am going to go in from the front because I can tell where it is lodged. If we can get it out in one complete piece, your husband has a good chance for recovery." He held Molly's shoulders as he added softly, "However, if the bullet shattered or if it damaged some organs, then I can't make you any promises."

Badger glared out the door at the men tied there while Old Man McNary cursed low in his chest and turned away.

Tears filled Molly's eyes and she began to sob. She finally took a deep breath.

"What do you need me to do?"

The surgeon studied her face and pointed toward the kitchen.

"We'll need boiling water and lots of it. Whiskey too if you have it. Scrub your kitchen table and then pour whiskey all over it. And wash your hands thoroughly. You may hand me my instruments as I need them. However, if you start to feel lightheaded, leave. I can't deal with a fainting woman while I am working.

"You two men—carry Mr. Rankin out to the kitchen and put him on that table once it is clean. Then get out. I don't need anyone in here but Mrs. Rankin—and she may stay only if she is helping me."

The young surgeon began. It took him nearly an hour to extract the bullet because it had lodged in a delicate area. Finally, he dropped the bullet on his tray. He examined it closely and began to suture the wound. When he finished, he studied the wound and then looked at Molly.

"The bullet remained intact, but because it was embedded so deeply, I am still concerned about internal bleeding.

"I am going to leave the laudanum here. Try to keep him as quiet as possible. However, use it sparingly because it can be addictive." The doctor took a deep breath as he touched Molly's shoulder and spoke quietly, "I will be back in two days. If he makes it until then, he should survive."

Molly stared at the doctor and her heart clenched in her chest. She took Lance's hand and pressed it to her face. "Lance don't leave us. We need you here," she sobbed.

After the doctor left, Badger applied more poultices and told Molly to try to keep Lance cool.

"Gotta watch fer the fever. It's a goin' ta come up an' we'uns have ta work ta keep 'er down." He patted Molly's shoulder and rushed outside.

The Rocking R riders had trickled in and were gathered around the horse tank. Talk was quiet and anger was evident in each of them.

Slim was the last to arrive. When he heard what had happened, his laughing blue eyes turned to ice chips. It was difficult to make Slim mad, but once he was pushed too far, he stayed mad for a long time.

Old Man McNary glared at the outlaws. His cold eyes swept over the tired riders.

"I think we should give these boys a trial right now. How about we head up to my cabin? Let's just get this over with." His eyes drilled into each of the three outlaws.

"I'll be your judge and these here riders will be your jury. Say your prayers, boys. I'm not sure what you can say to convince us you don't deserve to be hanged…even if we give each of you a bit of time to speak your piece."

The Rocking R riders cut the bound men loose from the corral and tied each man's hands with one end of a lariat. The other end of that rope was tied to a horse. The riders moved out at a brisk pace, and the outlaws were drug when they tripped. Not one of the riders talked as they rode up to Old Man McNary's cabin.

When they arrived at the cabin, the Old Man drug his kitchen table outside. He beat on it with a hammer.

"This here trial's now in order. Drag that closest man up here."

Tiny, the biggest and most gentle of all the riders was mad. He picked up the first outlaw and threw him across the yard to land in front of Old Man McNary.

Badger stepped up.

"Tell us yer name, ya' sidewinder," Badger growled.

The outlaw staggered to his feet. "My name is Joe Johnson and Hicks here is my brother. Smiley over there is our cousin. We fought together in the War of Southern Independence. When it was over, we headed west 'cause there ain't much need for Southern boys back home in Kansas.

"We met Cap an' his boys in Cheyenne. We was tryin' to get us ridin' jobs, an' Cap said he knew a feller south a town who needed help." Joe's eyes were sincere when he added, "We ain't never shot no one in the back, an' never planned to neither. Cap done that on his own. He did it so sudden that we didn't have time to think let alone stop him."

Badger glared at Joe and then at the other two men.

"An' why didn't you'ins leave after he shot my boy in the back? Ya stayed with 'im, didn't ya?"

Joe was quiet but Smiley spoke up.

"We was scared an' that's a fact. We shouldn't a joined up with these here fellers. We knew it about ten miles after we left Cheyenne. We was tryin' to think of a way to break loose when he spotted yore boy on the trail in front of us. Cap, he jist cut loose. Somehow, he knew yore man had a money belt, but I swear we didn't know it. We really thought we was headed to a ridin' job.

"When we met the three of 'em, Cap was already ridin' with the two fellers those women cut down with that scattergun. I ain't sure where they met or how long they was together though. We kinda stuck to our own selves an' they didn't talk much."

The faces of the three men were pale as they held themselves up. Each knew death was just around the corner, and everything depended on the men in this yard. As they looked around at the riders, they could almost feel the ropes around their necks. There was no mercy displayed on the hard faces of the Rocking R cowboys.

Old Man McNary was slowly calming down, and now he was in a quandary. He believed the three young men in front of him were as they said they were—in the wrong company at the wrong time. However, they had taken too long to cut loose from their first bad decision. Now here they were on trial for sanctioning a backshooting.

"Does anyone else have anything to say here?" he asked.

Several of the riders shuffled their feet while others shook out their ropes. They looped them over the large tree branch that hung out over the side of the yard.

Even Badger seemed to be short on words.

Old Man McNary barked, "Let's have a show of hands of who all believe these boys are guilty of sanctioning Lance's killing."

Nine of the thirteen riders raised their hands while the rest looked at the ground and dug at the dirt with the toes of their boots.

Old Man McNary asked, "How many of you think they took too long to grow a conscience?" All thirteen riders raised their hands.

The old man rubbed his chin and pondered a bit before he pounded the table with his hammer.

"These boys are guilty of bein' stupid, but I just don't believe that is enough to justify a hangin'. On the other hand, we do need punishment of some kind and I'm open for ideas."

Some of the riders looked relieved while others were furious. Slim threw his rope down on the ground and glared at the three men.

Muttering began among the cowpunchers. For the first time, the Rocking R riders were divided.

Badger spoke up. "Mebbie we'uns should jist hold off here fer a bit an' see how Lance gets on. If'n he lives, they live. If'n he dies, they hang."

Old Man McNary banged his hammer on the table. "That sounds fair to me. All in favor?"

Thirteen men raised their hands, and the sentence was passed.

Slim growled, "An' jist what do we do with 'em now?"

Old Man McNary locked his eyes on Slim, and his lean old face showed just the hint of a smile.

"Don't you have a house to build? I think you should start on that stonework. These here fellers will be glad to put in some long hours. Take four or five boys and head on down there. They can work until midnight, take a half-hour break, and start again. You boys spell each other. If they try to make a run for it, shoot 'em. Court dismissed!"

The old man banged the hammer again, and the riders grouped together as they discussed who was going where.

CHAPTER 4

SON, YOU FIGHT THIS

JOE, HICKS, AND SMILEY STARED QUIETLY AT EACH other. They couldn't believe they were still alive. However, they were afraid of the Rocking R riders and especially of Slim. They knew the next forty-eight hours were going to be dangerous. As Tiny moved toward them, Smiley backed up with large eyes and sputtered, "Jist—jist tell me where to go an' what ya want done! I'm a peaceable man!"

Tiny picked him up by the collar until he was eye level and snarled coldly, "So was I—till today." He dropped Smiley and pointed toward the Rocking R headquarters.

"Git on down there, ya crow baits, an' git on yore horses. I'm a volunteerin' fer this here job!"

Smiley, Joe, and Hicks rushed down the hill followed closely by the Rocking R riders. They quickly mounted. As the group headed out of the yard, Slim and Tiny along with three other riders could be seen crowding around the outlaws.

Hicks started to ask for a drink as they passed the tank, but Joe kicked him to shut him up.

Slim looked back at Badger and called, "One of us 'ill come down twice a day to check on Lance."

Badger nodded and the tight knot of men left the yard on a run.

They met Sadie and Martha coming up the lane. Sadie's brown eyes were large as she looked from Slim to the men crowded around him. Slim's face was cold. He only nodded at Sadie as he rode by.

Badger and Old Man McNary were in Lance's yard when the women arrived.

Sadie looked back at Slim. "Are they…are they going to hang them?" she asked.

"Not yet," spat Badger. "They's a gonna work hard an' pray hard that Lance makes it. If'n he don't, they hang."

Badger took Sammy and the Old Man took Paul as they helped the women down from the wagon. Martha and Sadie hurried to the kitchen to start supper. Dinner had been skipped so everyone would be extra hungry.

Badger and Old Man McNary went to check on Lance.

Molly's pretty face was stained with tears as she looked up at the two old men. They were both like fathers to Lance.

"I am so afraid," she whispered. "His breathing is so labored, and he is out of his head. I can't keep the fever down. Badger, can you make me some of your horrible concoction?" she pleaded as she looked at him with a trembling mouth.

Badger left the room quickly, and Old Man McNary leaned over Lance.

"Son, you fight this now. You have folks here who need you. You're a family man now an' you need to stick around." His old eyes were damp as he squeezed Lance's hand and kissed the top of Molly's head. He left the room quietly and went outside.

"Lord," he whispered, "I ain't much of a prayin' man but I am askin' you now to come down here an' help this boy. He's the closest thing to a son that I have, an' we need him here for a while longer. I ain't never needed no one, but I need this boy, an' his family needs him." Deep

42

sobs shook Old Man McNary's body, but no sound came forth as he bowed his head and cried silently.

He pulled himself up straight, wiped his eyes, and turned back into the house.

"Sammy, how about we go catch some fish for supper? Ladies, you tell Badger we'll meet him at the fishin' hole."

Sammy rushed out of the house and grabbed the poles that had never made it to the water that morning. Hand in hand, the boy and his grandpappy headed for the creek.

Sadie rocked Paul to sleep. She gazed down at the long eyelashes that lay on his soft cheeks as she breathed in his little-boy smell. She hugged him tighter and said a prayer of her own—for both Lance and for Slim.

"Please, Lord, keep our men safe and let Lance live. I have never seen Slim with such white, hot anger before, and I don't want him to do something he will regret when he calms down."

As Sadie moved to the kitchen to help Martha cook, she looked at Molly's pies. Once again, she teared up.

"Now, don't worry, honey," Martha whispered as she gave Sadie a hug. "I just don't think the Good Lord is ready for Lance yet—and fretting isn't going to help. Let's get these men fed. Then you take some food over to those men working on your house, and you sit with your man for a while. He needs your presence to calm him down, and you need his strength." Martha hugged Sadie again and kissed her cheek.

Sadie soaked up Martha's love. As she pulled back, she softly whispered, "Martha, you are such a gift to our family here."

Martha beamed and brushed her eyes.

"No more tears now. Let's get this meal ready. That we can do." Soon, the two of them were busy fixing a meal to feed fifteen hungry riders and three working outlaws.

When the meal was ready, Sadie knocked softly on the door to the bedroom.

"Molly, are you hungry? Martha and I fixed supper."

Molly was going to say no but then the aroma of the cooked meat filled the room.

"Maybe just a little," she answered with a slight smile.

As Sadie brought her a plate of tender steak and mashed potatoes with corn, Lance's eyes flew open. He almost focused them on Molly. Then he frowned and passed out again.

Badger arrived with his potion. "I had ta work with what I could find," he explained. "I'm a lackin' them thar buff'lo turds so deer scat 'ill have ta do." He soon had the evil concoction heated and mixed.

It was as foul smelling as Molly remembered.

Badger lifted Lance's head a little and Molly slipped a teaspoonful in his mouth. She was able to get five spoonfuls in before his eyes opened. He glared at her.

"Woman, are you trying to kill me? Tell my wife to come in here. She makes the best pies, and she sure wouldn't be trying to poison me with whatever it is that you're peddlin'!"

"Lance," Molly ordered, "Drink this. Your wife said it will make you better. She said if you drink it, you may have some pie."

Lance stared vacantly at Molly for a bit. Then he took the cup and drank the entire thing. He shuddered and grinned. Her pie is worth it." As he passed out again, a loose smile spread across his face.

Lance drifted in and out of consciousness the rest of the day and most of the night. Towards morning, his fever broke. Molly was asleep in her rocker by his bed when he awoke. His eyes were once again clear, and he could focus on Molly's pretty face. Her reddish-gold hair was down and hung softly around her face. The hairbrush lay on her lap. It had slipped from her hand as she brushed her hair. She was now sleeping.

He traced the tear tracks on her cheeks with his eyes and whispered, "Beautiful Molly. I just couldn't leave you and the boys. Oh, it would have been easy, but the Good Lord told me my job here wasn't done."

Lance whispered a prayer of thanksgiving as he drifted off into a restful sleep. When he awoke several hours later, he was hungry. The morning sun was shining in the east window. Even though he was sore, he felt more like his old self. As Molly sleepily opened her eyes, he grinned at her.

"Good morning, beautiful!"

Molly's tears came again, but this time, they were tears of joy and relief. As she leaned over the bed to hug Lance carefully, she sobbed, "Oh, Lance! I was so afraid! I was terrified you were not going to wake up. Once again, Badger's concoction seemed to do the trick!"

Lance stared hard at Molly and scowled.

"How much did I drink?"

"You drank an entire cup because you thought you would get some pie. Later, you drank a second cup." Molly laughed at the look on Lance's face.

"Well, that explains the terrible taste in my mouth. And I had better get some pie," he growled. "I smelled it all night long."

Sadie came in carrying a plate of food with a large piece of cherry pie on the side.

"I hid a piece in case you woke up today." She smiled softly at the two of them as she handed Molly the plate.

"Let me feed you," Molly urged. "Doc doesn't want you moving your arms until he checks you again."

Molly was worried as she looked up at Sadie. "Did the men get anything to eat yesterday?"

Martha popped her head into the bedroom. "The men are fine, and now Sadie and I making bear sign. Don't you worry about anything except helping your husband to get better."

"Do you think we can bring the riders home now?" Sadie asked. "Since Lance lived, those three men don't have to hang."

Lance and Molly both looked confused, so Sadie explained the trial and punishment.

Lance nodded somberly. Then he grinned.

"Say, if they are any good with wood, maybe we should keep them around awhile. I would like to do some work on the barn. Besides, I understand we are going to need an addition on the house."

When Molly stared at him, Lance grinned.

"Just because I was out of my head *part* of the time doesn't mean that I was out of my head *all* the time! Molly shared all kinds of information with me I think will be helpful down the road. Why, she even said some things that make me blush now."

Molly turned a dark red and glared at Lance.

"Lance Rankin, you had better not repeat anything I said. I didn't think you could hear me, or I wouldn't have been so uninhibited."

Lance tried to laugh but winced as he put his hand up to his chest.

"So, Mrs. Rankin, when is this new one going to show up?" he asked with a grin. He carefully stretched his hand over to touch Molly's stomach.

"My wife is beautiful, but she's even more beautiful when she's pregnant," he murmured softly as he touched Molly's cheek.

"In less than six months. We have Sadie's wedding first. Now Sadie, you bring those men home and tell them Lance is going to be fine!" Molly's blush became darker when she caught Lance's eye. He smiled and winked at her.

As Sadie darted out of the room, a yawning Sammy stumbled in. When he saw that Lance's eyes were open, he started to jump on the bed.

Molly caught him and pulled him onto her lap.

"Your papa is going to be fine, Sammy, but you can't jump on him for a while," she scolded gently, "and I think we should cook some of those fish you caught yesterday for dinner. I am sure he would like that."

Lance tousled Sammy's hair and pulled him in for a hug and a slobbery kiss.

"I sure would like that, partner. And isn't it nice to have your grandpappies so handy!"

Paul toddled into the room. He stared at Lance with somber little eyes.

Lance tried to pick him up. He grimaced as the little boy's weight pulled on his wound. He was about to lift him anyway, but Molly grabbed their son. A grin filled Lance's face as Molly lifted Paul close so he could kiss him.

"Good morning, Paul! How's my little man today?" asked Lance as he winked at the little boy.

Paul grinned and lunged toward Lance, grabbing him around the neck.

Wincing when a small knee hit him near his chest wound, Lance nevertheless smiled up at Molly. His eyes were warm and wet in the corners. "You were right—I couldn't leave yet," he whispered hoarsely as he pulled his little family close.

CHAPTER 5

HERE'S THE DEAL

MOLLY COULD HEAR THE RIDERS GATHERING IN THE kitchen. When she saw them peeking through the bedroom door, she invited all of them in. She moved away from the bed so each could come up and talk to Lance.

Slim and Tiny were the last ones to arrive.

As Slim gripped his hand, Lance asked, "So how are your stone workers?"

Slim looked surprised.

"They worked all night with barely any sleep, food, or water. I finally eased off an' give 'em some of the food that Sadie brought up—what was left, anyway," he added with a grin. "I'm pleased we didn't have to hang 'em. Joe an' Hicks grew up with a father who was a stonemason, an' they are handy with rock. Smiley is still mighty jumpy around Tiny, but he's a good worker too."

Lance's eyes opened wide. "Afraid of Tiny?" he asked in astonishment as he looked at Tiny.

Tiny blushed and Slim grinned.

"I have never seen Tiny mad, but he was mad yesterday. Dang, that boy is strong!" Slim grinned again. "Maybe we should keep him mad. He can really sling the rocks when he has a mad on!"

Tiny gripped Lance's hand. "Now, boys, I was just a little pre-turbed," he drawled with a slow grin. "I'm all over it now. 'Sides, they was jist little rocks." He held his arms out to show the size of the stones.

Lance laughed as he gripped Tiny's hand.

Slim looked at Lance seriously. "So, what do we do with those boys now? Yesterday, I was all for hangin' 'em. Old Man McNary pointed out that they was in the wrong place at the wrong time. He must be gettin' soft 'cause he wasn't fer hangin' 'em.

"We had a split vote. Finally, it was decided if y'all lived, they would live, but they had to work on my house till ya come to." Slim grinned again. "I have four walls 'bout halfway up. If we cin git Tiny mad again, I reckon we could finish it in a couple more days!"

Tiny shoved Slim, and the ornery cowpuncher nearly lost his balance. The three men laughed and visited some more. Then Slim and Tiny moved out so Old Man McNary and Badger could come in.

Badger's eyes were twinkling, and he was carrying some of his potion in a jug. "I brung more jist in case you'ins wasn't quite healed!" he offered with a grin.

Lance put up his hands. "No more, but I still am amazed at the healing qualities of that stuff. Don't even tell me what's in it—I don't want to be sick before I eat breakfast." He looked seriously at Old Man McNary.

"So, Judge, now what?" he asked.

The old man scratched his head. "I'm not real sure. They're just durn kids—one is nineteen and two are barely eighteen. I'm almost tempted to have you hire 'em. I'm just not sure how the boys will accept 'em though. There were some that felt plenty strong about hangin' 'em—first time I ever seen the boys split over anything big."

Lance looked carefully at the man who used to be his boss. He replied quietly, "You know some of those cattle rustlers we hung several years ago were about the same age. A fellow out here is considered a man grown by the time he is fifteen or sixteen."

Old Man McNary looked from one man to the other with a pained look on his face.

"Yeah, and what if it was Sammy or Paul just out raisin' cane, and they got caught up with the wrong fellers? Maybe I'm gettin' soft, but I just think we need to give 'em a chance." He shook his head again as he looked at Lance.

"You're goin' to lose some riders, you know. Slim is goin' to take some with him when he moves to his new place—Tiny will go even if Slim doesn't hire him outright. You are goin' to need some more hands."

Lance was quiet for a moment.

"Well, maybe we should let the boys vote. It has to be one hundred percent though or they go on down the road. We can explain what we are thinking at breakfast and hold the vote tonight. That way, the hands will have some time to think it over and discuss it with each other.

"Besides, the new guys may not even want to stay. They've had a touchy start."

Molly frowned. "I told you what the doctor said. He doesn't even want you to move your arms."

Lance growled, "I've been down long enough. If I don't move soon, my legs won't bend at all.

"That sawbones has me tied up tighter than an old calf. I reckon I can be up for a little while. I want to talk to the men myself."

As the men gathered for breakfast, Lance explained what he was considering.

The men began to mutter. Most of them were stunned and many were angry. Slim and Tiny were quiet.

Lance looked around at his riders. "Whatever we do, it has to be one hundred percent. If any one man of you is against this, it won't happen. I won't spit this crew with a decision like this, so talk it over today amongst yourselves. We will vote tonight."

Joe, one of the outlaws, stepped forward. "I'd like to say somethin' if ya don't mind."

Lance nodded and Joe faced the Rocking R cowboys.

"Fellers," he stated hesitantly, "We is plumb shocked that yore boss would give us a chance. We been on our own fer nearly six years. My daddy was a good man, but he died when Hicks an' me was twelve an' thirteen. Smiley's ol' man was never around an' our pa kinda considered him a son.

"When Pa died, Ma couldn't make it alone. She married up with a feller from back East. He didn't want no kids hangin' 'round, so she left us in Kansas. We scrapped around as best we could. We enlisted in the Confederate Army later that year. A feller was recruitin' an' we was hungry. We lied an' said we was all sixteen. We saw an' done things no kid should even think of—an' not all the fightin' stopped at the end of that war neither."

Joe's eyes settled on Molly and Sadie as he spoke. His neck turned red as he added, "We's plumb sorry fer scarin' yore womenfolk an' fer bein' part a the crowd that gunned down yore boss."

Hicks nodded in agreement.

"Those fellers that worked us last night showed us the value of friendship by how they treated each other. These here punchers is good folks an' we seen that as we watched 'em work an' help each other. We'd be plumb honored to be part of this here outfit, but we know we ain't deservin' of it. That's all we have to say."

The hands were quiet as Joe and Hicks talked. Slim slapped his hat against his knee and muttered under his breath.

Smiley looked around with a big grin.

"Say, we'd shore work a little more fer some vittles if ya wouldn't mind. That food last night was the best we had in a long time!"

Slim and Tiny had started to turn away, but they slowed and looked back at Lance. Lance waved a hand. "I need five riders to move cattle today and cut hay. The rest of you help Slim work on his house. Eat some breakfast before you head out."

Lance started to stagger, and Old Man McNary grabbed him around his waist. Molly was scolding him as she followed the two men into the bedroom.

Badger's eyes twinkled as he trailed along behind.

"I reckon you'ins jist done hired yerself three more hands."

Lance looked at him and frowned.

"That vote's not in yet."

"Sure, 'tis," drawled Badger. "Them hands was already a leanin'. When that thar boy wanted ta work fer no more food'n he ate last night, they jist plumb turned soft."

Laughing wickedly, the old man strolled out to find his grandson.

CHAPTER 6

GIFTS FOR OUR GIRLS

THE WOMEN HAD BREAKFAST READY, AND THE MEN ate quickly. Martha and Sadie had made tubs of bear sign early that morning. The biscuits and gravy were a hit as well. Some of the hands could barely walk as they moved away from the table, rubbing their bellies.

One of the younger hands, Jonesy, commented, "The vittles 'round here have sure improved since Lance got married. Yes sir, I'm shore likin' this here bear sign." He belched and grinned as he walked to his horse with a package of donuts that Martha had insisted he take with him.

Slim didn't give any orders as to who stayed. He figured he would let the men decide themselves.

In no time, a large work crew was headed back over to Slim's spread. Joe and Hicks really did know how to work with stone although neither of them talked much. The other men were impressed with their know-how.

Smiley always had a grin and would tackle any rock, regardless of size. He didn't talk much either but was always whistling under his breath.

Sadie brought over dinner of fried fish, mulberry pie, and fried potatoes. She sat with Slim for a while and watched their house take shape. Slim was once again the happy man she had fallen in love with.

"Jist look at it, Sadie! Ain't she gonna be a beauty! How many kids do ya think we cin fit in there?" he asked with a sly grin.

Sadie blushed and laughed. She squeezed his arm and Slim squeezed her.

"Sadie, ya smell like mulberry pie. I could jist eat ya up right here!" he whispered in her ear.

The men paused in their work and started to hoot at Slim when he kissed her.

Sadie pulled away as she blushed and Slim grinned.

"Boys, I jist cain't seem to focus on my work when this little gal is 'round!" He winked at Sadie as he climbed down, and she turned the wagon back to the Rocking R headquarters.

Molly and Martha had the kitchen cleaned, and a large package was sitting on the table when Sadie arrived. Martha was smiling.

"Sadie, Badger and I wanted to get you something special for your wedding, so I contacted Margaret Good back in Kansas." Martha looked over at Molly as she added, "She owns the dry goods store in Manhattan, you know."

When Molly nodded, Martha continued, "She and I were always quite close when I lived in that little town. I wrote her that I had a special young lady getting married who was an excellent seamstress." She beamed at Sadie as she added, "I told her you were like a daughter to me. I asked her to send me some quality fabric for your wedding dress. Martha pointed at the package and added, "This just came in on the train yesterday."

Sadie was speechless. She didn't have the money to spend on a wedding dress and had been trying to redo an old dress.

As she opened the package, lots of lace tumbled out onto the table. Light green combed cotton and dark green brocade followed. At the bottom of the package was a sheet that showed several different dress styles and brief instructions.

Sadie gasped, "Martha, I can't accept this. I could never pay you back!"

Martha's smile became bigger.

"Badger and I wanted to do something special for two of our favorite girls. I insist." She pushed the package toward Sadie.

Then she reached behind her and handed Molly a package.

"I told Margaret I wanted something for you as well. Luckily, she had written down your measurements. She adjusted them for no tummy—although you are going to have one soon again!" she added as they all laughed.

Molly opened the package and took out a dress. It was done in light blue with small daisies. It was the latest fashion with a tight waist, full skirt, and an open neckline.

Molly held it up and twirled around.

"Oh, Martha," she breathed, "It is beautiful! It is nearly the same fabric that Lance picked for me when we went through Manhattan two years ago!"

Lance heard his name and soon appeared in the door. He watched Molly with a smile on his face.

"Lance—it is like the fabric you chose in Manhattan! Oh, it is so beautiful!" Molly exclaimed as she showed it to him.

Lance pulled Molly to him and kissed her.

"Molly girl—you make my heart tingle," he whispered softly as she twirled away with the new dress.

Martha and Sadie were barely listening. Sadie was laying the fabric out and estimating amounts. She was jotting notes on her paper and could hardly wait to start.

Martha handed her another package with needles, thread, pins, tape measure, and scissors.

"Someday, Sadie, we are going to open a women's store in Cheyenne. You will do all the alterations and sewing so you must have the right tools." Martha smiled at both young women with tears in her eyes.

Sadie and Molly hugged Martha. As Martha wrapped them up in her arms, she looked up and whispered, "Thank you, Lord, for bringing these two women into my life."

Quickly wiping her eyes, Martha suggested, "Sadie, why don't you do your sewing at my house? You can spread things out a little more and not have so many interruptions."

They all agreed that Sadie should go to Martha's to work. She could sew there easier with no little boys underfoot and into everything.

"I can't wait to show this to Slim!" Sadie exclaimed as she folded the fabric and carefully wrapped it. "Or maybe I will just surprise him at our wedding."

Molly began to laugh.

"Well, that secret ought to keep him busy," she commented dryly. "You do know Slim is like a dog on a trail when he suspects something is going on."

Sadie giggled as she nodded. "Oh, Martha! I am so excited!"

As Lance eased into bed, he smiled. Listening to the women chatter, he thanked God again for these three special women who had completely changed his life.

My Molly can sure open doors, Lance thought as he drifted off to sleep.

CHAPTER 7

ALL IN FAVOR, RAISE YOUR HANDS

SUPPER WAS A LITTLE LATE THAT EVENING AS everyone waited for the cowboys to return from working on Slim and Sadie's house. The rock work was completed, and Slim was proud.

Sadie is going to be durned excited when she sees her kitchen, Slim thought to himself. He had even partitioned off a room for her to use as a sewing room.

Tiny offered to make a bed. Smiley said he was a fair hand with wood, and he would be glad to help. Tiny tried to glare at him, but he wasn't very successful when Smiley gave Tiny his big grin. Smiley was right though—he was a master with wood. While the other fellows were finishing the stone, Tiny and Smiley found a downed cottonwood tree and went to work. They peeled the bark and sanded down the knots in the wood. The resulting bed was a four-poster made from peeled logs. Smiley had found some sandstone and was using it to smooth out the surfaces. It was too rough to give a completely smooth finish, but the result was beautiful. They even roughed out some counters in the kitchen and made a large table.

When the roof was completed that night, the house had walls and even a few pieces of furniture. Slim would have to chink the walls to fill in the gaps, but it was going to be a fine house.

The men were tired. As they gathered their tools, the rest of the Rocking R cowboys stopped by to look at their work. The riders rode around the house and were amazed.

"Where did you find the rock?" one of them asked.

"We quarried it out of that ledge over there. Slim had some of it already stacked up, but Tiny moved the rest when he was mad," Jonesy answered with a grin. "Tiny can sure throw the rock when he has a mad on!"

The riders laughed, and the weary group of cowboys mounted their horses to head for home.

They could smell the food as they rode up.

One of the riders commented quietly, "I don't think I've ever worked for a spread that feeds you like this one does."

"And you won't find one," another answered. "Don't quit 'cause there's a waitin' list to work here!"

Smiley, Joe, and Hicks were quiet. They packed their bedrolls and had their horses ready to go. They were watering them at the tank when Martha hollered for everyone to come in. The three men hesitated before they mounted their horses.

As they started down the lane, Tiny hollered after them, "Hey! Don't ya fellers know it's bad manners to leave without thankin' the cooks? Git on back here an' git some food in ya. Ya earned it today, an' 'sides, ya need to show yore 'preciation."

The three young men slowly turned back. They tied their horses and tentatively climbed the steps to get a plate of food. The Rocking R riders basically ignored them, and they ate by themselves.

Lance was sitting in a chair. When the meal was almost done, he stood stiffly and began, "All right. We are ready to vote. Who wants to keep on Smiley, Joe, and Hicks? Raise your hands if you are in favor."

Some hands went up quickly and others followed more slowly. Two of the riders who had been with the cattle were not sure, but Tiny shoved between them. He raised an arm for each. They grinned and the rest of the punchers cheered. They clapped the new riders on the back and returned to eating. Lance smiled and Slim winked at Sadie. Badger laughed his evil laugh as he looked at Lance.

"An' ya doubted me!" he chortled. "Now watch this."

Badger turned Mule loose. Mule walked among the men sniffing each one. He stopped by the new riders and pulled their hats off with his teeth. When he reached Smiley, he rubbed his head against the smiling cowboy's back. Smiley stopped eating and scratched Mule's ears as he talked to him. Badger grinned.

"Never doubt the judgment of a durn good mule!" Badger whistled for Mule and prepared to go home.

None of the cowhands except Slim and Lance knew what Mule was capable of. However, most were leery of the big jack because he did have a cantankerous personality. Smiley liked mules though, and obviously, Mule returned that feeling.

Lance, Slim, and Old Man McNary were pleased with how the entire situation had ended. The Old Man was whistling as he headed for his little cabin.

As Badger came out of the barn with his wagon, he hollered, "Smiley, when ya git tard a workin' fer Lance, why don't ya come over ta my place an' help me raise mules? I won't work ya so hard an' we'll feed ya good!"

With another evil grin, he helped Martha into the wagon, and they headed for home. Badger rode close to the wagon, and they could hear him singing "Lorena" to Martha.

"The years creep slowly by, Lorena," but by the third line, he had changed it to Martha. "The sun's low down the sky, my Martha."

Martha smiled contentedly and reached out to hold her husband's hand.

CHAPTER 8

MYSTERY SOLVED!

THE NEXT MONTH PASSED QUICKLY. SADIE HELPED every day with breakfast before she rode to Martha's to work on her wedding dress. She decided to surprise Slim, and she listened with a smile to Molly's warnings every day about how Slim was on a mission to find out what was going on.

The visits weren't all sewing though. Sadie asked Martha to teach her to make cinnamon rolls. Cinnamon rolls were Slim's favorite dessert.

Today was the day she was making them with no help. Martha smiled proudly as Sadie removed the first pan from the oven. The nearly finished wedding dress hung on the wall behind where they were working, forgotten for the moment as they admired Sadie's fresh rolls.

Slim had slipped out behind his future wife when she left the Rocking R that morning. When he stepped through Martha's door, Sadie looked up in surprise. She was concerned he would see the wedding dress, but she began to giggle when he stared at the cinnamon rolls. His blue eyes went wide, and he eased up to the table.

"Yore makin' cinneymon rolls? I *love* cinneymon rolls!"

He still hadn't spotted the dress, so Martha casually stepped behind Sadie as Slim drooled over the large rolls Sadie was lifting out of the pan. He leaned over to smell them and rolled his eyes as he begged Sadie for one.

"Come on, sweetheart. Don't ya know I am so hungry I could chew on my saddle? Now here ya are jist a teasin' me with these here rolls!"

Sadie began to giggle and even Martha laughed at his pitiful pleading. Sadie cut out a large roll, and Slim closed his eyes as he savored the delectable treat.

"So, this here is why y'all been a comin' over here? To learn to make cinneymon rolls? Oh, I've died an' gone to heaven!"

Sadie laughed and Martha shook her head. Slim was so focused on the cinnamon rolls that he was paying no attention at all to the rest of the room.

Martha cut another cinnamon roll out for him.

"Now, you get out of here, Slim Crandall. You let this girl finish, or there won't be any for your supper!" Martha ordered.

Slim sauntered back out the door, munching delightedly on his cinnamon roll.

Sadie laughed softly as she watched Slim strut back to his horse, proud he had everything figured out.

Wide shoulders, blue eyes that sparkle with orneriness, curly blond hair, tall... Sadie sighed. She laughed again as she hurried to get the rest of the warm rolls out of the pan before they stuck. She knew Slim was pleased with himself for solving the "mystery" of where she went every morning. More than that though, he was excited his future wife would be able to make him his favorite treat.

Sadie cut off a small cinnamon roll from the corner and hurried after him. Her face was flushed, and she had flour on her cheek.

"Here is a small one if you have room for one more," she whispered as she kissed his cheek.

Slim grinned at her in delight as he took it, and Sadie rushed back inside to finish. Her brown eyes were soft with happiness and her smile grew larger when she caught Martha's eye.

"He's had my heart from the first day I met him," Sadie whispered softly.

Martha smiled and hugged her.

"And you had his as well. Now let's get these finished so maybe you will get home a little earlier today."

Sadie took her dress home that evening. All she had left was the hemming, and she knew that Molly could help her with that.

The ruffled, cotton skirt dropped in tiers from the waist. The bodice, short sleeves, and the skirt overlay were dark green brocade. The overlay was open on one side of the skirt, and a large ruffle finished the bottom. The neckline was open. It angled down to a point in the front and was wider on the sides. Sadie had added a bow to one shoulder she made from the combed cotton.

When Sadie tried the dress on, Molly stared in amazement.

"Sadie, your dress is fabulous! You have made a gown like those we see in the ladies' magazines from the East. When the women of Cheyenne see this, you are going to be busy with lots of dress orders!"

Sadie smiled shyly and turned so Molly could see all the details. Because she wanted to wear it for other occasions, Sadie had made the lace into a beautiful shawl instead of a veil. It could slip over her head like a scarf or drop over her shoulders. She added additional lace trim and beading to the bottom. The result was a sheer top dropping down to an intricate bottom.

Molly hugged Sadie as her eyes filled with tears.

"Sadie, you are beautiful in everything you wear, but you are going to be breathtaking in your wedding dress. Slim won't be able to speak!"

Sadie laughed as she turned slowly around.

Molly whispered, "I am so going to miss having you here." She wiped at her eyes as she rolled them, "And I know you are just going to be a few miles away, but still—I am going to miss you so much."

Sadie nodded. She giggled as she answered, "Me too but I don't think Slim would appreciate me coming back here every day after all the work he has done on our house."

The two women wiped their eyes, and Molly moved a chair to the center of the room for Sadie to stand on. The full skirt was going to take a lot of pinning and Molly wanted to make sure it was even all the way around.

Once they had the hem pinned, Molly asked, "Do you want to hang it in our bedroom? That way, you won't have to worry about little boys touching it."

Sadie laughed and agreed as she handed her beautiful dress to Molly.

When Lance came in that evening, Molly pointed at the dress. "Now don't you be roughhousing with the boys in this bedroom. I do not want something to happen to that dress before the wedding."

Lance grinned at her and his eyes twinkled. "How about their mother? Would she like to wrestle a little bit or do those rules apply to her in here too?"

Molly turned a deep red, and as she dodged his hands she whispered, "Lance, if the boys hear you say things like that, they will repeat it!"

Lance chuckled. He was nearly back to normal. He had a little stiffness in his chest, but overall, he was healed—not that he had stayed in bed as the doctor suggested. Three days was all he could handle. After a week of being housebound, he was back in the saddle and stayed there for a half-day. Molly scolded him for doing too much, but when he took both of their little boys down in a tickling heap, she gave up.

CHAPTER 9

A WEDDING SURPRISE

FOR NEARLY A MONTH, SLIM, TINY, AND SMILEY worked on Slim's house every night after being in the saddle all day. Finally, Lance gave them the last three days off before the wedding. The house was almost done, and Slim wanted to complete it before the wedding as his gift to Sadie.

None of the other riders complained about the men's special treatment.

"You'd better rest up some, Slim. Y'all will be too tired to enjoy your new wife if ya don't git some sleep before yore weddin' day."

Slim grinned good-naturedly but they were right. He *was* tired. Tiny and Smiley were tired too, but Slim stayed even longer to clean up after the other two called it a day.

His plan was to be up by dawn on Thursday. He looked at his two helpers and shook his head.

"Boys, I know yore both tired 'cause I'm plumb worn out. I would shore like to finish that house today though. Then we cin all rest up on Friday an' be fresh as flowers fer the weddin' on Saturday."

The three men dropped into their bunks Wednesday night. They didn't even stay awake to eat supper.

The other hands discussed Slim's house with Lance as they ate supper.

"Those three fellers ain't been gettin' no sleep, boss. They cowboy all day an' spend over half a the night a workin' on Slim's house. Mebbie we should take a little time off our own selves an' help 'em finish."

Lance looked surprised.

"How long has that been going on?"

"Oh, 'bout a month now. Ever since Smiley an' the Johnson boys showed up. They got so durn much work done that Slim decided he wanted it finished 'fore him an' Sadie moved in. 'Fore that, he figgered he'd have to work on it over time. He was jist hopin' he'd have the roof on it by the time they married."

Lance looked around at the riders. Most were Slim's long-time friends. The ornery cowboy had worked for Old Man McNary several years before Lance arrived, and most of these riders had too.

"I like that idea. Why don't you try to leave quiet in the morning and we'll let those fellas sleep in. Maybe put something over the windows to keep it dark in there.

"I'll give all of you one day and then we're back to work like normal. Make it count." He dumped his coffee and was grinning when he went into the house.

Molly was drying dishes and cleaning up while Sadie washed dishes. She started to ask Lance what he was smiling about but he shook his head slightly. He squeezed her arm as he walked by.

"Three more days before you are hitched for life, Sadie. You still have time to change your mind!" Lance put his arm around Sadie's shoulders as he smiled at her.

"That's not going to happen, but Molly and I certainly have a lot of cooking to do between now and then."

"Oh, it's not all up to us. We are just responsible for the meat. The women in the neighborhood will all bring food for the rest of the meal—kind of like a potluck." Molly glanced over at Lance. She laughed and added, "And I asked Barney Ford to fix the meat, so you and I are going to make dessert.

"I told Lance when you move out that he has to hire a ranch cook. I can't keep up with my work and cook for all those men too. This is my first step to make sure that happens."

Lance stared at Molly for a moment before he slowly nodded.

"I guess I'd better get on that. When Molly makes up her mind, I just agree, or things get mighty hard for me."

Molly snorted as she threw the rag she was using at Lance. He caught it as he laughed.

"I'm headed to bed. Tomorrow is going to be a long day. Good night, ladies."

CHAPTER 10

A LITTLE BIT OF SPOONIN'

WHEN SLIM, TINY, AND SMILEY AWOKE ON THURSDAY, it was nearly nine in the morning. The rest of the hands were gone. They had blocked the windows with sacks, so it stayed dark in the bunkhouse.

Grabbing their books and their britches, the three men rushed to saddle their horses. They raced to Slim's spread. Slim was cursing under his breath for oversleeping.

"I jist don't understand. How did all three of us sleep this long? Why, it's pertineer noon!"

Tiny agreed but Smiley just shrugged.

"We was tired and when folks is tired, they sleep when they can."

As they pulled their horses to a stop in front of Slim's house, they heard men's voices and wood pounding. All the Rocking R hands as well as Lance, Old Man McNary, and Badger were putting the finishing touches on the house. The floor was down, the last of the walls were chinked, and a bucket of plaster mixed with horsehair sat on the floor.

Nearly half of the rooms showed wet plaster. Joe was showing some of the hands how to apply the last of the sticky mess while others were painting. In fact, just about everything was done.

Slim walked around his house and stared in amazement. He stared from these men he had worked with for so long to his house. His only comment was, "Wahl, Dad gum. Y'all shore tricked me this mornin'." He rubbed his bristly chin and shook his head.

Lance slapped his foreman on the back.

"Now don't get all squishy on us, Slim. We did it for Sadie!"

The rest of the men laughed and teased Slim as they finished their work.

After Lance and his riders left Thursday morning, Molly asked Sadie to watch the boys for the day.

"I would like to do a little shopping before the wedding if you don't mind, Sadie. I will be back sometime this afternoon."

Sadie looked disappointed. She agreed even though she had hoped to ride into Cheyenne for a few things herself.

She sighed and herded the little boys back into the house.

"Come, you two. You need to finish your breakfast before you go outside to play."

Molly felt bad as she drove the wagon out of her yard. *Sadie looks so disappointed.* However, the plan was in place and Molly needed to do her part.

"I'll see you this afternoon!" Molly called as she hurried the team toward Martha's. Sadie was talking to the little boys as she pushed them toward the house. She paid no attention to the direction the team was headed, and Molly knew her plan was going off without a hitch.

She had purchased supplies last week for Sadie and Slim's new house. They were stored at Martha's, waiting for the house to be completed. Lance and she had decided to stock the new couple's kitchen as part of their wedding surprise.

Martha drove into Slim's yard with a feather mattress in her wagon as well as a new quilt. Slim stopped painting and stared as Tiny grabbed the mattress and hauled it into the house. He and Smiley placed it on Slim's new bed.

Molly's wagon followed Martha's into the yard. Slim climbed down from the ladder and stared at the wagonful of food and kitchen goods.

"I don't know how y'all planned this without me knowin', Molly, but I shore appreciate it. Y'all an' Lance too."

Molly smiled brightly at the surprised cowboy. "Slim, ride back to the ranch right away. Sadie is there with the boys, and she really wants to make a trip to Cheyenne. I will be there as soon as we unload these supplies, and then the two of you can have the rest of the day off."

Slim took off on his horse like something was after him. By the time Molly arrived, he had a horse saddled for Sadie and tied in front of the house. He was sitting on the porch beside her and was being mauled by two little boys.

As Molly pulled the wagon to a stop, Slim scooped Sadie up and carried her off the porch while Sammy hung on one leg and Paul drug on the other. After he set her on her horse and helped Molly down from the wagon, he picked the boys up and carried them back to the house. They were giggling and wiggling as he dropped them on the porch.

"Sammy," Slim whispered, "I'm goin' to take my gal to town. Do ya think I should take her dancin' or jist out fer supper?"

Sammy grinned. "Supper an' dancin' an' a little bit a spoonin' too!"

Slim began to laugh, and Molly looked around in surprise.

"Who told you about spooning, Sammy?"

Sammy answered with a grin, "Pa did. He said a feller should always spoon with his favorite gal an' his favorite gal is you, Ma!"

Molly blushed as Sammy added, "But I ain't real sure what spoonin' is. I think maybe it has to do with huggin' an' kissin' 'cause Pa sure does like to do that."

Molly grabbed Sammy and hurried him into the house as Sadie giggled and Slim laughed louder.

Lance had given all the riders the evening off, and seventeen cowboys were riding into Cheyenne for a night on the town. As they rushed to get ready, the bunkhouse was loud and rowdy.

When Lance rode into the yard, he could hear lots of commotion from the bunkhouse. The riders all pushed and shoved each other as they fought for first water.

Joe, Hicks, and Smiley stood outside and watched until a nearly naked Tiny hollered at them. "Ya boys git in here. The Rocking R is goin' out on the town an' we's all a goin'!"

As Tiny ducked back inside, one of the other hands threw a bucket of water at him. There was a roar from Tiny and some crashing of beds. Before long, Jonesy fell through the open door.

He winked at the three surprised young men and drawled, "I'd clean up at the horse tank was I you!" Then he dove back inside.

Slim and Sadie were the first ones home while the rest trickled in throughout the night. Tiny was the last to arrive. He was supported by Joe, Hicks, and Smiley.

Joe and Hicks weren't much on drinking. Smiley liked beer but he stayed away from the whiskey. Tiny wasn't usually affected by anything. However, his best buddy was getting married, and he had danced the night away with a redhead he'd met at the Cheyenne Billiard Hall.

"My little Cheyenne Rose loves me, boys! Why we jist danced all night!" Tiny slurred.

The other hands tried to tell Tiny that he paid to dance with her—it was her job to dance with cowboys—but Tiny was convinced she was dancing only with him. He was sure he was in love. It took all three of them to get Tiny off his horse and into bed.

CHAPTER 11

"Father!"

LANCE HAD THE MEN UP AT DAWN THE NEXT DAY TO catch up on the work that didn't get done on Thursday. He had hay to stack and cattle to move. They only had a short amount of time to get it done, especially since they all wanted Saturday off for Slim's wedding.

Molly handed each rider a couple of biscuits with sausage as they headed out. Bacon, as Sammy had called the pig, was now smoked, and the hams were in brine.

Lance watched Molly put her hands on her back as she walked back into the house.

"I need to hire a cook. Molly can make desserts for the men if she wants, but this is too much for her—especially with Sadie leaving. She shouldn't be doing all this cooking."

Once he had everyone lined out, Lance headed back to the house. "Molly!" he hollered.

Molly poked her head around the corner and shushed him.

"The boys aren't up yet," she whispered as she put her finger to her lips.

"I am headed into Cheyenne to hire a cook for the men. Do you want to go along?" Lance whispered loudly.

Sadie was fixing breakfast for the boys. She turned around as Lance whispered.

"Oh, Molly, take a day off and spend it with your husband!" she exclaimed. "The two of you have had no time together. I'll be fine here. I'll make those cakes while you are gone."

She debated briefly before she put on her new dress. *If I need to, I will wash it tonight.*

As Lance started to lift her into the wagon, he paused and whistled. "Molly girl, you just keep getting prettier by the day."

Molly smiled contentedly as Lance set her down. She took his arm as he jumped into the wagon, and they started for Cheyenne.

It was a bright, crisp fall morning. Molly took a deep breath.

"What a beautiful day. I so love the air up here. This fall weather is beautiful too. I hope tomorrow is as nice." She settled a little closer to Lance as she smiled. Her smile slowly faded as she thought of all she needed to do. *The wedding meal is a potluck. That makes it so much easier. Martha and I need to do some cooking in the morning though. Lance's shirt is done, and I can buy him new britches this morning. Still, I shouldn't be taking the day off. I don't have the shirts done I was making for the little boys!*

Then she looked at Lance's handsome profile and listened to his whistling as he drove. She snuggled closer and tried to push her thoughts of work aside. *I'll get the boys some shirts this morning. Right now, I just want to enjoy this day with my husband.*

"People before things," she whispered, and Lance grinned at her.

Cheyenne was bustling and busy. Lance talked to several men he knew as they drove by. He asked each one if they knew of any ranch cooks available. He had several possibilities by the time he left Molly at the dry goods store.

"I'll meet you at the Ford House in forty-five minutes."

Molly slowly picked out the items she wanted, savoring the quiet but missing the noise of her little boys. Suddenly, she heard a familiar voice. She lifted her head to listen more closely. A tall man with white hair was asking directions to the Rocking R Ranch.

"Father! You came!" Molly cried as she ran towards him.

Samuel Brewster turned as Molly cried out. His face crumpled as he gathered in the daughter he thought he'd lost.

With tears streaming down her face, Molly hugged her father. Tears were leaking from his eyes as he kissed her cheek.

"I missed you so much," Molly whispered as her father hugged her tightly. She quickly paid for her items and led her father to the Ford Restaurant.

"Oh, Father! I have so much to tell you! We have two sons and another little one who will arrive in about four months. I can't wait for you to meet Lance. Our friends, Sadie and Slim will be married tomorrow so you will meet all our riders and many of the neighbors!"

As Molly chattered on excitedly, she realized that she had asked her father nothing about himself or his trip. She took his hands.

"Tell me about your trip—how long will you be able to stay?"

Samuel Brewster smiled at his daughter and drank in her excitement. It had been so long since anyone had made him this happy. Slowly he answered.

"After you left, I didn't have any reason to stay in Georgia. It wasn't long before I put the ranch on the market. I had several offers, but I didn't accept any until I received Lance's letter inviting me to visit."

At Molly's questioning look, he explained, "Lance wrote me about two months ago and invited me out to the Rocking R. It was while, according to him, while he was 'stuck in the house' after he had been shot. I sold the ranch, liquidated my livestock, and now I am hoping to invest in land around here. I am moving to Cheyenne, Molly."

Molly squealed aloud, "Oh, Father! You are going to love Wyoming, and the boys will be so excited to have another grandfather!"

As Lance walked into the Ford Restaurant, he just followed the turned heads. They led him to his wife. Men always turned to look at

Molly when she walked by, but she was oblivious to their attention. As he strolled back to where she was sitting, he saw a distinguished-looking older man talking to her. When she looked up with tears of joy in her eyes, Lance knew who had arrived.

"Mr. Brewster, it is so nice to finally meet my father-in-law," Lance stated as he shook Samuel's hand.

When Samuel Brewster looked into Lance's eyes, he saw a strong man with a kind heart—a heart that was full of love for Samuel's little girl.

Samuel had never stopped regretting the day he had put Molly on that train for New Orleans. He had arranged for some friends returning to Georgia to meet her at the station and bring her back home. However, they never saw her disembark the train.

He was brokenhearted and so ashamed of himself. When he received the brief note from Molly saying she had married and the baby's name was Paul, he was relieved but even more sad. Sad he would never meet his grandson but happy that Molly was all right.

Lance's invitation to visit was second chance he needed. He decided immediately to move. In Cheyenne, he would be closer to the only daughter and living relative he had. He hoped she would eventually forgive him.

Samuel shook Lance's hand and encircled his son-in-law in a bear hug. "Thank you for loving my little girl and for keeping her safe," he whispered hoarsely as he put an arm around Molly.

"Did you bring anyone with you, Father, or did you travel by yourself?" Molly asked as she smiled at the two men.

"I only brought Gus," Samuel replied. "I was afraid good camp cooks would be hard to find, and Gus was open for a change."

Lance perked up. "You brought a ranch cook with you? Would he be willing to work for us until you are settled? We are in dire need of someone to cook for our ranch hands."

Just then, Molly saw Gus walking toward her with a smile on his wrinkled, black face.

"Gus!" she cried as she ran into his arms.

"Hello, little girlie! 'Ol Gus has sure missed you!" He held her off to look at her and with twinkling eyes he commented, "So a wee one is on the way. A little girl, I'm thinking!"

Molly blushed and straightened her dress. "Yes," she said, "in four months, but we will have to wait to see what I have."

Gus shook his head and said again, "It will be a wee little girl and you can plan on it." Then he looked around and asked, "So where are these small boys I have been hearing about. I have my pockets full of candy and it is going to melt if I don't get rid of it."

Molly laughed. "They are at home. Lance wanted to come to Cheyenne to find a ranch cook, but we sure didn't know we would run into you and Father!"

Gus grinned. "I suppose I could educate these cowboys on true southern cooking!" he drawled with a laugh. He turned to Lance.

"So, you are the cowboy who stole our Molly's heart!" Gus winked at Molly and stretched out his hand to Lance.

Lance grinned as he shook Gus' hand.

"I believe she stole my heart long before I wore her down." He put his arm around Molly and pulled her close.

The four of them talked and caught up as they ate. When Barney Ford, the owner of the Ford Restaurant, heard that Gus could cook, he tried to hire him on the spot.

Gus shook his head. "Sure now, I already have a job, but I will keep you in mind if something changes."

Lance grinned at both men.

"I guess it's a good thing I asked you first, Gus. Good cooks are in mighty high demand here."

CHAPTER 12

Gus

THE TRIP HOME WAS NOISY AND FULL OF LAUGHTER.
Gus rode beside Lance, and Molly sat by her father on the buckboard. Samuel quizzed Lance about the land, the railroad, the price of cattle, and what breeds he ran. Lance was excited to talk about his two greatest passions—land and cattle. Only Molly knew that pie came in a close third.

When Gus found out that Lance loved pie, he laughed. He was the pie master in their area, and he had shared that skill with Molly.

"You know, I taught our Molly to make pies. She didn't want to stay in the house, but her mother insisted on at least a half-day. Oh, it didn't happen every day, but when I figured out that Molly liked to cook and bake, we made all kinds of things. She didn't argue with her mother on those days. After Mrs. Brewster passed away, Molly helped more in the house. Some days though, I just sent her out to ride. She loves to ride horses, that girl does."

Molly and her father talked about Babe, the little boys, the wedding, the ranch hands, Badger and Martha, and finally, where Samuel would stay. Since Sadie was moving out, Samuel could bunk with the little boys and Gus would sleep in the bunkhouse with the men. Although

Molly had preferred to feed the men out of her kitchen, Gus said he'd use the small kitchen attached to the bunkhouse.

"Gus, the camp kitchen is small. You are welcome to use my kitchen too if you'd like," Molly offered.

"No, Missy, I will use the camp kitchen. That is what I'm familiar with and no wee ones will be in my space," Gus answered with a grin. "I did bring some of my own cooking tools, so I just need to see how it is stocked."

As the wagon pulled into the yard, two little boys rushed out to greet them. Paul pulled back when he saw the strangers, but Sammy climbed right up on the wagon. He stretched his hand out to Samuel.

"My name is Sammy Rankin. And you are?"

Samuel grinned at him as he answered, "Why my name is Samuel Brewster, but you may call me Grandpa if you want!"

Sammy's blue eyes became large as he looked around at Molly. "Another grandpappy!" he shouted. "I have three grandpappies?" Then he saw Gus.

"Are you a grandpappy too? Grampy Badger said a feller can't have too many grandpappies."

Gus grinned as he answered, "My name is Gus. How about you call me Uncle Gus?"

Sammy was delighted. "Another uncle! Paul, we have two uncles and three grandpappies! Holy Smokes! It just doesn't get any better than this!"

Then Sammy noticed Gus' bulging pockets.

"Say, whatcha have in yer pockets? Did ya bring candy?" he asked hopefully.

"Sammy, you don't ask people for candy," Molly scolded.

Sammy looked up at her with big eyes. "But I didn't really ask him fer candy. I just asked 'im if he *brung* any candy."

Gus was laughing and Molly shook her head. "That sounds like something Badger would say!" she muttered under her breath as Lance lifted her out of the wagon. Then she saw Lance's grin and she laughed.

Sammy adored all his grandfathers. As the little boy began to ply Gus with questions, Molly frowned. *Just maybe Father and Gus will be able to influence Sammy's speech a little in the right direction. He talks more like Badger every day.*

Lance helped Samuel carry in his bags and Sammy followed, asking questions. "Are ya goin' to sleep in my room? Can I sleep with ya? Do ya snore? Paul wets the bed sometimes, but I don't wet the bed. Do ya ever wet the bed? Is my Mommy yer kid? Did ya spank her when she was little? Papa says she's a pistol, but I don't really know what that means."

Samuel was grinning when Molly finally pulled Sammy away and sent him outside. Sammy immediately found Gus.

As he helped Gus carry his gear into the bunkhouse, Sammy asked, "Did ya burn yore face? Is that why it's so black? Do ya like to cook? My mommy's a good cook. My papa says she makes the best pies he has ever tasted!"

Gus picked Sammy up and set him on top of the fence.

"I didn't burn my face—the Good Lord made me this way just like he gave you freckles and yellow hair."

Sammy's eyes became big.

"I didn't know God made different colors of folks. Why, how many colors are there? Does he make some folks green? I think it would be fun to be green or blue."

Gus laughed as he shook his head.

"I have never seen any blue or green folks, but I guess the Good Lord could sure do that if he wanted to!" He smiled up at Sammy.

"You know, I taught your momma to make pies. When she was a little girl, I was the cook at her house. She used to help me. Her momma died when she was just a little squirt so I taught her a lot of the things her mommy would have. I love to cook, and I can show you how to cook too if you want to learn."

Sammy stared at Gus for a moment. He looked behind him to make sure his mother wasn't listening before he whispered, "Could ya teach me to make candy?"

Gus grinned. He leaned close and whispered, "Why I sure could! Maybe we will do that one day when your momma is gone for the day."

Sammy's big blue eyes were sparkling with excitement as Gus lifted him down from the fence.

Suddenly, Gus's eyes opened wide, "Say, could you help me with these pockets. I don't know what I have in them, but it needs to come out!"

Sammy emptied every pocket and as they ate the candy he found there, he decided he liked this new uncle.

Paul was peeking around a corner. Sammy grabbed him and drug him over to Gus. Gus lifted Paul onto his lap, and the three of them talked and ate candy until it was gone.

When Molly called the boys for supper, Sammy claimed he wasn't hungry.

"My tummy hurts, Momma. I think a rock is stuck in it."

Molly looked at Gus with suspicion and he grinned at her. He shrugged his shoulders as he winked at Sammy.

Sammy grinned back and then spent the next half hour trying to wink like Gus.

CHAPTER 13

HOPE IN A BOX

SATURDAY BROKE SUNNY AND CRISP. IT WAS A PERFECT September day, and the fall air was cooling quickly.

Gus had come up to the house the night before to pick up the supplies he needed. He was up before sunrise with hot food ready at the break of dawn. He banged the triangle and hollered for the men.

"Come and get it before I throw it out!"

Gus was in bed when the riders called it a night. The men were looking around cautiously to see who the new cook was. Some of them were grumbling as they were not excited about giving up Molly's meals. When the men slowly trickled into the camp kitchen to get their food, Gus grinned at them.

"Fill 'er up, boys! It's a plenty we have!"

Some of the hands whispered as they sniffed the air. "I hope it tastes as good as it smells," one cowboy muttered as he stepped up with his plate. He tasted the food tentatively, and then began to wolf it down.

Some of the hands standing in line asked him how it was.

He glared at them. "Terrible. I would skip breakfast was I you!" Then he began to gobble his food again.

Samuel Brewster quietly climbed out of bed and walked to the window. He was a tall man who looked immaculate even upon waking. He pushed his hand through his neat hair as he looked back at the two little boys stretched across the bed. He smiled. *Last night was not the most restful of nights, but what a joy to have grandsons.*

Sammy and Paul were still asleep. Both had climbed in bed with him during the night. Samuel's smile became larger as he looked at their innocent little faces.

"It has been a long time since I have been pummeled like that during the night," he muttered to himself as chuckled.

Samuel pulled a small box out of his travel bag. His smile faded as he stared at it.

He looked toward the door that led to the kitchen. He listened to the happy voices and the sound of his daughter's laughter. Then he opened the box and stared at the contents.

Samuel Brewster had been part of the reconstruction of the South when the war ended. He had worked closely with the organization that was helping the government to identify the bodies of dead Confederate soldiers. It saddened him to think of the number of young men who were buried in unmarked graves or misidentified because no one knew who they were.

Identification on any soldier was rare. Some of the sutlers' stores had started offering identification buttons toward the end of the war, and many of the Union soldiers purchased the small metal disks made of brass or lead. However, pay was in short supply in the South, and identification buttons were extremely rare among the Confederate soldiers. Even among the soldiers who did purchase them, the buttons were sometimes lost, or their importance was not recognized during the identification process. Identification was sketchy at best and was usually based on letters or pictures found on the fallen soldiers.

Paul Rankin's body had been identified by a letter found in his pocket from his brother, Lance Rankin. It was a letter from an older brother to a younger one telling him to keep his head down and to talk to his Maker every day. Lance mentioned the scar over Paul's eye resulting from a tree-climbing accident. He also told Paul not to be flashing his blue eyes at any of those northern girls or he might not ever be able to come back south.

The body labeled as Paul Rankin was listed as having no scars and brown eyes. After Lance wrote to Samuel and invited him out, Samuel contacted his friend in the reconstruction group. He asked if he could have the letter as the Lance who had written it was now his son-in-law.

He received the package just a week before he left for Cheyenne. In addition, his friend had included all the personal effects that had been on the body identified as Paul Rankin.

Samuel pondered how to address this. *Perhaps Paul is alive or perhaps the person writing down the details of the bodies was in a hurry and didn't see the scar.* However, the brown eyes were what had him wondering the most.

He finally decided to show the packet of items to Lance after the wedding. He would tell him what he knew. A small frown creased Samuel's face.

"I sure don't want to give Lance hope where there is none," he worried softly to himself as he studied the items on the bed.

Samuel rewrapped the small box and tucked it into his travel bag. He opened the door to the kitchen just as Lance kissed a giggling Molly. Watching them for a few moments, he said a quiet prayer of thanksgiving that the Good Lord had sent this man to take care of his little girl.

"Father!" Molly exclaimed as she blushed a deep red and stepped back. "Are you ready for breakfast?"

Samuel smiled at his daughter and kissed the top of her head.

"Never be embarrassed to show affection for the ones you love," he whispered softly in her ear. "Savor these moments and make them count."

As he hugged his only child, Molly smiled up at him.

"I have missed you so much, Father," she murmured. "I am so happy you will be living with us while you resettle here."

Lance watched them and was pleased. He didn't think Molly would be upset he had invited her father without telling her. However, his wife was truly delighted, and that made Lance a happy man.

"Martha will be here soon to start cooking for the wedding, so let's just eat with the men and save you some cleanup," Lance suggested with a grin. "I want my pretty wife ready to dance tonight!" He grinned and winked at her as he kissed her cheek. Then he whispered in her ear, "And maybe play a little after that!"

Molly blushed again as she shushed him.

"Lance! My father will hear you!" she whispered as she avoided his hands and rushed outside.

Lance grinned and Samuel smiled as the two men strolled through the kitchen door.

CHAPTER 14

A Finished Home

SLIM WAS ONE OF THE LAST IN LINE FOR BREAKFAST. His cheeks were flushed, and he was nervous. A smile filled his face even while he ate.

The other riders began to rib him. He grinned and took their teasing good-naturedly. As he ate, he watched the front door for Sadie. When she finally appeared towing two little boys, Slim dropped his plate and hurried to meet her. He gave her a long kiss while the men hooted and hollered.

Sadie blushed and laughed.

"Sadie gurl, let's go fer a ride an' see our new house," Slim suggested. His blue eyes were shining. He couldn't wait to show his future wife their finished home. "Ya haven't seen it since all the boys worked on it, an' I want ya to see it in daylight."

Sadie agreed excitedly.

Gus handed her a plate of food. He grabbed the little boys and took them back into the kitchen with him.

Sadie sat down beside Slim and ate quickly. She hurried back into the house to grab a jacket while Slim saddled the horses.

When they pulled their horses to a stop in front of their house, Sadie looked around in surprise.

"How did you get all this done?" she asked in amazement. "You told me we would have to finish some of it ourselves after we moved in!"

Slim laughed. "I know. The fellers all helped some. Tiny, Smiley, an' me worked this past month ever' night after we got done with the ranch work. Lance finally gave us Thursday an' Friday off. Then, before we woke up on Thursday, all the boys come over an' worked. It was pertineer done when they left. Tiny and Smiley helped me yesterday to add a few little touches." He led her into the kitchen.

"Look! Molly an' Lance even stocked us up with food an' cookin' things."

Tears of wonder filled Sadie's eyes. "How are we ever going to repay all these people, Slim?"

Slim pulled her close. "Family, Sadie. We're a family an' y'all don't worry 'bout paying folks back when you're family. Ya don't pay back— y'all help the next person out."

As Slim stepped back, he reached into his pocket. His blue eyes were serious as he smiled at his future wife.

"Sadie, I have somethin' special fer ya." He placed a beautiful gold locket in her hand. "It belonged to my ma an' now it's yores," he drawled softly.

Sadie's brown eyes were soft as she held up the locket and studied the details. When she opened it, she saw a black-haired version of Slim and a beautiful blonde woman with sparkling blue eyes.

"Oh, Slim. This is beautiful! Please tell me how your folks died? I know they are both gone." She held the locket up to her neck for Slim to fasten.

Slim's blue eyes were serious as he fastened the necklace. He rested his chin on Sadie's head and was quiet for a moment before he answered.

"They was both killed in an Injun raid down in Texas when I was small. Ma sent me an' my little sis down to hide in the creek bank under a tangle of roots. She pushed this locket into my hand as she shoved me out the back window. Josie, my little sis, she wasn't quite six at the time. I was a little older. I carried her most of the way on my back 'cause she couldn't keep up. The Injuns looked fer us, but they didn't find us.

"We waited a full day to come out. The Injuns was gone so I started diggin' a grave. Then some soldiers come. They finished diggin' the grave an' we put the folks in the ground together." He paused as he looked over Sadie's head through the open door.

"Ma had a prissy sister who lived in a town 'bout a hundred miles away. She took us in. I stayed fer a time an' then I ran away."

He looked down at Sadie and grinned, "An' now I'm a goin' to marry the purtiest gal around an' we are a goin' to fill this here house with little feet!" he whispered as he grabbed Sadie and twirled her around.

Sadie laughed and hung on. When they stopped spinning, she asked, "What about your sister? Have you talked to her since you left?"

Slim shook his head. "I wrote her a couple a times, but I never heard back. My aunt lived close to San Antonio when she took us in, but they might a moved."

Sadie looked up at Slim and softly asked, "Would you care if I write to her? I would love for us to get to know your sister."

Slim stared at Sadie for a moment before he hugged her.

"Sweet Sadie. That would be fine," he agreed as they walked out of their new home together.

CHAPTER 15

SLIM'S LITTLE SISTER

WHEN SADIE AND SLIM RETURNED TO THE ROCKING R, the ranch was in full-blown celebration mode. Lance, Tiny, and Smiley were setting planks of wood on barrels to make benches. When Lance asked Tiny where the wood came from, the big cowpuncher just grinned.

"Don't ya worry none, boss. I didn't steal it so that's all ya need to know."

Molly and Martha were cooking up a storm in the house while Gus was making the wedding cake in his kitchen. Both Sadie and Slim could smell the cake as they rode up.

Slim stuck his head into the camp kitchen and stared. He had never seen a cake like that before. "That-that cake is 'most a foot tall!" he sputtered.

Sadie peered in around Slim. "Gus! Your cake is beautiful! May I taste the frosting?"

Gus nodded and handed Sadie a spoon.

"Gracious, Gus! I guess you will be responsible for the cake from now on!" she exclaimed as she licked the creamy, white deliciousness off her spoon.

Slim moved off to help Lance, and Sadie rushed into the house to help Mollie and Martha. They noticed her locket right away. Soon the kitchen was full of chatter as Sadie told them all about her morning.

Badger had picked Paul and Sammy up early that morning. He was quite secretive, and the little boys barely talked before they left. They clamped their mouths shut whenever anyone asked them a question.

Gus moved the cake to the bunkhouse and prepared dinner for everyone. As they ate, Molly watched the lane that led to their house. Badger and the little boys were still not back. She was getting worried.

She started to say something to Lance, but he just grinned and winked at her. Molly knew immediately that he was in on whatever the secret was.

Just then, Badger appeared on the lane with the two little boys and a young woman. The riders who were trickling in for dinner stopped to stare at the girl in Badger's wagon. She was a tiny, blue-eyed blonde with dimples, lots of curves, and a friendly smile.

Slim stopped. He slowly took a step toward her.

"Josie? Is that you?"

The young woman jumped down from the wagon and rushed toward Slim.

"Charlie! Charlie Crandall" she cried while Slim turned a deep red.

Until that moment, very few on the ranch knew Slim's given name and only a few knew his last name. However, none of the cowboys heard what the young woman had called Slim anyway—they were too busy trying to absorb all the wonderful details of this new girl who had magically shown up at the ranch—and on the day of a party and a dance.

Tiny was the first to recover. His words were, "I think I'm in love!" as he rushed toward Slim.

Lance laughed with the rest of the riders and shook his head. *Those boys won't be able to focus on work for as long as she's around.* His mouth twisted into a wry grin. "Good thing she isn't staying!" He was still smiling as he moved forward with the rest of the men to meet Slim's little sister.

Badger had taken the boys for baths in Cheyenne, and Sammy had lots of details to share with everyone. They finally gathered that a wagon of scantily dressed women had driven through Cheyenne.

"Pa, those ladies forgot they was in town 'cause they was all wearin' their underwear! They was real friendly-like though. They even offered to let me go for a ride in their wagon, but Badger wouldn't let me."

Paul just grinned and ate handfuls of the candy that seemed to be falling out of his pockets.

Molly tried to glare at Badger, but he just winked at her and walked away whistling.

She hollered after him, "Thank you for taking the boys for baths, Badger!"

He waved at her over his head and continued to whistle as he headed toward the house to find his Martha.

CHAPTER 16

A WEDDING ON THE ROCKING R

SOON IT WAS TIME TO CHANGE CLOTHES AND GET ready for the wedding. Sadie was breathless and nervous. Her hands were shaking, and she kept saying she was hot. Martha sat her down at the table and told her to take some deep breaths.

"Just relax, Sadie, and enjoy the party along with everyone else." She took a bottle of brandy out of her bag and poured a small amount into a glass for Sadie to drink. Then Martha kissed Sadie's cheek and pushed her toward the bedroom to change. Somehow, Molly had managed to change during all the commotion, and she was laying out Sadie's dress on the bed.

Lance had taken a dip in the creek. As he came in to change, Molly shooed him into the boys' room. Molly had already set out clothes for the little boys, and Martha was helping them to dress. Badger had on his suit with tails, as well as his favorite top hat. He looked quite distinguished.

Lance took Sadie's arm as she came out of the bedroom.

"You look beautiful, little sister!" he whispered to the nervous Sadie. "Deep breaths now. Trust me, Slim is more nervous than you are."

Sadie truly did consider Lance her brother, and he was pleased to give her away at her wedding. He was going to double-duty it today as he was also Slim's best man. Molly would stand up with Sadie while Martha, Badger, Samuel, and Old Man McNary were in charge of the little boys. Badger handed each one of the grandfathers a sack of candy and winked at the boys. Sammy and Paul were quite contented to sit down with them. All the cowboys were angling for a spot next to Josie, and they made more noise than the little boys did.

When the preacher arrived, one of the neighbors started to play "When Tis Moonlight" softly on his fiddle. The music floated through the air and echoed away across the hills.

At last, Sadie stepped out of the house, escorted by Lance.

"I can hardly breathe," she whispered to Lance.

"Well, don't faint or Slim will join you. He's been stirred up all morning," Lance whispered back.

Sadie laughed softly as she looked for Slim. When she saw him, she smiled. His face was pale, and he looked like he might faint.

Slim stared at Sadie and appeared to have lost his ability to speak. He barely heard what the preacher said and stumbled through his vows.

Sadie's dress fit her perfectly, and she was wearing the locket he had given her. She was a beautiful bride and Slim's knees were shaking. The pastor read from the *Book of Psalms* and the wedding went off without a hitch. Slim did hear the pastor say, "You may kiss the bride," and he made it a good one.

Sadie was blushing and breathless, and Slim finally looked more like his ornery self.

The potluck meal was excellent, and everyone was amazed by Gus' cake, especially all the children. Little finger trails tracked all around the bottom it as every child there managed to take a swipe of the frosting when no one was looking.

Sammy was reaching his finger toward it when Molly caught him.

"Ah, Ma. I jist wanted to see if this here side tasted as good as the others. I think I like the backside the best. It has more of that white stuff on it. Paul likes that side the best too."

Molly shook her head as she wiped the frosting off the boys' happy faces. "Now don't touch that cake again or I will give your piece to your father," she scolded as she shooed them away.

Soon neighbors began to pull out their musical instruments. There were harmonicas, an accordion, two fiddles, and two boys who played spoons.

The men began to line up to ask Josie to dance and Tiny pushed his friends out of the way. He wanted to be the first in line.

"Miss Josie, would ya do me the honor of this first dance? I might be too skunked later an' I don't want to step on yore toes."

Josie laughed and Tiny swung her around the yard. His hours of dancing in the Cheyenne Billiard Hall had finally paid off.

The music was lively, and there was dancing long after midnight. Josie did not sit down for a single dance and was still enjoying herself.

Molly put the sleepy little boys in bed at ten. Lance and she retired three hours later, but the party showed no signs of ending. Finally, Slim bid everyone goodnight and took his bride to their new home. Josie was staying with Martha and Badger, but they did not seem to be in any hurry to get home. Molly could hear the music long after Lance and she went inside. She rolled over in bed to talk, but Lance was asleep. He smiled in his sleep when she kissed him and pulled her close.

Even though she was tired, Molly lay awake awhile and thought about the day. *Josie was the "Belle of the Ball."* Molly laughed to herself as she thought about the cowboys. *They will be so tired today. They were all convinced one of them could win her over if she stayed.*

"Now you be sure to come and visit again—and maybe stay awhile next time," Molly told Josie during the party.

"Oh, yes, I plan to come back next summer—perhaps Slim and Sadie will be expecting by then." Josie answered with a hopeful smile. "I want to stay longer and get to know Sadie better." She paused and added softly, "I can't wait to be an aunt. I am so excited to see my big brother as a father."

Now Josie was leaving in just a few hours much to the disappointment of every single man present. The cowboys had all been arguing about who would take her to meet the train, but Slim ended the arguments when he announced he would take his own sister to Cheyenne. He and Sadie would pick up Josie at seven Sunday morning so she could catch her ten-thirty train.

"What a long ride to make with almost no sleep," she whispered into the darkness. "That poor girl will be exhausted today and probably all week as well." Then she remembered Josie's laughter and she giggled out loud. "Josie had such a good time. I'm guessing she will believe her long trip was worthwhile."

Molly smiled contentedly as she fell asleep. She had enjoyed their first wedding on the ranch, and she hoped there would be many more. *I love our little community of family and friends.*

City Cemetery
Columbus, Georgia
October 1870

CHAPTER 17

HER SOLDIER

BETH WILLIAMS WALKED QUICKLY TOWARD THE Columbus City Cemetery. The sun's rays caught in her blonde hair and made it shine like spun gold. Her green eyes sparkled with a pure zest for life as she hurried down the street. Beth was four inches over five feet tall, and her slender body held a big heart. She was quick to spot sadness and always did what she could to make people more comfortable.

The October sun was setting on a soft Georgia evening. This was Beth's favorite time of the day. She had been coming to this cemetery since the Battle of Columbus had added the graves of soldiers from both sides of that terrible war.

Every week, she dreaded and yet hoped to see the name of her brother, Eli, on one of those stones. He had been declared missing and presumed dead. She and her older brother, Reuben, were the only remaining members of her immediate family.

Reuban didn't approve of Beth's weekly visits to the cemetery, but she looked forward to them. The cemetery was quiet and peaceful. She walked among the graves and read the tombstones. She often talked to the men who were buried there.

Beth came every week to visit and pray. In her heart, she believed Eli was dead. However, since his body had never been found, she kept a tiny spark of hope alive.

The flowers and gardening tools she carried were for the tomb of "her soldier." Somehow, Beth was drawn to the grave of Sergeant Paul Rankin. She didn't know who he was or anything about him. However, when walking by his tomb that very first time nearly three years ago, she had felt a catch in her heart. The weeds had grown up around the stone, and the grass over his grave was rough and untended.

Beth pulled weeds that first day and then sat back on her feet to rest. As she looked at the tidy grave, she felt a deep sense of sadness. Beth cried over his grave that day. She cried for the loss of a young man she would never know and for all the young men who were now buried there.

"So many wasted lives," she had whispered to herself as her tears fell. Lee had surrendered before the Battle of Columbus had ever taken place. However, communications hadn't made it through to the front lines and more lives were lost that day.

"Oh, Eli, if only you had known, maybe you would still with us—and Sergeant Rankin too."

Beth shifted her load as she reached to open the cemetery gate. A large stallion stood outside the fence. He reached his nose toward her, and she petted him without thinking. Then she pulled her small hand back.

Rueben has told me many times not to pet strange horses. Yet, here I am, petting this stallion, she thought to herself. Still, the horse seemed friendly. With a toss of her blonde curls, she reached over and scratched his ears.

"That horse is not tied in any way. He surely is a pet to someone," she whispered to herself as she hurried through the gate.

Beth looked like she was little more than a girl, but she was wise for her twenty-one years. She had helped her brother in his medical practice for nearly three years now. She not only kept his books but also assisted him in surgeries.

When people asked if she was a nurse. Beth's green eyes would sparkle with humor, and she would vigorously shake her head.

"Oh, no!" she always answered. "I am merely his bookkeeper."

However, Doc Williams disagreed. Beth's joyful spirit was a blessing and a gift to all his patients. She often sat with them after surgeries so they would awaken to a smiling face. Doctor Rueben Williams always became a little nervous when he thought about losing her. *Someday,* he thought, *Beth will find someone who will soak up the love she so readily shares. I just hope he will know how special she is. I know I will have a hard time replacing her.*

CHAPTER 18

THE STONE THAT BORE HIS NAME

A TALL MAN SQUATTED ON LONG LEGS IN FRONT OF A tombstone reading the words engraved there. His clothes were worn and dusty from travel. He had removed his black, worn cowboy hat and held it in his rough hands, turning the brim through his fingers. Finally, he pulled his fingers through his curly, black hair and shoved the hat back onto his head. He shifted his weight in his cowboy boots and rolled his wide shoulders. Paul 'Rowdy' Rankin stared hard at the stone that bore his name.

Sgt. Paul Rankin

Georgia Light Artillery

CSA

Died April 16, 1865

Battle of Columbus

The gravestone had the Southern Cross of Honor under the peak. The cross meant the man buried there had served honorably in the Confederate States of America. The stone itself was pointed on top "to keep the damn Yankees from sitting on the head of the Confederate soldier buried there" or so the Southern soldiers said.

Rowdy grinned ruefully as he read his own tombstone. *Not many people get to see their name engraved in stone,* he thought to himself with a low chuckle. He was jolted out of his reverie when he heard a sound behind him.

A young woman was carrying flowers and gardening tools. She stopped suddenly when she saw him.

"Oh, I am so sorry. I didn't mean to disturb you. Did you know Paul?"

Rowdy slowly nodded as he stood. "My whole life," he answered with a wry grin. He looked around at the other graves. Most were not as well-groomed as this one.

"Are you the one who has been taking care of this grave?" he asked with surprise.

The young lady smiled and nodded her head. Putting out her hand, she introduced herself.

"My name is Bethany Williams, but my friends just call me Beth."

Rowdy grinned as he took her hand. "My friends call me Rowdy." He paused as he looked at Beth. "So why this grave?" he asked with a backward nod of his head.

Beth smiled slowly as she stared out over the cemetery.

"My little brother died in that war, or at least that is what we were told. We believe he was in the Battle of Columbus. I come out once a week to look at the new markers to see if his name is on any of them. They are identifying more of the lost soldiers all the time, although not as many now as in the beginning."

She paused and softly added, "I don't know why I am drawn to this grave. Every time I come, I stop and visit this one. I pulled the weeds the first day I stopped and felt such a sense of peace. Now I come every week. I talk to him as I trim the grass and clean up his grave. I thought

I would bring some flowers today." Beth smiled slightly as she gazed over the lines of tombstones.

"I just love to walk through cemeteries. They are so peaceful," she murmured softly as she looked over the quiet field. Tears tried to fill her eyes as she whispered, "So many young lives cut short. I wonder what they would have become."

She glanced up to see Rowdy staring down at her intently. Beth blushed and ducked her head.

"I'm sorry. That sounds morbid, doesn't it? I don't mean it to be. I'm sorry if I offended you."

Rowdy slowly shook his head. "No, it doesn't sound morbid to me. I am sure the fellows lying here appreciate a visit, especially from a pretty gal who cares about who they were," he replied sincerely.

"Take this fellow. Maybe he grew up on a cotton farm right here in Georgia. He might have even had a brother who he fought with when he was young or who pushed him out of trees," he suggested as he grinned at her.

Then his face became more serious, "Or maybe he's not even the fellow whose name is on this stone. Maybe they buried a man and marked his grave with the wrong name."

Beth's eyes became large and she gasped.

"Oh, now I will have even more things to ponder when I visit next time!"

"Here," Rowdy offered, "Let me help you with those tools." He took the tools from her. Together, they began to trim the weeds and the grasses pushing up around the stone.

As they cleaned up the gravesite, Beth told Rowdy about her family.

"My older brother is a surgeon. He was in medical school when the war broke out, but he still volunteered as a doctor for the South. They seemed to be short on men of all kinds. He operated on some of these men," she stated softly as she waved her hand across the cemetery. "Now he has his own practice here in Columbus and is quite successful." Beth paused and frowned slightly before she continued.

"Reub is restless though. He is talking of moving. He wants to buy into a practice west of the Mississippi."

Rowdy paused his trimming to look up at her. "You don't want him to move away from you?" he asked.

Beth replied quickly, "Oh, I live with Reub. There were only my two brothers and me. Mother died of influenza five years ago and Father..." Her voice died off. "I think Father died of a broken heart. After Eli was declared missing and probably dead, Father just lost his will to live."

Looking at Rowdy, Beth asked, "Do you have any family?"

Rowdy shrugged. "I'm not sure. I only had one brother and he was older. Our mother died when I was born. Lance headed west at sixteen. Our father was mighty upset with him. He wanted Lance to take over the plantation.

"Lance didn't want to be a farmer though. He used to tell me that working in the fields made him feel like he was choking.

"I received a few letters from him during the war. In the last one, he said he was in Wyoming Territory working on a ranch somewhere around Cheyenne. He was cowboying and said he was doing what he loved. He had moved around quite a bit before then though, so I don't know if he is still there."

Rowdy paused and stared over the cemetery before he continued. "If Lance is alive, he is in the West somewhere. Our pa, or The Colonel as we called him, died before I made it home. Some folks called that war the Civil War but us Southern boys called it the War for Southern Independence.

"Our plantation was sold several years ago. My father only had one sister and she is dead. I don't know if Lance took care of the sale or if my aunt liquidated it.

"Who knows? There may not have been anything left to sell the way this state was decimated with all the fighting."

His gaze had been moving over the gravestones as he talked. Now he looked back at Beth and grinned. "So, you are looking at a twenty-six-year-old man with limited skills, no money, no family, and no prospects for any of those."

Beth looked up at him. "But you do have a great smile!" she answered with a smile.

Rowdy was surprised but he grinned, and together, they finished trimming the gravesite. When they were done, Rowdy removed his bandana and wiped off the stone.

As he stood, Beth asked shyly, "Rowdy, would you like to walk me home and stay for supper? Rueb is always telling me I need to bring friends home...and not to spend so much time with dead soldiers." Beth's eyes glistened with tears, but they were hopeful as she looked up at Rowdy and waited for an answer.

Rowdy wanted to say no. He really did, but when he looked at Beth's cute little face tilted up at him and her green eyes sparkling with such hope and anticipation, he caved.

"I'd be glad to. After all, you are talking to a man who, until now, didn't know where he was going to find his next meal," Rowdy drawled as he grinned.

Beth said she lived about a half-mile away, so Rowdy decided to tie the gardening tools to his horse. Smoke was waiting patiently outside the gate and nickered as Rowdy walked toward him.

CHAPTER 19

A WORLD OF DEBT

ON THE WALK TO HER HOME, ROWDY INTRODUCED Beth to his horse.

"Smoke is just about the best friend I have ever had," he added with a grin.

Beth smiled. "I knew he was someone's pet," she stated as they began to walk down the street. "He seemed so friendly."

Rowdy looked at her curiously. *Most folks don't use "friendly" and "Smoke" in the same sentence,* he thought as he grinned.

"He's friendly some of the time. Around me, he's a big pet. I don't even have to lead him. He follows me everywhere."

Beth led the way up the walk. The stately two-story brick house had a wide porch with white pillars and large double doors. Rowdy slowed and started to get fidgety.

"Beth," he said as his neck turned red, "I'm not sure this is a good idea. I have been riding for quite a few days. I could use a good bath and a change of clothes before I sit on anyone's chairs."

Beth stopped and looked up at Rowdy. Her small chin was determined as she shook her head.

"Nonsense. You are my guest. Please come in," she responded as she led the way onto the massive porch with white pillars and double doors.

As she threw the doors open, she called, "Rueb? I brought a friend home for supper!"

Rueben Williams stepped out of his study. The surprised look on his face turned to total shock. As a huge smile spread over his face, he quickly walked toward them with his hand outstretched.

"Rowdy! It's good to see you so healthy!"

Rowdy paused, his face pale as he stared.

"Doc? Doc Williams? I had no idea you were Beth's brother."

Beth looked from one to the other. "You know each other? Did you operate on Rowdy? Someone had better fill me in!" she exclaimed. She stared from one to the other with her hands on her hips as she smiled.

Reuben continued to pump Rowdy's hand. He finally caught himself.

"Come in. Come in and fill me in on all that has gone on with you since you were released from the hospital. I am guessing you did get your memory back?"

Reuben paused and turned to Beth.

"Rowdy was one of my first patients after I enlisted. I was standing behind the sawbones as the soldiers called the doctors—although this one certainly earned his name. They brought Rowdy in and were going to take off his leg and his arm. He was wounded badly and bleeding. He came to as the doctor touched his leg with the saw and started roaring. He pulled his gun and told the doc that—" Doc's face colored as he continued, "that special saw had better not touch him or the doctor wouldn't be around to do another surgery!"

Reuben shook his head. "Most of the doctors I worked with were excellent, but this guy was not. His table and his clothing were filthy. He even smoked as he did surgery, dropping ash on his patients. Of course, they were either too far gone to know or were anesthetized. Either way, they didn't know the difference."

Reuben frowned at the memory and then laughed as he remembered Rowdy's reaction. He gestured towards Rowdy.

"This guy was neither. I offered to do the surgery just to save the old doctor's life. I said a prayer as I cut away Rowdy's pant leg."

Reuben addressed Rowdy with a serious look on his face.

"I cleaned the table off and scrubbed you as best I could. Your leg was a mess, your arm was broken in three places, and you had taken bullets through your shoulder and upper chest. The deep bullet crease on your skull is what finally knocked you out. You really should have died. I am sure you would have too had you not been young and healthy. You were my first field surgery, and any time I think I have a tough surgery to do, I just remember you."

Reuben shook his head as he continued. "Your anesthesia wore off before I was done, and since it was rationed, we gave you a bottle of whiskey. You proceeded to anesthetize yourself!" he added with a laugh. His face became serious as he continued.

"When I was done, I put you on a table by the soldiers who did not survive and covered you with a sheet. The Yankees won that battle. They were ransacking the hospitals and surgical tents and taking all the wounded prisoners as they moved through. I knew you would not survive if you left that tent.

"Once the Yankees were gone, I moved you to the hospital. You were there for over a month. You had lost your memory, and no one there knew who you were. You did not have any kind of identification on you, no letters or anything. We called you Rowdy because of all the noise you made." Doc grinned and added, "You weren't a very cooperative patient.

"So, when did your memory come back?"

Rowdy looked at Beth and turned a little pale.

"Tell me about Eli. Maybe I can remember him, or I might know someone who does."

Beth took a picture from the mantle above the fireplace. "Father had this taken when Eli enlisted."

Rowdy stared at the picture. The face looking back at him was of a young Confederate soldier with blond hair and laughing brown eyes.

Rowdy turned around slowly.

"Was Eli a medic?" he asked.

Reuben's face became pale, and Beth gasped. "Yes! Did you know him?"

"He treated me on the battlefield and made sure I made it to one of the wagons," Rowdy answered quietly as he stared at Eli's picture. "The soldiers picking up the wounded were going to leave me there. They thought I was too far gone, but your brother insisted they treat me."

Rowdy looked at Beth and Reuben. "Your brother saved my life," he stated quietly with a haunted look in his blue eyes. "I gave him a letter from my brother that I had in my pocket. I asked him to give it to his commanding officer. I wanted someone to let my brother know if I didn't make it.

"I don't know what happened after I was carried off the field. Your brother was still there but that was the last I saw of him."

Rowdy looked at Beth and Reuben as the pain he felt showed in his voice. "Eli was a brave soldier. He was on the battlefield the entire time, treating men and praying with them."

Rowdy's face was tight. He pushed his shoulders back and took a deep breath.

"Your brother saved a lot of lives." His eyes moved to Doc Williams, and he added quietly, "Both of you did. I owe your family a world of debt." Rowdy gently set the picture back on the mantle.

Rueben's eyes were full of tears, and Beth was crying silently.

Rowdy turned toward the door. "I'll go now," he grated out, his voice breaking as he twisted his hat in his hands. When he reached the door, he paused and looked back.

"Thank you for your kindness to strangers," he said to Beth. He looked at Reuben Williams intently with haunted eyes. "You too, Doc. I will never forget what you and your brother did for me."

Beth started to protest and ask him to stay, but Reuben put his hand on her shoulder.

"Let him go," Reuben said softly as Rowdy walked toward his horse, stumbling a little as he climbed into the saddle. He hugged his little sister and kissed her wet cheek.

"You have such a big heart, Beth. You have loved the forgotten soldiers and now you showed this lonesome man that love and kindness as well." He put his hands on her shoulders and smiled down at her through the tears in his eyes. "I am proud to be your brother."

That night, Reuben talked to Beth again about moving West.

"Let's leave the sadness here, Beth. Let's start over. Maybe you will even find a good-looking cowboy out there," he teased as he tweaked her turned-up nose.

Beth laughed but she was thinking about a tall man with an ornery grin. A man whose blue eyes revealed the emotions he kept hidden from his face.

CHAPTER 20

HORSE SENSE

ROWDY CHOPPED WOOD THAT NIGHT FOR A MEAL and slept in the livery with his horse. As he drifted off to sleep, he saw a pert little face with a turned-up nose and green eyes. He shook himself and pushed the thought of Beth from his head.

When he awoke in the morning, he was thinking about what Beth had said about going West. *Why not? The railroad runs through clear to California now.* He smiled ruefully. *Maybe I will just ride the cars west until my money runs out.*

Rowdy didn't want to sell his horse or his guns, and he owned nothing else. He helped the hostler clean some stalls that morning and asked the old man if he knew where a fellow could get some work for a few days. The old hostler's name was Bandy.

Bandy studied Rowdy for a bit.

"Can ya ride?" he asked. "I have some new hosses comin' in today an' I need someone to break 'em gentle. Have ya ever broke hosses?"

Rowdy grinned. "I've broken more horses than most folks will ride. When do I start?"

Bandy growled, "Let's go eat some breakfast an' I'll line ya out." As he talked, Bandy's old eyes twinkled. He wasn't as tough as he let on, but he didn't want the word to get out.

Rowdy ate enough breakfast for three men and Bandy stifled a grin. *I knowed that boy was hungry, but I didn't know he could eat that much! He ain't afraid to work though.*

While Rowdy was waiting for the horses to arrive, he mucked out the rest of the stalls and laid out fresh hay. By noon, the barn smelled of clean hay and horses. He was fixing a loose board in the corral fence when Bandy called for him.

"The hosses jist come in on the train. Let's go get 'em." He handed Rowdy a thick ham sandwich and Rowdy wolfed it down in just a few bites.

Bandy muttered under his breath, "I'm mighty glad I ain't promisin' to feed ya as part of yer durn pay! I'd plumb lose money."

He received a grin for a reply and the two men sauntered down the street toward the train station.

Rowdy whistled as the four horses were unloaded. "Morgans!" he exclaimed. "I've ridden a few of them. Solid horse, smart with a good temperament." He looked sideways at Bandy as he stated, "Fancy horses like that will cost you a little extra."

"$50 each and nothin' more," Bandy growled. "I want 'em broke gentle an' they need to be broke in three weeks, four weeks tops."

Rowdy veiled his surprise. *I was going to ask for $35 each*, he thought. *Good thing I kept my mouth shut.*

"Do you have a place outside town I can take them? I'd prefer to have it a little less busy when I'm working with them."

Bandy liked that question, but his face was bland as he answered.

"My place is five miles south a town. I live alone an' rarely stay out there so make yerself to home. I don't have much fer food though so ya might want to pick up some provisions. Tell Beans over at the mercantile that I'll back ya fer credit."

As Bandy walked away, he was chuckling. He whistled to himself as he headed back to the livery.

"I am plumb glad that hungry cowboy asked me fer a job," he muttered to himself with a satisfied grin.

All the horses were halter broke when they arrived. Looking at their teeth, Rowdy determined that they were between three and four years old, three geldings and a filly. Rowdy paused as he studied the filly. "Women usually ride mares or fillies. Let's just break this one for a lady."

Rowdy spent the first few days just getting the horses used to him. He walked around the pen and talked to them. He fed them apples and scratched their ears as they ate. He worked with the horses ten to twelve hours each day, rotating from horse to horse to keep from wearing any of them out. It was hard work with lots of thinking, and he loved every minute of it.

Bandy rode out at the end of the first week. He watched Rowdy work with the blanket for a time. He rode back into town without saying a word.

By the time Rowdy was ready to saddle the horses, they trusted him and were comfortable with him around them. He saddled the horses and let them stand for a few hours before he took the saddles off. After doing that for several days, he mounted and rode each around the corral. At the beginning of the third week, he took the horses out of the corral and worked them individually.

He rigged a sidesaddle for the filly and tried to ride her that way. Even though she shied when he fell off the first few times, she adjusted to both the sidesaddle and riding astride. He even draped a blanket across her rump to acclimatize her to a long skirt.

Toward the end of the third week, Rowdy rode into town on one of the geldings, leading the other three Morgans. Smoke followed without being led. Even though the street was teeming with people, the horses stayed calm.

The gelding he rode snorted a couple of times and shied when a dog ran across the street. Rowdy talked softly to the animal and rubbed its neck. The horse flicked its ears back and forth, but it calmed down.

Bandy strolled out of the livery as Rowdy rode up.

"Yer jist in time to meet the owners!" Bandy grinned and nodded his head toward a couple walking up the street.

Rowdy looked up from the horses to see Reuben and Beth walking toward the livery.

Beth's eyes were bright with excitement.

"Rowdy, I didn't know you were breaking our horses! How wonderful!"

Reuben reached to shake Rowdy's hand.

"Anything I need to know before we take them off your hands?" he asked.

Rowdy slowly shook his head.

"No, I think you should be good to go. I broke the filly to ride sidesaddle and to ride astride, although I think Beth will probably be better at riding sidesaddle than I am," Rowdy drawled with an ornery grin.

Rueben looked startled. He laughed as he looked from the small filly to Rowdy.

"I wish I could have seen that. It would have been worth the trip out of town." Reuben laughed again. "Yes, I think Beth will be better at that than either one of us."

Beth's eyes were shining. "Rowdy, how did you know that I would be riding the filly?" she asked with surprise.

Rowdy grinned again. "Men don't typically ride mares or fillies, so I just assumed the rider would be a gal."

He turned his eyes toward Rueben again. "So where are you going to keep them? Do you have a place to keep them outside town?" Rowdy asked curiously.

Beth answered excitedly, "Oh, no! We are headed to the Wyoming Territory. Rueben sold his practice here and bought into a practice in Cheyenne with a friend from medical school. We were planning to take the train next week." She glanced up at Reuban and smiled before she continued, "Maybe we will be able to leave sooner though since you have our horses ready to go."

Rowdy smiled. "Good for you. Starting over in a new place just might be the thing to do."

Rueben pulled out his wallet and tried to hand Rowdy $250.

Rowdy shook his head. "You hired Bandy so settle up with him."

Rueben looked confused and a grinning Bandy spoke up. "Take the money, Rowdy. Ya done a good job. I'll charge 'em extry fer room an' board to make up fer my loss!" he drawled with a wink at Beth.

"$200 for breaking our four horses plus a $50 bonus for finishing in three weeks…as we agreed with Bandy." Reuben smiled as he placed the money in Rowdy's hand.

Rowdy stared at it for a moment before he pushed it into his vest pocket. He grinned at Beth and Rueben. As he dismounted, he drawled, "Thanks, folks. Pleasure to work with you. Now I am going to take a bath, get some clean clothes, eat a big meal, and maybe even sleep in a soft bed."

Tipping his hat to Beth, Rowdy led the Morgans into the livery. Smoke followed him.

"Well, Smoke, that was just about the best three weeks I have ever spent. Now you rest up because you and I are taking a long ride west on the cars."

CHAPTER 21

RIDE THE CARS WEST

ROWDY BOUGHT HIS TRAIN TICKET THE NEXT morning. The train would arrive that afternoon around three forty-five and leave about ten after four. It was now the end of October, and he wanted to get further west before the weather set in. He had never experienced cold weather where things froze and stayed that way for days. He was a little nervous about living in a place that could get that cold, but he figured if Lance could handle it, he could as well.

His second-class ticket to Cheyenne cost him $50, and the trip was to take around seventy hours. He was taking his horse so that would cost another $15. As he walked away from the train station, mentally counting his money, Rowdy muttered to himself, "I sure am glad Bandy hired me to break fancy horses!"

Startled by a woman's voice calling his name, Rowdy glanced around. Beth rushed toward him, excited as usual.

"Rowdy, would you like to eat breakfast with us? Rueb and I are leaving today on the train for Cheyenne!"

Rowdy grinned and drawled, "Why that would be just fine! Are you traveling first class? Probably safer for you as a woman."

Beth wrinkled her nose. "That is what Rueb told me too. Yes, we are. I have heard so many stories about riding on a train. Have you ridden a train before?"

Rowdy slowly nodded. "Yes, I have ridden the cars quite a bit. It's a good way to travel—it's faster and maybe even safer than going by wagon or horseback. I still prefer a horse though.

"Did you make arrangements for your Morgans? You will want to ask for a separate car so they don't pack them in too tight with other horses."

Beth frowned. "I think Rueb left it up to the ticketing agent." She paused and asked, "Do you think we should check?"

Beth was standing close enough that Rowdy could smell the soap she used for her bath. He backed up. He could feel himself blushing and that embarrassed him.

"I will make sure they're loaded correctly, and I'll see you in a little bit for breakfast."

Rowdy walked up the street toward the ticket agent's booth. Just as he arrived, the agent reached out and tried to close the window. He was scribbling in his book and growled, "I don't have any seats or cars left, and I don't have time to talk to anyone either."

Rowdy reached through the window, preventing it from closing, and turned the book over. His cold, blue eyes pierced the agent through as their eyes met.

"I am here to oversee the loading of four Morgan horses. They are to have their own car. Now tell me where to take them, and I will be back at train time to load them," Rowdy ground out.

The agent started to snort. Then he looked again at those hard, blue eyes.

"I haven't made any arrangements for them yet, but I am sure we can squeeze them in somewhere," he answered impatiently.

Rowdy pulled the book through the window.

"Perhaps you and I will take a look at what is available. Then, I'll tell you what works."

The ticket agent became quiet. He came out of his booth and showed Rowdy the cars that were available for livestock. "I thought we would put your horses up here," he said as he indicated the car directly behind the tinder car.

Rowdy knew that was the dirtiest car to ride on the entire train. He looked at the agent coldly.

"I think not. I believe we will put those horses in this car right here," he stated as he jabbed the book, "And while we are loading, we will put mine in there too."

The ticket agent started to protest. "But I am always supposed to leave that car open in case…" His protest faded away as Rowdy picked him up by his collar.

With his nose next to the agent's nose, Rowdy growled, "Doc Williams paid you for a private car for those horses, and I know he paid you well. Now you make sure that car is open and ready when the train pulls in. I intend to load them in that car, regardless of what is in it, on it, or around it. And make sure they have some hay as this will be a three-day ride." With that, he dropped the man and walked away without looking back.

A shifty-looking man slid up to the window as the agent was straightening his jacket. He glanced back at Rowdy before he whispered in a nasal voice to the ticket agent, "Joe, I have some horses that need to leave town fast. Be sure to have my car open an' ready."

Joe slammed the book shut. "The train is full today. I won't lose my job over stolen horses and a cantankerous man who knows too much about railroads!" He slammed the ticket window shut and stomped toward the station, muttering under his breath.

The horse thief looked surprised. His eyes narrowed down as he watched Joe walk away.

"We'll see about that," the man muttered to himself. "I intend to load those horses on that train today, and I expect my car to be available."

Beth waved to Rowdy as he came in and Doc Williams looked up with a smile.

Rowdy was almost embarrassed. "That girl just draws too much attention," he growled under his breath. *Still,* he thought as he grinned, *Those sparkly green eyes kind of pull a feller in though.* He was still smiling as he pulled out a chair.

Doc asked, "Are the horses taken care of?"

Rowdy kept his face bland as he answered, "All worked out. I put my horse in with yours if you don't mind. They will be in a larger car. We do need to check on them though as they will need some food and water on this trip. There will be a little hay but let's water them good before we load them."

Beth gave Rowdy a pretty smile and batted her eyes at him.

Rowdy almost blushed. He ducked his head into the menu to keep from looking at her, but he could still feel the red creeping up his neck.

Reuben looked from one to the other and tried not to laugh. He too ducked his head into the menu, but he was covering up a grin.

When the harried little waitress came to take their order, Rowdy ordered a stack of flapjacks, six eggs, some ham, fried potatoes, and grits. As he laid the menu down, he realized both Reuben and Beth were staring at him.

He grinned at them and drawled, "I'm hungry."

CHAPTER 22

SMOKE

AFTER BETH AND REUBEN HAD ORDERED, THE conversation turned to the train trip and Cheyenne.

Reuben asked, "So you are going West as well? Will you be stopping in Cheyenne?"

Rowdy nodded his head. "I will stop for a day or so. I want to see if Lance is there. If he isn't, I may ride the cars out to California. I haven't been west of the Mississippi so it will all be new country to me." He grinned as he added, "By then, I will likely have run out of horse-breaking money, so I might have to stop somewhere and get a job."

Beth looked at him sweetly.

"Maybe Rueb could hire you as a receptionist. You seem to be able to handle both people and horses."

She said it with such innocence that Rowdy stared at her. When he realized Beth was teasing him, he laughed out loud.

"I don't think Doc wants my people skills anywhere near his patients," he replied with a grin.

When the food arrived, Rowdy quit talking and gave his full attention to his plate. He cleaned it up with not so much as a crumb left. Rueben and Beth were once again looking at him with amazement.

Beth exclaimed, "I don't think I have ever seen anyone eat so much food in my life. Why you must have nearly starved in the war!"

Rowdy looked away. When his eyes returned to Beth, they were once again hooded.

"Food was mighty scarce," he agreed.

Reuben could see Rowdy didn't want to talk about the war, so he steered the conversation back to Cheyenne.

"So, Rowdy, if you do find your brother, do you plan to stay in Cheyenne?"

Rowdy chewed on a toothpick for a bit before he answered.

"It depends. If by chance he has his own place, I might. If he is a working cowboy, that will depend on his boss. What I would really like is to save enough to get a spread of my own. I'd like to raise horses.

"Before the war broke out, we crossed one of our big Thoroughbred studs with an Arabian mare. As a Thoroughbred, that stud already had some old Arabian blood in him." When both Beth and Doc stared at him in confusion, Rowdy added, "The Thoroughbred breed was created in the 1600s by crossing Arabian stallions with English brood mares. That cross made fine-looking horses.

"Both of the horses we crossed were gray, and my horse came from that union. That is why old Smoke is a dapple."

He paused as he thought about their plantation. His voice was quieter when he continued.

"The Colonel loved Thoroughbreds, and I like the stamina and the low-maintenance you get with Arabian blood. It proved to be a good cross." Rowdy stared off over the tables. "Smoke and I are a team. I took him with me when I signed up to fight, and he is still my best friend."

Beth listened quietly. *Roudy is so interesting and so wise and yet so unpretentious.* She was used to men trying to impress her, but Rowdy made no effort to impress anyone. She smiled. *He is a combination of roughness and gentleness.*

Rowdy heard loud voices and shouting coming from the direction of the livery. He looked toward the window. Suddenly, Smoke came racing down the street, and a saddle was hanging under his belly.

Rowdy walked to the door of the eating house with a hard look on his face. He leaned against the outside wall and watched. A man came running from the livery.

"Would somebody help me catch my horse? It spooked and ran off!" he shouted as he ran up the street.

Rowdy strolled out into the street. He picked up Smoke's reins and asked, "This horse?"

The man shouted, "Yes!" and tried to take the reins.

Rowdy moved the reins slightly as he stood there and chewed on his toothpick. He frowned a little.

"But how do I know this is your horse? For all we know, you're a thief and it belongs to someone else."

The man looked irritated and grabbed again for the reins.

Rowdy continued to hold the reins as he studied Smoke.

"So, what's his name? I mean, it is a stud, isn't it?"

The man flushed and stuttered, "Uh, he's uh, he don't have a name. I ain't named 'im yet."

Rowdy continued to look from the man to Smoke. "What breed is he? He looks like he might have a little Arabian in him. Good-lookin' horse."

The thief was getting more nervous all the time. Once again, he grabbed for the reins which Rowdy easily held aside.

"Tell you what," Rowdy commented casually, "How about you call him and see if he comes to you. Then I will try. Whoever he goes to gets to keep him." He grinned at the man.

"You can't lose if he is your horse. Now me—maybe I will win a horse today—if he's yours to bet with, that is."

The thief looked incredulously at Rowdy. However, the sugar cubes in his pocket gave him confidence. He held them out.

"Here, horse. Come and get a treat."

Smoke just stood with his head hanging and his ears flicking back and forth.

Rowdy stepped back and called, "Smoke!"

Smoke's ears flipped forward, and his head came up as he watched his owner.

Rowdy pointed at the thief and said, "Sic 'im!" Smoke wheeled on his hind legs and charged the thief. The man began to run down the street screaming. Smoke reached out with his teeth and grabbed the man's shoulder. He shook him like a dog with a bone and then tossed him in the air. As Smoke reared up on his hind legs, Rowdy whistled.

Smoke dropped to all four feet and waited as he watched Rowdy.

The horse thief was still screaming and holding his shoulder when Rowdy reached him. He looked coldly at the man writhing on the ground.

"Don't you ever touch my horse again or Smoke's feet coming down on you will be your last memory." He loosened the girth on Smoke and let the saddle drop to the ground. He did the same with the bridle. With no lead rope at all, Smoke followed Rowdy back to the livery.

The man lying in the street was the same man who had tried to get the ticket agent to give him a rail car. As the agent watched the scene play out, he felt a chill go through him. The sheriff had also been watching. In fact, the street was full of bystanders.

The sheriff jerked the thief to his feet and pushed him down the street towards the jail. Soon, small groups of men were muttering as they gathered in the street. Before long, a group of them rode out to the thief's shack a few miles out of town. In an hour, they were back with a remuda of stolen horses.

The horse thief's future was looking brief. Rowdy didn't care though. He had Smoke. The town and its laws were the citizens' problems.

Bandy appeared in the livery while Rowdy was rubbing Smoke down.

"Ya wouldn't want to stay on here an' help me break hosses, would ya?" he asked hopefully.

Rowdy shook his head. "Nope. I'll be on a train headed west by four this afternoon. I do want to thank you though. I'll keep you in mind if I'm back this way." He held out his hand to Bandy. "And thanks for letting me break those horses. Now I can travel on west with some pocket money." Rowdy grinned at the small, bowlegged man. He genuinely liked Bandy, and it showed on his face as he spoke to him.

Bandy shook Rowdy's hand and grinned back.

"Things shore been more entertainin' since ya come to town. Ya come on back any time, even fer a short visit," he declared as he gripped Rowdy's hand.

When Rowdy finally made it back to the hotel to pay for his breakfast, he was told that Doctor Williams had already paid. Rowdy frowned, but he thanked the waitress.

"I don't like to be beholden to anyone," he growled as he left the hotel.

CHAPTER 23

So Many Questions

ROWDY WAS ANXIOUS TO GET ON THE TRAIN. HE NEVER was much on standing around nor was he used to free time. He finally decided to take another bath. He stopped in the dry goods store and picked up a couple more shirts and some new britches as well as a pair of longhandles and socks. As he soaked and smoked a cigar, he stared out over the mountains.

"I will miss Georgia. Of course, I can always come back if I want. I might not even like the West." He frowned and added, "Especially if I don't find Lance." He soaked until the water was cool and his skin was wrinkled. As he sauntered back up the street, he grinned. "Clean clothes and a bath can sure make a fellow feel like a new man."

Dinnertime found him back in the hotel. Again, he loaded up on food in the restaurant. He also asked for a couple of sandwiches to take with him.

"I think this train ride is going to be a long one," he muttered to himself.

Beth and Reuben came in as he was finishing. Rowdy stood to greet them.

"Thanks for paying for my breakfast. I forgot all about it until I had Smoke taken care of." He signaled to the waitress for two menus. "This meal is on me," he drawled with a grin.

For once, Beth was quiet. She kept looking at Rowdy and ducking her head. The ornery cowboy knew she couldn't stay quiet for long, so he waited for her to speak. Finally, a question spilled out.

"Did you train Smoke to charge like that?"

Rowdy looked somberly at Beth. "I taught Smoke lots of things but some behaviors he acquired on his own. He doesn't like to be handled by strangers, but he's as gentle as a baby if he takes a liking to you. He's a little notional. He kind of does as he pleases unless I whoa him down."

He grinned at her knowing more questions were coming.

"Did he ever save your life?" she asked.

Rowdy nodded.

"Many times during the war. He found me after every battle. He'd break loose if he was taken, and I would hear him snuffling through the trees. Several times when I was wounded and fell off, he stopped and stayed beside me until I came to."

Rowdy paused and added softly as he looked over Beth's head. "Smoke and I have been up and down the river together. He's my horse and I'm his people."

He nodded his head toward the livery as he spoke seriously, "Your Morgans are capable of that kind of loyalty, but you have to spend time with them.

"Riding once a week and stabling them in between won't do it. You have to develop closeness. They must be excited to see you. They have to love you," he explained softly.

Beth could feel her heart beating heavily in her chest as Rowdy talked. She had never met a man like him before. Again, she thought of the scene in the street. *To Rowdy, that was nothing special. To me, it was amazing.* She sighed deeply. *I wish we could ride together on the train so I could talk to him more.*

Reuben looked over at his little sister and smiled. *Beth is falling in love with a rough man who hides a tender heart.* He slowly shook his head. *Life is tricky that way.* He pondered on that as he waited for their food to arrive.

CHAPTER 24

TOO MUCH TACK

ONCE THE MEAL WAS COMPLETED, ROWDY DECIDED to check the horses to ensure everything was ready to load.

He walked down to the livery with the Williams. When Reuben showed him what they were planning to take, Rowdy stared incredulously. He had never seen so much tack.

"Six saddles? You have four horses, and you can only ride two of them at one time."

Reuben's neck turned a light red. "Two are jumping saddles," he explained as he glanced sideways at Rowdy.

Rowdy restrained the urge to growl at him. He ground out, "I didn't teach your horses a thing about jumping or dressage. Leave those saddles here. You are going to have to haul all this to where you are going to live once we hit Cheyenne. Sell this stuff to Bandy if you can."

He went through the rest of the tack and weeded out what the Williams didn't need. The pile to leave behind was almost as large as the pile to take.

Reuben was embarrassed. However, he was glad to have Rowdy's help sorting. *It would have been worse to have hauled unnecessary items that far with nowhere to sell them on the other end.* He blushed again as he thought of how he might have been ridiculed in Cheyenne. *If Rowdy could see the lack of necessity here, how might folks in Cheyenne have laughed when we unloaded there?*

Bandy did laugh, especially at the dressage saddles. In the end, he offered Reuben $50 for everything. The young doctor nearly turned him down, but when he looked at Rowdy's face, he agreed.

Rowdy had their horses at the station a little after three that afternoon. They had been watered and fed. He saw some hay stacked in front of the car and he grinned. *That ticket agent might be a slow learner, but he gets it down eventually.*

Rowdy had his warbag, tack for his horse, and his guns. He thought his pile was too big until he saw the Williams pull up in a wagon. He slowly walked toward them as he muttered under his breath, "They will for sure need a private car if they plan to take all that along!"

Reuben looked from Rowdy's pile to their full wagon. He laughed ruefully. "And this is after sorting five times!" he said as he looked at his little sister.

"Do you already have a house in Cheyenne or where are you going to store all this?" Rowdy asked as he looked the wagon over.

Reuben nodded his head. "We do have a house. My business partner said we will have to do a little work on it. Even though it will be smaller than our house here, I am sure it will be adequate. Cheyenne is a prosperous town."

Rowdy was not convinced, but houses were out of his area of expertise. He only shook his head and walked back to the horses.

The train whistled loudly as it pulled into the station, and a wave of excitement went through the people gathered there. Rowdy held the halter ropes of the four Morgans tightly. He knew the noise and hissing would be loud as the train stopped. Smoke's rope trailed on the ground.

The ticket agent was directing the passengers. He already had the livestock cars open, and he pointed toward the Williams' car. As Rowdy led the horses up the ramp and into the car, he could see there was a small stall on one end. He was relieved. Smoke was a stud, and Rowdy was a little concerned to have him around Beth's filly for the entire trip. *I hope she doesn't come into heat during the three days we'll be on this train.* "Darn females!" he muttered.

Rowdy put Smoke in the stall and turned the other four horses loose in the car. He stacked the saddles and the rest of the tack in the front of the car. He stepped back and stared from the nervous horses to the pile of saddles. Not satisfied, he grabbed some old boards and wire that were lying close to the train. He constructed a makeshift fence to separate the tack from the horses. He put some hay out for them to eat and tossed more behind the saddles. He had purchased some bags of oats, and those he put under the saddles. When things looked satisfactory, he went back for his warbag and guns.

Reuben was staggering from the wagon to his train car with loads of "stuff." Rowdy stifled a grin and went to help his friend. When he saw the piano at the bottom of the pile, he stopped. The old piano was huge. *Beth must play or they wouldn't be dragging this thing along.* He shook his head. "We are going to need more help to stow that." Rowdy left and was back in a few minutes with three stout men.

Reuben directed, and the rest of the men did the heavy lifting. The young doctor did offer to pay the men, but they just grinned at him and chuckled as they walked away. Finally, all the Williams' personal items were loaded in their car.

Rowdy looked around as he dropped the last items inside the door. He had never been inside a first-class car before. He whistled under his breath. *They should be well-rested when they arrive. They will be riding in the lap of comfort.*

He jumped down and helped Beth up the train steps. He tipped his hat when she thanked him. Reuben waved before he pulled the door shut.

"She is such a pretty, happy little gal," Rowdy commented to himself as climbed into the second-class car. When the cowboy next to him grinned, Rowdy knew he had spoken out loud. He grinned back and settled into his seat.

CHAPTER 25

I'd Rather Ride a Horse

THE NEXT SEVENTY-TWO HOURS WERE LONG. THE temperature inside the train car fluctuated between cold and hot although the further northwest they rolled, the cooler it became.

Rowdy decided he was going to have to buy a coat in Cheyenne, and that was something he had never worried about before. *Several shirts and a vest usually do me just fine. The nights are for sure getting colder though.*

Several stops were longer, and he took advantage of those to water the horses as well as give them some oats and hay. He even managed to shovel the manure out of the car a couple of times.

Rowdy frowned. He was going to run out of feed before they arrived and that bothered him. He was more worried about the horses than the fact that he hadn't eaten anything but the sandwich since the trip started.

He stretched to his full height and flexed his muscles. His back ached and the rushing around at every stop meant he was getting very little sleep. *Not to mention I'm dang hungry.*

Finally, in Omaha, there was a little eating place next to the tracks. He hurried in to buy some food. The cold beer tasted good. He drank it quickly and refilled the bottle with water.

It was five hundred sixteen miles from Omaha, Nebraska to Cheyenne so they should arrive in Cheyenne around a little after four the next day.

Rowdy was ready to get off the train and back on his horse. *At least on a horse, I decide when to stop. This train seems to stop about every half hour.* His mind churned with all the things that had taken place in the last few weeks. Between that and the hard seat, he couldn't get comfortable. Finally, around four-thirty in the morning, he fell asleep and slept for four hours straight.

His stomach was growling when he awoke. Willow Island, Nebraska didn't have much to offer people, but there was a water tank right by the tracks. The stop was short, but Rowdy was able to water all the horses and buy a little hay. He didn't make it back to the passenger car before the train pulled out, so he rode with the horses to North Platte. This time, he was able to get food for himself.

As he settled back in his seat, he muttered, "This would sure be more relaxing if I was doing it on horseback."

The same cowboy who had grinned at him earlier laughed, and a second cowboy agreed. The first cowboy's name was Tab, and he was headed home to Julesburg. He talked a little before he pulled his hat over his eyes. He was asleep at once.

The other cowboy was from Texas, and he seemed ready to visit. He went by Stretch and had just trailed a herd of cattle from Kansas to the railhead in Omaha.

"Thought I might amble on up to Cheyenne 'fore I head back down to Texas for the winter," he stated with a grin.

"I shore have spent a winter up north," he answered in response to Rowdy's question. "Omaha's as far as I went, but Kansas can be bad too. I'm a southern boy m'self an' I like to head south when she gets cold," he stated seriously.

"I been workin' with a cattle buyer I met in the war. His name's Jack Sneld. Y'all will pro'bly meet 'em if ya settle in Cheyenne. He works with some of the bigger ranchers supplyin' beef to Denver."

Rowdy was surprised. He hadn't seen Jack since the Battle of Columbus. Jack had been wounded but the last Rowdy saw of him, he was still shooting.

So, Jack made it through safely. Rowdy was pleased. However, he didn't tell Stretch that Jack had been his best friend before the war. He wasn't much on sharing personal things about his life and even less likely when it involved that war.

Stretch helped Rowdy water the horses at Julesburg, Colorado. The terrain was changing, and it was getting even more chilly. Rowdy finally put on a second shirt and added his vest. At Sidney, Nebraska, the two men grabbed a quick meal and made it back on the train before it left. *These stops are mighty brief,* Rowdy thought. *Whoever planned this schedule didn't waste around any.*

At last, the next stop was Cheyenne. Rowdy was glad they were going to arrive in the daylight. He grinned as he thought of Doc and all his "stuff." *I sure hope his buddy brings a big wagon. Wait till he sees that piano*, Rowdy thought and he chuckled out loud.

CHAPTER 26

A Smooth-Talking Texan

AS SOON AS THE TRAIN PULLED INTO THE STATION, Rowdy was out the door and in the car with the horses. He hooked ropes to their halters and led them off the train.

Stretch unloaded all the tack. He pulled down the fence Rowdy had built and tossed it on top of some trash by the tracks. It was much easier with two men working together and Rowdy appreciated the help. Stretch didn't seem to mind helping either.

Rowdy waited by the train until the door to Beth's car opened.

"I'm going to take these horses down to the livery. I'll put them under Doc's name."

Beth smiled sweetly and thanked him.

Stretch stared from Beth to Rowdy and whistled softly.

"No wonder yore willin' to stay in Cheyenne through the winter!" he exclaimed with a good-natured grin. Rowdy grinned in return even though he felt heat creeping up his neck.

The livery in Cheyenne was large and well stocked. Rowdy visited with the hostler and was able to find stalls for all the horses. The hostler's name was Rooster, and he seemed to have his finger on the pulse of

Cheyenne. Again, the Morgans were put together and Smoke was penned by himself.

Smoke was starting to snort and paw when he came close to the filly.

Rowdy frowned and shook his head. "Yep, she's coming into heat. Females! They are always messing with a feller's thinking," he growled as he gave the horses hay and oats.

Stretch agreed and laughed. "An' we just keep a comin' back for more." He slapped Rowdy on the back as the two of them left the livery.

When they returned to the train station, Rowdy saw a wagon backed up to the train car. Reuben and another man were trying to lift the piano so Rowdy and Stretch moved quickly to help. It was incredibly heavy, and all were out of breath when they finally settled it in the wagon. Beth smiled at the men and Rowdy decided that smile was worth all the straining he did to lift her piano.

Stretch doffed his hat and gave Beth his most charming southern smile. He was as smooth as butter when he spoke.

Rowdy snorted. *How can he do that? I don't think I have that kind of charm anywhere inside me.* He scowled and looked away.

Beth wasn't done though. "Rueb, how about we buy these men supper if they help us unload this piano?" she asked with a pretty smile.

Stretch quickly agreed. As they loaded the rest of the items into the wagon, he talked easily with Beth.

Rowdy had never been envious of anyone in his life, but he decided he was jealous of Stretch. *A smooth tongue and says all the right things.*

Stretch kept the conversation going and there were no awkward silences. Rowdy talked less and less as he listened to their conversation. Stretch knew Beth's life story by the time the wagon was unloaded, and she took his arm as they walked to the Ford Restaurant.

Rowdy followed quietly. He was surprised at himself. *What is it about that little gal that gets me so tangled up,* he wondered. He glowered, looking at the ground as he walked behind them.

"That Stretch is a smooth one," he muttered.

CHAPTER 27

THE BOSS THINKS YORE DEAD!

SATURDAY NIGHT IN CHEYENNE WAS BUSY. THERE were lots of riders in the Ford House. Reuben had been told it was the best place in town to eat, and he was hoping they were right. Both Beth and he were hungry, so Rowdy had to be ravenous.

A group of loud riders arrived after Rueben's party. They headed to a table in the back like they went there often. They were all obviously part of the same outfit because there was lots of teasing and joking. Suddenly, they spotted Beth. The table became much quieter as they all stared at the new woman in town.

Rowdy had the feeling that they were studying him as well, so he glared at them. His eyes always looked cold when he was irritated, and he was plumb irritated tonight.

"And you have no good cause either," he muttered to himself.

Finally, the biggest of the riders stood and pushed through to their table. "Beggin' yore pardon, ma'am. We don't mean to look like we was starin', but this here feller has an on-canny resemblance to our boss." He turned his eyes to Rowdy and added, "In fact, when ya looked up an' stared at us, it was like Lance was in yer chair!"

Rowdy was quiet as he thought about how to respond.

Beth had no such qualms. "Rowdy! Lance is here! Your brother is here!" she exclaimed.

The rider's eyes opened wide. "Brother! You's Paul? But the boss thinks yore dead!" he blurted out loudly. Both tables went silent, waiting for Rowdy to respond.

Rowdy's face was pale as he looked up at the man in front of him. He frowned slightly as his eyes moved to the table of riders.

"Fellers, I was pretty much a goner and Doc here pulled me through. He is the surgeon who saved my life.

"Lance being here is as much of a surprise to me as me being alive will be to him. I lost track of him some time ago. I received his last letter nearly six years ago. He said he was working on a ranch near here, but I wasn't sure if he would still be around." He paused and added quietly, "I am pleased to meet all of you, but I would appreciate you not telling Lance I'm here. I would like to do that myself."

The noise at the Rocking R table worked up to a crescendo as Tiny rejoined his friends. They were all discussing how things would change now that the boss had a brother.

Rowdy cursed silently to himself. He didn't want charity from his brother, and he sure wasn't coming here to demand half of a ranch. Even though he was hungry, he was leaving. He looked along the table at Reuben, Beth, and Stretch. His voice was rough when he spoke.

"If you all will excuse me, I think I'll get some air," he growled as he strode out of the restaurant.

Once outside, Rowdy could breathe again. He cursed under his breath again. *Lance sure moved up—boss of a bunch of riders like that. I guess that means he owns a big ranch.* Rowdy was proud of his brother, but once again he was reminded of how little he had in this world.

He shook his head and rolled a cigarette. He had picked up the habit during the war, but he rarely smoked now. It was only when he was really strung tight that he even reached for them.

"I just need to get back on that train and continue on west," he growled to himself. The part of him who loved and missed Lance started to argue though. He took a few puffs on the cigarette, looked at it with disgust, and ground it out in the dirt.

As he leaned against the wall of the Ford House and watched the shadows, Rowdy decided he liked the cool evening air of Cheyenne. *No wonder Lance thought he was suffocating in Georgia. I understand that now.* Slowly, he turned down the street. He would go talk to Smoke. That horse was the best listener he knew.

As Rowdy entered the livery, a whinny from the back greeted him. "You're right, Smoke. We need to move on. And I would rather ride you than ride the cars. We'll just mosey on out tomorrow and head on down the road. We won't come back here until I have something I can hold in my hands and say is mine."

He tossed his tobacco and the rest of his cigarette papers on a pile of manure as he walked by. He climbed into Smoke's stall and bedded down beside his horse.

Rowdy didn't hear someone enter the barn quietly, nor did he hear the man saddle a horse and ride out of town on a run.

PAUL'S ALIVE!

SLIM KNEW WHAT WAS GOING THROUGH ROWDY'S head. He had been there, and he didn't want his best friend to miss seeing the brother he thought was dead. He was going to go against this lost brother's wishes and tell Lance that Paul was back.

It was nearly ten that night when Slim rode into the ranch headquarters. The house was dark and quiet.

Slim shook his head as he thought about Paul. He saddled Lance's mustang and switched his own horse out for a fresh mount before he knocked on the door. There was no sound, so he knocked harder a second time.

A rifle appeared through a crack in the door. Then the door swung wide to show Lance's startled face.

He had sent Slim and ten of the hands to Cheyenne with cattle to ship on the cars. He had given them the night off, and most would be staying in town since they didn't have to be back at work until noon the next day. Slim had taken his hands, Tiny and Smiley, along as well.

"Slim! What's wrong? Who's hurt? Where are the boys?" Lance asked as he peered behind Slim.

"Nothin's wrong. I have good news, but it's a goin' to shake ya some." The moon shone on Slim's face as he exclaimed, "Paul's alive!"

Lance's face turned white. "No, his body was identified. It can't be!"

Samuel stepped out of the house to join the men on the steps.

"Yes, Lance, it is possible. I did some checking into Paul's records after you wrote to me. The identification markers on his body were off. I decided to wait to tell you until I was sure. I didn't want to get your hopes up if I was wrong. I kept waiting for more information, but nothing came.

"I do think the body that was buried under Paul's name was not Paul. Your brother may very well be alive."

"He's the image of ya, Lance," Slim stated quietly. "He has those piercin' blue eyes like y'all. We saw 'em when he glared at us. He is a mighty serious-lookin' feller, but he looks jist like ya. Maybe an inch shorter but the walk is the same. Yore brother is alive!"

As Lance tried to process this news, he stared at Slim in confusion.

"So why didn't Paul ride out with you tonight? Is he in Cheyenne now?"

Slim was quiet for a moment. When he looked at Lance, pain showed in his eyes.

"He's in Cheyenne. He come in on the train this evenin', but he ain't a goin' to come out. Yore brother has a great, big load a pride he's a haulin' 'round. Come mornin,' he'll be gone. He has nothin', an' he ain't a goin' to look like no beggar." Slim's voice was soft when he added, "I know this 'cause I done it my own self. If ya want to see yore brother, ya need to ride in right now or he ain't a goin' to be there."

Lance rushed into the house and threw on some clothes. Slim heard a stir of voices followed by Molly's sharp exclamation, "Oh, Lance! You bring your brother home!"

The two men headed down the lane at a run. Luckily, the moon was bright because they had fifteen miles to ride in a hurry.

The clouds toyed some with them that night. They kept covering the moon making the ride to Cheyenne just a little slower. It was nearly eleven-thirty when they arrived at the livery.

Rowdy awoke at the sound of horses snorting and coming into the barn. When Smoke perked up his ears and began to nicker excitedly, Rowdy knew who was there. Smoke was moving around so much that Rowdy finally stood. As he faced the open livery door, the man's face in front of him was hazy. However, Smoke's reaction was all he needed.

When Lance said, "Hello, Paul," Rowdy's heart turned over.

He slowly climbed out of the stall and met his brother with a handshake. Lance grabbed him and wrapped him in a bear hug. He was trying not to cry as he hugged this brother he thought was dead.

Paul was quiet. His face was tight, and Lance could see that the ornery, happy brother who had gone off to war had come home a different man.

"Paul, I am pleased you stopped tonight and plumb happy you are alive. Part of me would have just broken off and died if I had found out you stopped in Cheyenne but didn't come to see me." Lance pulled Slim forward. "This is the cayuse who busted you, and I am darn glad he did."

Slim reached forward to shake Paul's hand.

"Paul, I'm sure sorry I couldn't foller yore wishes, but Lance here is like a brother to me. I jist couldn't do it to 'im." Slim looked seriously at Paul and added quietly, "I been where y'all are."

Paul looked in amazement at his older brother. Lance was still wiping at tears.

Lance grinned at Paul a little sheepishly. "Blame it on my wife. She has made me just plain soft." He slapped his brother on the back.

"Now that we're both up, let's go have some breakfast. Barney will cook us something special." Lance grinned at his brother again.

Paul didn't argue. His belly was talking to him. He had been looking forward to a good meal when he arrived in Cheyenne, and he was even hungrier now.

Barney agreed to fix the men a big breakfast. However, when the Saturday night partiers started coming in as well, he shooed them away. He finally relented and let the Rocking R riders in after they all clustered around the windows with their faces pressed against the glass.

Those men sure like Lance. He must be a great boss. Rowdy was amazed. He hadn't experienced that kind of friendship in a long time. *Even during the war, I worked mostly by myself. I've plumb forgotten how nice it is to have friends.*

Lance's riders crowded around him.

"We want to meet yore brother, boss. Then we'll be on our way." The big man who had talked to Rowdy earlier reached out his hand.

"I'm Tiny an' the little runty feller next to me is Jonesy. We're mighty pleased to make yore acquaintance, Paul." The big man waved over his shoulder toward the blond cowboy who had raced to find Lance.

"That there is Slim. He has him a little ranch right next to Lance's spread. Smiley there, him an' me work fer Slim. The rest a these fellers are riders fer the Rockin' R.

"Joe, Hicks—the rest a ya git on up here an' say yore names yore own selves."

One by one, the riders came forward with a smile. Each told Rowdy his name and welcomed him to Cheyenne.

When Slim came forward, he grabbed Rowdy's hand. His grin was ornery, but his eyes were sincere when he spoke.

"I shore hope y'all will stick around. I been pards with Lance ever since he showed up at the Rockin' R. I heard a lot 'bout ya durin' that time. The rest a yore family too. I shore hope y'all are here to stay."

Slim waved his arm toward the grinning riders.

"Come on, ya snoopy fellers. Let's give these brothers some peace. They have things to say we ain't part of." Slim winked at Rowdy as he followed the rest of the loud cowboys out the door.

The riders all decided to go home that night. As they rode, they discussed how Paul's arrival might change things on the ranch.

CHAPTER 29

ROWDY'S STORY

LANCE GRABBED ROWDY'S SHOULDERS AND SQUEEZED. "I just can't believe you are here. I've missed you so much. Now tell me everything. I want to hear it all. Everything that happened to you after your last letter." He frowned and scratched his head. "I reckon that was close to seven years ago."

Rowdy finally pulled the plug. He told Lance everything from almost dying on the battlefield to the long recovery.

"The hardest part was not knowing who I was or where I was from. I couldn't remember anything except waking up in that field hospital. I vaguely remembered being hauled off the battlefield but that was it. I didn't even know where I was hit.

"I didn't have any type of identification on me that said who I was, not even your letters." Rowdy frowned and shook his head. "They must have gotten lost somewhere. I kept them tied up in a string, and they were inside my shirt all the time.

"Your last letter I had just received, and it was in my vest pocket. I gave it to the fellow who treated me on the field. I asked that you be notified in case I died, but I'm not sure what happened to it after that.

"Doc Williams, the surgeon who saved my life in the field hospital, he's the one who gave me the name of Rowdy.

"No one there recognized me. The other fellers in that hospital told me I must have been a sniper because of the gun I carried. That's all anyone knew.

"'Course, ol' Smoke knew me. He wouldn't leave. He ran back and forth outside that hospital and made a heck of a ruckus. He wouldn't let up. Doc finally broke his rules once I came to and brought Smoke in so he could check on me. I guess I rambled on about my horse while I was out of my head. That's how they knew Smoke belonged to me.

"Once I talked to him, he settled down." Rowdy chuckled and shook his head. "That durn Smoke. I can't tell you the number of times we were separated. He always found me. Just tracked me down.

"I wasn't pleased about being stuck in bed. I guess I raised a little Cain while I was in that hospital." Rowdy's eyes glinted and he gave Lance a grin. "My memory is a little spotty about my stay there.

"I was concerned about getting my memory back, but Doc wasn't too worried. He said I'd get my memory back in a year or less." Rowdy frowned and shrugged. "Doc Williams is an excellent surgeon and a fine man, but he was wrong about that.

"After two years, I gave up. I kept up the name Rowdy and never told folks a last name. I figured I'd have one name for the rest of my life.

"Last year in Virginia, I got in a fight. It was a little burg. I don't even remember the name of the town. A fellow in a saloon there was smacking a woman around. I shoved him and made some suggestions about his lack of proper behavior. He tossed me against the bar, and I slammed my head. I guess that thump cleared some spider webs out because my memory started coming back."

He grinned at Lance when he added, "I still pounded the guy for hitting a woman though. He was a Yankee to boot and was making derogatory comments about the qualities of Southern ladies. I took offense.

"I went by our plantation and saw it had been sold. I didn't know if you had sold it or if Aunt Kittie had. She had passed by the time I made it down there."

Finally, Rowdy talked about going to the cemetery in Columbus, Georgia and finding his name on a tombstone.

"I can't quite explain the feeling that went through me when I saw that marker. I sure didn't think I would ever read my own gravestone." Both Lance and Rowdy chuckled over that.

"I met a little gal there. Beth Williams. She visited that cemetery every week and talked to the soldiers buried there. She kept things trimmed up some too.

"She is a sister to the surgeon who fixed me up. Her brother bought into a practice here in town. They came in on the same train I was on tonight."

Rowdy was tired by the time he was done telling his story. However, the weight he had been carrying around was finally starting to slide off. Watching the emotions course across his brother's face warmed Rowdy's heart. *My brother's glad to see me.*

CHAPTER 30

TOO MANY PAULS

LANCE WAS QUIET AS HE LISTENED TO ROWDY SPEAK. When his brother finished, he pulled an envelope out of his pocket and slid it across the table. Rowdy frowned and started to push it back.

"I am not here for charity," he ground out through clenched teeth.

Lance shook his head. "No, it is your half of the plantation. I worked there for over seven months. I rebuilt the fences and some of the buildings. I was able to get $100 an acre for the plantation." Lance added softly, "I used my half to buy this ranch, but Molly and I decided to save yours in case you came back. We both knew it seemed crazy since you had been declared dead, but we just couldn't make ourselves use it.

"There you are. One thousand acres sold at $100 per acre. Your half is $50,000 less a little bit for the restoration expenses." Lance placed the envelope in Rowdy's hand and pushed his fingers around it as he gripped his brother's hand. He looked at this brother he loved and commented softly, "Now you can make the decision of where to settle. The money is yours to buy a place wherever you want. We would love to have you around here, but the money is yours free and clear. You buy where you want. Welcome home, Brother!" exclaimed Lance as he gave his brother a big grin.

Paul "Rowdy" Rankin was speechless. This night hadn't turned out as he had expected at all. He picked up the envelope and his eyes began to water. Paul Rankin cried for the first time in nearly nine years. As quiet tears ran down his face, they washed away the anger, the doubt, and the sadness that he had carried with him since the war. Rowdy was on the road to recovery. Embarrassed, he wiped his face, but Lance looked away and pretended not to notice.

When Barney brought their food, Lance introduced Paul. Barney assumed Paul was a brother because the family resemblance was uncanny. However, he could tell from Lance's face that this was more than just a casual visit. Barney put out his hand, "Welcome to the Ford Restaurant, Paul. We're glad to have you home." He was back shortly with another plate of food.

"I thought since you polished that first plate off so fast, maybe you were hungry enough for second helpings of everything." Barney gave Paul a big smile and hurried back to the kitchen to clean up.

Both Rankin brothers were tired when they arrived at the Rocking R at two-thirty that morning. Paul insisted he sleep in the bunkhouse.

"It's too late to figure out sleeping arrangements, Lance. Besides, Smoke will behave better if I am there," he said with a grin.

When Gus rang the breakfast bell at six, only four men showed up for breakfast, and Paul was one of them. The rest of the riders slept right through it.

Paul went to the creek and took a bath before he walked up to the house. He was looking forward to meeting Lance's wife and he was not disappointed.

Lance had referred to the "little boys" the night before, but Paul didn't realize they were *Lance's* little boys until Molly told him he was an uncle.

His brother laughed and nodded.

"It's a long story and not one to worry about. I will catch you up when you have more time to just sit." He grinned and pointed toward one of the bedrooms.

"They are coming now so be prepared to be mauled!"

Sammy came rushing into the kitchen with his hair poking out in every direction and talking as fast as he could make words. Little Paul followed him, dragging an old blanket and sucking his thumb. He pulled it out long enough to grin at everyone.

"Sammy, how would you like to have another uncle?" Lance asked.

Sammy's eyes went wide with delight. "I would love to have another uncle because Slim and Gus are my uncles, and they are lots of fun!"

Lance laughed as he explained, "Well, Paul is my brother, so he is your uncle!"

Sammy looked from big Paul to little Paul.

"Well, I think that is too many Pauls. We need to give you a different name," Sammy told his uncle seriously.

Paul's eyes twinkled as he answered, "How about Rowdy? That's what my friends call me."

Sammy shouted with excitement, "Yes, we'll call you Rowdy! Why that's a fine name!" Sammy put out his hand very seriously and introduced himself.

"My name is Sammy Rankin, and you are?"

Paul grinned as he shook Sammy's small hand.

"My name is Rowdy Rankin."

Sammy collapsed on the floor laughing. "Your name is Rowdy, and we are both Rankins!"

Lance lifted little Paul onto his lap. "This fine young man is Paul Broken Knife Rankin. One of these days you will meet our other brother whose name he bears," Lance added with a smile.

Molly and Lance were watching their boys as they laughed, and Rowdy was beginning to understand why Lance was getting "soft."

CHAPTER 31

WELCOME HOME, ROWDY!

MOLLY DECIDED THEY NEEDED TO HAVE A BEAR SIGN Party to introduce all the family to Rowdy. She had asked Sadie to make a bear sign flag last winter. It was a brown bear footprint with bright blue clouds around the outside. Lance mounted a flagpole on top of a hill not too far from the house. When the flag on the hill went up, anyone who could see it would know Molly and Martha were making bear sign that day.

It was easily seen from all directions and soon friends, neighbors, and even a few stray cowboys were riding in.

Broken Knife came by with some of his braves as well as Molly's friend, Blue Feather.

Lance introduced Broken Knife and Rowdy. He pointed at Rowdy and then at himself. "Brothers." Then he pointed from Broken Knife to Rowdy. "We are all brothers."

Broken Knife stared from Rowdy to Lance. Then he pointed at Rowdy and said, "Same. Great Spirit confused. He make two the same." He slid from his horse and stalked over to Rowdy. Putting out his hand, he grunted, "Broken Knife and Same will be brothers as well."

Rowdy watched as Broken Knife talked to Molly.

The fierce-looking brave pointed at her stomach and said, "Another brave."

Molly shook her head.

"No. A girl child to make warriors behave."

Broken Knife laughed. As he took his bag of bear sign, he pointed at Lance. "Someday. Someday she cut your heart out!" He rode away, still laughing.

Rowdy met everyone. Badger, Martha, Sadie, Samuel, and Old Man McNary were the first to introduce themselves. All the Rocking R cowboys came to visit as well, although Tiny couldn't tell the two brothers apart.

Lance even sent a rider to town to invite Rueben and Beth Williams. When the Williams drove in the yard, the party was in full swing. The tables were loaded with food because a party at Rankin's ranch always meant lots of food.

Rowdy was standing next to the food table. That way, he didn't have to walk far to go back for more.

Beth cautiously approached him. For the first time since Rowdy had met her, her eyes weren't sparkling with happiness. She looked pale and nervous.

"Rowdy—er—I mean, Paul, I want to apologize for speaking out of turn at the restaurant. I didn't mean to upset you." Beth's voice was trembling, and her pretty eyes filled with tears.

Rowdy put his plate down. "Here now. There is no cause for tears." He smiled as he held her shoulders. "You forced me to face myself, and I've avoided doing that for a long time. I should thank you.

"Had you not spoken up, who knows where I would be today." He grinned at her as he added, "I'd probably be working for some rich widow woman, helping her break her horses and heal her broken heart!"

Beth's mouth fell open. When she realized Rowdy was teasing her, she began to laugh.

"Oh, Paul, I am so glad you aren't mad. When you left so fast, I just knew you were gone for good."

Rowdy looked at Beth intently before he looked away.

"That was my intention, but Slim rode out here and told Lance I was in town. The two of them showed up at the livery at midnight, and Lance messed up all my plans to run away." He looked around the noisy yard and added quietly, "It appears I have quite a bit of family in this area."

Rowdy pointed across the yard to where the kids were playing. "Those two little fellows are Lance's little boys, Sammy and Paul. Sammy was excited to get another uncle. He told me last night that we only need one Paul though, so I'll still be called Rowdy."

Beth followed Rowdy's eyes. She could see that some of the sadness had lifted, and it made her heart happy to see him happy. She answered softly, "You have a lovely family, Rowdy."

Rowdy nodded as he looked around the yard.

"Yes, I do, don't I?" As he watched Beth from the side of his eye, he totally forgot he had an entire plate of food just waiting to be eaten.

Rowdy felt something pulling on his britches. Little Paul was standing below him with his arms up. "Up," he demanded as he tugged again on Rowdy's pants. Rowdy lifted the little boy up. He had never held a baby and had no idea what to do with him or how to position him.

Paul had no such problem. He wiggled until his curly head was on Rowdy's big shoulder. Then he encircled Rowdy's neck with his little arm and promptly went to sleep. Rowdy tried to turn his head to look at the little boy. His face filled with surprise, and he patted Paul's back awkwardly.

Beth was giggling at the confused look on Rowdy's face when Molly hurried up.

"Here, I will take him," Molly offered as she reached out her arms.

Rowdy looked at the sleeping little boy in his arms. "Naw. He's fine. I'll just hold him awhile." Molly smiled and nodded before she hurried into the house to bring out more food.

Rowdy followed her in and sat down in the rocking chair. "I've never held a baby before," he said softly as he began to rock. "This is kind of nice."

Molly's tender heart was full. She put her arms around Rowdy's shoulders and kissed him on the cheek.

"Welcome home, Rowdy!" she whispered softly as she left the kitchen.

As Rowdy rocked the little boy, he pondered all the events that had taken place in just a few days. He didn't know where he was going to start his horse ranch, but he knew it wouldn't be far from here. He squeezed Paul a little closer as he rocked quietly in the empty kitchen.

When Molly came in later to check on them, Rowdy let her lift Paul out of his arms and place him in his crib. Paul pulled his knees up under his tummy and continued to sleep.

Rowdy watched them and said quietly, "I can see now why Lance has gotten soft."

His comment startled Molly. When she turned around, Rowdy was looking at Paul with a tender look on his face. She linked her arm through his and laughed. "Kids change you, Rowdy, and in a few months, we will have more changes!" she exclaimed as she touched her stomach. "Come on. Let's go outside and join your party!"

Rowdy was grinning as a laughing Molly pulled him through the door. She whispered, "You should probably eat some more anyway!"

Lance looked up as Molly drug his brother out of the house. Both were laughing. He felt his heart go still, and he sent up a quick prayer of thanksgiving. "I have my brother back!" he said softly as he walked toward them.

The party broke up in time for everyone to go home and chore before dark. Lance went up the hill to take the flag down and Rowdy walked with him.

"Where do you think I should start if I want to build a horse ranch?" Rowdy asked.

Lance thought for a moment. He pushed his hat back before he answered.

"Let's ride over to Badger's place in the morning. That man has more connections than anyone I know." He paused to look at his brother. "I guess this means you are going to stick around here?" Lance asked with a grin.

Rowdy laughed. "Yeah, Paul convinced me that I didn't want to move too far away."

Lance clapped him on the back, and the two brothers discussed Rowdy's future ranch as they walked down the hill.

CHAPTER 32

YEE HAW!

GUS WAS BEATING THE TRIANGLE LOUDLY AT SIX THE next morning. As the men ate breakfast, Lance lined them out for the day. A cougar had been bothering some of the cattle in the West Pasture.

"I need a couple of you who can track to go get a cougar today."

Joe and Hicks quickly stepped forward. "We cin track," offered Joe. "Do ya want the hide?"

When Lance looked at him in surprise, he grinned. "It makes a difference on the shot we take is all I'm a sayin'," Joe explained. "We cin blow it all to—" He turned red when he realized Molly was listening. "Beggin' yore pardon, Mrs. Rankin."

"I would love a lion hide," Molly answered with a smile. "Thank you, Joe."

As the men saddled up and prepared to leave, Rowdy walked out to the tack building where Joe and Hicks were loading a pack horse. Joe had picked up Rowdy's rifle from where it was leaning against Smoke's saddle and was looking it over. He whistled softly as he set it down.

Rowdy picked up the gun and balanced it in his hands.

"She a fine gun. Shoots true and never jams." Rowdy ran his hands over the smooth gun stock and started to put it down. Then he paused and asked Joe, "Would you like to borrow it?"

Joe's eyes lit up, but he shook his head. "Naw. It's a purty nice gun. I don't want to mess it up."

Rowdy gave a dry laugh and handed it to Joe. "Take it. This gun needs a new life as much as I do," he said softly, and he walked away.

Joe picked up the rifle and slid it into the boot on his saddle. Hicks was looking at his brother with a strange look on his face.

"Yeah, I recognized 'im too. He was one of the best sharpshooters we had on our side. He was never the same after he shot that kid though. Durn kid. Wearin' an officer's coat an' chargin' a line of tough Rebs. I will never understand folks."

"But cats…" he grinned, "those we do understand! Come on, Hicks. Let's go get a skin fer the boss' wife." As the two men rode out of the yard, Joe turned around in his saddle and saluted Rowdy.

Rowdy lifted his hand in a wave and turned to walk back toward the house.

"I knew I recognized those boys," he muttered to himself. "They were just kids in a man's war. Guess we all have a few scars that can't be seen."

Samuel and Molly wanted to go with Lance and Rowdy to the McCunes, so Lance saddled Babe while Rowdy saddled a horse for Samuel. Rowdy looked over as Lance was throwing a saddle on his mustang.

"That horse has some miles under it—bet it still doesn't have a name," he commented with a sideways grin. "I never could figure out why you refused to name your horses. Guess we're lucky your kids have names!"

Lance laughed.

"Maybe I'll name the next horse, but this old fellow still has a few good miles."

Sammy was standing on the bucket he used to get on Barleycorn when Lance asked, "Sammy, how would you like a saddle of your own?"

Sammy's big blue eyes lit up. "Say, I would like that jist fine!"

He jumped off the bucket and ran around Barleycorn. Taking the Shetland's head in his hands, he talked excitedly to the little pony.

"Did ya hear that, Barley? We are gettin' us a new saddle! Now we cin rope an' chase cattle with Pa!"

Lance pulled a new saddle out from behind some hay and handed it to Sammy. Sammy staggered a little but hung onto it. Lance laid a bright red blanket over it. He grinned and pointed at Rowdy.

"Have your Uncle Rowdy help you saddle that horse. Your uncle breaks horses for a living. In fact, I don't know anyone who knows more about horses than him."

Lance clapped Rowdy on the back as he left the barn, and Rowdy proceeded to show Sammy how to saddle a horse.

Rowdy could see the Shetland was ornery, so he waited for Barleycorn to release his air before he tightened the girth. "Don't hurry your horse, Sammy. Let your mind think with him." Rowdy adjusted the stirrups after Sammy was seated.

"There you go, cowboy. Spur 'im like you mean it an' ride 'im like ya stole 'im! Yee Haw!"

Sammy swung Barleycorn around and they raced out of the barn. His feet were drumming small horse's sides, and he was yelling, "Yee Haw! Yee Haw!"

Rowdy was on Smoke and waiting when Molly and Lance came from the house carrying Paul. Molly mounted Babe and reached her hands down for Paul.

Paul kicked his feet and cried. He twisted his body and reached towards Rowdy.

Rowdy moved Smoke closer. "How do I hold him?" he asked as he reached for the little boy.

"Just put him in front of you. He will hang onto the saddle horn," Lance answered with a grin. "Looks like you have a new partner."

Paul looked up at Rowdy with a look of pure joy. He took hold of the saddle horn and began to drum his small legs against Smoke's sides. Smoke turned his head to look back at who was on him and snorted.

Rowdy patted Paul's legs. "Here now, partner. Let's let Smoke do his job in peace," he suggested with a grin.

CHAPTER 33

HORSE BUSINESS

IT WAS A BEAUTIFUL FALL DAY, BUT ROWDY STILL HAD on two shirts along with his vest and longhandles. When Lance started to tease him, Rowdy replied, "Now I'm a southern boy, and it's going to take me a while to get used to this chill."

He breathed deeply as he inhaled the crisp air. *Georgia is nice but I still don't believe I will be going back*, Rowdy thought as he eased Smoke up to ride beside Molly.

Badger was working with his mules when the little group rode into the yard. Rowdy sat on Smoke and watched. He had never worked with mules, but he liked what he saw. Badger walked over to the fence and leaned against the bars.

Rowdy dismounted, lifting Paul down.

Badger's sharp blue eyes were twinkling.

"So you'ins be wantin' ta git into the hoss raisin' business, is ya?"

Rowdy looked at the little man with a surprised look on his face and Badger laughed.

"Now don't go a thinkin' I'm a smart one now. I jist like the way ya handle yer hoss an' a feller needs a business!" Badger grinned as he climbed spryly over the corral bars.

As they walked up to the house, he added, "The other thing you'ins needs ta be thinkin' on is a wife…but mebbie that there's a done deal considerin' the way that little bright-eyed gal was a lookin' at ya!"

Rowdy blushed a deep red and shifted Paul in his arms.

When Badger laughed his evil laugh, Lance turned around. He grinned. *Badger is one of the wiliest men I have ever met. He's a good friend too, and I'm durn happy he likes Rowdy.* Lance continued to grin as he reached to shake Badger's hand.

Samuel had gone into the house with Molly and Martha, so Badger cut right to the chase.

"I been a thinkin.' What you'ins needs is a hoss ranch, an' I think we ought ta talk ta ol' man Hutchins. His wife is sickly an' he's tard a fightin' with 'er. She don't like the weather an' she's got the lonelys."

Rowdy looked at Lance. He had no idea where the Hutchins' place was, but his brother probably knew the location.

Lance slowly nodded.

"I think you might like it, Rowdy. It is quite a ways out though. It's between here and Laramie. It's on the other side of Slim and a little to the north. You would be closer to us than to town but it's still over a twenty-mile ride." He grinned at Rowdy before he added, "But what's twenty miles on a good horse?"

Rowdy nodded. He could feel the excitement surging in him. He pushed it down and asked, "What does land sell for around here?"

"How does $7 an acre sound?" Lance asked with a grin. "I think Hutchins owns around twelve hundred acres, but you should pick up more if possible." He frowned slightly and added, "You will want to look over how the land lays as well as the water sources. I'm not familiar enough with that area to know where the water is.

"When do you want to leave?" Lance was almost as excited as Rowdy about buying more land.

Before Rowdy could answer, Badger added, "I'm a comin' too so don't you'ins make all yer plans 'fore ya include me!"

Rowdy looked at these two men who were going to drop everything to help him. A broad smile spread across his face.

"How about tomorrow? I want to buy a coat first though. I don't think I am going to survive the fall, let alone the winter out here."

As they stepped into the McCunes' home, Molly looked up at Lance excitedly.

"Father is going to buy into the livery!"

Samuel smiled and nodded. "Molly is correct. I decided I wanted to buy or start a business in town. I have been looking around and happened to be in the livery several days ago.

"Heck Reel and J.C. Abney were both in there. When I mentioned I was looking to invest in a business, Heck offered to sell me his half of their livery. He said he wants to buy a ranch and live where things aren't quite so busy. I am going in this week to finalize the details. As soon as that's done, I will be moving to my own place in Cheyenne."

Lance, Rowdy, and Badger stopped inside the door. They were surprised by the news.

Rowdy commented dryly, "Well, I guess I had better get busy and buy that horse ranch. Next thing, Molly will be wanting me to move up to the house and sleep with the boys." Rowdy grinned at Molly and everyone laughed.

Martha invited the Rankins to stay for dinner. When they finished, everyone but Sammy headed home. Sammy and Badger were going fishing.

The trip home was faster than the one over. Molly wanted to put Paul down for a nap, and Rowdy seemed to be in quite a rush to get to Cheyenne and find that coat.

Paul rode with Lance and fell asleep in the saddle. Rowdy was amazed at how Lance could hold a baby in the saddle, talk about land prices, and still be so relaxed.

Old Man McNary came down that afternoon to see what the plans were for the week. It was decided that Rowdy's group would leave at seven the next morning. Rowdy wanted to travel slowly to see the lay of the land, and the other men agreed. Old Man McNary offered to run things while everyone was gone.

Rowdy looked over at Samuel. "Want to go with us Samuel? We might run into a little snow, but you are welcome to come along."

Samuel shook his head. "No, tomorrow is Tuesday, November 1, and that is when we are going to hash out the details in my contract for the livery."

Lance was a little worried about being gone. *I have a good crew of men but no foreman. Still, Old Man McNary will keep an eye on things.* Lance frowned slightly as he put his pack together.

"I need to pick a foreman, but I don't have time to do that before I leave. I sure do miss Slim. And if we keep marrying fellows off, I am going to lose more help," Lance commented to himself with a chuckle.

Molly came into the bedroom to see if he needed any help. "Talking to yourself again, Lance?" she asked with a smile.

Lance pulled his wife close and kissed her.

"The worst part about this trip will be leaving you here," he whispered into her hair. Then he bent and kissed her growing stomach.

"Be nice to your mother, little one. No emergencies while I'm gone."

Molly smiled and Lance went back to making a pile of what he wanted to take.

"Most of our snow comes in the spring, so the weather should cooperate. You need to watch out for one of those northers though. They can come in fast, so watch the sky. Better yet, talk to the Old Man before you leave the house for long," he told Molly as he packed.

Lance headed to the kitchen to grab some food. They were going to take a pack mule so they could cook on the trail. He looked back at Molly and added, "I don't think we will be gone more than three days, maybe less." He dumped his supplies in the corner of the kitchen and went outside to help the men.

Once their plans were finalized, Rowdy headed for Cheyenne. He wanted that coat before he left as well as another blanket since they would be sleeping on the ground at least part of the way.

"I might even stop in and see Doc Williams," Rowdy commented to Smoke casually as he felt the heat climb up his neck.

Smoke snorted. It was almost as if he was rolling his eyes at Rowdy.

CHAPTER 34

SLOW DOWN, HEART!

BETH SAW ROWDY RIDING INTO TOWN BEFORE HE reached their house, and she rushed out to greet him.

"Rowdy!" she called as she waved at him.

Rowdy grinned as he pointed Smoke in her direction. *I intended to get my coat first, but this will work too,* he thought. His heart felt light and happy. Smoke snorted again.

As Beth came out to the street, she asked breathlessly, "What are you doing in town? Do you need to see Rueb? Is everything all right?"

Rowdy crossed his hands over the saddle horn and grinned at her.

"Actually, I wanted to see you. I wondered if you would like to have supper with me tonight?"

As Beth stood there looking up at him with her green eyes sparkling, Rowdy thought she was the prettiest gal he had ever seen.

"I would love to, Rowdy!" she exclaimed.

Rowdy sat on his horse a little longer just watching her. He finally chuckled.

"I'll see you at five-thirty then." He tipped his hat. As he turned his horse around, Beth put her hands over her heart.

"Slow down, heart, or you are going to beat right out of me!" she gasped as she tapped her chest.

Running inside, she popped her head into Doc Williams' office.

"I have plans for supper tonight, Reub. I'll be leaving at five-thirty!" she exclaimed. Blushing, she ran up the stairs to get ready.

Doc Williams stared after his sister before he hurried to the window. He could see Rowdy riding away. He walked slowly back to his desk and frowned slightly as he tapped the pen he was using on the desktop.

"Rowdy Rankin. Well, if this is the one, I won't complain. He's a fine man."

Rowdy rode slowly up Cheyenne's main street. He stopped at Herman's Mercantile. Shopping had never been something he liked to do, and he could feel himself growling as he looked at the blankets and coats. A young woman asked him if she could help him. He stared at the stacks for a moment. He finally turned to her with a frown.

"How long have you lived here?" he asked.

The young clerk was startled but she smiled as she answered, "My whole life."

Rowdy looked relieved and the young woman was even more confused.

"I'm a southern boy and this is the farthest north or west I have ever been. I am plumb cold now and I need a coat to get through the winter. Think maybe you can help me?" Rowdy asked seriously.

The clerk looked him over and she laughed out loud.

"I'm sorry. I just don't know what size to tell you." She paused and giggled again as she added, "You already have on so many clothes."

Rowdy looked down. Longhandles, two shirts, and a vest. He was just about comfortable. He grinned back at her.

"Well, let's make it fit over what I have on. I don't see any signs of me getting any warmer!"

When Rowdy left, he had two heavy shirts, another heavier vest, a sheepskin coat, and a couple of thick blankets. As he tied his bundle onto Smoke, the horse looked around to look at him.

"Now don't you argue with me, Smoke. I am plumb tired of being cold."

The horse snorted and Rowdy grinned.

He turned Smoke south. He wanted to get a bath and a shave before supper.

"And don't you be blowing in my bathwater today. I don't have time for all your foolishness this trip."

Smoke snorted again and flicked his ears back and forth as they headed toward the bath area.

Rowdy stopped at the Ford House as they rode by. It was early for the supper crowd, and the eating house wasn't busy. He waved Barney over and asked, "I'm bringing a little gal in here for supper, Barney. Think you could give us a side table where it won't be quite so crowded?"

Barney smiled in agreement. "And two plates for you, Mr. Rankin?"

"That would be just fine, Barney. But no mister. Just Rowdy," he replied with a grin.

When Rowdy knocked on Beth's door at five, he had on a new red flannel shirt, a bandana, and a black wool vest. He had even taken off his longhandles for the occasion. The bath was refreshing, and Rowdy felt good.

Doc Williams answered the door with a smile. "Come in, Rowdy. Beth will be down in a minute. Would you like a whiskey or some water?"

Rowdy nodded as he answered, "Water will be fine. I might have a beer with supper." As he looked around, he could see some remodeling had been completed. Other projects were just started.

"Do you plan to keep your office here, Doc, or are you looking for a place closer to the downtown area?" Rowdy asked.

"I am looking for something downtown. I think I found what I want, but I need to get a little more business before I buy another building." He grinned at Rowdy and added, "I am trying not to buy things I don't need."

Rowdy raised his eyebrows and Doc commented casually, "Business is picking up but it is mostly cowboys with made-up ailments so they can talk to Beth."

Rowdy was startled and then he laughed. "I can see how that would be," he replied seriously as his eyes twinkled.

Just then, Beth came hurrying into the room. Her blonde hair was wrapped in twists around her head with soft curls hanging below the twists. The green dress made her eyes look even greener.

Rowdy caught his breath. His chest felt tight, and he could hardly talk. He looked down and coughed before he put out his arm. He cleared his throat and asked, "Shall we go?"

Beth took his arm as they walked out the door. She whispered, "Rowdy, you have the biggest, strongest arm I have ever held!"

Rowdy stopped mid-step and looked down at her. She was smiling, and he resisted the urge to kiss her.

As he stared at her intently, Beth's eyes opened wide.

"Oh Rowdy! I am so thankful I met you at your grave," she whispered with a giggle.

Rowdy grinned down at her. "I am too. I don't know that I've ever made a friend at a cemetery—and certainly not one as good-lookin' as you." He pointed down the street.

"I was going to rent a buggy, but I thought you might like to walk. It's a nice evening."

Beth nodded and Rowdy pulled her arm a little closer.

Barney had set up a special table for them. It was off to the side and in a corner—the closest thing to private in the entire eating house. Barney worked hard to make his customers happy. Besides, he liked Rowdy and was glad to help out.

After Rowdy placed his order, the waitress paused. "Is a third person joining you?" she asked.

Rowdy looked confused, but Beth giggled. "No, it's just the two of us, but don't worry—there will be nothing left to throw away."

As they waited for their food, Rowdy told Beth about the ranch he was going to look at. He told her everything he knew about it so far including how it was a little isolated. His eyes were excited as he talked about breeding, raising, and breaking horses.

"I want it to be a horse ranch, Beth. I think there is potential to build and grow in this area, but…" his voice trailed off as he looked at her.

"But what, Rowdy?"

"Well, it's out a ways from town. The fellow who is selling says his wife hates the isolation. I am just not sure a woman would like it there," he explained cautiously.

Beth put her hand on his arm. "Rowdy, I think the right woman would like it there just fine," she replied sincerely as she looked at him.

Rowdy stared back at her and neither of them spoke. Finally, he picked up Beth's hand and kissed it.

"Beth, I think you are the girl I didn't think I would ever find," he said softly as he squeezed her hand.

Once again, Beth's heart felt like it was going to explode. Rowdy didn't let go of her hand, and she liked it that way.

As they walked back up the street to Beth's house, Rowdy was quiet. Beth had her arm linked through his and she was content to just be with him. When they reached her porch, Rowdy turned her toward him.

"Beth, would you let me be your fellow, like the most important fellow in your life?"

Beth put her hands on each side of Rowdy's face and whispered, "You already are my fellow, Rowdy. You have been since the day I met you."

Rowdy kissed her and it wasn't a quick peck.

When Beth pulled away, her heart was exploding, and her breath was coming quickly.

They stood there for a moment. Then Rowdy touched his heart and whispered softly, "You make my heart happy, Beth." He squeezed her shoulders and turned to lope down the steps. As he swung Smoke around, Rowdy raised a hand to wave. Beth blew him a kiss and Rowdy pretended to catch it. He was smiling when he rode away.

Beth stood watching him for a moment. Then she quietly opened the door and went inside.

Reuben watched her as she walked by his study without speaking. He stepped out with a laugh. "Good night to you too!" he called after her. "Anything you want to talk about?"

Beth paused and turned around. "Oh, Rueb. He is just wonderful," she whispered softly. She smiled at her brother before she turned toward the stairs.

Doc went into his office and sat quietly. Then he drummed his fingers on the desk.

"I had better start looking for a receptionist. I think I am going to lose this one quite soon." He began a list of possibilities, but it was short and not too promising. He frowned slightly and then smiled.

"At least I know my little sister will be loved and cherished by a darn good man."

CHAPTER 35

A Ranch for Rowdy

GUS BEAT ON THE DINNER BELL AT SIX O'CLOCK SHARP. The morning air was crisp and cool. Rowdy already had Smoke and Lance's mustang saddled. He had a pack saddle on one of Lance's mules. He was leading all three of them to the hitching rail in front of the house when Lance opened the door.

Lance laughed as he pulled on his boots. He drawled, "I think I am going to like traveling with you, Same. I just hope we can pack enough food with us."

Rowdy grinned and the two brothers walked into Gus's kitchen together. Each picked up a plate. Gus filled Lance's and put nearly twice that amount on Rowdy's. He winked at Rowdy, and Rowdy looked pleased.

The hands drifted in slowly, followed by Old Man McNary.

The Old Man started barking orders, and Lance held his face still to keep from laughing.

"Listen up, fellers! The Old Man's back in charge."

Once breakfast was finished, Lance went back inside for his bedroll and the sack of food. He threw it over the mule, and Rowdy tied it in place.

As the hands watched the two brothers work together, one of them muttered, "Same," and they all laughed.

Lance went back into the house again to tell Molly goodbye. Neither of the little boys was up yet, and Lance kissed each one softly. He hugged Molly one more time and was walking out the door when Badger rode in on Mule.

Badger added a few things to their pack and Rowdy cinched it down.

Mule and Smoke snorted at each other a couple of times, and the three men were on the trail by six-thirty.

The first mile was fairly quiet. Finally, Badger looked at Rowdy with devils sparkling in his eyes and asked, "So when's the weddin'?"

Lance looked from Badger to Rowdy with surprise on his face, and Rowdy turned red.

As the red continued up his neck, Rowdy coolly stared from one man to the other and replied with a lop-sided smile, "Soon, I hope."

They all laughed, and conversation started.

Rowdy quizzed the two men about the winters and what a person needed to do to prepare. He liked to plan and anything unknown gave him a worry. He only had one shirt on under his vest this morning, but his sheepskin coat was inside his bed roll.

"The first things to look for are water and winter feed. Horses are different from cattle, but they still have to eat through the winter. Summer graze is important but that is usually available." Lance continued, "Then look at the buildings. You are going to be foaling so you will want some place warm to put the mares while they foal. You'll need stalls too if the weather is bad when they are born. You will probably have to build your working pens, but that can come later."

Badger nodded and added, "Jist 'remember this here feller wants ta move. His wife ain't happy an' ya know she's a makin' his life mighty rough. Whatever price he throws at ya, think on it an' come in lower. He wants ta sell worser than ya want ta buy."

Badger paused and added, "Hutchins an' his wife each filed on six hundred forty acres. Ya need ta do that too but make shore yer land has water." He grinned again, "An' when ya git that little gal yore thinkin' on locked down, ya have her file too."

Rowdy turned red and they all laughed.

The men covered nearly twenty miles before they stopped. They were winding their way through the hills and riding slowly. Rowdy liked what he saw so far.

After they were back on the trail for about six hours, Badger pointed ahead. "We ought ta be comin' up on Hutchins' place real soon. Let's us make camp 'round here so's we cin ease on down that in the mornin'."

They turned all the animals loose to graze and made camp. Neither of the horses nor Badger's mule would roam far, and Lance's pack mule would stay close to the other animals.

Coffee, biscuits, and beans. Rowdy grinned. He hadn't had that for some time, and it tasted good.

Rowdy leaned back against his saddle. The coffee tasted good, and the fire was cozy. He was glad he had purchased extra blankets though. The air was crisp and clear as he drifted off to sleep.

There was frost on the ground in the low places the next morning. The men were slow to climb out of their blankets, but the coffee warmed them. Lance had bacon frying and made more biscuits.

Rowdy caught their mounts. Even though Badger's mule acted docile, Rowdy kept an eye on him.

"There is something a little fierce about you, Mule," Rowdy told him as they walked. Mule ignored him.

Badger gave Rowdy his evil grin.

"Don't mind Mule. He's a feelin' peaceable this mornin'."

Rowdy still didn't trust the large mule.

They rode into Hutchins' ranch headquarters around eight-thirty that morning. Harold Hutchins was surprised to see visitors.

As they sat on their horses, Rowdy went right to the point.

"Mr. Hutchins, we heard you were thinking of selling your ranch. We were riding by and thought we would stop in and talk if you had a little time. This is my brother, Lance Rankin. That's Badger McCune and I'm Rowdy Rankin."

Hutchins shook hands. "I'm Harold and my wife is Louise.

"Louise!" Harold hollered. "Some boys out here who want to talk to us about buyin' our ranch."

"*Maybe* buying," Rowdy corrected. "We are just looking things over today." He looked toward the house when Louise Hutchins appeared in the doorway.

"Good morning, ma'am," Rowdy greeted her as they all tipped their hats.

Louise Hutchins was a grumpy-looking woman. She had a sour expression on her face, and Rowdy guessed she had a sour disposition to go with it. He kept his face void of expression as she studied the three of them.

"Sell it," was all she said before she walked back into the house.

The house appeared a little small, but both the house and the buildings looked solid.

Rowdy could feel his excitement growing as Badger spoke.

"So, where's yer water come from? Does you'ins have a well or fetch it from that there creek?"

Harold Hutchins pointed up to the hills north of the house. "There is a spring-fed pool up there. I filed on it as part of my six hundred forty acres and the wife filed on another spring to the west." Harold's face was still as his eyes moved over the hills.

"I like this place, but the wife thinks it's too far from people. I guess she wants to move to Denver although I don't know what I'll do there. All I know is cattle and farming." Hutchins sounded and looked defeated as he stared across his small ranch.

The rest of the men were silent.

Lance finally asked, "What is your winter graze like?"

"There are protected little valleys scattered all over in those hills. The first few years we were here, I cut grass for hay, but I haven't had to do that for several years now. There is another nice little spring with good grass around it just over those hills. Was I you, I'd file on that if you decide to buy this place. That would give you ownership of the three main water sources in this area."

Rowdy felt sorry for the man. He obviously had a lot of knowledge and loved what he did. *I guess he just married the wrong woman… or brought the right woman to the wrong place*, Rowdy thought with a twinge of panic.

Hutchins offered to show them around the ranch. He called his wife to tell her, but she didn't answer.

Lance and Badger rode on each side of Hutchins and Rowdy rode behind. He could hear most of what they talked about and was able to look around without appearing rude. Some of the ground was rough but little grassy valleys were scattered all over.

Rowdy heard Lance ask, "How much snow do you get in a winter here?"

"Oh, about five to six feet total and around eleven or twelve inches of rain. Sometimes, the rain is less. That's why water is so important."

Badger asked, "How do yer horses handle the wind? Ya got wind, ain't ya?"

"The wind can be brutal. That's why we built the headquarters where we did.

"Winter in general can be vicious, but it can be easy too." Hutchins shrugged. "It's just winter. I've been through a couple of winters down in Kansas, and they ain't so great neither."

The men rode around the ranch all morning and made it back by one in the afternoon. Louise Hutchins didn't come out of the house, nor did she invite them in for dinner. Lance was embarrassed for the man.

Finally, Badger asked the question Rowdy had wanted to hear. "How much ya askin' fer this here operation?"

Hutchins paused and looked toward the house. He cleared his throat and answered, "$7 an acre but if you can have cash by next week, I'd take $6."

The men were silent, and Lance slowly nodded.

"We'll think on it. Thanks for your time and we'll let you know."

As they rode away, Lance turned to look at Rowdy.

"Well? What do you think?"

Rowdy was trying to keep the excitement from showing on his face.

"I like it, but I think I am a little too desperate to buy a ranch. I want to buy as much as he wants to sell."

Lance laughed and suggested, "Let's check with the land office in Cheyenne and see what it would take to pick up that last water hole. I think I can find that location on a map. We hash it over at Barney's.

"If it sounds good, you could ride back up there tomorrow and finalize the deal. We are about twenty-five miles from Cheyenne now. Do you want to skip dinner and just ride on in?"

The consensus was to keep going, and they reached Cheyenne just a little before five. The land office door was still open, and the men went in.

The clerk was just getting ready to close for the day, but he opened his maps when they told him what they wanted to see.

"Harold Hutchins? Yes, here is his land. He proved up on two sections, here and here," the clerk said, pointing at the map.

"How about that section there?" Lance asked as he pointed to where the other water hole was.

"Let's see…Yes. That's available. Do you want to prove up on it or buy it outright? If you buy it outright, the price is $8 an acre."

Lance slid to the side so Rowdy could see as well. "Is there any more open land available around those three sections?" Rowdy asked.

"Two more sections. One to the north and one to the east. Each of those sections would be $7 per acre."

Rowdy studied the map and nodded.

"We'll talk it over and be back tomorrow. What time will you open?"

"We officially open at eight in the morning Monday through Saturday, but I'm usually here a half-hour earlier. Just knock. If I'm here, I'll let you in."

The men thanked him and walked down the street to Barney's.

After they ordered, Rowdy pulled out a piece of paper and wrote down all the numbers.

"That land will cost $21,760 if I buy it this week. That number includes the three extra sections. It would give me thirty-two hundred acres, but it would leave me with less than $28,000 for working capital. What do you think?" he asked.

Lance grinned. "I like land so I would do it, but Badger has a money mind. What do you think, Badger?"

"I don't think that east section's goin' ta give ya a lot a benefit even though it does sit right next door. Fer sure the other two pieces," Badger replied as he studied the numbers and the descriptions on the paper.

The men ate supper and talked some more. Rowdy was still mulling it over.

Lance and Badger decided to go on home while Rowdy opted to stay in town. He wanted to be at the land office first thing Thursday morning.

"I might mosey on over and visit with Doc Williams," he drawled casually, studying the floor as red crept up his neck. When he raised his head, both men were laughing at him. He joined them as the red rose higher.

Lance slapped Rowdy's back and laughed.

"She's a fine little gal, Same. We'll look forward to that wedding."

CHAPTER 36

A QUESTION FOR DOC

BETH WAS SURPRISED WHEN ROWDY KNOCKED ON the door around seven that evening.

"Rowdy!" she exclaimed excitedly, "Come in!" As he followed her into the dining room, Reuben stood up from the table and stretched out his hand.

"Have a chair, Rowdy. We are just finishing up but there is plenty." He smiled as he added, "Beth always seems to make too much, but it is too good not to eat."

Beth blushed happily and Rowdy sat down.

Beth set a full plate in front of him.

I don't need to eat, but it sure smells good.

Rowdy tasted Beth's cooking that evening for the first time. He took a couple of bites and put his fork down as he stared at his plate.

Beth's face paled a little. "Is there something wrong?"

Rowdy looked up and answered seriously, "Beth, that is the best food I have ever eaten in my life. I think I'm just going to slow down and savor it a little."

Beth was all smiles and dimples as she sat down. She pulled her chair a little closer to Rowdy's.

He told them about the trip to look at the ranch.

Beth's eyes were shining, and Reuben knew without a doubt that he was going to need a new receptionist. *The question is how fast,* he thought with a twinge of sadness as he looked at her bright eyes and happy face. *This house is going to be lonely.*

Once Beth started to clear the table, Reuben invited Rowdy back to his study for a drink. Rowdy agreed to the whiskey, but after he accepted it, he just turned it in his hands.

Reuben knew what was coming so he made small talk until Rowdy found the words he was looking for.

"Doc, I want to ask your sister to marry me, and I would like to have your permission first." Rowdy's hands were gripping the glass, and his face was tight as he watched the man in front of him.

Doc was pleased. He grinned as he slapped Rowdy on the back.

"Rowdy, I can't think of anyone I would like more for a brother than you," he answered sincerely as he reached to shake Rowdy's hand. "How fast is this going to happen? I am going to need a new receptionist, you know," he commented wryly.

Rowdy grinned. "I have never been one to put things off, but I guess I will let Beth decide that."

Just then, Beth walked into the room.

"Beth decide what?" she asked as she looked from one to the other.

Reuben didn't answer and Rowdy stood to take her arm.

"How would you like to ride out to that ranch with me tomorrow morning when I close the deal?"

Beth's eyes opened wide. "Oh, Rowdy, I would love to! What time should I be ready?"

Rowdy laughed as he looked down at her. "I will bring your filly by around eight. We'll eat some breakfast at the Ford House and head out. Once we sign the papers, we'll come right back. It's about four hours out there though so we'll be gone most of the day."

Beth's eyes were shining. "Rowdy, let's have a picnic! I will pack a lunch and we can take it with us!"

Rowdy looked down at Beth and smiled. "That would be just fine." He wanted to kiss her but instead, he touched her cheek with his hand and turned out the door.

Beth stood in the door and watched Rowdy take the steps two at a time. As he climbed onto Smoke, she called his name softly and blew him a kiss.

Once again, Rowdy pretended to catch it. This time, he laid his hand over his heart. He tipped his hat as he rode down the street.

Beth rushed back into the house. As she ran by her brother, she gushed breathlessly, "Reub, I will be gone all day tomorrow. I know you have appointments and I'm sorry. I'm making food and I'll leave you some!"

Soon, Reuben heard pans banging and his sister's pretty voice singing.

"Probably next week," Reuben pondered out loud as he drank Rowdy's full glass of whiskey. "Yes, I think it will be next week."

Doc rocked back in his chair and stared at the ceiling for a moment before he opened his medical books. He had a surgery to perform in two days, and he wanted to see if there was any way he could make the process easier. *And maybe take just a little less time too,* he thought. The practice of medicine was improving, and Doctor Williams wanted to improve along with it.

CHAPTER 37

A Genuinely Kind Man

SAMUEL BREWSTER WAS WALKING OUT OF THE LIVERY as Rowdy rode up on Smoke.

"Rowdy!" he exclaimed, "Today went well?"

Rowdy gave him a sideways grin and nodded his head. "I am heading out tomorrow to sign papers."

Samuel was smiling as he asked, "So do you have a place to stay tonight? I just took possession of my house today. I bought it fully furnished and it's right down the street. They even left the sheets so I have an extra bedroom ready if you would like to spend the night."

Rowdy was surprised. Samuel was a genuinely nice man, but he was reserved around most people. The two men had never talked much.

"I would like that, Samuel. If you can wait a little bit, I will put up my horse and be right out."

Samuel agreed. He had wanted to talk to Rowdy alone for some time and this might be that time.

Rowdy talked to Smoke as he rubbed him down, and Samuel could hear from where he stood.

"Now, Smoke, tomorrow we are going for a ride with a special gal, and I want you to be on your best behavior. I know that little filly is

199

purty and all, but don't you be botherin' her. You'll have plenty of time for that after we marry."

Smoke snorted in response and Samuel almost laughed.

"Why that horse acts like it understands what Rowdy is saying!" he murmured.

Rowdy wrapped his arm around Smoke's neck, and the stallion nuzzled him. He handed the horse an apple and walked back out to meet Samuel.

"I sure appreciate this, Samuel."

As the two men started up the street, Rowdy asked, "So is the livery half Brewster now?"

Samuel smiled and nodded.

"It sure is, but I came in as a silent partner so the name will be J.C. Abney, Livery Feed & Sale Stable. I have experience in feed and shipping, and that was the part that Heck ran. I don't want my name on it and J.C. has an established reputation. We agreed this would work out well for all of us."

The older man rubbed his hands together in the brisk fall air. "I don't know about you, but my southern bones are still getting used to this cool weather.

"And as much as I love my little grandsons, I am ready for a place of my own. There is a part of me that will miss those cold little bodies showing up in my bed around midnight every night though—and some of the time with wet britches!"

Samuel chuckled, and Rowdy joined him.

"Yes, those two little boys are mighty special," agreed Rowdy. He thought about Paul falling asleep on his shoulder. "Paul is the one who convinced me I needed to stay. Family is just downright important."

Samuel was quiet for a bit. Then he stopped walking and turned to the man next to him.

"Rowdy, I have something I want to give you. After Lance invited me to visit, I wrote to a friend of mine whose organization was helping the government identify fallen Confederate soldiers. I asked for the letter Lance had written to you since the Lance in that letter was now my son-in-law. My friend sent me everything found on the man's body identified as you.

"I want to give it all to you. Perhaps someday, you can give it to your children and tell them your story. There is no point in sending it back, and it is more yours than anyone else's. Once you get settled, I'll bring it by."

Rowdy was quiet for a moment. "I would like that, Samuel, and I appreciate the work you did to help those boys. You know, I met Beth at the cemetery in Columbus, Georgia.

"After I regained my memory, I started backtracking and found my own grave." Rowdy's mouth twisted in a wry grin. "Gives a fellow a funny feeling to read his own tombstone.

Rowdy paused before he continued softly. "Beth visited that cemetery every week and somehow came across my grave. She kept it trimmed down and even planted some flowers. She was coming to spruce it up the day I happened to be there."

Samuel was quiet. He had never talked to Rowdy much, but he knew he knew the young man carried scars inside of him.

Rowdy turned to look at Samuel. "I am going to ask Beth to marry me tomorrow after I sign the papers on my ranch," he shared softly.

Samuel gripped Rowdy's hand. "Well, that is fine, Rowdy. That is just fine."

The two men walked on toward Samuel's house without talking.

Rowdy was comfortable around this quiet man. He didn't know why he had told Samuel he was marrying. It just seemed right.

Then his mouth turned up in an ornery grin. *Maybe since I don't have a father-in-law, I will just steal Lance's. Same,* he thought. He almost chuckled as he followed Samuel into the house.

CHAPTER 38

WHERE TO, COWBOY?

ROWDY WAS UP EARLY THE NEXT MORNING. HE LEFT Samuel a note and thanked him for the night's stay.

As he walked down to the livery, he could feel a new crispness in the air. His walking slowed as he thought about Beth.

"Shoot! I forgot to ask Beth what saddle she wanted to ride today," he growled. "I don't even know if she rides astride." As he slowly walked into the barn, the hostler walked out chewing on a piece of hay.

"Say," Rowdy commented, "I am taking Miss Williams for a ride today, and I forgot to ask her if she wanted to ride astride or use a sidesaddle. Do you know which she prefers?"

The hostler grinned. "I know which she prefers, an' I know which she most often rides. Which one do ya want?" The hostler was an old cowboy, and he'd had several talks with Beth about a feller she was sweet on. *She is ass over teakettle fer that feller an' this jist might be the cowboy.*

The hostler added, "Her brother wants her to ride like a lady, an' she does when she rides out with a feller." Rowdy scowled and the hostler grinned.

"Now when she comes to git that filly by her own self, she rides astride. So which kinda feller are ya? One that wants to chit chat or one that wants to *ride?*

Rowdy grinned. "Ride!"

The hostler brought Beth's saddle up and led the filly out. The horse recognized Rowdy and was eagerly nosing him.

"Looks like that little filly may be some familiar with ya," the hostler commented.

"I broke her," Rowdy explained softly as he scratched the filly's ears.

The hostler perked up. "Say, if ya want some breakin' work, I cin set ya right up."

Rowdy looked over at the man with his piercing blue eyes and replied quietly, "I break gentle, and I only break for people who will treat their horses gentle."

The hostler grinned again. *Yep, this is my little missy's feller,* he thought. He put out his hand. "The name's Smith, Fred Smith." The hostler's sharp blue eyes were twinkling. "But ya cin call me Rooster."

Rowdy took the small man's hand. He gave the hostler a wry grin. "I've known a few Smiths in my time. Glad to meet you, Rooster."

Rowdy talked to Smoke again as he saddled him. Then he put his arm around Smoke's neck. "I'm going to ask her today, Smoke. I'm counting on you to help me say the right words."

Rooster had exceptional hearing, a sense that he often exercised to keep it in prime working condition. His old eyes sparkled with humor as he listened, but he was whistling tunelessly when Rowdy led Smoke out.

Rooster acted a little too innocent, and Rowdy looked at him suspiciously.

"I wish ya luck, boy!" Rooster grinned and walked away laughing.

Rowdy stared after him and chuckled as he shook his head.

"Rooster Smith, my eye," Rowdy muttered to himself. "I'm guessing he was a rooster in his day but, but his last name sure wasn't Smith."

Rooster turned to wave as Rowdy left and winked at him.

Rowdy lifted his arm in return. He was smiling as he headed up the street to the land office. It was just a little after seven, but he thought he would see if the agent was in.

The agent answered quickly when Rowdy knocked. In answer to Rowdy's questions about filing versus purchasing outright, he explained, "You need to show some work. The legal description says irrigation, but most of this land doesn't have any regular water so that rule has a little give." He pointed at the section to the east on his land map. "That is going to be a hard one to prove up on. No water for miles, and the grass is a little short. On wet years, the grass is good but on dry years, she's bone dry. It would be durn hard to farm, and the graze is sketchy."

That made up Rowdy's mind. He showed the agent the two sections he wanted to buy.

"The name is Paul Rankin. I am buying Harold Hutchins' ranch today. If you can get that paperwork ready, I will try to be in before five this afternoon. I will have the cash then."

As he started to walk out, the agent called after him, "If you want more land further north, there's a fellow scraping by with a passel of kids who might sell. His land lays just to the west of your north sections and would give you a nice amount of land all together. Name's Hatch." He paused and added, "Something to think on."

Rowdy nodded and thanked him. As he left the land office, he checked his pocket watch.

"It's just seven-thirty. I'll be a little early but maybe Beth will be ready." His eyes sparkled with humor as he laughed. "And if she's not, I will just watch her rush around. That might be fun too."

Beth wasn't quite ready, but she was excited. Her split riding skirt told Rowdy she thought the same way he did about the saddle. He followed her into the kitchen and watched her as she packed the lunch. Finally, she turned to look at him. Her face was pink, but she was smiling.

"If you are going to just sit there and watch, then come around this table and help me," she ordered with her hands on her hips.

Rowdy laughed. He helped Beth pack the picnic lunch. He was hungry and was pleased Beth had fixed lots of food.

Doc Williams was with his first patient of the day, so they left quietly. Rowdy loaded the food into his saddlebags. He still had his bed roll behind his saddle, and he sent Beth inside to get a heavier coat. He wasn't taking any chances with the weather.

As they rode toward the Ford House, Beth greeted everyone she met.

Finally, Rowdy looked at her and asked incredulously, "Do you know everyone in the entire town of Cheyenne?"

Beth giggled. "Not yet but give me time!"

Just as Rowdy dismounted in front of restaurant, Slim Crandall stopped his wagon beside them. Sadie was sitting close beside him. Rowdy greeted them and turned to Beth.

"Beth, these are friends of mine. Lance's best friend and past foreman, Slim, and his wife, Sadie." He put his hand on Beth's horse as he pointed toward her.

"Beth Williams, Doc William's sister. I think you met her at Badger's the other night."

Sadie leaned forward. "Beth, it is so nice to see you again. I hope we will see more of you."

As Slim and Sadie drove down the street, Beth commented softly, "You know a lot of people too, Rowdy."

Rowdy watched as the Crandalls drove away. Then he turned to look up at Beth.

"I owe Slim." As he lifted Beth down, Rowdy kept his hands on her waist for just a moment as he added softly, "I sure am glad I stayed."

Beth blushed and Rowdy had to resist kissing her right there on the street.

The Ford Restaurant was nearly full, but Barney led them to the Rocking R table. Joe and Hicks were there. After introductions, Rowdy asked about the mountain lion.

"Did you get it?"

Joe gave a sideways grin and his eyes lit up. "We shore did. I could get attached to that gun a yores! We sighted right in on that big cat. Four hundred yards an' we took 'im down! Now Mrs. Rankin has that cat hide she wanted. We shot several wolves too." Joe frowned. "There were some big lobos harassin' the cattle."

Rowdy introduced Beth and she asked how they knew Rowdy.

Joe paused and Hicks replied, "We work fer Lance." His eyes twinkled as he gestured at the table. "That's why we git to sit at the Rockin' R table!"

Everyone laughed and the conversation quieted as the men ate.

Finally, Hicks looked up at Rowdy and asked, "So where are the two of ya headed today?"

"We are riding up towards Laramie to look at a ranch."

"And, we are planning to have a picnic as well," added Beth, her eyes sparkling with excitement.

Hicks frowned. "Don't mess around. I think we are goin' to git a storm today."

Rowdy was surprised, but he was glad for the advice. Then he frowned. *I don't know how to read this weather at all,* he thought. *That is something I sure need to learn.*

As the four of them left the restaurant and headed for their horses, Joe pulled Rowdy's rifle out of the boot on his saddle. He held it reverently as he handed it to Rowdy.

"Thanks fer loanin' us yer gun an' fer watchin' our backs." He started to salute but changed it to a wave.

Rowdy watched them quietly as they rode away. Beth came up to stand beside him.

As she took his arm, she looked up at him with tears in her eyes.

"You knew them in the war, didn't you? That is a sharpshooter's rifle. Eli described one to me in one of his letters," she whispered softly as she wrapped her arm tighter around Rowdy's.

"You are a good man, Rowdy Rankin. A good man with a kind heart." She stood on her tiptoes and kissed his cheek. Then she stepped back with pink in her cheeks and asked, "Where to now, cowboy?"

Rowdy stared at Beth for a moment before he smiled. He took her arm, and they crossed the street to the bank. Rowdy withdrew $7,680 and tucked it into the money belt he had around his waist. He was almost light-headed when they reached the horses. *We are going to buy a ranch!*

The ride went quickly. They arrived at Hutchins' ranch a little before noon. Once again, Louise Hutchins did not come out of the house, nor were they invited in. Harold Hutchins had the deed ready and signed.

Rowdy noticed that Louise's name was not on the deed, but he said nothing. He paid and Harold Hutchins shook his hand. Rowdy followed Hutchins' eyes as the man looked over his little spread.

When Hutchins looked back at Rowdy, he had tears in his eyes. "Good Luck—I sure hope you make it pay. We will be gone in two weeks if that works for you."

Rowdy agreed. He was quiet as he and Beth turned their horses southeast to head back to Cheyenne.

CHAPTER 39

A Picnic at Midnight

BETH HAD BEEN QUIET THE ENTIRE TIME, BUT NOW she looked at Rowdy with fire in her eyes. "How could she do that to him? She didn't even come outside. Why, he is giving up his dream for her, and she didn't even stand beside him or invite you in to eat!"

Rowdy pushed Smoke closer to Beth's horse and reached his arm around her waist. He pulled her off her horse and across his saddle in front of him. As he held her and looked into her surprised eyes, he asked, "Beth Williams, will you marry me and stay with me forever on my ranch?"

Beth smiled as she put her arms around his neck. "Our ranch, Rowdy. And only if my name is on the deed too!"

Smoke was on his best behavior as he walked quietly beside the little filly. He did look back from time to time though to see just what his "people" were doing back there.

Finally, Rowdy set Beth back on her horse. They were both a little out of breath. His smile slowly faded as he looked up at the sky. The clouds were rolling in and the air was much colder than it had been.

"Beth, let's skip that picnic and get on back to Cheyenne. The wind is picking up, and I'm not too familiar with this weather yet."

They had only gone a few miles when the rain cut loose, and the wind began to blow in gales. Rowdy was looking for an abandoned cabin or shelter of any kind. He spotted a line shack off the trail and pushed the horses against the wind. As he tried to force the door open, the wind sucked it closed, almost smashing his hand. Pushing his way in, he saw there was enough room for the horses. He quickly pushed Beth in and then followed with both horses. Smoke he turned loose, but he kept the bridle on the filly. After he unsaddled them, the horses shook off the water, and the heat from their bodies helped warm the room.

Rowdy looked around. Whoever had stayed there before had left wood ready for a fire with more stacked inside. *Good thing*, he thought. *There is no wood close so they must have hauled that in.*

Beth was shivering so Rowdy opened his bedroll and took out his heavy coat. He wrapped her in it. He dug through his saddlebags until he found a rag, and he rubbed the horses down.

Beth watched as Rowdy talked to Smoke just like one would talk to another person.

"Smoke, you did alright today. I'm real proud of how you behaved around that little filly. Now you leave her alone tonight. Durn females," he muttered as he turned around.

When he saw Beth laughing, he grinned. "Smoke and I have been together so long that I forget he's not a person," Rowdy tried to explain as the red moved up his neck. Then he moved closer to Beth and whispered softly, "Durn females!"

Rowdy wrapped the blankets around them as the fire died down. The horses stamped impatiently, and the wind continued to howl.

A noise awakened Rowdy, and he was alert instantly. Smoke faced the door, and his ears were pricked forward. Rowdy listened. He could hear howling outside. It sounded like a pack of wolves, and they sounded close.

Then he heard a child cry. Rowdy slid into his boots, grabbed his rifle, and rushed out the door. As he followed the sound, he saw two small children backed up to a rock. Three wolves were in front of them. The oldest, a boy, had a stick that he was shoving at the wolves. Tears were running down his face as he yelled. A small girl was cowered against the rock. She was seated, and her knees were pulled up to her chin. She was crying as she hid her face.

Rowdy aimed and shot the first wolf. A second shot took the second one. The third wolf was running, and Rowdy's third shot brought it down. As Rowdy moved closer, he called to the children.

"Everybody okay there?"

The boy turned to face him. He was thin and shivered in the cold. Neither child had a coat, and their clothes were threadbare.

Rowdy looked around but he saw no adults. As he walked slowly the children, he asked, "How did you come to be out here tonight? Where do you kids belong?"

The boy answered, "I'm Rudy Hatch and this is my little sister. Her name is Maribelle."

Rowdy recognized their last name. As he led the kids back to the shack, Rowdy's confusion increased.

"You kids live way up north—what are you doing down here?"

Rudy's eyes filled with tears. "I forgot to shut the gate an' the milk cow got out. Ma sent Maribelle an' me to look for her. That storm came up an' I got lost. Then the wolves started to foller us. I was tryin' to find somewhere I could hold 'em off." He took a deep breath as he tried not to cry. "I sure am glad ya came along."

Beth was standing in the doorway as Rudy was telling his story and she pulled the children inside. Her bright eyes sparkled as she looked at them.

"You know, we were going to have a picnic today, but the storm came up and we missed it. How would you two like to join us for a picnic right now? I know I'm hungry and Rowdy is always hungry!" she exclaimed as she pointed at him with a smile on her face.

Maribelle's eyes opened wide, and Rudy licked his lips. By the time Rowdy had taken off his boots, Beth had her picnic blanket spread on the floor and was setting out the food. Maribelle was smiling at Beth shyly while Rudy stood back and watched.

"I ain't never been to no picnic before," he said quietly.

Rowdy grinned at him and whispered, "Neither have I."

Rudy smiled for the first time, and they all sat down around the blanket. Beth kept a happy conversation going as the children ate hungrily. Rowdy held off until the young ones had their fill, and then he ate a little of what was left. Maribelle was starting to fall asleep sitting up, so Beth wrapped her in a blanket and laid her on the floor. She put Rowdy's huge coat on Rudy and pulled it around him.

Rudy looked down in wonder. "I ain't never had a warm coat before." Soon his head was bobbing, and Rowdy eased him down by his sister.

CHAPTER 40

MEET THE NEIGHBORS

AS THEY WATCHED THE CHILDREN SLEEP, ROWDY looked at Beth and grinned. "Well, I just ruined your reputation by keeping you out all night *and* having a picnic at three in the morning. I guess you are going to have to marry me now."

Beth giggled and moved closer to Rowdy. He pulled the second blanket up and wrapped his arms around Beth. As she laid her head on his chest, he thought, *I could sure get used to this.*

Rowdy was up early. The sun was shining and there was no indication anywhere of the storm that had come up so fast the day before. He found a sinkhole that had filled with water and led the horses out to drink. He had packed two canteens of water, and both were still three-fourths full.

Beth opened what was left of the food and spread it out on the blanket again. The two children eyed it hungrily.

Rowdy had barely eaten anything the night before and he wasn't going to eat this morning either. *It is going to be a long trip to get these kids back home and they are certainly hungrier than I am.*

When Beth offered him a piece of chicken, he shook his head as he patted his stomach. "I'm still full from last night," he stated even as Beth heard his stomach growl.

She didn't eat either and the Hatch kids cleaned up the food in no time.

Rudy asked, "Was that fried chicken? I ate fried chicken one time, but it didn't taste near as good as that."

Rowdy drawled, "That's because Beth here is the best cook around!" He winked at Rudy and whispered loudly, "And that's why I'm going to marry her!"

Rudy looked from one to the other and slowly smiled.

As they repacked the saddle bags and Rowdy rolled up his blankets, he took off one shirt for Rudy to wear. Beth put her coat on Maribelle, and Rowdy wrapped his heavy coat around Rudy.

Rowdy had the horses saddled and loaded in no time. He laid out wood for another fire and they were ready to move out. Beth put Maribelle in front of her and Rudy rode behind Rowdy.

As they headed northwest, Rudy began to talk.

"Pop got hurt last winter. He broke his leg on some ice. It didn't heal right, and he has a mighty hard time walkin'. Ma's been tryin' to do his work. I'm the oldest so I been helpin' as much as I can. There are six of us kids. I'm ten, Johnny's seven, Merle and Sarah are five—they're twins. Maribelle is three and Jolly, he's the baby. He ain't one yet.

"Pop said we should just sell out, but Ma says our little spread is Pop's dream, an' she wants to do whatever she can to keep his dream alive."

Rowdy listened and let Rudy talk. His stomach tightened when Rudy talked about eating one meal a day because there was no food as well as being cold all the time.

Once they were close to Hutchins' ranch, Rudy knew where he was and was able to guide Rowdy. The grass looked better the further they rode.

Finally, Rudy called out, "There's Ma! Hey, Ma! We're okay!"

He slid off the back of Smoke and pulled Maribelle down as he ran to meet his mother.

Mrs. Hatch shaded her eyes and then ran to her children. As she pulled them close, tears ran down her face.

"Oh Rudy! I was so worried. The cow came back at milking time, but you kids didn't show up. I was so afraid for you out in that storm."

Mr. Hatch hobbled up. His face was drawn with pain, but he put out his hand.

"Much obliged to you for bringin' the young ones home." He lifted Maribelle up and kissed her. "Pa sure missed his little Mari," he murmured softly as he held her. Maribelle beamed and wrapped her arms around her father's neck. Mr. Hatch reached over and squeezed Rudy's shoulder.

Rudy looked up at his father.

"Pa, I'm sorry. I got us lost in the storm. Rowdy here shot all three of the wolves that were a followin' us an' then we spent the night in their shack."

"An' we had a picnic on the floor!" Maribelle added.

Rowdy chuckled and put out his hand. "I'm Rowdy Rankin and this is my future wife, Beth Williams. We are going to be your neighbors—we just bought the Hutchins place. We were headed back to Cheyenne and were caught in that storm."

Mrs. Hatch had come to stand by her husband. She smiled at Beth and Rowdy.

"Would you like to come in and eat? We were going to fix breakfast."

Rowdy shook his head and Beth smiled.

"No, thank you, Mrs. Hatch. We had breakfast this morning with Rudy and Maribelle."

Mr. Hatch put his free arm around his wife.

"I am John, and my wife is Marlene. We will look forward to having you as neighbors. We sure do appreciate you bringing the kids home."

He frowned and his face blanched as he added, "I wish there was something I could do to repay you."

Beth spoke quickly.

"Actually, Mr. Hatch, there is something you can do." As he looked at her and waited, she continued, "You can come into Cheyenne on Monday morning and meet with my brother at his office. He is a surgeon, and he can fix that leg for you."

Rowdy was surprised. He ducked his head to stifle a smile.

John Hatch looked stunned. "I can't afford a surgeon," he replied with embarrassment as he shook his head.

"No," Beth explained, "it would be a practice surgery. My brother is very good, but he is always testing new innovations to make surgery more successful and less stressful for the patient. You can repay us by letting him test a new method he has been studying on you."

Hatch frowned and Rowdy spoke up.

"Doc William is a mighty good surgeon, John. The boys were going to leave me lay after a battle back in Georgia because they didn't think I would make it. Doc Williams removed the bullets and saved both an arm and a leg. It might be a practice surgery, but you would receive care from one of the best surgeons around," Rowdy assured him.

John Hatch looked from Beth to Rowdy. *That is the craziest repayment I have ever heard of. Still, if that doctor could make this leg just enough better to farm again, it would be a good thing.*

Marlene was looking at her husband with hopeful eyes and he slowly nodded his head.

"But only for the surgery. We don't accept charity."

Beth nodded her head. She and Rowdy waved as they turned their horses to ride back towards Cheyenne. Rowdy stewed for a little bit as he thought about being in Cheyenne for another night. Then he thought about spending more time with Beth and he smiled. *It might be a long ride, but with the right person by your side, it will be just fine.*

CHAPTER 41

WHEN'S THE WEDDIN'?

I T WAS NEARLY EIGHT THAT EVENING WHEN ROWDY and Beth rode into Cheyenne. They were both tired, but Beth's eyes were still sparkling.

"Oh, Rowdy! Thank you so much for taking me with you! I had such a fun time, and we were able to meet our new neighbors."

Rowdy dismounted. His face was rough, and he was quite sure his eyes were bloodshot. Even Smoke was drooping a little, and here Beth was talking about how much fun she had. As he studied her face his smiled.

"Beth, you look like you were at a party instead of stuck in a shack during a storm!"

He lifted her down from her horse and held her close for just a moment. She smiled up at him and he could feel his heart thumping.

As he walked her up the steps to her house, Doc Williams pulled the door open with worry all over his face. "What happened? I expected you home last night!"

Beth started talking as fast as she could, and Rowdy just let her. He was too tired to explain anything.

Finally, Reuben nodded and reached to squeeze Rowdy's shoulder. "Thank you, Rowdy. Thank you for bringing my sister home safely."

Rowdy grinned at his future brother-in-law.

"You are welcome, but you know you are going to lose your receptionist."

Beth's eyes shined even more brightly.

"Rowdy, let's don't wait. We can move to our new ranch in two weeks. Let's get married then!"

Rowdy smiled at Beth.

"That would be fine, Beth. That would be just fine." He took her face between his hands and kissed her gently.

Beth watched him as he walked toward his horse. She called softly, "Rowdy!"

Rowdy turned around and she blew him a kiss. He caught it and placed his hand across his heart. It was still there as he rode down the street.

Rooster was mucking out a stall when Rowdy rode up. He took the filly's reins without asking any questions. "I'll go ahead an' rub 'er down. Don't ya worry 'bout a thing," he offered as he led the horse to water.

Rowdy watered Smoke and rubbed him down before he dropped down in the hay beside him. When Rooster brought Smoke some oats, Rowdy didn't even stir.

It was nearly seven the next morning when Rowdy climbed out of Smoke's stall. His mouth felt like sandpaper and the sidewalls of his stomach were rubbing together.

Rooster looked at him and grinned. "Those northers cin sneak up on a feller." His grin became wider as he asked, "So when's the weddin'?"

Rowdy grinned at the ornery hostler. "Two weeks," he answered as he saddled Smoke and headed down the street.

He stopped at the dry goods store and bought another shirt and longhandles. Then, he added some britches and several bandanas. He needed a bath and didn't want to put dirty clothes back on.

"I need to start washing my clothes," he muttered to himself with a wry grin.

As he soaked in the tub, Rowdy planned his day. *Breakfast will be first, then the bank and the land office.* He scowled. *I'll be lucky to be out of town by noon.*

Smoke was sticking his nose in the bath water and snorting.

"Dadgum it, Smoke, quit blowin' bubbles! Just let me sit here and enjoy this bath." The horse didn't stop though. Rowdy finally gave up and stepped out of the tub, still talking to Smoke.

"Well, Smoke. We are landowners now. And just maybe, you will get to breed that little filly since she will be coming to our house in two weeks."

Smoke snorted and blew more bubbles in the water. He pushed Rowdy with his head as they walked up the street.

Breakfast was good as usual, and Rowdy told Barney just to keep the plates coming.

After four plates were sent to Rowdy's table, Barney came out of the kitchen to talk. Rowdy had just finished the last crumb, and he leaned back contentedly.

"Barney, how would you like to come to a wedding where you didn't have to cook anything?"

"Your wedding?" Barney asked with a smile.

Rowdy nodded as he grinned. "My wedding. In two weeks. I don't even know what day it is, but I'm guessing I will be told soon enough. We'd be plumb tickled to have you and your missus there. I do appreciate good food."

Barney nodded in agreement as he shook Rowdy's hand.

"We'd be pleased to come, Rowdy. You just let me know the day and where it will be." Barney patted Rowdy's shoulder before he hurried back to the kitchen.

Rowdy grinned at this man he considered a friend and dropped some money on the table. He walked out, leaving a smiling Barney behind him.

CHAPTER 42

WHAT'S THE OCCASION?

THE $9600 ROWDY HAD IN HIS MONEY BELT FELT HEAVY as he left the bank and headed to the land office.

The clerk looked up. "I thought you'd changed your mind," he commented as he pulled out the paperwork.

Rowdy shook his head. "No, but it was a long two days for sure. We got caught in that norther that blew through."

He handed the clerk the deed for the Hutchins ground.

"Now I want my wife's name on everything too. We will be married in the next week or so. Her name is Beth."

The clerk nodded. "I will write it up and leave a place for her to sign."

"Welcome to Wyoming Territory, Mr. Rankin," and he shook Rowdy's hand.

Rowdy's smile was huge, and he was almost lightheaded as he left the land office.

Badger and Martha were in town to do some shopping. As they watched Rowdy mount Smoke and head out of town, Badger suggested, "Why don't we jist go by Doc's office. We cin invite him an' his little sis out fer supper."

His blue eyes were sparkling, and Martha laughed as she listened to this man she knew so well.

"We'uns cin make it a family gatherin'."

Martha nodded her head in agreement and immediately began to plan the meal.

When they knocked on Doc William's door, Beth answered with a bright smile.

"Badger and Martha! How good to see you. Please come in. Are you here to see Doctor Williams?"

Badger grinned at her. "Naw, we come ta invite you'ins out fer supper. I wanna git ta know the little gal that done melted ol' Rowdy's hard heart!" He winked at her and grinned while his ornery blue eyes snapped.

Beth's mouth opened in surprise, but she laughed. "I would love to but let me check with Reub."

She returned quickly. "What time and what can I bring?"

Martha smiled as she answered. "You just bring yourselves. Come out when Doc Williams can get away. We'll plan to eat around five or six depending on when everyone gets there."

Badger grinned bigger and added, "We'uns be havin' us a party ta celebrate yer marryin'!"

Beth's eyes opened wide as she answered, "I didn't know Rowdy had told his family yet."

"Oh, he didn't have ta tell us," Badger assured her as his ornery eyes twinkled. "I know'd this day was a comin' the first time I saw ya lookin' at 'im with them purty eyes. Ain't no man coulda resisted that, not even one as coldhearted as Rowdy!" He grinned at her again and Martha beamed.

Color moved up Beth's face, but she laughed when Badger winked at her again.

As the McCunes turned to walk down the steps, Badger was doing a jig. He finished it just as they reached the buggy. He bowed deeply to Martha. She took his hand as he helped her in and fanned her heart while they both laughed.

Martha waved at Beth before she turned toward Badger and listened attentively. He was talking with lots of animation and hand motions as they turned down the street.

Beth waved back and smiled. Reuben came out to stand beside her, and they both watched Martha and Badger turn their buggy south.

"What a delightful couple. I am guessing they have been married for years. I hope Rowdy and I still act silly when we are old—so happy with each other and still so in love."

Reuben commented dryly, "You are certainly marrying into an interesting family!"

Beth smiled as she shut the door. "Oh, I am. A wonderful, big family."

Rowdy hadn't been home for very long before Badger and Martha drove into the yard. Badger informed everyone that the McCunes' were having a party that night so everyone needed to be there by four-thirty. Rowdy looked at Badger suspiciously, but Badger said nothing more.

"I will do the cooking so just come and enjoy!" invited Martha. She added innocently, "I invited Doc Williams and his sister. She seems like a very charming girl," and she smiled sweetly at Rowdy.

He snorted. *Martha is almost as ornery as Badger.*

Paul and Sammy were excited because Badger always had candy. When the men came in to eat dinner, Molly told Lance about the party.

"What's the occasion?" Lance asked innocently.

Rowdy growled as he turned to face Lance and Molly.

"All right, you snoops. I'm getting married. Beth said yes, and the wedding is in two weeks.

"Somehow, Badger must have figured it out because Martha and him are planning a party." Rowdy shook his head as he muttered, "I didn't tell him anything. I swear, there are no secrets around here."

Everyone cheered and Lance clapped his brother on the back. "Congratulations, Same!" he exclaimed as his blue eyes sparkled.

"I sure am glad you made that trip west."

CHAPTER 43

A Wonderful, Big Family

REUBEN HAD NEVER BEEN TO BADGER'S HOME, SO Beth and he stopped by the Rocking R. Rowdy rode with them when they left.

Paul wanted to ride along too. He raced out of the house behind Rowdy, yelling "Me go! Me go!" Rowdy laughed as he lifted the little boy to his shoulder. Paul sat on Rowdy's lap and sucked his thumb. Occasionally, he would remove it and give Beth a big smile. Then his left thumb would go right back into his mouth.

Samuel drove out and brought Rooster.

Rooster's wise old eyes sparkled as he commented, "So ya must a chosen the right saddle, huh, Rowdy?"

Beth looked confused, but Rooster just winked at her.

Sadie, Slim, and all the riders came. Tiny still could not tell Lance and Rowdy apart.

Smiley finally exploded and hollered, "Jist look to see which gal he's a kissin' on an' then you'll know which one he is!"

"When is the wedding?" Molly asked.

Rowdy looked at Beth and waited for her to answer.

"We can't move into our new place for two weeks so it will be after that."

Samuel was listening and quietly commented, "If you are waiting for the Hutchins to move out, they are already gone. They sold their horses and wagons on Thursday. They were on the nine-thirty train this morning headed south."

Beth's eyes lit up. "Then the wedding will be next Saturday if that works for everyone! At one?"

Rowdy's smile was wide as he moved up beside Beth.

"It works for me, and we are the only ones who really have to be there," he drawled as he squeezed Beth closer to him.

Everyone began talking and laughing. The men surrounded Rowdy and the women pushed Beth inside.

Doc Williams watched with a smile on his face. He picked up his drink and followed the men. *They sure like Rowdy,* he thought. *Yes, Beth is marrying into a big, noisy family, and our house is going to feel empty.*

The women were full of questions. Molly asked Beth if she had a dress in mind.

Beth's pretty eyes sparkled as she answered. "I have my mother's dress but it's too big." She giggled and added, "Mother was taller and more endowed than I am!" Beth held her hands in front of her chest as she demonstrated. "I will have to take it in but that is what I want to wear."

All the women in the room turned to look at Sadie who smiled and leaned forward.

"I would love to help you work on your dress, Beth. Maybe I could come in tomorrow and we can fit it for you."

Molly's eyes lit up. "Let's all go! I can leave the boys with their grandpappies. We can all help. What time shall we meet?" she asked Martha and Sadie.

The two women agreed to meet at Molly's right after dinner. They'd ride together to Cheyenne around one.

"Where are you going to be married, Beth?" Martha asked.

Beth responded slowly, "Rowdy and I haven't talked about that yet. I would like to be married in the little church in town. If the weather was warmer, I would have the reception outside, but Reub said we need to have everything inside."

Beth rolled her eyes. "He wants to reserve the Rollins House. Reub promised Mother that he would give me a proper Southern wedding, and he intends to keep that promise." Beth frowned a little and looked at Molly nervously.

"I'm not sure what Rowdy will think about all the fuss though."

Molly took Beth's hands. "Beth, all Rowdy cares about with this wedding is that you are there," she stated softly. "Let your brother give you the reception your mother wanted. And I am excited to have another sister!" she exclaimed as she hugged Beth.

The men had all kinds of questions for Rowdy about his ranch. Lance wanted to know if he bought the east section.

Rowdy shook his head. "I talked to the land agent a little more and decided against it."

He told them about finding the two Hatch children and taking them home. "John Hatch is in a bad way," he added with a frown.

Doc nodded and smiled. "I heard about that. Beth told me she volunteered my services to help him."

Rowdy was quiet for a moment. Then he looked intently at Reuben.

"I hope you can help him. The land agent told me I should try to buy his place, but I just couldn't do it. He loves what he does, and they have a nice family. They were all so excited to have Rudy and Maribelle back. They have six little ones, and those kids were hungry."

He looked around the group of men. "Rudy told me they only eat one meal a day now since John was hurt, and yet Mrs. Hatch wanted us to come in for breakfast to say thank you." Rowdy shook his head. "Good folks," he added with admiration in his voice.

The men were silent, and Lance thought about Louise Hutchins.

Rowdy continued, "Mrs. Hatch is doing her best to keep things going because it is her husband's dream, and I want to have neighbors like that." Rowdy's face was sincere as he looked around the little group.

The men shifted their feet, and no one spoke. They all knew what it was like to go through hard times. Rowdy was right—those were the kind of neighbors you wanted. They all hoped Doc would be able to fix John Hatch's leg.

CHAPTER 44

THE OLD MAID FROM TEXAS

SLIM LOOKED AT DOC WITH JUST A LITTLE TOO MUCH innocence on his face. "So, what are ya goin' to do fer a helper, Doc? Y'all better be hustlin' to find one since yore losin' Beth in a week."

Doc Williams frowned. "I honestly don't know. I haven't really met anyone who has the experience Beth does, and I dread taking the time to train someone. The person I hire can't just be good with people. She needs to be able to help me with surgeries as well as organize and keep my accounting books."

Lance looked at Slim and hid a grin. He knew what Slim was doing and he was glad to help.

Lance drawled, "Slim, when is Josie comin' back out? Doesn't she work for a doctor or someone like that in Texas?"

Slim looked surprised as he exclaimed, "Say, yore right! Maybe we should invite 'er to Rowdy's weddin'! We cin see if she'd mebbie stay an' help out fer a few weeks till Doc finds someone."

Rowdy knew exactly what game they were playing, but Doc Williams was oblivious. He listened intently as Slim described his older, spinster sister.

Slim became more and more descriptive of the old maid until Lance couldn't keep a straight face. All the Rocking R cowboys stared at Slim with disbelief.

Tiny started to protest, but Smiley elbowed him hard.

Finally, Slim agreed to send a telegram to Josie right away.

"Shore now, she has a job as an ol' nurse maid but since she ain't got no social life, she jist might be able to git away fer a few weeks."

Badger was grinning with evil lights in his eyes. He even offered to send the telegram himself since he was going to Cheyenne the next day to pick up a new mare.

Lance and Slim were quite pleased with themselves, and Rowdy snorted as he headed toward the house.

As Rowdy walked away, he heard Doc tell them that he would be glad to pick her up at the train station if they needed him to.

The Rocking R cowboys all started to volunteer but Lance drawled, "If you boys want the afternoon off for the wedding, you'll all be working that morning."

Doc still didn't catch on, and Slim almost collapsed laughing as they all moved to the house.

On the way home, Beth shared with Rowdy all about the wedding plans the women had made. She was hesitant as she asked him about the location of the reception.

Rowdy wasn't in favor of a fancy reception, but Reuben asked quietly, "Please let me keep my word to our mother, Rowdy. She put money back and wanted it to be nice. There is even enough to have a prepared meal, so the ladies don't have to cook that day."

Rowdy was quiet for a little bit. He smiled as he looked at Beth. "You know what I would like? I would like a hog in the ground, sweet tea, and grits. Let the women bring whatever food they want. That's how they welcome you into the family, so let them do it." He paused and looked at Reuben.

"Doc, if you want to have the reception at the Rollins House, that's fine, but I would like a down-home, country party with good food and no fuss. Gus can do the pig. Molly would love to plan the meal so you can turn that over to her." Then he added, "And I want Barney to come as my guest."

When Reuben looked confused, Rowdy explained, "Barney—he owns Ford's House. I want him to come to our wedding as a guest. I don't want him to work that day."

Beth had tears in her eyes as she looked up at Rowdy.

"Oh, Rowdy. You are such a wonderful man!" she exclaimed softly as she squeezed his arm.

Rowdy looked surprised and Doc smiled. He nodded as he looked at Rowdy. "A down-home, country party it is, Rowdy!"

After everyone left, Badger told Martha about the Hatch family. Hungry children concerned both of them, and Martha's eyes began to sparkle when Badger told her what he had in mind.

Badger headed to Cheyenne early on Saturday. His first stop was the telegraph office. Slim didn't tell him what to put in the wire, so Badger used his imagination.

The telegram read:

Josie come quick. Need Nov. 11. Plan to stay a bit. Town doc will pick ya up. He's cranky, deaf, bald, old, and cain't see. Might have a cane. Slim

The telegraph operator stared at the message and shook his head. He never knew what Badger would send when the little man came in his office. *Oh well. I'll send it. I sure don't know what doctor he is talking about though.*

Badger was laughing as he walked out of the telegraph office. He was still chuckling when he headed home, his ornery blue eyes dancing as he thought about Doc Williams and Slim's little sister.

CHAPTER 45

HER MOTHER'S DRESS

BETH'S WEDDING DRESS WAS LOVELY. HER MOTHER had truly been a southern belle and Beth was going to be a beautiful bride. The dress was mostly old lace and draped from the waist. The short sleeves just caught the top of her shoulders, and the neck was scooped low.

"Do you want to leave it all the same or do you want to make any changes?" Sadie asked.

Beth covered her bare chest and blushed. "I don't want it to be this low. Maybe you can add some fabric up here. Rowdy would be able to see all the way to my toes!"

Molly tried not to laugh, and Sadie hid her smile. Beth was correct though. The neckline was very low. Sadie quickly began to create a higher one with lace.

Beth looked behind at the long train. "And I really don't want that thing dragging behind me," she whispered.

Molly laughed out loud, and Sadie giggled with them. Martha stood to the side and beamed at the young women.

Sadie suggested adding a jacket. "The sleeves are quite short for November. A jacket would give you a little more warmth and cover your shoulders. If you don't want the train, I can use some of that fabric to make a jacket. Thanks to Martha, I have some lace left from my wedding veil as well. I can add some of that to the jacket if you'd like." Sadie smiled at Martha whose smile became even bigger.

"Do you like the veil, Beth?"

Beth paused. "I don't really like veils. I would like something with beads in my hair, but I don't want anything getting in my way."

Sadie showed Beth how she could take the beading off and make the hairpiece.

"Why don't you use your veil for the jacket since it's lace? You can always save your train and make a christening gown for your babies," Molly suggested.

Beth blushed but her eyes sparkled. "Oh yes. Let's do that."

Sadie measured and tucked while the women pinned and pulled. In no time, they had the dress pinned and ready for Sadie to work her magic.

Beth agreed to let Sadie take the dress home with her to finish.

"Maybe you can come out this week sometime, perhaps after Slim's sister arrives. We can check the fit then," Sadie said with a smile.

Molly looked at Sadie in surprise. "Is Josie coming for the wedding? How wonderful!"

Beth added distractedly, "Yes, Rueb told me he is going to ask her to stay on for a few weeks until he can get someone hired. Slim told him she is much older and doesn't have many social commitments since she is a spinster."

As Molly stared at Beth with her mouth open, Sadie poked her. She buried her own face in the dress. Martha coughed and left the room for a drink of water.

Molly turned her head as she tried not to laugh. *Poor Doc,* she thought. *He won't even know who he is supposed to pick up. Those men,* and she almost giggled out loud.

The women were in Molly's buggy by three. The wind was blowing in gusts, and they could feel moisture in the air. Molly hurried the horses.

Even though Rowdy had offered to drive the women home, both Badger and Slim were waiting for their wives when the women arrived at the Rocking R.

The wind blew hard all night, and there was a light blanket of snow in the morning. Winter had arrived.

CHAPTER 46

A HELPFUL STRANGER

JOHN HATCH BROUGHT HIS WAGON TO TOWN ON Monday morning so he could take home a few supplies. He was going to leave it at the dry goods store while he was at Doc's.

An older man just happened to be in front of the store when John drove up. He was a friendly fellow. They visited some and he offered to give John a ride to Doc's.

"I ain't too busy today. I cin drive ya up ta Doc's if'n ya want so's you'ins don't have ta walk. I cin leave yer wagon down ta the dry goods store. Isaac Herman owns this here place an' he cin make shore it's a waitin' fer ya once it's filled."

Hatch had no idea who the man was, but he seemed to know everyone in town. He nodded hesitantly.

"I guess that would be fine. I'd sure appreciate a ride if you don't mind."

Rowdy rode Smoke into Cheyenne that morning around nine. Samuel had told him about some horses that were going to come up for sale, and he wanted to look at them. *Besides, any excuse to see Beth was a good one,* he thought with a grin.

He saw the wagonload of supplies parked in front but paid little attention to it. Doc's office was getting busier all the time.

As he dismounted, he studied the older wagon. It was packed with supplies from staples to clothing.

"I wonder if that is the Hatch wagon. Today is when John was supposed to come in for his surgery. I sure hope so. His family could use those supplies."

Beth met him at the door with her finger over her mouth.

"Reub is examining Mr. Hatch today," she whispered. "He asked me to be extra quiet. He didn't want any kind of noise to disturb them. He is concerned Mr. Hatch won't want to do the surgery."

Rowdy nodded as he followed her into the kitchen.

Doc Williams examined John's leg. *That leg will have to be rebroken or the bone possibly cut as it is misaligned.*

"Can you be gone for a week, John? I can fix this, but it is going to require surgery. Once the surgery is done, you need to stay down for a while."

John's face turned pale. "I need to get supplies home to my family. Maybe I can come back later."

Doc Williams studied the man in front of him for a moment.

"Let me check on something."

Beth had made a pie, and Rowdy was just finishing his second piece when Doc asked if he could get the wagonful of supplies to Mrs. Hatch. Rowdy only hesitated a moment before he agreed.

Doc was back in the examination room in a few minutes. "If we can get the supplies to your wife, will you agree to do the surgery today and stay down for several days?"

John's face tightened as he stared intently at the doctor. Finally, he looked away. He winced in pain when he tried to move his leg.

"Marlene told me to have the surgery done right away if you could fix my leg," he answered quietly, "but she needs those supplies."

Doc Williams patted his arm. "We'll make sure she has those supplies. Now let's get that leg fixed."

Rowdy shoveled in a third piece of pie before he stood and pulled his hat on. Beth wanted to go along but he refused.

"It is going to be a long, cold trip, and I don't want to take a chance with you out in the weather." He kissed her and added with a grin, "You need to stay healthy for our wedding."

Beth laughed softly. "You take this with you, Rowdy Rankin. If you get delayed again, I don't want you to go hungry."

She pushed a package of food into Rowdy's hands as he headed out the door, taking the steps three at a time. He needed to hustle if he was going to make it out to Hatch's and back before dark.

Rowdy passed Badger as he was headed out of town. Badger promptly offered to ride with him, and Rowdy was glad for the company. Badger turned Mule loose beside Smoke. Both animals would follow the loaded wagon. Rowdy cracked his whip, and they headed northwest.

Rowdy pointed over his shoulder at the full wagon.

"I sure am glad John was able to stock up some provisions before winter."

When Badger made no comment, Rowdy looked hard at him and chuckled.

Badger waved his arms and grinned. "Now don't you'ins go assumin' I filled this here wagon. I jist happened ta be in town this mornin.' Fer all I know, ya done filled it yer own self."

CHAPTER 47

EXTRA PROVISIONS

THE WAGON WAS OLD, BUT THE MULES WERE IN
decent condition. Still, it was a slow trip, and they didn't arrive until
after three that afternoon.

Mrs. Hatch was shading her eyes to see who was driving their wagon.
When she recognized Rowdy, she waved. She called behind her and the
kids came rushing out of the house.

Rowdy wished he had brought something for them as they crowded
around the wagon. However, Badger was prepared.

"Ya young'uns want some candy?" he asked as he winked at them.
He pulled some bags out of his coat pockets and held them out. The
children's eyes were bright with anticipation, but they waited until their
mother nodded before they accepted.

Mrs. Hatch asked with concern, "Who do all these supplies belong
to? I only had five things on my list for John to pick up."

Rowdy scratched his head and shrugged.

"If this is your wagon, these are your supplies. I happened to be at
Doc's office this morning when he was checking your husband over. John
was concerned about staying so Doc asked me to bring your supplies

out. He said to tell you John will be laid up for three days. You can pick him up on Thursday."

Mrs. Hatch was still fretting about the supplies, so Rowdy gently reassured her, "Marlene, I don't know who filled your wagon, but someone must have. Now your kids need some food, and we have it here. Let's just unload the wagon. Maybe someday you can do a good turn for someone else."

Marlene Hatch straightened her shoulders and Rowdy thought she was going to cry. Then she clapped her hands. "Children! Let's unload this wagon quickly…and thank these nice men for bringing it all the way out here!"

As the kids quickly began to unload the wagon and chorused thank yous, Mrs. Hatch urged the men to go.

"Please go home. I have lots of help here to carry things in, and I know you will already be traveling after dark."

Rowdy and Badger quickly mounted. They waved goodbye, and six smiling, candy-covered faces waved back at them.

When they were about a mile down the road, Rowdy exclaimed, "Durn it! I forgot to introduce you, Badger. I'm plumb sorry."

Badger grinned and answered, "I didn't really want them folks ta know who I was anyhow." His happy whistle echoed around them as they hurried toward Cheyenne.

Both Mule and Smoke were anxious to go home, and the men made good time. They rode through Cheyenne around six and headed home in the dark.

Rowdy sighed. *I'll have to ride into Cheyenne another day since I didn't get to look at those horses.* He had almost forgotten about the food Beth had sent, so they ate it while they rode those last fifteen miles home. Rowdy was glad to finally see the lights of the ranch house, and Badger was glad he just had five more miles to go.

Marlene Hatch arrived Thursday morning to take John home. She had brought along some blankets for him to lie down on in the back of the wagon in case riding on the seat became too painful. John Hatch was healing nicely, and Doc Williams was pleased with his most recent surgery.

"Doctor Williams," Marlene asked, "do you know anything about the extra supplies in our wagon?"

The confused look Doc gave her told Marlene he had nothing to do with it. As she helped John into the wagon, she told him about the wagonful of food, coats, clothing, and staple items. John was quiet as he listened.

"I think our new neighbor had something to do with it."

Marlene paused, "Or perhaps that older man who was with Rowdy when he delivered it."

John looked surprised. "What was his name?"

Marlene gasped softly, "Why I don't know. He didn't introduce himself, and I have never seen him before." They were both quiet as they drove out of town.

"Perhaps we can do something nice for Rowdy and Beth when you get to feeling better."

John smiled and squeezed her hand. "That is an excellent idea," he agreed as they began their long drive home.

CHAPTER 48

MISS CRANDALL?

JOSIE RECEIVED THE CRYPTIC TELEGRAM FROM SLIM and immediately bought a ticket to Cheyenne. Her train was to arrive at four-fifteen in the afternoon on Thursday, November 10. She sent a wire back telling Slim when she would arrive. However, since Doctor Williams would be picking her up, she addressed it to him.

The train arrived on time, but Josie didn't see the elderly doctor anywhere. A nice-looking younger man was waiting with a buggy. He smiled and tipped his hat to her, but she saw no older gentleman anywhere. As Josie settled down to wait, the young man came forward.

"I see you are waiting on someone. I am as well. Perhaps I may wait with you?" he asked politely.

Josie agreed and they began to visit.

Just then, an older woman walked in. Her hair was in a tight gray bun and her face was quite severe with an almost permanent frown.

The young man smiled at Josie, "If you will excuse me?" he asked as he rose. He walked toward the older woman.

"Miss Crandall?" the young man asked. "I am Doctor Williams. I believe I am to pick you up today?"

The woman stared at the young doctor for a moment before she responded, "My name ain't Crandall, but I sure wish it was!" She winked at him and gave him a huge grin.

Josie began laughing.

Doctor Williams turned to look at her. A dark blush moved up his neck and he was very confused.

Josie stood up and curtsied as she giggled, "Doctor Williams, I am Miss Crandall, Miss Josie Crandall." Her blue eyes filled with laughter, and she laughed harder as Doc Williams looked from the older woman to Josie and then back.

He started to speak. Instead, he just bowed to the woman and backed away.

The older woman winked at him again and her grin became bigger.

Josie stepped up to take his arm and they walked outside to where Doc's buggy was parked. As Doctor Williams looked at Josie and then back toward the station, Josie laughed again.

"I am guessing my brother gave you a rather detailed description of me?" she asked as her eyes filled with humor.

When Doc Williams nodded and his blush became more pronounced, she pulled out her telegram to show him who she was waiting for. "He's cranky, deaf, bald, old, and can't see. Might have a cane," she read. Josie began to giggle again. "We were both played, and I am guessing some of my brother's friends were in on this as well!"

Reuben Williams was beginning to smile. He shook his head and chuckled as they walked toward the carriage. When they arrived, he bowed deeply.

"Miss Crandall, my name is Reuben Williams, and I am delighted your brother's description was so absolutely wrong. Before we go, would you like to eat supper as they call the evening meal here, and go out to the ranch tomorrow? Or would you prefer to go to your brother's right away?" He smiled at her and waited for her response.

Josie paused as she looked up at him. *Tall, curly blond hair, brown eyes, nice shoulders…* She gave Reuben a pretty smile with her best dimples, "I believe I will stay in town tonight if you don't mind, Doctor Williams. Would you have time to take me to the ranch tomorrow?"

Reuben Williams was more than happy to comply. He left her for a moment to arrange for a room at the Rollins House before he escorted her to Ford's for supper. He had scheduled Friday off to help Beth with last-minute wedding preparations. However, he was sure he could squeeze a carriage ride in. *After all, Beth is going to need to go out for a final fitting with Sadie.* Doc smiled.

This is all working out quite nicely, he thought as he took Josie's arm. *Just maybe I can convince Josie to stay for two weeks until I find a new receptionist.*

As they followed Barney to their table, Reuben suggested, "I believe we should plan something to repay your brother." They both laughed and were soon visiting like old friends.

CHAPTER 49

SLIM'S LITTLE SISTER

BETH WAS UP EARLY ON FRIDAY AND READY TO RIDE out to Sadie's to pick up her dress. Reuben laughed as he slowed her down.

"First of all, we need to take a surrey or else you will need to ride your filly because we will have another passenger. Slim's sister came in on the train yesterday afternoon, and she will be riding with us."

Beth's green eyes lit up with excitement. "Do you think she will fill in for two weeks? I understand she is an older woman, so she should have lots of experience."

Just then, Rooster pulled up in front of their house in a surrey and lifted a pretty blonde down. As he took her arm and dramatically escorted her up the steps to the porch, Beth's eyes opened wide.

"Surely that is not Miss Crandall!" she exclaimed in disbelief. She looked back at her brother.

Doc's mouth twisted in a wry grin and a touch of red showed on his neck.

"Yes, she is not quite what I was expecting either."

Reuben opened the door and Beth quickly stepped up beside him.

"Rooster, thank you for delivering Miss Crandall. This is my sister…"

Beth interrupted him with a squeal of delight. "Josie! We thought you were older! Please come in and I...we will show you around!"

As Rooster stood to the side with an innocent look on his face and his ornery eyes sparkling with laughter, Beth gave him a hug. "Rooster, you are coming tomorrow, aren't you?"

He hugged Beth back. *I shore like this spunky, happy little gal.* "Ya cin bet on it. I wouldn't miss this here deal fer nothin'. I want to make sure that cranky cowboy treats my special gurl right!" He smiled at Beth and pecked her cheek. Beth gave him another hug.

"Thanks, Rooster," she whispered. "You are a great listener!"

Reuben recognized Rooster because he worked at the livery, but he didn't know Beth knew the old hostler so well. Then he smiled. *Well, Beth makes friends wherever she goes,* he thought as he chuckled softly.

Josie Crandall watched the exchange between the three of them and smiled. She was a beautiful woman and was used to lots of attention from men. However, at heart, she was still the little sister of a cowboy. As such, she loved warm and friendly people.

When Reuben stepped aside and invited her in, she looked around the big house with approval. It was tastefully decorated, and she loved the large piano. As she stepped over to look at it, she ran her fingers softly across the ivory keys.

Reuben smiled and Beth stepped forward quickly to stand beside her. "Do you play?" Beth asked.

"Oh, yes," replied Josie. "My aunt raised me after our parents died, and she loved music." She covered her mouth to suppress a giggle as she continued. "She tried to get Charlie—or I mean Slim to play, but he climbed out the window and left a trail of 'city clothes' behind him. When I finally found him that night, he was up in a tree with only his unders on. He said he was going to run away."

Her eyes clouded a little as she continued. "Slim hated it there, and he did run away when he was almost twelve. I missed him but he was so unhappy. No horses, lots of people, and in his words, 'stuffy card parties with old, rich women.' Our aunt was a good person, but she had never married and had no idea what to do with a wild boy like Slim."

Josie laughed again as she continued, "Oh, the stories I could tell you! I loved music as much as Slim detested being inside, and our aunt was delighted to teach me." Josie paused. "I love to sing and to play the piano. I play the organ at our church as well as the violin."

She looked at the two of them and asked in wonder, "How in the world did you get this huge piano to Cheyenne?"

Beth and Reuben both laughed as they thought of the look on Rowdy's face when he spotted the piano that day in the Columbus train station.

"It wasn't easy and neither of us plays," Beth shared with a giggle. "It belonged to our mother. She loved to play but neither of us learned.

"As children, Reuben was busy with his experiments, and I refused to practice. However, we couldn't bear to part with it when we moved from Georgia, so it came west with us in our train car." She looked at Reuben and laughed again.

"Rowdy would have made us leave it had he known we didn't play. We didn't tell him, and he didn't ask. He had already made us sort out our tack. We had to leave most of it behind." Beth ran her fingers over the old keys. "You will certainly have to play while you are here."

Josie sat down at the piano and began to play a soft waltz. The music was beautiful, and Reuben's eyes were soft as he watched her.

When she finished, he asked, "Who wrote that? I don't recognize that composer."

Josie blushed. "I wrote that one evening after a ride in the country. I call it 'Alone with the Sunset.'" She looked up at Reuben and blushed again.

Standing quickly, she asked, "Do you have time to show me around before we go?"

As Reuben showed her his office and the examination room, Josie noticed the open book on his desk. "You are studying that surgery?" she asked with surprise.

Beth spoke up before her brother could answer.

"Reub is an excellent surgeon. He not only studied that surgery but performed it successfully on a man just this week. His patient went home yesterday and was doing well four days after surgery. Reub even made notes of small changes to be incorporated next time."

Josie looked at Reuben in surprise, and he shrugged.

"I was a surgeon in the war, so I have quite a bit of field experience. I just took some of the things that worked there and tweaked them with this new procedure."

Josie looked down at the book again and then once more at Doctor Williams. *I believe I would like to work with this man,* she thought.

"Do you have any medical training, Josie?" Beth asked.

"Yes, I am a nurse, although I don't practice it much where I work. I mostly do the books and arrange schedules for the three doctors who work together. They have a busy practice, so they hired a nurse to help during the week. I sometimes help on the weekends although I am not called in very often."

Reuben said nothing as he smiled at her, but Beth was excited.

"Oh, Josie! I hope you will be able to help here for a while! I am getting married tomorrow and leaving Rueb in a jam. We truly are excited to have you here, and you are welcome to stay a little longer if you would like."

Josie laughed.

"Well, I did take off three weeks after Slim—or whoever—sent me that wire. I guess I can help that long."

She smiled at Reuben, and he looked pleased.

Beth squealed and clapped her hands. "Thank you so much, Josie!" she exclaimed. "Now let's hurry out to Slim's so you can see your brother, and I can try on my wedding dress."

CHAPTER 50

PERTINEER

ROOSTER HAD LEFT THE SURREY IN FRONT OF DOC'S house with all of Josie's bags in the back. Reuben helped Beth in first. She climbed into the back while Josie sat in front beside Reuben. Beth leaned forward in her seat, and the three of them began to visit.

"Tell us about Texas, Josie. Reub and I have never been there. Georgia is so different from Wyoming. We are still trying to adjust to the openness here. Is Texas open like the land around here?"

Josie laughed.

"Well, Texas is quite large, and it has just about every type of landscape you can think of. As you head north, it is wide-open land, but around San Antonio where I live, it is more settled. San Antonio is one of the oldest cities in Texas. It was founded as a mission in 1718. It is now the largest city in our state."

Beth asked, "I have read that there are many German immigrants around that area. Is it hard to communicate with them?"

"Some speak only German, but many speak English as well. Auntie was adamant that I learn to speak other languages, so I speak both German and Spanish. It was easy to learn growing up as both languages were prevalent. Of course, the children I played with were all learning English, so we learned together."

Doc nodded and asked, "How about cattle? Texas is a cattle state, isn't it?"

"Cattle is a huge industry in Texas. Since the War for Southern Independence, the prices for beef there have been very low. We have many cattle ready for market, more than can be consumed in Texas, and those excessive numbers have glutted the market.

"Some of the ranchers there are sending herds north, some as far as Cheyenne. I saw many cattle grazing around the city as I came in on the train. They looked so beautiful, just miles and miles of longhorn cattle." Josie smiled at them.

"I love the city, but I think I am still a country girl at heart. I get tired of all the people sometimes and just want to leave. That's when I go riding. I love the rolling grasslands. We have them in Texas too." She shivered and added with a laugh, "Of course, it is much warmer there than here. I rarely need more than a jacket. Auntie insisted I purchase a heavy coat before I came, and I am glad that I did."

Josie moved the conversation to Reuben's practice.

"I am guessing your practice here is growing, but why did you leave Georgia?"

Beth responded before Reuben could answer.

"Reub told me I spent too much time at the cemetery with the dead soldiers. He said I needed to spend more time with the living." Tears filled her eyes as she added, "We lost our little brother at the Battle of Columbus, and we were hoping to find some word of him." She wiped her eyes and smiled.

"I met Rowdy at that cemetery—in front of a tombstone that bore his name. I didn't know until later it was his name on the stone, but that is where we met. And now, our wedding is tomorrow!"

Soon, Josie and Beth were talking excitedly about the wedding, Beth's dress, and Rowdy's meal requests.

The miles went by quickly, and in no time, they were pulling up at the Rocking R headquarters.

"I suppose you will want to stop here, won't you, Beth?" asked Reuben teasingly.

Beth laughed and jumped down before Reuben could help her. As she ran toward the house, she called back, "Don't leave me—I will only be a minute!"

Rowdy stepped out of the small open building they used as a blacksmith's shop when he heard Beth's voice. He grinned at her as he wiped his hands on his pants. When she ran up to him, he held out his hands to stop her. "No closer, Beth! I'm mighty dirty."

Coming to a stop, she pointed at the surrey. "Slim's sister arrived yesterday. We are taking her over to his ranch, and I'm picking up my wedding dress from Sadie." Beth's eyes opened wide as she paused and added, "I just realized neither Reub nor I know how to get there."

Molly had come to the door. "I will ride with you," she offered with a laugh. "Both of the little boys are with their grandpappy so let me grab my jacket. We can tell Old Man McNary what we are doing as we go by."

As Molly climbed in, she looked from Reuben to Josie and began to laugh.

"I see you managed to make connections," she commented dryly.

Rowdy sauntered up to help Beth into the surrey, and he was grinning as well.

Reuben looked at the two of them and shook his head. "Yes," he agreed ruefully, "I am sure it was all you hoped it would be and more!" His neck was red as he clucked to the horses, and all the women were talking as they drove away.

Old Man McNary had built a swing set, and both boys were swinging as the surrey went by.

"I will pick them up after dinner," Molly called as she waved.

The Old Man waved back, and the boys didn't even see their mother.

Molly sat back in her seat. *It is so wonderful to have grandparents so close,* she thought with a smile.

Slim was not at home, but Sadie came out to greet them. "Please stay for dinner. Slim will be home before too long. I know he would love to see all of you."

Sadie's smile was friendly, but mirth showed in her eyes as she looked from Doc to Josie.

Doc Williams frowned slightly before he asked carefully, "So just how wide was this joke?"

Both Sadie and Molly began to laugh. Doc shook his head as a smile creased his face.

"Well, you sure fooled us, but I want you to know, we intend to get even!"

Josie laughed as she agreed with Doc.

"Yes, we do. It may take some time, but we will get even."

Doc secured the reins and helped the women down.

He tied the team to the hitching rack and followed the chattering women inside.

Sadie had Beth's dress hanging in the doorway to her sewing room as they walked in. Beth gasped as she stared at her dress and Molly gave Sadie a hug.

"Sadie, you are amazing!" Molly exclaimed softly.

Sadie had made a short jacket from the long veil and embellished it with some of the lace left from her own wedding shawl. The dress had a small waist and flowed out as it reached the floor. It was nearly sleeveless, and the lacy jacket draped softly with a tiny ruffle of gathered lace around the outer edge.

Beth's eyes were shining as she touched it. "Sadie, it is all I had hoped for. You are incredibly talented!"

Josie moved forward to look at it. Her face showed her amazement as she touched the dress. She turned to look at Sadie.

"Sadie, I don't know if you have thought of this, but you could make a lot of money creating garments like this for women, and not just those from Cheyenne. This is fabulous!"

Sadie blushed and smiled.

"Beth, if you would like to try it on, you may take it into that room behind you."

Beth rushed into the sewing room followed by Molly and Sadie. Beth and Molly were talking excitedly as Sadie smiled.

Reuben and Josie were alone in the kitchen when a tired Slim walked through the door. When he saw his sister, his face lit up. Then his ornery eyes settled on Reuben.

"Doc," he drawled, "I see y'all figgered out who my little sis was. I hope it wasn't too difficult." Slim's eyes were innocent as he tried not to smile.

Josie rushed to give him a hug and Doc Williams' neck turned red as he laughed.

He stepped forward to shake Slim's hand and answered blandly, "No trouble at all. She was just as you described her." Josie's head turned in surprise, and both men were laughing when Beth opened the sewing room door.

Slim whistled. "Beth, yore pertineer as beautiful as Sadie was on our weddin' day…pertineer," he said with a grin as he pulled Sadie close.

Sadie laughed. She pulled away to turn Beth around. The dress fit beautifully. Sadie then lifted a beaded headpiece out of a small box.

"I made this from the beading around your veil," Sadie said softly as she placed the headpiece on Beth.

The women gasped in unison and Beth ran to look in the small hand mirror in the sewing room.

They all heard her exclaim, "Oh Sadie, how can I ever thank you!"

Reuben smiled. "Well, we certainly need to pay her," he stated as he reached for his wallet.

Sadie shook her head.

"No, it is our wedding gift to you. Slim and I both consider Lance a brother so that makes Rowdy a brother as well. Welcome to the family, Beth." Sadie gave Beth a soft smile as she reached out her arms to hug her new sister.

All the women were tearing up and Slim headed for the door, followed closely by Doc.

Doc Williams looked back at the stone house admiringly. "Did you build this yourself, Slim? And where did you find all the stone?"

Slim grinned. "There was shore lots a time an' sweat went into this, but it weren't all mine. All the hands on the Rockin' R helped, an' some a those fellers are purty good at stackin' rock.

"An' as far as the stone goes, we found some jist stacked up. The rest we quarried outta one a those draws," Slim stated as he pointed behind him.

When Tiny and Smiley came in for dinner, Sadie hurried to set the food out. She had fresh bread as well as roast beef and gravy. She set her canned green beans on the table and put Slim's favorite food next to him—a full pan of cinnamon rolls.

Slim rolled his eyes and rubbed his stomach as he hugged his wife. "I'm a tellin' ya, boys. This here marriage stuff is jist all right!" He grinned and kissed a blushing Sadie.

Once dinner was over and cleanup was done, Doc, Molly, and Beth were ready to head back to the Rocking R.

Beth hugged Sadie and thanked her again for reworking her mother's wedding dress.

"It's beautiful, Sadie. It just couldn't be more perfect."

CHAPTER 51

A Pig in the Ground

THE WOMEN WERE HELPED INTO THE SURREY, AND Rueben clucked to the horses. He hoped to be back in Cheyenne before dark and they needed to get on the road.

"I can't wait to show Rowdy my dress!" Beth exclaimed. She clutched the box that held the dress tightly against her as they rode back toward the Rocking R.

Surprise showed on Josie's face. She asked, "Don't you want it to be a surprise on your wedding day?" she asked seriously.

Beth blushed and laughed, "I can't keep surprises. So, no. I want to show him tonight."

Josie was intrigued. *I thought it was a hard and fast tradition that the groom didn't see the dress or the bride before the wedding. I guess some traditions aren't that important,* she mused to herself.

Reuben laughed as he looked at Josie's confused face.

"Beth doesn't worry too much about what should or shouldn't be, and I don't care. Mother wanted her to have a big, southern wedding and we are…sort of…doing that. I doubt she would have approved of a pig in the ground and grits on the table. Out here though, things are maybe a little more practical."

"A pig in the ground?" Josie asked incredulously.

"Yes. Cooked over coals!" gushed Beth. "Gus put it in the ground this morning, and it will be cooking all night!"

Josie was surprised but intrigued. She smiled at Beth.

"That sounds absolutely delicious. I can't wait to taste it."

Molly invited everyone to stop at the Rocking R for supper. Doc was going to decline, but he changed his mind after he looked at Beth's excited face.

As the surrey came to a stop, Beth jumped down and ran towards Rowdy. He had cleaned up and was leaning against the porch banister.

"I have my dress and it is beautiful!" she exclaimed. She held the box out to him. "Would you like to see it?"

Rowdy grinned at Beth. He set the box down as he pulled her in for a kiss. "Only if you are in it," he replied with an ornery smile on his face. Beth blushed as she melted into Rowdy.

"I love you, Rowdy!" she whispered softly as he pulled her in for a longer kiss.

Paul insisted he sit on Rowdy's lap during supper while Sammy sat between Beth and Reuben. Rowdy ate the food the little boy as he pulled food off his plate and stuffed in his mouth. He shifted Paul a little higher. *I sure do like this little fellow. I am going to miss these meals.*

Rowdy insisted Reuben, Beth, and Josie be on their way back to Cheyenne by six. He lit the lamps on the side of the surrey because they would already be driving in the dark.

"Just give those horses their heads. They are sure-footed and will be able to pick where to walk better than you can guide them." He handed Beth two heavy blankets and watched them leave with a look of concern.

Molly stepped up to take his arm. "Don't worry, Rowdy," she whispered, "Those horses know their way home even if Doc gets lost."

Rowdy looked down at his pretty sister-in-law and relaxed. He put his arm around her and gave her a quick hug. "Thanks, Molly."

CHAPTER 52

HEAVEN IN EVERY BITE

THE ROCKING R RIDERS WERE LATE COMING IN. LANCE was starting to run some fence around parts of the ranch. The herds moving up from the south were encroaching on his grass, and fences were becoming necessary to separate his land from open range. Badger, Slim, and Lance worked together to keep the water holes open and accessible to all their cattle.

Gus had supper prepared when the tired fencing crew dragged themselves home after they finished that night. Building fence was a hard job that required lots of manpower and muscle.

The hog for the wedding was in the ground, and Gus was working on the wedding cakes. He decided to make long cakes since they would have to be transported to Cheyenne in the back of a wagon. The cowboys looked longingly at the pans of chocolate cake, but Gus glared at them. When he threatened them with his meat cleaver, they quickly backed off. Gus grinned as they walked away grumbling. He loved his cowboys, but food was serious business. *Especially when I like the couple getting married,* he thought with a grin.

Rowdy wandered in and stared at the cake. *Chocolate cake is my favorite! Why, I haven't had any since before that war.*

Gus looked up as Rowdy came in and saw the look of surprise on his face. He winked at him.

"Lance told me chocolate cake used to be your favorite. Samuel was on a mission and managed to get the cocoa in here on short notice." He handed a big slab of cake to Rowdy to try.

Rowdy almost stopped breathing. He swallowed slowly with a look of pure delight on his face.

"Gus, that is like heaven in every bite!" Rowdy exclaimed.

Gus gave him a crooked grin. "Wait till you taste the hog."

He led Rowdy out to the pit. The smell was amazing, but the pig wouldn't be done until Saturday morning. Gus frowned slightly.

"The hard thing will be keeping it warm till the wedding," he muttered with a perplexed look on his face.

Rowdy thought for a moment.

"Maybe we could put a tank in the back of the wagon and lay some small rocks or coals down in the bottom on a bed of sand. We could get some hot rocks and lay those on the coals. Put the meat on top. Throw some blankets over it and it should stay warm," Rowdy suggested as he swallowed the last bite of cake.

Gus slapped his leg with his hand. "By George, Rowdy, that just might work. You get that tank rigged up for me and I will have this pig ready to load by nine tomorrow morning. And the grits too," he added.

Rowdy nodded and slowly walked toward the house with a smile of complete satisfaction on his face.

Lance was just sitting down for supper when Rowdy entered.

Rowdy had wiped his face but missed a crumb of cake.

"How was the chocolate cake?" Lance asked innocently as Rowdy licked off the last crumb.

"First chocolate cake I have had in over nine years, and it tasted better than I remembered," Rowdy replied as he slapped his brother on the back.

"Thanks, Same!" He grinned as he headed to bed. He paused and turned around.

"Say, do you have an old tank around that we could put sand and rocks in to keep the meat warm in the back of a wagon?"

Lance thought a moment and slowly nodded.

"There is a leaky one in the loft of the barn. It is smaller, so it should fit."

Rowdy thanked him. He waved his hand to Molly and went into the bedroom.

Just then, Paul and Sammy came racing into the house looking for Rowdy. Molly shushed them.

"Uncle Rowdy just went to bed, which means you can both play outside for another half hour before you come in for the night," and she shooed them back out the door.

Rowdy slept well and was up by five-thirty. He tried to slide the tank down from the loft, but he wasn't having much luck by himself. Joe heard the banging and grunting in the barn. He poked his head in the door to see what was going on. He was still rubbing the sleep out of his eyes, but he guided the tank as Rowdy slid it down the ladder from the loft. The two of them rolled it over to the wagon and set it in the wagon bed. Rowdy hitched the mules, grabbed a couple of buckets, and headed down to the creek to get some sand and rocks. Joe rode with him.

When they returned, they pulled the wagon over to the pit, unhitched the team, and led them back to the corral.

"Don't worry, mules," Rowdy commented as he turned them loose, "you will earn your keep on the trip to town."

Gus was out by the pit when they returned. He had dug a second pit. He had the coals hot and was ready for the stones. As they dropped the stones in, Rowdy wondered how they would get them back out, although this pit wasn't nearly as deep as the hog pit.

Rowdy turned to Joe with a grin. "Thanks, Joe. I didn't expect to have help so early in the morning, but it was appreciated."

Joe gave Rowdy a slow smile and shook his hand. "Glad to help, Sarge," he replied. He added sincerely, "I'm glad to be part of this ranch."

Rowdy slapped him on the back and the two men headed for breakfast. The smell of the roasting pig was even stronger now, and Rowdy's stomach started to growl. Lance came out of the house to join them as the rest of the men slowly drifted up to eat.

The two brothers strolled over to the corral with their plates. Soon, they were both leaning against the fence with the heel of one boot hooked in the corral fence. Once again, the men were reminded of the similarity between Lance and his brother. The men pointed and laughed as they took their plates.

"Same!" they said in unison as the brothers continued to talk.

CHAPTER 53

MEMORIES

LANCE'S EYES WERE TWINKLING AS HE ASKED ROWDY, "Remember when Granny Mac wanted to teach us to dance?"

Rowdy laughed. "Yea, we came up with those dance moves as a surprise for her on her birthday and she loved it."

Lance nodded and then his eyes grew more serious.

"She promised Mother she would teach us to dance, and Granny Mac took promises seriously."

Lance laughed as he added, "She had the moves, didn't she? She moved so fast she made that old calico dress pop like a whip. We couldn't believe all the bopping and bending she could do because we thought she was older than dirt."

The two men linked elbows and did a fast version of fancy footwork that ended with them bowing to each other. They were laughing when they finished.

Rowdy's smile remained as he commented, "I haven't thought of that since I left home."

"Maybe we should entertain our wives today with the 'Rankin Rollick,'" Lance suggested as his face lit up with humor. He slapped his brother on the back and headed to the kitchen to get his breakfast.

Rowdy laughed again as he agreed. He looked out over Lance's pasture and smiled. He could still see Granny Mac standing in their kitchen back on the plantation. *Now ya boys listen up. We's a gonna learn ya to dance like yore mammy asked me to do. Now put that foot over there an' take hold a my hand.* Rowdy's smile slowly faded.

Granny Mac. I wonder what happened to you, Granny? He shook his head. *That war was hard on all of us.*

"We loved you like a mother, but we didn't want to learn to dance. I'm sorry we didn't cooperate better, Granny. We were bratty boys, but you loved us anyway. You could go from a waltz or even peeling potatoes to bouncing and scraping all over the kitchen. That part we loved. In the end, you did teach us to dance, and we learned to love it."

As he packed his bedroll after breakfast, Rowdy was again reminded of how little he owned in the world. He smiled.

"But I have a ranch and soon I'll have a wife," he told himself as he thought about the day. He stopped so quickly he almost tripped. Running out of the house, he grabbed Lance.

"A ring!" he whispered hoarsely. "I don't even have a ring!" Molly heard the panic in Rowdy's voice and came over to see what the crisis was. She smiled at him and patted his back as she went k into the house. When she returned, she was carrying a small box which she handed to Rowdy.

"Doc Williams left this yesterday. It belonged to their mother. Beth doesn't even know it is still around. Their mother gave it to Doc as she was dying and asked him to save it for Beth." Molly smiled tenderly at Rowdy. "He wanted to give it to you himself, but Beth wouldn't let you out of her sight."

Rowdy opened the box. It was a simple gold band. Engraved on the inside was *Love lives in you.* Rowdy hugged Molly and then he hugged his brother. He rubbed his eyes as he growled, "I don't even have kids and I'm getting soft."

Lance laughed and Molly kissed his cheek as she hurried back inside to finish her cooking for the wedding.

With his bedroll under his arm, Rowdy whistled as he sauntered toward the barn. Smoke nickered as he entered. He curried Smoke, talking to him about his plans for the day.

"We are riding into town around nine, and you need to be on your best behavior," he told his horse as he brushed him. Rowdy had arranged for the Honeymoon Room at the Rollins House that night. He almost blushed just thinking about it.

"A married man!" he exclaimed to Smoke. "In just a few more hours, I will be a married man. I didn't see that coming."

Smoke snorted and Rowdy continued, "We will leave for the ranch first thing on Sunday morning." Then he paused. "Beth wants to go to church first and that's all right. It sure will give us a late start though," he remarked as he brushed Smoke hard enough that the horse turned around to nibble his hand.

"Doc offered to drive a wagon out with all of Beth's things—or some of them anyway," he added with a wry grin. The grin became bigger as he thought about the piano.

"Good thing we don't have to haul that heavy thing out!" he exclaimed with a laugh. Beth had told him just a few days ago that neither she nor Rueben knew how to play it. Rowdy shook his head.

"I just don't know why they would haul something that big clear out here, especially when neither of them even knows how to play the durn thing.

"I'm guessing that wagon will still be full though. And a full wagon is going to make it a slow trip." His smile faded and he shook his head as he thought about Louise Hutchins.

"I hope that house is cleaned up and ready to stay in," he muttered to himself.

Lance and Molly had offered to ride along with Rowdy and Beth to their new ranch. They wanted to make sure Doc made it back to town since this was another area he had never been to before. Besides, Molly wanted to see where they were going to live. They were all hoping there would be enough food left after the wedding to pack a lunch for the trip.

Molly was excited about going to church. All three grandfathers were going with them, and they were to oversee the boys for the rest of the day.

"Church services and a nice little visit on the way out," Rowdy told his horse. "It is going to be a good day."

CHAPTER 54

FRIENDS OLD AND NEW

GUS WAS CHECKING THE PIG WHEN ROWDY LED SMOKE out of the barn. The whole, unskinned hog was on an iron grate and the smell was amazing. Gus had already lined the bottom of the water tank with rocks and now he was working to pull the pig up. He had attached wire loops to the grates and was stringing rope through them to create a levy system. As the cowboys gathered around, Gus explained what he wanted them to do. He placed four men on each side with himself at the snout and Rowdy at the tail to hoist the pig up and out of the pit.

As it sizzled and steamed, the men leaned forward to get a closer look. Some of the cowboys had never seen a pig cooked in a pit before.

Gus climbed into the wagon and started giving orders. This time, two ropes were attached to each hook to lift the rack high enough to go over the tank sides as Gus guided it into position. As the large pig settled down on the hot rocks, the men cheered. Heavy blankets were used to pull more rocks out of the smaller pit. Those rocks were set around the pig and heavy blankets covered everything. More rocks were rolled onto the edges of the blanket to hold it down.

Lance hitched a second wagon to carry the cakes as well as the grits. Molly handed Gus clean tea towels to cover both of those for the ride into town. Once Gus had the cakes and grits loaded, Molly brought out the food she had made. Those pans were placed around the edges. The tailgates to both wagons were raised, and the food was ready to be hauled to town.

Gus drove the wagon with the pig while Joe and Hicks offered to drive the second wagon. The wagons were on the road before nine and were expected to arrive in Cheyenne by noon.

Rowdy rode beside the wagons for the first hour. He was too nervous to ride slowly though and pushed Smoke into a lope. He wanted to take a bath and change clothes before the wedding.

He bought a new red shirt and a pair of black britches. He also added another pair of socks. After a soaking bath, he beat the dust out of his hat and vest and shined his boots. He pulled on his hat and was ready for the day.

He resisted the urge to go see Beth and went into Ford's for dinner instead.

Barney greeted him with a huge smile. "Big day, Rowdy!"

Rowdy grinned and nodded. "You will be there, won't you?"

Barney smiled and nodded. "I am shutting down soon for the rest of the day. In fact, I am going to lock the doors and put out my sign now. My wife and I are looking forward to a day off."

Barney brought Rowdy three plates of food. Rowdy didn't even order any more when he went to the Ford House. Barney knew what the hungry cowboy liked, and he kept it coming. As Rowdy leaned back in his seat after he finished, he noticed a familiar face.

Jack Sneld, his best friend from home and now a cattle buyer, was eating quietly at a table in the front of the room. Rowdy dropped some money on his table and walked that way.

As he stepped around in front of Jack, Rowdy grinned and put out his hand. "Hello, Jack!"

Jack dropped his fork, and his face went white.

"Paul? It can't be you. I saw you die!" He pushed his chair back with a lurch and stood as he reached for Rowdy's hand.

Rowdy shook his hand and gave Jack a wry grin as he dropped into the seat opposite his old friend. He shook his head as he drawled, "Naw, you saw me fall!" As Jack stared at him, Rowdy told him the story of how Doc Williams and Eli had saved him.

Jack nodded his head. "Private Williams saved a lot of boys that day. He put their care in front of his own safety. When we retreated, he was still on the field. I never did know what happened to him."

As he studied Rowdy, Jack commented, "You are sure all gussied up today. What's the occasion—you gettin' married?" Jack teased.

Rowdy's neck turned red as he laughed. "Actually, I am," he answered. "I'm marrying Doc Williams' little sister."

"The wedding will be at the little church south of town at one o'clock today. We'll have dinner and a party at the Rollins House afterwards.

"I'd love to have you there if you can make it."

Jack was still in shock at seeing Rowdy, or Paul as he called him, and the fact that he was marrying added to the surprise.

"Paul, I will try but I don't think I can make it work. I have quite a few ranches to visit as Denver needs more beef all the time. Now if I could just find a steady supply of horses, I would be good."

Rowdy looked at him in surprise, "Well, that is what I am going to run on my ranch here. I am going to raise and break horses. Beth and I just bought a ranch north and west of Cheyenne. We are moving out there tomorrow. I don't have any livestock yet, but I want to catch some of the mustangs running loose. I also have some raw-broke horses coming in by train next week."

Jack slapped his knee, "That is excellent news. I know how you treat your horseflesh, and we can make this a great business venture for both of us. I will stop by next week when I come back through this way."

As both men stood up, Jack gripped Rowdy's hand. "Paul—" he started to say.

Rowdy shook his head. "Call me Rowdy—that is what I am known by here."

Jack raised an eyebrow as he laughed. "Rowdy, it is so good to see you alive!" he exclaimed as he gripped his friend's hand. His smile was large when he pulled his old friend in for a bear hug.

As Rowdy watched Jack walk away, he smiled again. "It was good to see Jack. We spent a lot of time together as kids."

He was soon headed for the livery with Smoke trailing behind him. Rooster was cleaning a stall, and he whistled as Rowdy walked up.

"My, ya shore do clean up good," he commented as the devils danced in his eyes.

Rowdy gave him an ornery grin. "I just stopped by to make sure you were coming to the wedding. We'd sure like to have you there."

Rooster's eyes twinkled as he drawled, "Your little gal done already told me to come an' I plan to be thar." His grin became bigger as he added, "Doc Williams' already rented two wagons to haul her things in. Are ya a wantin' a third?" Rooster cackled an evil laugh as Rowdy's mouth fell open.

"Oh, I'm jist a funnin' ya. I'll have a third wagon ready though jist in case. I know how they come into town, an' I'm a guessin' all that stuff didn't belong jist to Doc!" Rooster was still chuckling as he slapped Rowdy's back.

CHAPTER 55

An Unusual Groom

ROWDY STARTED TO PUT SMOKE IN A STALL BUT changed his mind. Mounting, he rode up the street to Doc's house. As he knocked on the door, Doc Williams answered with a smile on his face.

"Rowdy, I suppose you want to break another tradition and see Beth before the wedding," he said with a smile as he turned toward the stairway.

There was a flurry of footsteps on the stairs and Beth rushed into Rowdy's arms. Her hair was loose and hanging around her shoulders, and her dress looked like she had just dropped it over her head. As he pulled her in close for a kiss, he breathed softly in her ear, "Beth, I am a lucky man."

Beth blushed. After the second long kiss, she pulled away breathlessly.

"Rowdy, I must get ready. You are going to make me late for my own wedding!" As she turned to run back up the stairs, she blew him a kiss. Once again, Rowdy caught it and placed it over his heart.

With a contented look on his face, he turned to walk out the door. Doc followed him.

"Did Molly give you the ring?" Doc asked. "I hope I wasn't too forward in thinking you might use it."

Rowdy gave him a lop-sided grin and patted his pocket. "Actually, you saved me. I forgot all about a ring and this one is perfect. Besides, I know Beth will love it. She likes things that have a special meaning."

Doc nodded and reached for Rowdy's hand. "Thank you for loving my little sister," Doc stated sincerely as he gripped Rowdy's hard hand. "I can't think of a better man for her to marry."

Rowdy paused and looked down. As he looked back up at Doc, his eyes were misty. "Funny how this all worked out, isn't it?" he commented quietly.

Doc Williams nodded his head. He watched Rowdy lope down the steps to his horse. He lifted his hand in a wave before he turned back into the house.

Beth watched from the window. She held her hand over her heart as she whispered, "Rowdy, I've loved you since the day I met you in the cemetery." She was still smiling as she hurried to fix her hair.

The food wagons were pulling into town as Rowdy rode up to the Rollins House. He offered to help Gus unload, but the old cook shook his head.

"The Rocking R cowboys are right behind the wagons. Those fellows can help me unload." He grinned at Rowdy and waved his hands. "This is your wedding day. You get on out of here."

Rowdy led Smoke into the livery and Rooster took his reins with a grin. He shooed Rowdy away as well. It was not quite twelve-thirty, and Rowdy had nothing to do for half an hour.

He walked to the small church set back off the street. It was a short walk from the main street but was still a little way out of town. The pastor looked up as Rowdy walked through the door. He was wiping the seats down with a cloth.

"We have a wedding here today, and I don't want anyone to get dirty sitting down," the pastor explained with a smile.

Rowdy nodded and laughed. "I'm the groom," he said, and he reached out his hand. "Rowdy Rankin."

"I am Pastor Roland and I hope to see more of you, Mr. Rankin," the pastor stated as he took Rowdy's hand.

Rowdy looked around and asked, "Need help with anything? I have a little time before this deal starts."

Pastor Roland was surprised. *Most grooms don't volunteer to help before their weddings.* The pastor nodded.

"I could use some help. We had to move some pews to replace some broken floorboards, and they never were moved back to the right spot." He showed Rowdy where they were to go, and the two men swung them back into place. As Rowdy stared around the church, it reminded him of his father and the little church in Georgia they had attended.

The smell of flowers wafted past Rowdy's nose and he sniffed. *Lilacs! Someone found lilacs in November and this little church smells wonderful.* Rowdy shook his head.

"We sure have a lot of friends who have worked to make this day special," he muttered to himself as he turned to walk out the door.

Guests were beginning to arrive, and Rowdy greeted each one as they came in. Most of them he knew, but a few were friends of Lance and Molly whom he had not yet met.

A man with a limp was walking toward him with a smile on his face. He was followed by a beaming wife and a passel of kids. Rowdy's face lit up as he recognized John and Marlene Hatch.

"Welcome, neighbors!" Rowdy exclaimed with grin. As he looked at John, the pain he had originally seen in the man's face was gone.

"The leg is healing well, John?" Rowdy asked.

John Hatch grinned. "Almost as good as new," he replied. "Another week, and I think I will be back to normal."

As the two men shook hands, Marlene smiled and touched Rowdy's arm. "We have a surprise for you," she whispered mysteriously. She stepped into the church followed by their six little ones.

Rowdy wanted to ask about the surprise, but Marlene had already moved on.

He grinned at the kids and asked, "Who likes chocolate cake?" Then he leaned toward them and whispered, "When you see folks lining up for food, come find me. I will put you in the front of the line!" He gave them a big wink.

The kids were all smiling shyly. Maribelle looked over her shoulder with big eyes and a bigger smile as they followed their parents into the church.

CHAPTER 56

THE RANKIN ROLLICK

THE LITTLE CHURCH WAS SOON FULL, BUT PEOPLE continued to squeeze in. Before long, guests were standing around the inside walls of the church. Rowdy was getting worried when Lance and his family arrived.

"I don't know where you are going to sit," he whispered. "The church is clear full!"

Lance squeezed his brother's shoulder.

"That is because you have lots of friends, Rowdy," Lance answered softly. Rowdy's neck began to turn red, and Lance laughed as he herded his family inside.

Pastor Roland had saved the front seat for family. It was full by the time Slim, Badger, Martha, Molly, Old Man McNary, Samuel, and the little boys squeezed in.

Lance was best man, and Sadie was standing up with Beth. Rowdy was fidgeting more all the time. Finally, he saw Doc pull up in his carriage. He started to go outside, but Lance grabbed him and pulled him to the front of the church.

"Doc will walk her up. You need to stay here," Lance whispered.

When Beth stepped into the back of the church, Rowdy sucked in his breath. Her dress was beautiful because she was in it, and she was carrying a small bouquet of lilacs. *I'm truly a lucky man,* he thought as Beth smiled just for him.

A family headed west to the gold fields had donated a pump organ to the church. It was over seven feet high and red fabric showed behind the beautiful design of the wood. Carved spindles and spirals added to the intricate woodwork.

Josie was playing her heart out as Slim listened and looked on with pride. Doc Williams was smiling, and Beth looked like she was ready to burst with happiness.

Josie began to play, "Here Comes the Bride." Everyone stood to watch as Doc Williams escorted his pretty sister up the aisle. As Rowdy stepped forward to take her arm, Doc shook Rowdy's hand and then squeezed into the seat next to a grinning Slim.

"Sis' music is purty, ain't it? Makes ya jist want to melt." Slim's eyes went from Doc to Josie, and he gave Doc a wink. Doc's neck began to turn red, and he faced forward as the ceremony began.

Rowdy was quiet and nervous. When he took the ring from his pocket to place it on Beth's finger, her green eyes filled with tears, and he thought she was going to cry. He almost dropped the ring because his hands were shaking. Beth helped him slide it on her finger. She squeezed his fingers and smiled up at him.

"I love you, Rowdy Rankin," she whispered, and Rowdy calmed down. Slowly, he began to enjoy himself.

Finally, it was over, and Rowdy was able to kiss Mrs. Paul Rowdy Rankin. As he pulled her close and then bent her backwards, the little church was filled with laughter and applause.

Josie began to play "Alone with the Sunset." As the sweet music lifted through the church, Rowdy escorted his bride down the aisle and into the sunshine. Doc almost forgot to stand because he was so caught up in Josie's music. Slim poked him.

"Stand up, Doc. This here deal is over an' done. Open yore eyes an' don't look so durn dreamy." Doc quickly stood and Slim laughed wickedly.

Rowdy helped Beth into the carriage and Doc waved to them. As they left for the Rollins House, the people followed.

Reuben Williams stood inside the door of the church and listened to Josie play. When she finished, he walked up to the front and offered to escort her to the party. As Josie closed the organ, Reuben stated softly, "I think your song is now my favorite song."

Josie looked up in surprise. When she realized the young doctor's compliment was sincere, she blushed. She smiled at him as she took his arm, and they walked toward the Rollins House, visiting easily.

Gus had the pig on the table with an apple in its mouth. As the guests began to arrive, he started to carve it.

Rowdy was delighted when he saw steam rising from the meat.

"It stayed hot!" he told Beth with excitement.

Beth smiled up at him and laughed softly. *Food just excites Rowdy*, she thought with a giggle.

As people began to line up, Rowdy grabbed the Hatch children and pulled them into line in front of him. "Take as much as you want," he whispered as he gave them a wink. Their eyes were big as they looked at all the food. Each had a full plate when they left the food table, and every plate was wiped clean when they finished.

The food was all delicious. Rowdy had three pieces of chocolate cake. He ate each one slowly, rolling his eyes in delight.

Beth laughed and made a note to herself to talk to Samuel about ordering some cocoa.

As people finished eating, some of the guests began to pull out their musical instruments.

Suddenly, Lance was beside Rowdy and Beth. An ornery light shone in his eyes as he tried not to smile.

Rowdy stood and the two of them walked to the middle of the dance floor.

Lance began, "Our mother died when Rowdy was born. Before she died, she asked our nanny, Granny Mac, to make sure we learned to dance.

"Neither of us was too excited about those lessons, but we did love Granny Mac. This is something we created in Georgia a long time ago as a birthday present to her. Today, we do it for our wives. We call it the 'Rankin Rollick.'"

As the brothers linked arms and began their fancy footwork, the harmonica and accordion joined in. When they finally finished with a bow to each other, the crowd cheered and the Rocking R cowboys yelled, "Same!"

Molly and Beth were laughing even though both were quite surprised.

The two brothers grinned at each other and pulled their wives onto the dance floor. Both Lance and Rowdy were excellent dancers—Granny Mac had taught them well.

Barney and his wife sat with the Rocking R cowboys and joined in the merriment. Rooster had come with Samuel and was sitting next to Badger. As Rowdy and Beth danced by, Rowdy wondered what kind of trouble two old rascals like Rooster and Badger could cook up.

When the sun began to go down, people gathered their children and their kettles. Most of their guests had chores to do, and many lived a distance away.

By five-thirty, nearly everyone was gone. Lance and Molly had decided to stay in town with Samuel, so Beth and Rowdy helped them clean up. The cake was gone, but there was a little meat left.

Rowdy and Lance each had another plate of food before they helped Gus load all the empty pans and racks into the last wagon. Joe and Hicks had already taken one wagon home. Molly and Beth both gave Gus a hug and thanked him for all his hard work.

"I did it for my family," he replied with a huge, wrinkled smile.

CHAPTER 57

A Brother, a Tombstone, and a Husband

FINALLY, THE BIG ROOM WAS QUIET, AND EVERYONE was gone. Lance looked sideways at his brother and winked. "Well, Same," he drawled, "I think we will go over to Samuel's for the night. He might even have the boys in bed by now. We might play some cards, eat some of Molly's pie, and chew a little fat…if you want to join us for a while."

Rowdy looked at Beth and grinned.

"Mrs. Rankin, would you like to visit a while…or what?"

Molly covered her mouth to hide her giggle as Beth blushed.

"I would love to visit for a while. It is early, so an evening of visiting would be fun."

The men took their wives' arms, and the four set off down the street toward Samuel's new house. The boys were not yet in bed and came charging out of the house to greet their parents. Martha and Badger were there, along with Old Man McNary.

When Paul saw Rowdy, he grabbed his leg to ride it into the house. Sammy jumped on the other one, and Rowdy staggered up the steps, dragging the boys as they shouted with delight. He finally scooped them both up and dropped them on the floor where they all began to wrestle.

Molly looked at Beth and laughed.

"Rowdy sure has fun with the boys, and they love their Uncle Rowdy."

Beth watched with soft eyes. *Rowdy is going to be a wonderful father.*

When Rowdy finally made it off the floor, Samuel waved him toward the kitchen. He pointed toward a small box. "Those are the items I talked to you about," he stated softly. "Be sure to take them with you when you leave."

Rowdy stared at the box silently. He started to set it aside when Beth asked, "What is that?"

Rowdy paused and Samuel answered, "I talked to Rowdy about this before.

"These are the personal items found on the body of the soldier who was identified as Rowdy. The letter from Lance was in his pocket—that was how they identified the body. Now no one knows who he is.

"When I asked for Lance's letter, they sent me everything they had." Samuel looked around the room and added softly, "That boy was buried in a grave with the wrong marker, so he'll probably never be identified. Rowdy here was the closest connection anyone had to him, so all his personal items were sent here with Lance's letter."

Beth's pretty eyes had tears in them. "Let's look in the box, Rowdy. You know how I love my soldiers."

Everyone gathered around Samuel's table while Rowdy opened the small box. He emptied the contents onto the table.

There was a comb, a razor, a wallet with a few Confederate dollars, and a small metal pill box.

When Rowdy opened the pill box, Beth gasped and went completely white. There was a curl of blonde hair twisted inside the pill box.

Taking the pill box from Rowdy, she lifted the hair out and began to sob.

"Oh, Eli!" she cried as she stared at the hair. As she lifted her eyes to Rowdy, she whispered, "He wanted something from me to keep next to him, so I cut off a curl."

Rowdy put his arms around his wife as she cried softly.

Suddenly, she stopped crying and her eyes opened wide.

"That is why I was drawn to the grave with your stone! My little brother was buried there. He brought you to me!"

Rowdy squeezed her tightly as she alternated between sobs and smiles.

Looking up at Rowdy with hopeful eyes, Beth asked, "Do you think maybe we can go back to Georgia in the spring and put a proper tombstone on Eli's grave?"

Rowdy kissed his wife and nodded. "And I can bring mine back with me—no point in letting a good tombstone go to waste." Rowdy added seriously as the humor glinted in his eyes.

Around eight, Molly and Lance put the boys down.

Rowdy took that as their time to leave. He shook Samuel's hand and thanked him for working so hard to identify the soldiers. He slowly shook his head and said with some amazement, "I guess the Good Lord just wanted me to meet Beth."

Samuel was quiet, but he knew the Good Lord had guided Rowdy many times to bring him to where he was today.

As Beth and Rowdy walked back to the Rollins House, Rowdy pulled his wife close. "Now I owe your brother again," he whispered softly as he kissed the top of her head. "We might not have met but for Eli keeping Lance's letter."

When Beth looked up at him, he kissed her as he had wanted to for a very long time. They were both a little breathless when he released her. The rest of their walk to the Rollins House was just a little faster.

CHAPTER 58

LOADED AND READY

CHURCH SERVICES WERE AT ELEVEN ON SUNDAY morning. Rowdy wanted to load the wagons before church and make sure everything was tied down.

He was up at six and kissed his sleeping wife as he tried to slip out of the room. Beth woke when he opened the door and insisted she go with him. Rowdy forgot he was in a hurry as he watched Beth dress, and both were still laughing when they walked into the livery around seven.

Rooster offered to drive one wagon up to the Williams' house, and all three were knocking on Doc's door by seven-thirty.

Beth's pretty eyes were full of sparkles, and she wanted to fix everyone breakfast. She had already packed her things, and her stack of items to take was large.

As Rowdy eyed the huge pile, he was hoping two wagons would be enough.

Rooster looked at the stack, and his eyes filled with humor. He said nothing as he struggled not to laugh.

Suddenly, he slapped his leg.

"I 'most fergot to tell ya! I have a feller what wants ya to break five horses. They be here on the train in two days. He says they's halter broke.

That feller looks plenty green though, so I ain't even shore if 'n he knows what that means. They's fancy though an' I told 'im yer fee was $50 a head with money up front."

Rooster paused as he grinned at Beth and Rowdy. "See'uns as we don't know this here feller, I figgered we'd jist make 'im pay first."

Rowdy looked hard at Rooster. "And how much of that is your fee?" he asked dryly.

Rooster tried to look shocked, but his ornery eyes gave him away. "Oh, I have a finder's fee of $2 a head but I'll let 'er slide this time as a weddin' gift to that thar little green-eyed gurl ya married. See'uns how I'll kinda be like a grandpappy an' all mebbie one a these days!" Rooster's face broke into a huge grin, and he winked at Beth.

Beth hugged him and gave him a kiss.

"Rooster, you know I would love for you to be grandfather to our children."

Rowdy stared in surprise and finally he laughed out loud.

"Just so you try to keep our kids on the right side of the law, Rooster."

As Rooster tried to look innocent, Rowdy laughed again and shook his head. "Rooster as a grandfather—I just don't know."

Beth remembered Rowdy's box from the night before. Running out to the wagon, she brought it in to show her brother.

Doc recognized the wallet before she showed him the pill box. He picked it up and reached under a hidden flap to pull out a picture of their family. As he stared at it, Beth's eyes filled with tears. Doc's eyes were red as well.

"Father gave Eli this wallet when he enlisted." He flipped up the hidden flap, and his voice was soft when he continued. "It belonged to our father, and Eli was always fascinated with the 'secret hiding place' in it. Father put in a little money, hid the picture, and gave it to Eli before he left." He held the wallet up to the light.

"If you look closely, you can just see a 'W' on the front."

Doc looked at Rowdy and added, "It surely is good to know where our brother is. Now we'll have to put a marker up there."

Beth exclaimed excitedly, "Let's all go to Georgia in the spring!" She smiled, and her eyes crinkled at the corners, as she added, "Rowdy wants to bring his stone back home. I'm not sure where we should put it though."

Doc looked surprised, and Rowdy pretended to be serious.

"Well, it just seems like a waste to throw a nice stone like that away, especially with my name on it and all. Maybe we could put it in a garden or something," he said as he winked at Doc."

Beth rolled her eyes and Doc shook his head.

Rooster chuckled and agreed with Rowdy.

As soon as breakfast was finished, the men began to load the wagons. Rowdy wanted to allow room in one wagon for the provisions he had ordered earlier. Isaac Herman was going to open the back of his dry goods store at nine. As the second wagon began to fill, Rooster started laughing.

"Want me to get that third wagon down here or should I jist back 'er up to Herman's so ya don't have to work so hard here?"

Rowdy scowled and piled things higher. He had no intention of taking three wagons of "stuff" to their ranch.

Finally, all of Beth's things were loaded.

She came hurrying out of the kitchen with a big basket of food for the trip. "I left food for you too, Reub, so don't worry," she told him with a bright smile as she kissed his cheek.

Rowdy's irritation faded when he saw the basket his wife was carrying. *This is going to be just a plumb enjoyable trip after all.*

Isaac Herman was waiting for them, and both wagons were soon heaped over the sides.

Rowdy bought some rope to tie things down, and the wagons were pulled into the livery to be picked up after church.

Rooster would make sure the mules were ready to go by noon.

Rowdy checked on the horses and decided to go ahead and saddle them for the trip.

Beth had put on her riding skirt, and her cheeks were flushed with excitement.

A new ranch, a happy wife, lots of food, and good weather. It's a great way to start our first day together, Rowdy thought. They mounted up and rode up to Samuel's since they had some time to kill.

Paul and Sammy were digging holes in the yard when they arrived.

"We're lookin' for gold," Sammy explained.

Rowdy walked over to where they were digging. "Probably shouldn't dig so close to the house. Maybe dig out there," he suggested as he pointed toward the middle of the yard. "The folks who built this house would have found all the gold by the house when they built it."

As the boys rushed to dig a new hole, Rowdy kicked the dirt back into the first holes. He chuckled as he thought of Samuel's face when he saw all the holes in his yard.

CHAPTER 59

STAMPEDE!

PASTOR ROLAND WAS AN ANIMATED PREACHER. HE jumped around and pounded on the podium.

Badger had fallen asleep and was awakened when the pastor hit the podium and hollered at the same time. After that, Badger began to yell, "Amen!" whenever the podium was banged. Before long, Badger was standing up and jumping around as he yelled his amens.

Paul and Sammy tried to mimic both men. The pastor seemed to calm it down some after the little boys joined in. It was an exciting service though and most of the congregation were smiling as they left.

Sammy asked, "So, when is the next hollerin' session goin' to be, Pa? That feller was mighty loud, but he didn't act like he was mad. I guess he was jist a yellin' fer the fun of it. Paul an' me had fun. Let's do that again."

Molly was a little embarrassed, but Lance and Rowdy were laughing.

Beth had jumped every time Pastor Roland slammed the podium, and Rowdy's arm felt bruised where she had gripped it. Still, it was a good way to start their day as they all headed to the livery for the long drive to Rowdy's ranch.

Rooster was sitting in a new wagon with two mules hitched to it and a satisfied look on his face. The loads from the first two wagons had been split, and the new wagon was filled as well.

Rowdy's face narrowed into a glare, but Rooster just grinned.

"These here mules is a weddin' gift from Badger an' Martha. Some a the neighbors thought ya needed a new wagon as well. Ain't polite to look a gift hoss in the mouth so ya jist have to hire me to drive 'er out!" he stated loudly.

Rowdy stared and his frown became deeper.

"Rowdy," Beth whispered, "They are gifts from your family. How nice is that." She smiled at Rooster. "We would love to have you drive our new wagon for us, Rooster." Her smile became larger when she added, "Perhaps we should discuss your terms first though."

Rooster looked at Beth and his eyes were soft.

"Jist fer ya, little gal, I'll drive 'er fer free. I'll add it to my weddin' gift fer you'ins an' that sour-faced cowboy ya done hitched up with."

Rowdy shook his head. The tension slowly flowed out of him, and he relaxed. He reached for Rooster's hand and gripped it hard.

"This darn place has me all mixed up about the difference between taking charity and accepting gifts," Rowdy muttered as he helped Beth on her horse. He turned to face Lance and Molly who were already in the first wagon.

Lance was smiling. "A successful rancher needs a good wagon, Brother. Besides, you never know when you will have to start hauling kids," he drawled, and Rowdy's neck turned red.

Rowdy gripped his brother's hand.

"Thanks, Same. And you too, Molly. I'm not used to all this giving, but it is appreciated."

Doc arrived to drive the second wagon. He had invited Josie to ride with him. Her eyes were sparkling as she greeted everyone.

Lance was amazed at the mannerisms she shared with Slim. She had all his charm with a touch of his orneriness in addition to his curly blond hair and twinkling blue eyes. Josie's country-girl heart showed when she was among friends.

It was going to be a chilly day, so everyone wore coats or jackets. Molly had some extra blankets as well.

Folks waved and hollered at them as they left town.

Rowdy growled, "We look like a durn parade."

Lance laughed as he agreed.

"Stuff, Rowdy. I don't know when you started to collect so much stuff. You used to be a simpler fellow."

Rowdy glared at his brother.

"At least you didn't have to bring the piano," Beth whispered with a giggle.

Rowdy looked over at his happy wife and slowly smiled.

"You're right, Beth. I have no cause to complain."

Rooster had hooked four mules to the first two wagons. Rowdy's new wagon was loaded lighter, and his new mules were hitched there. They moved out briskly in the crisp afternoon air.

Lance had hoped to unload and be back home by dark but that changed when they left after church.

Molly wasn't concerned. "If we see it is too late, we will just have to spend the night," she whispered and she scooted closer to Lance with a smile.

When they were within a half-mile of the ranch, Smoke began to snort and pull at the reins. Rowdy stopped and turned to look around them. He couldn't see anything, but he could hear a noise that he didn't recognize.

Lance stood up and yelled, "Buffalo! Get the wagons on high ground close to those rocks!"

The men raced the wagons to the top of the hill and pushed them towards the rocks and brush on the right side of the trail. As they crested the hill, they saw a wagon below them. It was coming down the lane from Rowdy's house. When the driver saw the wagons crest the hill, he waved and turned his wagon towards them. Rowdy and Lance began to yell and point behind them. The man stood and looked behind his wagon. Seeing nothing, he continued to drive his team up the hill. Just then, the herd of buffalo topped the hill and charged down the other side toward the wagon. The driver frantically tried to turn his team as the buffalo bore down on them.

Molly and Beth watched in horror as the stampeding buffalo crowded the lone wagon on both sides.

Beth cried, "What can we do?"

Lance ground out, "Not a thing. You can't turn buffalo."

Rowdy dropped to the ground and started to shoot down at the buffalo that were closest to the wagon to try to turn them away. Lance and Doc were holding their teams tightly because the mules wanted to run.

The driver tried to push his wagon to the outside of the herd, but he was overtaken by the huge beasts. The running buffalo pressed against the wagon, and it began to tip and bounce from side to side. The driver was frantically whipping his team to keep from being overrun, but he was soon in the middle of the herd.

Rowdy mounted Smoke and began to race down the hill, shooting buffalo to the side of the wagon, hoping to turn the herd around the wagon. However, the animals at the back of the herd just jumped over the downed bodies and continued to crowd the wagon.

A large bull snorted and slammed the wagon with his head, lifting the right side of the wagon off the ground. Other buffalo following him continued to push and the wagon slowly flipped over, twisting the tongue and throwing the team to the ground. The surge of panting bodies spilled around the downed wagon. Several smaller bulls tried to jump over the wagon bed. They crashed through it, pawing their way out the other side. As the buffalo raced on, Rowdy reached the wagon. He dropped to the ground before Smoke skidded to a stop.

He strained to lift the mangled wagon bed, and Lance led the three wagons down the hill.

CHAPTER 60

DEATH COMES QUICKLY

THE OVERTURNED WAGON WAS SO BROKEN THAT Rowdy couldn't flip it. He was tearing boards away when the rest of his group arrived.

Lance handed the lines to Molly and jumped to the ground to help his brother.

The mules didn't like the smell of buffalo or blood. They were fighting the traces and trying to run away.

When the men finally pulled the wagon bed up, it broke apart in the middle uncovering a bruised and battered John Hatch. The wagon had crushed him, and he was unable to move. Beth quickly dismounted and took Doc's wagon lines as he rushed forward.

John waved Doc away as he gasped, "My family! My family is still under there!" He pointed at the crushed wagon seat.

Rowdy and Lance strained to pull the wagon seat up and then paused as it lifted. Marlene and her children were under the seat, and no one was moving.

Doc gently checked each person as he removed them. Marlene was still holding baby Jolly, and both were dead. He found the twins, Merle and Sarah, along with Johnny. All three had been crushed when the wagon seat collapsed.

From below, there was a small cry. As Doc lifted the bodies of the other children, the face of a small girl stared up at him, sobbing. It was Maribelle. Doc gently lifted her out and laid her on the ground.

Rowdy rushed over. "Maribelle!" he cried as he leaned over her. Maribelle lifted her little arms and gripped Rowdy around the neck. He leaned back as he held her tightly.

John Hatch was trying to turn his head to see.

He gasped, "My family! Are they all right?"

Rowdy moved over to his side. Tears formed in his eyes as he took John's hand.

"John, Maribelle is going to be fine but…" Rowdy finished his sentence with a soundless sob. Tears welled out of John's eyes.

"We had just gone over to your place. The missus wanted to make sure it was all cleaned up and ready for you. When we saw you coming over the hill, we decided to go meet you." His body was racked with heavy sobs. "It's all my fault. They're gone and it's all my fault."

Doc Williams knelt beside the man. "John, Maribelle is just fine. She sprained her arm, but it isn't broken."

Maribelle slipped out of Rowdy's arms and held her father's face. "Papa," she cried, "Momma won't wake up!"

John Hatch tried to lift his arm to put it around his daughter, but he couldn't move it. Rowdy lifted it for him.

He looked up at Rowdy as he quietly stated, "I'm all busted up inside, Rowdy. Someone needs to take care of my little girl," and tears coursed down the father's face. Beth moved forward and lifted Maribelle up. As Maribelle buried her face on Beth's shoulder, Beth and Molly took her back to their wagons.

Rowdy asked John with fear in his voice, "Was Rudy with you?"

John nodded weakly as he answered, "I knew the wagon was going to flip, and I told him to slide onto the mules. I tried to cut the traces, but the buffalo came on us too fast." Then his eyes focused, and he asked with panic in his voice, "Have you found him yet?"

Rowdy and Lance rushed to the front of the wagon. They could see a shoe laying in the dirt beside a dead mule. The other mule was down and thrashing.

While Rowdy looped a rope on Smoke's saddle to pull the dead mule aside, Lance tried to calm the second mule. Its legs were tangled in the traces, and it was thrashing to get up.

"Rowdy, hold up until I get this mule loose—it could hurt someone kicking this way," Lance hollered. When the mule was finally untangled, it surged to its feet. One leg was twisted at an odd angle, but it was calm.

Lance kept the rope in place on the dead mule while Rowdy led Smoke.

As the mule was pulled aside, they could see Rudy's body.

Doc Williams moved quickly to examine him, and Rudy opened his eyes.

"Rowdy," he said with a weak smile, "We was just at your place. We have a surprise for you." His nose was bleeding, and his ankle was twisted. However, his body had fallen into a rut in the path, and that kept the mule from crushing him. He was trying to get up, but Rowdy held him down.

"Stay down, Rudy. Let Doc check you over first," Rowdy told him quietly.

Rudy stared vacantly at Rowdy but stopped moving.

Doc moved his hands over Rudy's torso and stomach, checking and listening.

He finally looked up with sheer amazement on his face. "He has no broken bones, nor do I feel any internal injuries. A slight concussion but he is going to be fine."

As Rowdy reached to pull him up, Rudy asked dazedly, "Where am I? I remember hitchin' the wagon when we left your place but that's all. I don't know where I am."

Rowdy put his hands on Rudy's shoulders. He tried to talk but no words would come out. He just hugged Rudy tightly and led him back to his father.

Maribelle had wiggled out of Beth's arms and was crouched by her father's face. Once again, she had his face in her hands as she leaned over him. "Papa, I'm scared, Papa."

Doc Williams leaned back on his heels after he examined John. His face was grim when he looked at Rowdy. He gave his head a slight shake, and he tried to make John as comfortable as possible.

Rudy crouched on the ground beside his father. "Pa? Are you goin' to be okay?"

Then he looked around. His eyes passed over his mother as he asked, "Where's Ma?" He looked back at the body of his mother lying quietly with Jolly in her arms. "That ain't Ma. Where's Ma?"

John's eyes were full of pain as he gasped, "Rudy, listen to me. I ain't gonna make it, an' you're the man of the house now. You be strong for Maribelle." John wheezed as he continued, "You go on home with Rowdy till they find you a new home."

Rowdy put his big hand on John's shoulder and gave it a squeeze.

"They already have a home, John. They can live with us. Beth and I would be honored to raise your children."

John smiled weakly as Rudy held his hand and tried not to cry.

Rowdy looked at the boy and spoke softly, "Tears don't mean you're weak, Rudy. They just show that you love deep inside. Those tears are that love leaking out."

Rudy gripped his father's hand as the tears flowed, and Rowdy picked up Maribelle. She pushed her face against his neck and squeezed him tightly. The wheezing was louder, and John opened his eyes.

"Rudy, you get the deed to the land and give it to Rowdy."

Rowdy shook his head, "No, that land will remain Hatch land. We will work it, but it will always be Rudy's."

John Hatch looked up at Rowdy and almost smiled.

"I knew you would be a good neighbor. The missus and I was lookin' forward to havin' you close by."

Rudy felt a slight squeeze of his hand.

John Hatch opened his eyes wide and asked in amazement, "Are those angels? Can you hear that music?" As his eyes slowly closed, the dying father left the world with a smile on his face. He knew his family would be cared for.

CHAPTER 61

WALDO

DOC COVERED MARLENE AND THE CHILDREN WITH blankets from Rowdy's wagons while Rooster moved supplies to make room for their bodies. The little group was silent as the men lifted the bodies of the Hatch family and placed them in the bed of the wagon.

Maribelle clung to Rowdy, her eyes big while Rudy stood to the side and said nothing. He held himself straight. His face was pale, and his hands were clenched as he watched.

Rowdy looked back at the mule and spoke softly to Lance, "His leg is broken. We should put him down."

Rudy's head jerked up, "You can't kill Waldo! I raised him from a baby! I'll take care of 'im," he cried as tears began to fill his eyes.

Rowdy looked at him helplessly and then at Doc. He knew broken legs on mules and horses rarely healed. Still, he didn't want to force any more death on Rudy.

Doc patted Rudy's shoulder. "I don't know anything about mules, but I do have some chloroform. Maybe I can check his leg if we put him under."

Rowdy was muttering under his breath when Beth put her hand on his arm.

Smiling up at Rowdy she suggested gently, "Let's use the chloroform and let Reub check him out. See if you can find a splint of some kind. If he can make it to the ranch, Rudy can take care of him."

When Rowdy started to say it wouldn't work, Beth kissed him and added softly, "For Rudy." She took Maribelle out of Rowdy's arms and walked over to where Molly was standing.

The men estimated the young mule's weight to be between eight hundred and nine hundred pounds.

Doc shook his head as he measured out the required amount of chloroform. He looked at Rudy.

"I am going to do my best, Rudy, but this may not work."

Rudy's face was tight as he stood in front of Waldo, talking to him. However, he nodded his head.

Rowdy and Lance held the mule tightly, one on each side. When Doc administered the chloroform, Waldo wrinkled his nose and let out a loud sound, almost like a moan. His body went limp, and he would have dropped to the ground had he not been supported by Lance and Rowdy. They held him up to protect his leg.

Doc found the break in the long pastern bone just below the fetlock, the large joint on the mule's front leg.

Rooster cut off the end of a tea towel. They wrapped the leg in the towel and then attached a wood splint—one strip of wood behind the leg and one on each side. Rudy wanted to stay with the mule until the chloroform wore off.

Lance suggested quietly, "Let Rudy grieve in his own way. He will talk things over with his mule, just like you do with Smoke."

Rowdy looked surprised but slowly nodded in agreement. Maribelle wouldn't let go of Rowdy, so he set her in front of him. As the three wagons moved down the final hill toward the ranch, Rudy sat down in front of Waldo and began talking to him.

Molly and Beth hurried the food items into the kitchen. Lance's smoked ham and Martha's fresh bread were going to be appreciated.

CHAPTER 62

A New Family

THE WOMEN HURRIED MARIBELLE INTO THE HOUSE while the men dug graves. Molly set her down at the table and gave her a cookie.

"You eat that, Maribelle." She kissed the little girl's cheek as she hurried to help Beth unload the wagons.

As they put items away, the women looked around the house with approval. It was well-built and had two bedrooms. Louise Hutchins had taken hardly anything with her. Even the rough-cut furniture and large kitchen table were still there. The kitchen was clean with a small can of wildflowers on the table.

Beth's eyes had tears in them as she looked around. When she peeked into the larger of the bedrooms, she saw a four-poster bed with a beautiful patchwork quilt covering it. On top of the bed was a note written in a woman's neat hand that read,

Beth and Rowdy — Welcome to your new home. We are looking forward to having you as neighbors.

John, Marlene, and children

As Beth read the note, a sob caught in her throat. "Oh, Molly! The Hatches—they were here cleaning and preparing our house when they were caught in the stampede!"

Molly read the note over Beth's shoulder. She hugged her new sister-in-law as Beth cried. Finally, Molly suggested softly, "Beth, let's prepare something to eat. It has been a long and difficult day, especially for the children."

When they returned to the kitchen, Beth gasped, "Maribelle! She's gone!" She rushed outside. Josie was holding Maribelle as Rowdy looked for shovels to use to dig the graves. Beth reached to lift the little girl from Josie's arms. "Where is Rudy? Is he home yet?"

Lance put his arm around Beth's shoulders and explained softly, "Not yet. We'll check on him later. We'll see if his mule is going to make it."

Maribelle clung to Beth as she carried her back into the house, followed by Josie.

Molly appeared with a bright smile and asked, "Maribelle, how would you like a sandwich? Are you hungry?"

Maribelle's eyes were huge as Molly cut a thick slice of bread and folded it over a slab of ham. However, she would only eat if Beth was holding her. Soon, her head was nodding. Molly lifted her out of Beth's arms and laid her down on the bed in the second bedroom. As she pulled the soft coverlet over Maribelle, Molly looked around the room with surprise. The room was bright and happy with colorful curtains on the window and a rag rug by the bed. A patchwork quilt lay across the base of the bed.

"But the Hutchins' didn't have any children," she whispered as Beth and Josie looked over her shoulder. Beth picked up the corner of the quilt where something was embroidered and read, "For our first son, May 10, 1865."

Beth covered her mouth as her eyes filled with tears. "Poor Louise. Rowdy said she was a bitter, angry woman but I think she was just very sad."

As they softly shut the door, the women began to prepare a quick meal for the men.

The men gently laid the bodies of the Hatch family on the ground, and Doc wrapped them tightly in blankets.

The Hutchins had started a small cemetery several hundred yards from the house. A white fence was around it and a small tree had been planted there. Lance and Rowdy read the stones as they looked for a place to dig the graves. When they read the names and ages on the markers, both men were a little quieter.

Louise Hutchins had buried four children in her time on the ranch. Rowdy was ashamed of himself for thinking poorly of her. *I guess she carried scars too that no one knew about.*

The men discussed how they should bury the family. They finally decided one grave would be suitable. Mrs. Hatch was still holding her baby, and John's greatest concern had always been for his family. It was decided since they had lived and died as a family, they would be buried as one too.

Rowdy rode Smoke out to find Rudy and his mule while Lance followed with an empty wagon. They weren't sure if the mule would even wake let alone be able to walk. Waldo was starting to stir, and the men were undecided if they should try to lay him in the wagon or help him stand. Either way could damage his leg further.

In the end, it was Rudy who decided. "I will just walk back with him," he told the men. When Waldo struggled to stand, Lance and Rowdy lifted from each side to take the weight off the young mule's leg. Waldo nuzzled Rudy, and as the young boy walked toward the ranch, Waldo followed awkwardly.

Rooster and Doc had laid the Hatch family in the large grave, and everyone was gathered around. Doc had his small Bible open to *Psalm 23* and Josie stood beside him. The little group waited quietly for Rudy and his mule.

Maribelle didn't sleep long. When she awoke, she stood in the doorway of the house and cried until Beth hurried to pick her up.

She was clinging to Beth but as Rowdy dismounted, she wriggled to the ground and ran to him. When he picked her up, she wrapped her arms tightly around his neck. Her little body shook with great sobs, but no sound came out. Rowdy patted her back and pulled her closer. He talked softly to her until she became quiet.

Once Rudy arrived, Doc began to read, "The Lord is my Shepherd, I shall not want…"

When Doc finished, Rowdy asked, "Rudy, do you want to say anything?"

Rudy paused and cleared his throat as he began strongly, "Pa was a fair man. Ma always said he never skinned nobody an' I reckon that was a good way to meet the Maker.

Ma loved us kids an' even though we never had much, she made sure we knew we was special to her an' we was all loved." His voice caught as he added. "I'll miss 'em, every one of 'em."

The group was quiet. Rudy was right about his parents. The little family would be missed. As the men stood with their hats in their hands, Molly started "Amazing Grace" and Josie harmonized. Soon, everyone was singing. The music echoed over the ranch and through the small valleys. As the sound faded away, everyone but Rudy headed to the house.

Maribelle still clung to Rowdy, and he sat down on the steps of the house with her on his lap.

"Maribelle, how would you like to come live with Beth and me?" he asked.

She looked at him with big, brown eyes, "And be your little girl?" she asked.

Rowdy could feel his heart crumbling. He nodded and smiled, "And be our little girl."

"But I don't know what to call you," she whispered as she looked at Rowdy.

"What would you like to call me?" Rowdy asked.

Maribelle smiled for the first time since the accident.

"I'd like to call you Papa," she whispered.

Rowdy hugged her tightly. "Well then, that is what you can call me. What would you like to call Beth?"

Maribelle frowned a little. "Do you think I could call her Momma? Since my momma is in the dirt, I don't think I have a momma anymore."

Rowdy looked into the little girl's eyes. "You will always have your momma. You can hear her when the birds sing, and you can smell her when you smell the flowers. She will always be watching over you."

Maribelle's eyes were large. "Will I see her?"

Rowdy shook his head, "No, but she will see you."

Maribelle thought for a moment. "Do you think my first momma would like Beth to be my momma now?"

Rowdy smiled. "I know she would," he answered.

Beth had come to the doorway to call Rowdy in. She listened to the entire exchange. Her heart was full as she watched Rowdy with the little girl, and she covered her mouth to keep from sobbing herself. When Maribelle looked up and saw Beth, she climbed out of Rowdy's arms and ran to her.

"Would you like to be my momma?" she asked, as she looked up at Beth with a shy smile.

Beth reached down and scooped Maribelle up. She kissed her and whispered softly, "I would love to be your momma."

Maribelle smiled and wrapped her arms around Beth's neck.

Rudy had put Waldo in the barn. As he approached the house, he heard the exchange between Maribelle, Rowdy, and Beth.

Rowdy stood and looped a big arm over the young boy's shoulders. Rudy shyly smiled as the four of them walked into their new home.

CHAPTER 63

A Milk Cow and New Treats

ONCE THE MEAL WAS COMPLETED, LANCE AND ROWDY went outside to discuss what needed to be done next.

As they stood by the corral, each had his arms folded over the top corral bar and one leg up on the fence.

Molly looked out the window and covered her mouth as she laughed softly.

"Look," she exclaimed to Beth, "Same!"

Beth and Doc didn't understand, but Rooster laughed.

Rudy joined the men at the corral with a look of concern on his face. "I need to milk the cow, but I don't know if I can get her in by myself. I usually take Waldo." Both men looked at Rudy.

"Well, let's go get her," Rowdy answered. "Lance here loves milk cows."

Rowdy' blue eyes twinkled, and he slapped his brother's back.

"Come on, Lance. You can help. I know how much you love milk cows," he drawled.

Rowdy hitched up the new wagon with his mules and saddled the horses while Lance went in the house to tell the women where they were going. It was too late to head back to town, so Doc and Rooster offered to go with them.

Rooster was driving the wagon, Doc was riding shotgun, and Rudy was sitting in the wagon bed.

It was five miles to the Hatches' house. The men could see that even though John Hatch had done a lot of physical work, it was still a hardscrabble ranch.

The milk cow was waiting by the gate, and she followed Rudy into the barn. Rudy forked what little hay there was into a small pile. Then, he went into the house and came out with a bucket for milking.

Rooster suggested, "Why don't we jist milk that cow when we get back to Rowdy's? Be mighty hard to haul milk in a wagon with it sloshin' all over the place."

"That's a fine idea, Rooster. Rudy, you get everything you need to chore with, and we'll put it in this wagon." Rowdy said. He and Lance walked into the barn and looked around.

Rudy nodded. He hurried into the barn and came back quickly with kickers and a lead rope for the cow.

Lance watched him for a moment before he asked softly, "Anything here you kids want to take to your new place—things that would make the two of you more comfortable?"

Rudy stared from Lance to the house. He walked slowly toward the old house, tripping several times as he wiped his eyes.

Rowdy looked at Lance in surprise and slapped Smoke's reins against his leg. "I don't know about any of this parent stuff," he muttered with some embarrassment.

Lance gave him a wry grin. "Neither did I but you'll learn."

The two men hurried to catch up with Rudy. Lance put his hand on Rudy's shoulder.

"Rudy, how about you show us where you kids sleep. We can load up anything you want."

All the kids slept in the small loft. Rudy came down with two blankets and a battered doll. He showed them where their clothes were. Had it not been for the new things Badger and Martha had given them in secret, the children would have had nothing worth taking. Rudy looked around the small house. He lifted an old rifle off the wall. "I don't think we need anything else," he stated quietly as his lips quivered.

Rowdy squeezed his shoulder. "Let's go look in the barn."

Rooster had already forked the hay into the wagon bed. He pointed at the chicken coop beside the barn. "What about the chickens?" he asked.

Rowdy scratched his head and looked at Lance. "Any ideas?" he asked.

"Let's put them in that old crate," Lance suggested as he pointed at a wooden box. "We can break the coop down and rebuild it at your place."

The men soon had the few chickens in the crate, and the coop dissembled. After the wagon was loaded, Rudy climbed in on top. He looked around with tears in his eyes and sat down. "Let's go," he stated quietly.

The men were quiet as they turned down the lane with the Hatches' few possessions in the back of Rowdy's wagon.

It was nearly dark when the little group arrived at Rowdy's ranch. They found a place with a little protection and quickly nailed the chicken coop back together. They set the chickens on their roosts and hooked the door.

Beth was excited to have chickens and a milk cow. She whispered to Molly and Josie, "I have never milked a cow or collected eggs."

Josie looked surprised and Molly laughed. The three of them hurried to the barn to watch Rudy milk the cow. Beth was excited to learn while Rowdy laughed and Lance scowled.

Lance glared at Molly. "Don't be getting any ideas. I am not going to milk a cow!"

Molly smiled at him and batted her eyes as she took his arm. "But think of the children, Lance. Milk would be so good for them."

As she stood close to him, looking up and smiling, Lance shook his head. He pretended to glare at Rowdy.

"And this is how they get what they want," he growled as he squeezed his wife.

Rudy watched the two couples quietly. *Our folks never hugged an' kissed on each other as much as these folks do—an' they sure didn't do it in front of us kids. Sometimes, we would sneak in an' catch Pa givin' Ma a kiss, but these people don't care who watches them being silly.* He pushed his head into the cow's flank. *This place might take some gettin' used to, but I think I am goin' to like it.* When Rudy looked up again, Lance winked at him. Rudy ducked his head as he grinned.

As soon as the milk was in the house, Molly showed Beth how to strain it. Then they made pudding. Beth gave Rudy the bowl to clean out, and he didn't think he had ever tasted anything so delicious. Beth didn't know how to milk a cow, but she did know lots of ways to use fresh milk.

Molly cleaned an old butter churn she found. The women planned to skim the cream off the milk in the morning and make some butter.

Beth caught Rowdy's eye and gave him a dazzling smile.

Rowdy grinned back at her. *Beth is such a happy little gal. Everything is an adventure for her,* Rowdy thought. His face lit up with pride as he watched her.

Maribelle was falling asleep in her food, so Rowdy picked her up and put her in bed. Rudy watched him somberly.

"She'll wet the bed if ya don't wake her up. She does it 'most ever' night."

Rowdy was surprised but turned to Molly.

"Any suggestions?"

Molly found a chamber pot. She picked Maribelle up and told her, "Sit on the pot, Maribelle. We don't want you to wet the bed."

Maribelle's eyes never opened but a tinkling could be heard in the metal pot. Molly lifted the little girl up and placed her in bed.

"You need to help her clean her teeth. I can show you how I mix baking soda and salt to clean them. She has pretty little teeth, and we don't want her to lose them too early," Molly commented as she smiled at the sleeping little girl. She glanced over at Rudy and added, "And you too, Rudy. You are a handsome young man, and we want you to stay that way."

Rudy blushed and ducked his head as he followed Rowdy out of the bedroom.

The men decided they would sleep in the barn that night, and the women would share the two bedrooms. Beth offered to sleep with Maribelle if Molly and Josie wanted to share the bigger bedroom.

After the sleeping situation was settled, Molly put her hands on her hips as she looked around.

"Beth, it's still early. Let's get your kitchen set up tonight while we are here. There is no point in sitting around and you working harder tomorrow."

Soon Molly and Beth were busy discussing how to organize things to make the kitchen as efficient as possible.

Josie watched and helped where she could. Her aunt employed someone who did the cooking so even though she enjoyed cooking, she had never done much. She was amazed at the wealth of knowledge Beth and Molly shared when it came to food and managing a household. When the other two women saw Josie's interest, they pulled her into the work. She was soon on the floor stashing pans and storing food items along with them.

CHAPTER 64

ROOSTER SMITH

THE MEN WENT OUTSIDE. WHILE ROWDY AND LANCE wandered down toward the corral, Rooster walked to the top of a little hill. He looked back at Rudy and grinned.

"Did ya know this here place was once a hideout fer outlaws? That there hill over yonder was the lookout point. Why a feller cin see miles in ever' direction on top a that hill. They's caves all over here an' some a those caves hook up underground. Why they's 'nough explorin' 'round here to keep a smart feller like yerself busy fer a long time."

Rudy stared at the old man. He walked slowly up the hill until he stood beside Rooster. Even the small rise they were on gave them a good view of the lane that led to the house. Rudy looked in the direction Rooster pointed. He could see the hill Rooster was talking about.

Doc had followed Rudy and he looked at Rooster in surprise.

"Were you part of a posse that came out here, Rooster, or did you live in this area? You seem to have a lot of knowledge of the terrain."

"Why shore now, I did live out here fer a time, but mostly, I jist passed through. A feller learns a lot 'bout the land he travels, or he better if he intends to survive. Ya need to know the waterholes an' where to hole up if a-a norther is to come through.

"They's caves all over out there that cin give shelter, an' some has they own water too. Good water—fresh an' cold right outta the rocks."

The old man's eyes took on a far-off look as he stared across the hilly terrain.

"I was jist a young whippersnapper when I first come up on this place. I 'most settled down then an' I should have. Met me a nice little gal an' plumb fell in love. Her pappy didn't like me none though. He threatened to shoot me if'n I was ever to show up on his place again."

Rooster winked at Rudy.

"His place wasn't too far from where yer folks homesteaded. He had him a sod house dug outta the side of a hill. That ol' man was a cranky ol' feller but he worked hard.

"He was right to run me off too. 'Course, I didn't see it at the time. When I come through six years later, he had 'im a nice house an' my little gal was married up to his foreman."

Rooster was silent for a moment and Rudy stood quietly as he waited for the old man to go on.

When the Rooster didn't speak for several minutes, Rudy asked, "What happened to 'em? I ain't never seen no big house 'round here, an' I been all over those hills."

Rooster's eyes were bleak when he looked at Rudy.

"My little gal's baby got sick an' then he died. She died not long after—they thought it was the cholera but no one knowed fer shore. Her young husband died when his horse went down that winter.

"The old man burned the house down. Burned it to the ground an' left. He jist up an' left an' no one knowed where he went. He didn't sell or nothin'—jist walked away."

Rudy's eyes were wide as he stared at Rooster.

"I seen that place. A bunch of burned timbers over a stone foundation, and three graves together under an old, skinny tree." He paused as he continued to look at Rooster. "I asked Pa what happened, but he didn't know. He said they died 'fore he come into this country. Pa told

314

us to stay away from there. He was afraid the sickness could still be in the ground."

Doc Williams was quiet. He had seen his share of heartache and death during the war, but his life before and after had been quite shielded. He shook his head. *This is a hard land. It takes strong people to survive out here, let alone succeed.* His eyes moved to watch Lance and Rowdy leaning on the corral fence as they talked.

A smile creased Doc's face. *Strong men like Rowdy and Lance, and yes, strong women too, like Molly.* He frowned. *I hope Beth is strong enough to survive here.*

Rudy was looking at him and speaking when Doc looked up.

"I'm sorry, Rudy. I didn't hear what you said. What did you ask me?"

"I jist wondered what ya thought they died of—those folks that built the house over yonder? What kind of sickness takes a ma an' a baby but leaves the pa?"

Doc's brow creased as he pondered how to answer. He put his hands on Rudy's shoulders and smiled at the serious young man.

"Rudy, the Good Lord decides when it is our time to go. We doctors can help sometimes, but every sickness is different. Many times, even as doctors, we don't understand sickness at all." Doc paused and looked at Rooster before he looked back at Rudy.

"Sickness hits folks in all kinds of ways. Chances are, that little momma had some complications after birth, but we'll just never know. We do know some sickness comes from dirty bodies, so washing often and cleaning your teeth is a good thing to do."

Doc patted Rudy's back before he turned back to Rooster.

"How long have you been in Cheyenne, Rooster? I know it is a young town, but you seem to have been around here for a long time."

Rooster grinned at his two companions.

"I bumped 'round all over these here hills an' beyond fer most a my life. When the first plots a land was sold fer Cheyenne, I bought up all I had money fer at $150 each, an' that was a number of 'em. My friends thought I'd done lost the last piece a brain I had. The price a those plots jist kept a goin' up though. I sold most of 'em for over $3000 each, an' my little 'vestment made me more money than all the banks I ever—I—than all the banks I ever saved money in." His grin became bigger as he added, "'Course, I kept the best ones. Now they's worth way more than that, an' I'm jist a lettin' 'em grow."

Rooster's old eyes were gleaming. "I bought me a little place outside a town an' I settled down. A feller gets bored when he's by his lonesome though, so I got me a job in the livery. I like hosses an' mules better than most folks, so it suits me fine."

He grinned evilly at Doc. "I do what I durn well please there. Now, if a highfalutin' gal comes in with 'er nose in the air. Then I jist give 'er the orneriest hosses I have. Same with the menfolk. If they think they's too important fer other folks, I set 'em up with a team that'll keep they hands busy." Rooster winked again at Doc.

"Now ya take little Beth. She be a fine little woman an' she's a gonna make it here. A happy little gal like her cin weather the hard times an' come out on the other side with a smile.

"She softens up ol' Rowdy an' makes 'im a better man. An' he'll help her git stronger. That's what married folks is s'posed to do. They makes the other person better."

He slapped Rudy on the back.

"Now I been pontificatin' long 'nough. I need to quit my blabberin' so us fellers cin git us some sleep."

The three walked down the little rise to the barn and spread their blankets out on the hay. Rudy didn't have a blanket of his own, but someone had left an extra for him. The blanket was a new one. It was big and heavy. He was going to be warm that night.

Rudy lay down on the soft blanket and rolled up. *Yep, things are goin' to be different, but I think I'll like it here.*

CHAPTER 65

THANKS TO BANDY

ROWDY HAD LOTS OF PLANS FOR HIS RANCH, AND HE shared them with Lance.

"You know I bought some green-broke horses but check this out." He pulled a piece of paper out of his pocket and handed it to Lance.

When his brother looked at him in surprise, Rowdy gave him a crooked grin.

"Samuel gave me the letter last week, but I don't know how Dodge heard of me."

The note read:

Mr. Rowdy Rankin,
Come out to Fort Russell. I would like to negotiate a horse contract for the army with you. You were recommended by a colleague of mine back East. I want to discuss numbers and prices.

General Grenville Dodge

"The general sent that note with one of the soldiers at Fort Russell. As the troops passed through Cheyenne, the soldier was instructed to give the note to Samuel Brewster at the livery.

"Samuel told me General Dodge didn't know how to get hold of me, but he had been told I had family in Cheyenne. He just took a chance and started at the livery."

Lance smiled at his younger brother and squeezed his shoulder.

"I'm proud of you, Rowdy. You're an honest man. Folks remember that. Someone Dodge respected recommended you. Who knows who it was, but you are a good man, and the word is getting out."

Rowdy's neck turned red as he stared at his brother. He wasn't used to receiving compliments, especially not from this brother whom he admired and respected. Rowdy turned back around to face the fence and was silent for a moment.

Lance was right although neither of them would ever know. Rowdy had received a glowing recommendation from an old Union soldier who ran the livery back in Columbus, Georgia. Bandy Jackson had served with General Dodge in the Atlanta Campaign. General Grenville Mellen Dodge was the head of the blossoming military intelligence movement, and Major Bandy Jackson had been in his command.

Bandy contacted General Dodge after Rowdy left Columbus and headed west. Dodge received a post from Bandy that read,

general, i have a cowboy ya should look up fer breakin yer army mounts. he worked here fer 3 weeks an i coulda kept im busy all winter after the job he done on those 4 hosses. he broke em gentle an was honest. hard worker an wont tolerate abusin animals. his name be rowdy rankin an he was headed west when he left here. talked some of settlin down in the cheyenne area.

318

has him a brother round there by the name a lance.
talk to rooster smith at the livery there.
                                        bandy jackson

Lance grinned at Rowdy and bumped him with his shoulder.
"So?"

Rowdy turned his head. "What?"

"Have you met with Dodge yet? Do you have the contract all tied
up?"

Rowdy nodded as he grinned at his brother.

"I met with him. He was coming through Cheyenne and sent a wire.
We met in town and the contract is in my saddle bag."

Before Lance could ask another question, Rowdy laughed and added,
"And yes, I am pleased with the contract. The Army needs horses and
mules, and they offered me a fair price. It also means steady income
while I build this place up. So yes, I'm pleased." He bumped Lance with
his shoulder. "Maybe someday I will own as much land as my brother.
Shoot, maybe our ranches will connect."

The two brothers grinned at each other as they turned toward the
barn.

Doc, Rooster, and Rudy were already bedded down and asleep when
they slipped quietly through the big barn door.

The brothers spread their bed rolls and blankets on the floor. The
barn was snug and warm. The smell of the horses and a milk cow filled
the air along with the scent of fresh hay.

Rowdy laced his fingers behind his head as he looked over at Lance.

"I'm thinking of catching some of those mustangs that roam across
here. Tomorrow, I want to look the ranch over. I want to see where I
can capture and pen them. Interested in helping?"

Lance grinned at him. "I know you think my mustang is old, and
that is why you are offering."

Rowdy just smiled and chewed on a piece of hay.

"Sure, figure it out and I'll bring some of the boys along. We need to add some horses to the remuda. You won't even need to break ours. Slim can do that. I'll bring him along too." Lance grinned as he bumped this brother. "Slim is the only man I ever met who has as much horse sense as you. He's a mighty fine rider too."

"I've seen at least thirty head in that herd led by a big, black mustang with the star on his face. I know there is a second herd around here as well with some Appaloosa blood, but I don't want to mix the two herds if I can help it. I would hate to see that big black take on another stallion. They are brutal when they fight, and the loser is usually crippled or dead when they are done." Rowdy added softly, "I'd sure like to own that black stud."

Lance muttered a response and rolled over. He quickly fell asleep, but Rowdy was awake several more hours as he ran numbers and projects through his mind.

Rudy was awake too. He had listened to the brothers' conversation about gathering horses. He could feel the excitement bubbling through him, and he tried to hold himself still. *Rowdy is a smart man, and he's nice too.* Then he said a silent prayer that Waldo's leg would heal. His mother's face flitted in front of him as he drifted off to sleep. She smiled down at him and he smiled back.

Maribelle woke several times during the night and cried until Beth pulled her close. She tucked her little body tightly against Beth and finally stayed asleep the rest of the night.

CHAPTER 66

THE RIGHT MAN

THE NEXT MORNING, SMOKE CAME TO GREET ROWDY when he opened the barn door. The two of them had a full-blown conversation about the day. When Rowdy looked up, Lance was grinning, and Rudy's eyes were wide with surprise.

Rowdy grinned at Rudy and tousled his hair.

"That horse is the best friend and partner I have ever had."

Rudy looked at Waldo. *That's what I think of Waldo* too. He walked over to the young mule and rubbed his neck. Rowdy followed him and bent down to study the broken leg.

"Rudy, get some of that horse liniment over there by the barn door. I am going to show you how to rub his legs and work those muscles. He is going to have to wear this splint for some time since we want him to put as little weight on it as possible."

Rudy hurried to get the liniment and Lance held the lamp as Doc and Rowdy took the splint off.

Waldo stood quietly, while Rudy held his head.

Rowdy looked at Doc Williams.

"What do you think, Doc? How often should he take this splint off and apply the salve?"

Doc Williams felt Waldo's leg and studied the broken skin around the break.

"I would change that bandage at least every other day. Maybe even once a day if Rudy can keep him still. We don't want that leg to get infected, so make sure to use a clean rag when you wrap it back up. Use a little corn whiskey to clean it out if you need to. Rowdy can show you what to look for."

Doc started to show Rowdy what to do, but Rowdy shook his head and stepped back.

"Rudy, you need to learn this. Waldo is your mule and your responsibility."

Doc smiled as he carefully showed Rudy how to apply the salve as well as how to wrap the leg before the splint was reattached.

Once the leg had been wrapped, Rowdy showed Rudy how to rub the liniment into the muscles.

"Rub his legs every day, Rudy. Rub all four of them, not just the broken one. He needs to stay in this small stall so he moves around as little as possible.

"Breaks in a leg on a horse or a mule rarely heal well. You are going to have to take special care of Waldo if we are going to save his leg." Rowdy talked quietly as he watched Rudy work the liniment into Waldo's legs. His eyes were bleak when he stood up. *I don't think that mule is going to make it, and that will break Rudy's heart.*

Lance's eyes met Rowdy's. Both men believed any action was futile.

Rudy was working on Waldo and didn't see the men's expressions. He was convinced Waldo would heal, and he wasn't going to give up on his mule without a fight.

The young mule nibbled on Rudy's ear and sniffed his pockets for treats. Rudy laughed and pushed Waldo's muzzle away as he buried his face in the mule's soft neck.

Rowdy's mouth lifted in a crooked smile as he watched the young boy and his mule communicate.

Yep, Waldo is Rudy's special companion. I sure hope we can save that leg. He shrugged his shoulders and stifled a grin. *If not, I guess we will have a three-legged mule on this place.*

Rowdy tousled Rudy's hair again, and the men headed up to the house for breakfast.

All the adults were in a hurry that morning. Doc and Lance wanted to get home, and Rowdy wanted to ride the ranch to look things over. He had spotted an old saddle last night in the back of the barn, and he was going to show Rudy how to restore the leather. He had a feeling it might be the first saddle Rudy had ever owned.

Beth, Molly, and Josie fixed a big breakfast. Josie showed the other two women how make stuffed burritos, and they were a new dish for everyone. The women skimmed the cream off the milk, and Molly made butter.

Lance and Rowdy were both very motivated by food, and they stared in appreciation at the meal. Fried slices of ham, burritos, thick bread with butter—they grinned with pure happiness and began to eat.

Beth put her hand on Rowdy's arm. "Rowdy, would you lead us in prayer before our first breakfast in our new home?"

Rowdy paused in his eating. His neck turned a little red as he put his fork down.

"Lord, we thank you for this fine food and for the family gathered here. We thank you for Maribelle and Rudy as well as for giving Beth and me the opportunity to settle on this ranch. We pray for the safety of those who travel to and from this place. We pray for those who lived here before and for those buried here. In Jesus' name, Amen."

It was a fine prayer, and everyone began to eat.

When Rudy saw the fat burrito on his plate, he was surprised. He looked around to see who he needed to share with.

Rowdy whispered to him, "Eat up, Rudy. We have plenty of food."

Rudy pulled his plate closer and started to shovel his food in. Then he slowed down and tried to mimic the way Rowdy and Lance held their forks. Last night, he had been full when he left the table, and it looked like he might be full again this morning.

As he eyed more bread, Lance picked up a large slice, slathered it with butter, and handed it to the little boy with a wink. Rudy took it silently. He stared at the bread for a moment before he began to eat.

Maribelle was also eating steadily, but she scattered lots of questions between mouthfuls.

"What's your name?" she asked Lance.

His eyes wrinkled at the corners. He looked seriously at her and answered, "Why I am your Uncle Lance, and that lady is your Aunt Molly. Maybe next Sunday you can come over for dinner and meet your cousins."

Maribelle's brown eyes were large, and her mass of dark curls bobbed as she looked around the room. "I have cousins? Are cousins kids like me? How big are they? Are any of them as big as me?"

Rudy snorted.

"Maribelle, you ain't even four, an' that is not big!"

Maribelle glared at him.

"Three is big. I can take care of the chickens by myself, dress myself, an' wipe my own bottom. 'Sides, someday, I am goin' to read. Just 'cause you're bigger don't mean that three is little!" She was gripping her fork and glaring at Rudy from angry, brown eyes. He glared back at her but looked around in surprise when everyone laughed.

Meals just might be a little more exciting from now on, Rowdy thought as he smiled over their heads at Beth.

Once breakfast was over, the wagons were hitched. Beth and Rowdy promised to ride down to the Rocking R for dinner on Sunday. Doc was smiling as he thought about working with Josie for two weeks as well as the long wagon ride back to town with her. Even Rooster was anxious to get back to the livery.

When Rowdy started to pay him for the use of the wagons, Rooster shook his head. "Samuel took care of it. He said to tell ya that his house always be open when ya come to Cheyenne if ya need a place to stay."

Rowdy was grinning when he looked at Lance.

"Brother, I like your father-in-law. I think I will just share him with you since I don't have one of my own."

Lance looked startled. He shook his head as he laughed. Molly was beaming, and Beth was looking at Rowdy with adoring eyes. As Doc watched his little sister, he knew she had found the right man, and he was glad that man was Rowdy.

CHAPTER 67

THE R4 RANCH

ONCE THE WAGONS PULLED OUT, RUDY HEADED TO the barn with the milk bucket.

Beth called to him, "Just a moment, Rudy. I want you to show me how to milk."

Rudy turned to look at her in surprise, but he waited. He proved to be a patient teacher and Beth was an excited learner. When they returned to the house, Beth and Rudy were both carrying the milk bucket while Maribelle held Beth's other hand. All three were smiling.

Rowdy was walking the pastures to see where to keep the milk cow. One small pasture had a fence around it although it was down in several places.

"Rudy, let's fix that fence. Then we can turn the cow out today," Rowdy suggested as he inspected the gate.

Rowdy turned both mules and the horses loose. Since Badger had broken the mules, he hoped they would stay close. *Even if they like to roam, Smoke won't go anywhere, and mules like company.*

Maribelle stayed close to Beth most of the morning but was starting to venture away a little more. She had been delighted to get her doll back. She slept with it along with her old, threadbare blanket.

Rudy followed Rowdy as he fixed the fence, and Rowdy soon had him hammering nails and holding the wire in place. Once they were done, Rudy led the cow out to her new pasture. A little stream ran out of the spring in the hill and collected in the bottom of a draw. Rowdy leaned on the corral fence as he watched with his arms folded over the top bar and one leg up. When Rudy returned, he leaned on the corral fence as he mimicked Rowdy's stance. Beth could see them from the window and her heart gave a happy jump as she watched them talk.

"Rudy, I think we will try to pipe some of that water a little closer to the house." He looked over at the young man and asked, "Have you ever seen a windmill? One of those might be mighty handy to bring water in for the stock." He grinned at the young man and nodded toward the house.

"Why don't you ask Beth if she would like to go for a ride this morning. I want to look the ranch over, and I think she might like that."

Rudy didn't move and Rowdy looked down at him. "Do you want to say something, Rudy?"

Rudy paused as he looked up and asked tentatively, "Can I come too?"

Rowdy looked surprised. "Of course, you can come. We're going as a family!" he exclaimed as he reached over to tousle Rudy's hair.

Rudy raced for the house, hollering as he ran. "Beth! Let's go for a ride! Rowdy said we can all go!"

Rowdy was laughing as he headed to the barn. He whistled for Smoke as he walked in the door. He pulled out the old saddle and hung it over a sawhorse he had found. It needed to be oiled, but otherwise, it looked solid.

"Yep, I am going to show Rudy how to oil that when we get back," he muttered softly.

Rowdy walked out of the barn with Smoke and the filly following him.

"I think it's time Beth gave a name to this little filly. We need to know what to call her."

As they walked up to the house, Beth rushed out with a basketful of food, a blanket, and a couple of canteens. Rowdy looked at her with surprise.

She smiled at him. Her face was bright and happy as she laughed.

"I thought the children would like to have a picnic since it might be late before we get back. And I packed enough food so even you can get full this time."

As Rowdy looked down at her, his heart lurched. *What did I ever do to deserve this sweet woman,* he wondered? He leaned over and kissed his wife as he took the food and the blanket from her.

"I'll put the food in my saddle bags, and we'll tie the blanket behind your saddle. Now…what are you going to call your horse? I think she has gone long enough without a name," he drawled as he smiled down at her.

Beth had jackets for all of them and as Rowdy gave her a leg up, she smiled at him.

"I am going to call her Sister. I never had a sister, and I always wanted one. Sister will be her name."

Rowdy kept his hand on Beth's leg as he looked up at her. "Sister is a fine name." He squeezed her leg and lifted Maribelle up to ride with her. Then he mounted Smoke and pulled Rudy up behind him.

As the Rankins's rode out to look at their ranch, Rowdy looked around at his family.

"I believe our ranch needs a name too. Anyone have an idea?"

Rudy had been thinking about that. *I always wanted to name our place, but Pa said it was the Hatch place. He said that was good enough.*

He leaned around Rowdy to look at him and suggested, "How about the R4? There are four of us and we are all Rankins now."

Beth looked at Rudy with tears in her eyes, and Rowdy answered quietly, "I like that name just fine, Rudy. R4 it is."

CHAPTER 68

A RAWHIDE OUTFIT

ROWDY BROUGHT HIS MAPS ALONG SO HE COULD trace the boundaries of their property. He was excited when he saw how close they came to one of the railroad's refueling stops. "Beth, we might be able to ship and receive horses from here instead of going all the way to Cheyenne."

Beth smiled at him. *Rowdy is always thinking of ways to improve and make things better. Why, he is just like Rueb except he does it with land and horses instead of people.*

They rode through a protected nook and Beth asked, "Can we stop for a little bit here, Rowdy? This is such a pretty area, and the sun feels so good."

Rowdy looked over at Beth and smiled as he nodded.

"We'll stop here. Ten-thirty is early for dinner, so you kids can play awhile. Be careful of that creek and stay off the ice. It's not thick enough yet. There are plenty of other places to play and explore though." He pointed toward a large rock.

"I'll bet if you climb to the top of that, you can see for miles."

As Rudy slid off, he hollered, "C'mon, Mari—let's go explore!" Maribelle followed him toward the big rock. They climbed it quickly

331

and were back down. They ran to the creek to see if there were any fish under the ice.

Rowdy leaned back against a rock. As he chewed on a stem of grass, he commented softly, "Maybe we should get them a dog. Kids should grow up with a dog. And Rudy needs a horse."

Beth kissed his cheek as she sat down on his lap. "You already sound like a father, and it has only been a day," she murmured softly as she kissed him again.

Rowdy pulled her close. "They make it pretty easy," he replied with an ornery grin, "but that doesn't mean we aren't going to keep trying for more." He pulled her closer for a long kiss, and they were laughing when Rudy ran up.

His eyes were worried, and his voice was high as he exclaimed excitedly, "We found a dog! It's stuck in the water and can't get out!"

Rowdy slid Beth off his lap and stood.

"You found a dog? Out here? You'd better show us where."

As Rudy raced off, Rowdy and Beth followed. When they rounded a turn in the small stream, they saw a puppy in the water. It was trying to climb the bank, but with all the ice in the water, the open spots were too steep. It kept falling back into the water. It was shivering and shaking as it tried time and again to climb out.

Rowdy reached down and grabbed the dog by the scruff of its neck. He pulled it out. As he lifted it up, he looked at Beth in surprise. "Why this is a Collie. How in the world would it get clear out here?"

Beth took the dog and wrapped it up in the blanket she had around her shoulders. She rubbed it vigorously to dry it off as quickly as possible.

Suddenly, they heard voices downstream. Several men were coming their way. The dog wiggled and yelped as it tried to get loose. Beth set it on the ground, and it promptly ran away. Rowdy pushed his family into the bushes. He turned to face the approaching men. Beth crouched down with the children and put her finger over her mouth.

Rowdy stood casually, blocking the path. He greeted the two men with a single, abrupt, "Howdy," as they walked toward him. His blue eyes were cool, and his face was still. This was *his* land, and he didn't want uninvited people on it.

The two men paused before they continued slowly toward Rowdy. Their eyes shifted from one side of the trail to the other. Once they decided the man in front of them was alone, they spread out a little as they approached. Both were dusty and wore tied-down guns.

One looked younger than the other, but his hat was over his eyes and Rowdy couldn't see his face. The older of the two men kept shifting his eyes away.

Putting his finger to his lips, Rowdy gave a shrill whistle. Smoke came charging up the trail and stopped beside him.

Rowdy asked quietly, "What are you boys doing way out here?"

The oldest one answered, "We was just passin' through. We been thinkin' on buyin' some land an' thought we'd look this piece over."

Rowdy continued to look hard at them and didn't answer.

The second man added, "We ain't lookin' fer no trouble. We lost our dog an' come to look fer 'im."

Rowdy nodded toward the puppy. It had stopped and was facing toward the men. "There's a dog. That the one you're looking for?"

When the older man started for the puppy, it growled, tucked its tail between its legs, and ran down the trail as it yelped.

Rowdy's eyes narrowed. "I'll walk with you back to your camp," he offered. "A feller could get hurt wandering around out here."

He lifted his rifle off the saddle and indicated for the men to turn around. The shorter man stared from Rowdy to the gun. He ducked his head as he walked.

Smoke was snorting, and Beth was terrified. She kept one arm around each child. As soon as the men were out of sight, she hurried them back to their picnic site. She grabbed Sister's reins and led her off the trail.

Beth very much wanted to follow Rowdy, but she knew he could take care of himself. She needed to keep the children safe.

Behind the large rock was a dip in the ground surrounded by bushes. Beth pulled the bushes aside and hurried the children through the opening. Sister didn't want to walk through the brush, so Rudy held the bushes apart while Beth pulled on Sister's bridle. The horse finally snorted and pushed through the small opening. Beth found more bushes on the far side and hurried the kids behind those, following with Sister.

Rowdy looked around the camp. It was a rawhide outfit. A cinch ring lay on the ground and was black from being used in the fire. Honest cowboys sometimes used their cinch rings to brand on the range but so did rustlers...and these men didn't look like working cowboys. Two men were lounging around the fire as the three of them walked up.

Rowdy's rifle casually covered them as he talked. "Howdy. My name is Rowdy Rankin and you boys are on my land. Maybe you can tell me what you all are doing here."

As the men by the fire slowly stood and started to spread out, Rowdy stepped away from his horse and pointed the rifle at the one by the fire whom he thought looked the most dangerous. Without warning, he cracked the rifle butt over the head of the young man in front of him. As the man dropped to the ground, Rowdy stated quietly, "Your number is looking better to me. Now who is going to start talking?"

The man to the right of the boss went for his gun and Rowdy shot him. The other two men looked stunned as they stared at their companion. The man Rowdy had shot was down, and he wasn't getting up.

Rowdy didn't shoot to warn—his warning was done when he dropped the first man. He levered another bullet into his rifle and stepped around the man closest to him to get a clear shot at the boss.

Smoke snorted and stepped closer. His nose was almost touching the man's back. When the man turned, Smoke's ears went back. He snorted again as he shoved the man with his head. The outlaw staggered across the clearing, almost falling into the fire.

As the man regained his balance, he cried, "Keep yer hoss away from me! He acts like he could hurt somebody!"

Rowdy stared at the two men and answered quietly, "I suggest you tell me what you rawhiders are doing here before I turn him loose and find my answers when I go through your packs."

The boss stood quietly and didn't answer, but the man Smoke had shoved spoke quickly. "We's jist passin' through. We ain't hurt no one an' didn't know this was yer land. We cin pack up an' be outta here in a shake."

Rowdy shook his head. "That cinch ring says otherwise."

The man who had spoken growled a curse and went for his gun. Rowdy touched Smoke's neck and the stallion charged. The man was shaken like a dog and then thrown up in the air. His screaming ended when Smoke's front feet stomped the life out of him.

Rowdy clicked his tongue and the horse backed up to stand beside him without taking his eyes off the last outlaw.

The last man standing didn't move. He stood still, careful to keep his hands away from his guns. He asked quietly, "Do you mind if I get a smoke from my pocket?"

Rowdy nodded but he followed the man's movements with his gun.

The outlaw lit his cigarette and stared at it for a moment before he looked up at Rowdy.

"Yore right. We're rustlers. We're a workin' for a big outfit down by Cheyenne. Yore a gonna have to kill me. If I tell ya who's runnin' this here deal, he'll kill me slow. Then he'll kill y'all an' all yore family. This here operation is bigger than ya know."

The outlaw on the ground had begun to stir and Smoke walked over to him. He rested his nose on the man's back and nibbled his shirt.

The standing outlaw looked at Rowdy and threw down his cigarette.

"Let's get this over with," he ground out and went for his gun.

Rowdy muttered a curse as he shot the man. The outlaw dropped and Rowdy moved over to kneel beside him.

The dying man looked up at Rowdy. His breath was coming in short gasps, but his voice was calm.

"I remember ya an' I remember that gun. Ya saved my bacon several times." As he grimaced in pain, he clutched Rowdy's shirt and gasped, "I shore didn't expect I'd ever die by yore hand."

As the outlaw fell back, Rowdy looked over the scene with bleak eyes. The man he had hit was coming to and Rowdy pulled him up.

He stared at the young man in surprise and grated out, "Paige, what are you doing with this outfit?"

The young man he called Paige was little more than a boy.

He muttered, "Sarge," with a hint of shame in his voice.

Rowdy stepped back from the young man.

"Private Paige, you have yourself in one heck of a spot," he growled. Frustration and anger were heavy in his voice as he stared down at the young man.

PRIVATE PAIGE DIED TODAY

PRIVATE PAIGE'S FACE TURNED PALE AS HE HELD himself upright.

"Sarge, no explanation would be good enough, but I'll tell ya anyway. I was ridin' the grub line with Spotty there," Paige explained as he pointed toward the dead man by the fire. "We wasn't pards, but we hired on together on several spreads. Then we come up on Morris in Laramie last month. He said he'd found a job an' they was hirin' riders. We was hungry, an' with winter comin' on, we decided to ride along." His face went bleak as he pointed toward the man Smoke had killed. "I didn't like Smithy, but Morris said he was alright. Ya remember Morris, don't ya?"

When Rowdy nodded slightly, Paige continued. "I always liked Morris. He saved my life at Shiloh an' I figgered I owed 'im." He looked around the fire at the bodies. "My old ma will be so ashamed of me," he stated quietly as he looked down.

Rowdy cursed silently. He pointed at the saddled horses and ordered, "Well, let's get some graves dug. I don't know what you are going to use but we'll need four."

Private Paige's face became even paler, but he nodded. He went to his horse and pulled out a shovel. When Rowdy looked at the shovel in surprise, Paige blushed. "We buried the hides of the cows we shot to eat."

Rowdy knew the inside of a cow hide would show that the brands had been reworked, and that was a sure sign of rustling in the area. He glared at Private Paige but didn't respond as he collected the guns. Then he left the private alone to dig the graves while he went back down the trail to get Beth and the children. He met Beth as she was coming out of the little copse.

The men's voices carried well down the hill. Beth heard most of their conversation as well as the gunshots. She was leading Sister with both Rudy and Maribelle mounted on the filly's back. As she looked at Rowdy's face, she could see the hardness and the sadness around his eyes. She moved quickly to his side and took his arm.

"Oh, Rowdy. We heard everything. Can we please save the boy? He sounded so young."

Rowdy looked at her grimly. He was thinking the same thing, but he just hadn't worked it all the way through.

Slowly, his eyes began to gleam, and his face lost some of its tightness. Taking Beth's arm, he whispered, "I think I have an idea."

As they walked back into the clearing, Private Paige looked up from his digging. He dropped his shovel and quickly removed his hat at the sight of Beth.

Rowdy pointed at the young man. "Beth, this is a fellow I knew some years back. We were in the same cavalry unit for a time.

"Private Paige, this is my wife, Beth. These are our kids, Rudy and Maribelle."

Private Paige looked a little confused, but he just nodded. He stood uncomfortably until Rowdy turned away. As he went back to his digging, he thought, *Sarge didn't have no wife or kids in the war. Shoot, he didn't even have a girl that I know of. An' his wife looks too young to have a son that boy's age—why that kid is eight or ten years old.* He shrugged his shoulders and dug deeper in the hard ground.

He paused once as he muttered to himself, "I sure wish I had stuck with Sarge instead of takin' up with Morris. My ol' ma will be mighty ashamed if she ever finds out I was hung fer rustlin' cattle."

Rowdy had Beth take the kids back to the little cove they originally camped in for their picnic. He sent the puppy with them, and he could hear their happy cries as they played with the little dog. He went over to where Paige was digging.

"That's deep enough," he said. "Take off their gun belts and roll them in those three holes."

As Private Paige covered their bodies with dirt, he thought more of his bleak future. *Sarge was never one to shirk a duty or to deal out pity,* he thought to himself as he covered the graves.

Rowdy brought up four markers. He set three of them in the ground on the mounds of dirt. One read Smithy, the second read Spotty, and the third read Private James Morris. The fourth was marked Private Hank Paige and each had the date: Nov. 14, 1870. Paige paled a little when he looked at his own marker.

Rowdy let him study it awhile before he ordered, "Fill that grave in and put the marker on it. Private Paige died today, so you will need to come up with a new name."

He turned away and walked out of the clearing, leading the four horses.

Hank Paige stared at Sergeant Rankin's back. That wasn't the Sarge he remembered.

There would have been no mercy given by the man I knew during the war, Private Paige thought. *Maybe someday, I can write my old ma a letter an' tell her I'm all right.* He slammed the shovel into the ground and cussed himself for being such a fool. Then he thanked the Good Lord for giving him a second chance.

A New Puppy

BETH HAD THE BLANKET SPREAD ON THE GROUND for a chilly picnic when Private Paige walked cautiously into the clearing carrying his shovel. Rudy and Maribelle were chasing the puppy, and the dog seemed to be as delighted as they were.

Rowdy looked up at him. "So, what do we call you?"

Private Paige paused a moment. "My ma's maiden name was Kraus and my pa's name was Henry. Just call me Hank Kraus."

Rowdy stood to shake his hand as he looked sternly at him. "It is a new beginning for you, Hank Kraus. Welcome to the R4."

Beth smiled at Hank.

"Would you like a sandwich, Hank? Rowdy's brother shared a smoked ham with us, and this is the last of it."

Hank looked at Rowdy and his face slowly paled again. "Lance Rankin is your brother?" he asked cautiously.

Rowdy looked hard at Hank, and the ice came back in his blue eyes. "Sure is. How many of his cows did you steal and where are they?"

"About eighty head. They are penned by the tracks. They are to be picked up this afternoon when the train stops to refuel."

Rowdy looked hard at Hank, and the man dropped his head as red crept up his neck.

"I'm sure sorry, Sarge. I knew it was wrong when I helped. I just kept thinkin' Morris would never do anything that dishonest. I told myself there had to be a reason for his actions."

Beth placed her hand on Rowdy's arm as he stared at Hank.

"Rowdy, we just need to get down to the tracks and turn them loose, don't we?" she interjected brightly.

As Rudy and Maribelle rushed up with the puppy, Rudy asked, "What is yer dog's name? We sure like 'im. Do you care if we play with 'im?"

Hank shook his head, "He's not my puppy. I reckon ya can call him whatever ya want."

Rowdy watched them run back towards the creek. "What's the story with the dog? Was he stolen as well?" he asked sarcastically.

Hank blushed again as he answered, "No, he was left behind when the train went through. Smithy claimed him as his dog. He was a mean man though, and the pup was afraid of him." He paused and added, "Smithy wanted to make the pup a fightin' dog, so he said we should all be mean to it. I don't take to hurtin' animals though an' I told him so.

"It didn't do no good, so I dropped the pup in the creek when Smithy took a—a—when Smithy relieved himself," he explained, as he looked at Beth with embarrassment. "I thought the dog would swim downstream an' climb out, but I forgot how cold the water was. I didn't think about the big chunks of ice either.

"I was just tired of Smithy a kickin' that pup. When he saw the pup was missin', he sent Spotty an' me to look for it. That's when we come up on y'all."

Rowdy stared at Hank for a bit before he spat out, "Any man who abuses animals will likely go on to do worse things. You should have left those boys. You could have even taken the pup with you."

Hank looked directly at Rowdy. "I swear, that was my intention. I was goin' to sneak off tonight an' head south. I knew the pup would come to me if I whistled an' that was what I was goin' to do.

"Morris watched us close though. I think he was suspicious when the dog disappeared." Hank paused and looked again at Rowdy.

"I messed up, Sarge. I don't know what ya have in mind fer me, but I know I don't deserve kindness from ya or any of yore family."

Rowdy cursed under his breath before he asked abruptly, "When did you pen those cattle and who all saw you do it?"

"Jist before ya come up on us. We was the only ones there. We did it fast an' cut out.

"Somebody on the train is part of it though 'cause there are always four open cars on the days we pen cattle. Nobody ever asks no questions neither. We show up to help 'em load, an' then we're gone until the next group is gathered."

"How often do you 'gather' cattle?" Rowdy asked as his eyes burned into Hank.

"We was only with Morris fer two weeks an' we shipped six herds of seventy to eighty head each time." Hank paused and his neck began to turn red again. "But only the last herd had the Rocking R brand."

Rowdy studied Hank and then shook his head. He got up and walked over to the horses. Two of them carried military brands and the other two had brands he didn't recognize.

"Which horse is yours?" he asked.

Hank indicated one with an Army brand. "We was each able to keep a horse when we mustered out."

"That one is mine an' the other army horse is Spotty's," Hank said as he pointed at the horses. "Smithy and Morris rode the nicer horses. Those brands are from a spread down in Kansas, but I don't know if they was stolen or not."

Rowdy glared at the young man and then grated out, "First, we will get Lance's cows, and then we are riding into Cheyenne to report this. We'll need to remember those horses' brands in case the sheriff can track them down.

"I want to get Lance's cows back to him. We'll ride over there tomorrow morning because I don't think the two of us can take them all the way back to his spread. Then, you, me, and Lance will have a heart-to-heart talk about your future." Rowdy scowled as he looked hard at Hank again.

Beth stood and said firmly, "Rowdy, you have three adults who can ride. If Rudy can handle a horse alone, let him ride one of the extra horses. Maybe the four of us can move those cattle."

Rowdy looked at Beth with surprise. He frowned but slowly nodded. "We just might be able to," he agreed as he thought it through. "Let's eat first. Then we'll head down to the tracks and collect those cattle."

He whistled for the kids and Smoke looked up with surprise. He knew that wasn't his whistle, but he wasn't used to Rowdy whistling for anyone but him. Rowdy laughed and petted his horse.

"Smoke, you are the best horse I ever owned."

As Rudy and Maribelle came on the run, Rowdy asked Rudy, "So do you think you would be able to handle a horse by yourself? I need an extra hand to move cattle."

Rudy's eyes grew large, and his face glowed with excitement.

"I can ride a mule by myself, so I reckon I can ride a horse." As he sat down to eat, Rudy was full of questions.

Rowdy laughed as he held his hands up.

"Whoa down there. Let's eat first. We are taking Lance's cattle back home. If you can help, that gives us four hands."

The meal was a quick one even though there was an argument ongoing the entire time about the puppy.

"I think her name should be Dolly. She's pretty an' she's fun to hold like my dolly is at home," stated Maribelle as she folded her arms and stuck out her lip.

Rudy was disgusted. "It's a boy dog, Mari! Ya can't give a boy dog a girl's name! I think we should call it Scout since we found it in the creek. He was probably explorin' an' fell in so Scout would be a good name."

Maribelle pushed out her bottom lip farther. "Okay, we can call him Scout, but sometimes, I am goin' to pretend he is a girl dog, an' I am goin' to call him Dolly!"

Rudy rolled his eyes and Rowdy grinned.

Beth smiled at them and pointed at the food.

"Let's talk about Scout later. Right now, you both need to eat so we can load the horses."

CHAPTER 71

A Real Cowboy

RUDY LOOKED AT ROWDY AND ASKED SHYLY, "DOES this mean I get to ride one of the horses by myself right now?" He paused and added with a grin, "It would be good practice for trailin' the cattle."

Rowdy laughed as he tousled Rudy's hair.

"Yes, it would be good practice. You help Beth clean up here while Hank and I get the horses packed. Then we will see if we can get those stirrups short enough for you."

Rowdy loaded all the outlaws' supplies and gear onto one of the extra horses. It would be inconvenient to lead horses while they trailed the cattle, but he couldn't see any other way. Maribelle was too small to ride by herself.

They found the cattle standing in the pens as Hank had described. They were bawling for water. Hank turned them out, and Rowdy kept an eye on them as they crowded around the tank to drink. Once they all drank their fill, Rowdy began to push them southeast. The cattle seemed to know where they were going and moved easily across the grass picking out a cow trail as they went.

Rowdy watched the cows, and the wheels in his mind began to spin.

He rode over to Beth. "Maybe we should just take the cattle on to Lance's right now. It isn't quite noon. We can be there in five or six hours, and they are moving easily."

Beth shook her head. "What about the milk cow and Waldo? His bandage needs to be changed."

Rowdy slowly nodded.

"We are only about three miles from our house now. Why don't you take the kids and go on home. I think Hank and I might be able to handle them from here."

Rowdy frowned as he looked over Beth's head and added, "I may be gone several days. It depends on how things go in Cheyenne."

Beth smiled up at him. "We will be fine, Rowdy, and we will be waiting for you when you get home."

Maribelle was sagging in the saddle already and Beth called to Rudy, "Come on, Rudy! We are going to head home and do chores. Hank and Rowdy can take the cows on from here by themselves. You need to milk the cow and check on Waldo."

As they rode away, Beth looked back and called out softly, "Rowdy." When he looked back, she blew him a kiss.

Rowdy grinned as he caught it. He kissed his hand before he put it in his pocket. Then he waved his hat to Beth and turned back to follow the herd.

Beth watched Rowdy's back as he followed the cattle. "How I love that man," she whispered to herself. She turned Sister around. Rudy was leading the horse with all the extra provisions and guns from the outlaw camp while Rowdy still led the second horse with the other Kansas brand.

Rudy was disappointed he wouldn't be going on a real cattle drive. Still, he was able to ride a horse by himself, so it wasn't all bad.

When Rowdy gave Rudy the reins of the extra horse, he ordered, "Keep a firm grip on the reins, but if that horse jerks his head, let him go. I would rather he get loose than you get hurt trying to lead a horse you aren't familiar with."

The horse followed easily though, and Rudy felt proud. *I'm riding a horse all by myself and leading one as well.*

"I know the way from here," and he said as he led their horses west.

"Your father would be so proud of you, Rudy," Beth said softly. "He loved all of you so much. He was a fine father. His dream was for you to grow up to be a good man."

Rudy thought about that. *Well, Pa liked Rowdy. I want to grow up to be like Rowdy.* He smiled shyly at Beth, and they rode for a while in silence.

Scout was getting tired, so Rudy carried him for the last two miles. He needed his hands free, so he tucked the little dog inside his jacket with just its head sticking out.

CHAPTER 72

CINCH RINGS AND CATTLE THIEVES

HANK WAS RELIEVED THEY WERE TAKING THE CATTLE back right away. He just wanted the entire ordeal to be over. *And if Sarge's brother is anything like him, it won't be good.*

They cut across the corner of Slim's ranch, and Tiny met them on the trail. He looked at the cattle and then at the brand. "Are ya in the cattle business now, Rowdy?" he asked in surprise.

Rowdy shook his head, "Nope. We came across some cattle thieves, and they were holding Lance's cattle. They'd reworked the brands. We had a little altercation, and they came out on the dead side. Hank here is helping me take them back to the Rocking R."

Tiny looked hard at Hank and then back at Rowdy.

Hank looked down at his horse's neck. *I feel guilty an' act guilty 'cause I am guilty,* he thought.

"I'd be glad to help if ya think ya need some. They seem to be movin' easy though."

"Naw. We're almost there. Thanks for your offer though." He pushed Smoke to a trot to catch Hank. "Tell Slim and Sadie hello," Rowdy called back as he rode away.

It was nearly dark when Lance heard cattle coming up the lane. As he stepped out of the barn, he recognized Rowdy. He squinted harder and then stood upright.

"Those are my cattle!"

He opened the gate to a small pasture and the cattle walked in, stopping to grab mouthfuls of grass as they headed for the water tank. Lance looked at Rowdy and then he looked hard at Hank.

"So, what's the story with the reworked brand?" he asked quietly as he studied the two of them.

"Let's talk over by the corral," Rowdy suggested.

As Lance led the way, Hank could feel the panic rising in his throat. Lance had the same hard blue eyes that the Sarge had, and they looked like they could be just as angry.

As they stopped at the corral fence, Lance and Rowdy leaned sideways with Hank between them.

Lance straightened to face Hank and asked coldly, "So what outlaw band were you with when you stole my cattle and used a cinch ring on my brand?"

Hank's face turned white, and he dropped his head. He slowly pulled himself erect and told Lance everything he had told Rowdy.

Rowdy added what Morris had said about connections to someone in Cheyenne.

"Whoever is heading this up must be mighty powerful because Morris was willing to die rather than face the ringleader."

Lance looked again at Hank. "I want you to write down all the brands you created with those cinch rings. You are going to draw them out on paper. I want an accounting for every single one," he stated coldly.

Then he looked at Rowdy. "What happens to him?" he asked as he pointed at Hank.

Hank's stomach was knotting as he waited for an answer.

Rowdy studied Hank. His face was still when he looked at Lance and answered quietly, "You know, I have been thinking about how well Joe and Hicks worked out for you...Smiley too. Think maybe there is some hope for Hank as well?"

A frown covered Lance's face, but a slow smile tugged on the corners of his mouth. His eyes glinted but he held his face hard.

"You had to bring that up, didn't you? Well, I don't need any hands although I am guessing you could use a man with all the horse business you have managed to put together.

"So how many graves are up there in your Spring Pasture?"

Lance laughed when Rowdy held up four fingers. He looked seriously at Hank.

"You are walking a fine line, Hank. If the ringleader of this rustling operation ever figures out you worked with Morris, your life won't be worth a plugged nickel. And if he figures out that you shared information, you are a dead man already."

Hank nodded slowly. "So, what are you going to tell the sheriff?" he asked.

Rowdy looked at him with a sly grin. "Why, everything you told me—you talked before you died, didn't you?" he asked with a glint of humor in his eyes. Then he added. "You work for me. You were riding the grub line just like you said, and I hired you."

Rowdy looked seriously at Hank and added quietly, "I won't lie for any man, but we can leave out a few details as long as you learned your lesson. Just know there won't be a second chance."

Hank looked at the two men. They looked enough alike to be twins instead of just brothers. He knew he'd made a big mistake, and he couldn't believe these two hard men were willing to give him a second chance.

He put out his hand to Lance. "I'm shore sorry I stole your cows. You have ever' right to hang me an' I'm plumb grateful for the second chance."

Then he turned to Rowdy. "An' you too, Sarge. I'm ashamed of myself, an' I will shore keep on a steady path from now on."

The men turned away from the corral just as Gus banged on the supper bell.

Lance pointed toward the ranch kitchen. "Let's go eat. Molly asked me to eat with the men tonight. She is still a little tired from our trip to your place."

He looked at Rowdy intently and asked, "How are the young'uns?"

Rowdy smiled. "They seem to be doing all right. Maribelle sticks close to Beth. Hank here gave them a stray puppy, and they are both excited about that. I wanted to get Rudy a horse and now we have an extra one from one of the bandits, so Rudy is pleased about that as well.

"And a big plus for us, he even likes to milk the cow!" Rowdy gave Lance a sly grin as he elbowed him.

Lance frowned. "Yeah, thanks for that. Molly has been on me to get a cow ever since you inherited yours. I am going to talk to Gus to see if he would want to milk it. I refuse to milk a cow," Lance growled with a surly look on his face.

The men headed into Gus's kitchen. A huge smile covered the old cook's face when he saw Rowdy. He loaded the hungry cowboy's plate to overflowing. Rowdy thanked him, and the two brothers headed up to the house to eat.

Hank stood to the side with his plate, trying to eat while standing.

"Come on," drawled Joe as he grabbed Hank's arm. "You cin eat in the bunkhouse with the rest of us."

Pausing inside the door to the bunkhouse, Joe introduced him.

"Fellers, this here is Hank. He's Rowdy's new hand." The men hollered out greetings around their food, and Hank began to eat. He paused, stared at his plate, and then ate faster. The rest of the men laughed.

"The grub is good here. Miss Molly cin cook too." Hicks added with a laugh, "We was some worried when Gus took over, but we ain't worried no more."

Joe had heard the conversation between Lance, Rowdy, and Hank. He was working in the blacksmith shed. He was building a gate and had just quit for the evening. As he quietly cleaned up and put his tools away, he listened to Hank's story.

The Rocking R was now his home, and Joe was grateful every day for the chance he had been given. The Rocking R riders accepted both Hicks and him, and it seemed like Lance was giving him more responsibilities. He was loyal to the brand as well as to Lance and Molly.

Joe knew how low Hank felt because he remembered his first day on the Rocking R as well. He remembered Hank too, although he doubted if Hank remembered him.

Hank had joined the outfit Joe was in shortly before the end of the war. Hank's unit had been ambushed, and Joe's unit, the 1st Regiment of the Georgia Reserves, found Hank wandering in the forest as they moved through. He was disoriented and hungry.

Joe pointed at an empty bunk. "You can throw your bed roll on there, Hank," he offered, "That bunk is an extry."

Hank nodded and thanked him.

When Hank had finished eating, he took his horse to the corral and unsaddled it.

Joe joined him as Hank was slinging the saddle over the corral bars.

"The Rankins are good folks," Joe stated quietly, "an' ya ain't the first hand they've given a second chance," he added as he looked intently at Hank.

Hank dropped his eyes and began to rub his horse down as Joe continued to talk.

"Folks make mistakes an' if yore lucky enough to git a second chance, ya take it an' ya move on. Us riders here, we ride fer the brand an' we ride tall.

"Don't mess up a second time or the Rocking R hands will come fer ya. You understand now how it's to be." Joe slapped Hanks' shoulder and added, "See ya inside," as he walked back into the bunkhouse.

Hank curried his horse and rubbed it down. As he petted it and turned to leave, the horse nuzzled his arm.

"Patch," Hank muttered, "You an' I have been together nigh on ten years. I think it's time we found a spread to make home. We need to quit this wanderin' 'round."

CHAPTER 73

HOW MANY BRANDS DOES ONE MAN NEED?

THE MEN WERE UP EARLY. LANCE DECIDED TO RIDE into Cheyenne with Rowdy and Hank to talk to the sheriff as well.

Hank had drawn out all the brands he had seen used, each on a separate piece of paper. As Lance studied them, he could feel the anger boiling up inside him. There was a cinch brand to cover just about every brand around Cheyenne, certainly for all the larger operations.

"Whoever is running this swindle has full knowledge of our area," Lance commented as he studied the brands.

Rowdy agreed, but besides reporting the stolen cattle, he also wanted to talk to the railroad about shipping horses closer to his place. Thanks to the cattle thieves, he knew the area that would work.

"Maybe I will be able to rattle a few timbers myself if I start asking questions," he added with a scowl.

Once again, Rowdy, Lance, and Hank ate with the men. They were on the road to Cheyenne by seven that morning. Rowdy and Lance hashed over every angle they could think of, but no ideas of who was in charge surfaced.

Finally, Hank spoke up. "Mebbie the Kansas horse brands mean somethin'. Do ya have a brand inspector in Cheyenne? He could mebbie tell ya where they come from."

Both men looked at him with their piercing blue eyes, and Hank was instantly agitated.

He looked from one to the other and said seriously, "Ya fellers need to quit drillin' me with yore eyes. It's a plumb uncomfortable feelin'."

Rowdy looked surprised and Lance chuckled.

"We have heard that before," Lance agreed, humor glinting in his eyes. "You keep coming up with good ideas, and we'll try harder not to glare at you."

When the three arrived in Cheyenne, they decided the brand inspector would be their first stop.

Lance showed the brands to the inspector, and he looked surprised.

"Why all those brands are registered to one man. He is a businessman right here in Cheyenne. His name is Berger, Emmett Berger. He owns one of the larger watering holes, the Bucking Horse Saloon."

Lance scowled a moment before he asked, "Does he own a ranch?"

The inspector nodded his head, "Yes, he has a little spread just west of town two or three miles. It butts right up to the railroad tracks. I don't think he has a wife, but he is quite social. He always has lots of guests coming and going out there it seems."

Rowdy looked hard at the inspector. "Don't you think it a little odd that a man needs that many brands?"

The inspector turned a little red as he responded slowly, "I guess I never thought much about it."

When Rowdy snorted, the brand inspector turned a deeper red.

As the men left, the inspector called after them, "Berger should be in the Bucking Horse by ten. He usually takes his breakfast there about that time."

Lance and Rowdy said nothing as they left the brand inspector's office. Once they were outside, they both turned toward the rail station without speaking.

Hank shook his head in amazement as he followed them. *These two men act alike and think alike.*

At the rail station, Rowdy asked who he needed to talk to about loading and unloading horses at a refueling point between Cheyenne and Laramie.

The station agent paused before he spoke. "We don't do that very often," he answered slowly, "and before it takes place, it must be approved by Mr. Johnson. Charles Johnson. He's not in yet, but you might catch him at the Wild Horse. He sometimes eats there."

Rowdy's face tightened, but he managed to grind out a thank you as the three left.

Lance commented dryly, "Well, the net just keeps getting a little tighter now, doesn't it? Who all wants some breakfast? I think I'm feeling a little hungry, and I know Rowdy can eat any time."

He gave the two men a hard grin as he elbowed his brother.

Rowdy growled an answer, and the three men walked back up the street to the Bucking Horse Saloon.

The crowd was small at nine. As the men walked in, they saw a gentleman with a railroad insignia on his jacket sitting by himself.

Lance led the way to his table. He pulled out a chair and sat down with a smile. "Howdy. Breakfast good here? I hear you take your meals here pretty much every day."

The man looked up. His eyes went from the taller of the two men who looked alike to the second one and then back to the first. Another man was standing behind them. He said nothing.

Lance reached out his hand. "My name is Lance Rankin, and we were told you might be here. Mr. Johnson, isn't it? We just want to talk to you a little over breakfast. We are interested in shipping some horses through one of your refueling points between here and Laramie. We understand you are the man to talk to if that is going to happen."

Lance's face was bland, and he was smiling. However, if Molly had been there, she would have been patting his arm to calm him down as fury was just below the surface.

Rowdy was not as good as Lance at masking his anger. His blue eyes bored into the man as he glared at him.

Charles Johnson ignored Lance's outstretched hand. He picked up his napkin and gently dabbed his lips. *Who do these cowboys think they are? I am an important man, and I won't have my breakfast interrupted by men who make their living following the hind end of a cow.*

Johnson's disdain came across clearly on his face. Lance could feel Rowdy starting to growl. He dropped his hand but kept smiling as he waited for Johnson's answer.

Charles Johnson looked at the men in front of him coldly and replied, "We don't pick up livestock on the sidetracks. You will need to ship from Cheyenne or Laramie like everyone else. Now if you will excuse me?"

As Johnson started to stand, Lance's smile disappeared, and his hard hand shoved the railroad man back in his chair. He leaned across the table putting his face close to Johnson's.

"Well, that is mighty interesting," Lance growled. He spat the words at Johnson as he continued, "We just found eighty head of my cattle in a pen waiting to be picked up this morning at one of those very stops. Now I understand you are the man who makes those stops happen, so you must be the same man who makes sure there are four empty rail cars available on just the days when cattle are penned there."

Johnson's face blanched white. He shrank back in his chair as Rowdy stood and circled the table to stand close to him. Charles Johnson found himself two men who looked exceptionally dangerous to him.

Just then, Rowdy saw a tall, over-bearing man with pale skin and a gold watch hanging over his large chest push through the doors of the saloon. As Rowdy locked eyes with the man, he could feel a reckless fury rising inside him.

The bartender nodded at the large man. "Good morning, Mr. Berger." Berger looked briefly toward Johnson's table. Then he went around the bar and through a door to his private office.

Rowdy turned quickly to follow. As he reached for the doorknob, the bartender jerked his arm and Rowdy exploded. He slammed the bartender's face against the bar and broke his nose, dropping him with one hand. Then he walked behind the bar and pulled out the sawed-off shotgun that was hidden there. With the shotgun in his hands, Rowdy kicked the door open.

A gun fired from inside the office as Rowdy sprang to the side and then jumped through the doorway, covering Berger with the shotgun. Emmett Berger was lifting his pistol for a second shot when Rowdy leveled the shotgun at his stomach and stepped closer.

"You do what you think you should, Berger, but was I you, I would do anything I could to avoid buckshot in the belly. That is a hard death, even for a lowdown thief like you."

As Berger dropped the gun, he sneered at Rowdy.

"You got nothin' on me. Go ahead and take me to jail. I'll be out by supper time."

Rowdy stared at him and thought a bit before he responded calmly, "Yes, you might at that as we don't know just how deep this deal goes. However, there is a United States marshal coming through here this week. We just might make an appointment with him."

Rowdy winked and gave Berger an evil grin. "Of course, we could take you to Fort Sanders by horseback since that's the county seat. I'd even let you ride my horse.

"Smoke's a canny judge of character, and he just plumb goes crazy if he don't like you. Notional, that's what he is, just notional."

Berger's face paled at the implication. It turned even whiter when Rowdy shoved the shotgun directly into his stomach.

"Get up," Rowdy growled as he pushed him again with the shotgun. "Let's go talk to your railroad buddy out there."

As Rowdy shoved Berger through the office door, Charles Johnson grimaced and dropped his arm. Hank slammed his gun down on the man's wrist knocking a Derringer loose from his sleeve.

As Johnson grabbed his hand and cried out in pain, Lance jerked him up and slapped him across the face. "You lowdown coward! You don't even deserve a good punch." Lance proceeded to slap Johnson three more times, so hard that the man's head whipped back and forth.

The bartender was shaking his head and trying to stand when Rowdy's fist smashed him, dropping the man a second time.

Several of the patrons stared at him and Rowdy grinned at them. "He keeps poor company."

As Rowdy and Lance shoved the two men outside, Lance told Hank to get a hammer and some nails. The proprietor of the dry goods store handed them to Hank with no questions and followed him outside to see what was going on.

Lance nailed the pictures of the brands to the outside of the Bucking Horse Saloon.

Men began to gather out of curiosity, and Lance turned around to face the crowd.

"These brands are all registered under Emmett Berger's name. They can all be created with a cinch ring and can cover nearly every brand in this area." Lance paused as the men in the street began to murmur.

"We just found eighty head of my cattle penned by the tracks between here and Laramie. You will find four marked graves several miles from the tracks where the rustlers were found. Johnson here is the man who controls what and where the railroad picks up and drops off at those refueling stops." He let that sink in before he added, "And every time a herd of cattle shows up in the pen there, he just happens to have open cars on his train."

Lance waited a moment until the noise in the crowd died down. "Berger has a little spread east of town two or three miles. I can't believe he would be stupid enough to hold cattle there, but it does butt right up next to the tracks. It might behoove some of you to check that out."

Several cowboys headed for their horses. Within minutes, ten riders were racing out of town.

Lance continued, "We have a sheriff here, but he is out of town for three days. A United States marshal is supposed to be riding through about that same time. I guess the question is what to do with these fellows? I know I am too busy to play nursemaid to them until the law gets back."

He looked over the crowd and then back at the rustlers.

"Who all here is missing cows?" Hands began to go up as those present called out the names of their ranches or brands.

A quiet man in the front suggested, "Why don't we wait until those riders get back? Maybe they will have more cattle. They might even find someone who will testify."

There was some grumbling but most agreed. Lance and Rowdy shoved the two men into jail cells, and the quiet man offered to watch them until the riders returned.

The ten cowboys were back in an hour. They were driving about two hundred head of cattle they had found penned on Berger' place. They also had three prisoners who were found with the cattle. One of the ten cowboys had a ledger, and another had broken open the safe in Berger's house. He was carrying cash that had been found there.

The three outlaws were quiet and pale. Their hands were tied to their saddle horns, and they made no effort to defend themselves or get away. The ledger and cash were taken to the bank and locked in the vault. The cattle were penned and counted before they were sorted to go back to their original owners.

Volunteers offered to build gallows. However, there was a large tree in the middle of town, and the citizens decided that would work.

The telegraph operator sent an urgent message to Laramie. He asked for a marshal and a judge to be sent as soon as possible.

A few minutes later, the telegraph operator rushed out into the street waving the response as he shouted, "The judge will be here this afternoon! He is coming in on the four-fifteen train from Laramie."

The quiet man who was guarding the prisoners urged the crowd to move inside.

"The judge will be here in four hours. Let's let justice take its course. You men go on now. We'll have a trial, and you can all attend."

CHAPTER 74

Judge William T. Jones

JUDGE WILLIAM T. JONES ARRIVED AS PROMISED THAT afternoon, perhaps because the telegraph message read,

All Hell breaking loose in Cheyenne. Large rustling ring cracked. Ringleaders may be lynched.

The judge announced that court would be held at seven the next morning.

He was hoping to be back on the nine-thirty train to Laramie that same morning. His wife was due to have a baby any time, and he didn't want to be the recipient of her wrath if he missed the birth of their first child.

Justice Jones, at age twenty-seven, was young for a judge. However, he was known as a cool and impartial man. His tolerance for lawbreakers was low, and he believed that thievery was among the vilest of crimes.

He met with Berger and Johnson immediately. They both were able to hire lawyers, and he suggested they do so. His next visit was to the three cowboys who were found with the cattle. None of them had any money. All were riding the grub line and had hired on for an easy winter job. They were subdued, but one asked if all three could get off if they told what they knew.

The judge looked at them hard. "What information do you want to share?" he asked.

The cowboys looked at the judge and then at each other. One slowly stated "The men you have on trial are not the ringleaders. It goes way higher, and we have the name of that person."

The judge stared at them before he replied, "I will have a lawyer appointed for you. Tell him your story."

His next stop was the bank where he picked up the ledger. He checked to make sure no pages had been torn from it.

"I wish this had been sealed before it was locked up," he muttered to himself as he tucked it under his arm. He checked into the Rollins House and asked for an evening meal to be delivered to his room. He asked young hotel clerk, "If you were in trouble, who in Cheyenne would you want to hire as your lawyer?"

The young man paused for a moment before he replied, "John Street is one of the best when he's sober."

Judge Jones nodded his head. "Can you arrange for Mr. Street to meet me in my room as soon as possible?" he asked.

The young man nodded his head, and the judge thanked him. As he settled in for a night of studying, Judge Jones was amazed at the amount of money Berger and Johnson had siphoned out of Cheyenne. He was also amazed not only at their audacity but at their ability to rustle undetected for over a year.

John Street knocked on Judge Jones' hotel room door at seven that evening. His eyes were bloodshot, but he appeared to be sober.

The judge glared at him.

"Three young men in the jail need your services. The trial begins at seven tomorrow morning. I suggest you meet with them immediately and in private—even if you have to pull them out of jail and take them somewhere else."

He scribbled a note giving the jailer permission to release the prisoners in the custody of their lawyer.

"We will pick a jury in the morning at seven sharp. I am sure we will have a deep bench to choose from looking at the crowd in the street. Stay sober tonight and don't be late!"

John Street rubbed his stubbly face with a shaky hand as he agreed. He backed out of the room and walked quickly to the jail. He presented the paper to the jailer and escorted the three cowboys to his office down the street.

The three young men told what they knew, and Street's hands shook as he wrote down their testimony. He looked at the three with clear eyes when they finished.

"You fellows be ready tomorrow to tell your story just like you told me today. I can't make you any promises because cattle rustling is a hanging offence. However, the information you gave me could possibly break this ring, and that might account for something."

CHAPTER 75

JUSTICE IN CHEYENNE

COURT WAS CONVENED IN THE LARGEST SALOON IN town which was the Gold Room Saloon. Gaming tables had been moved and extra chairs were set up. The judge didn't know the names of many residents around Cheyenne in 1870, but he did have the ledger. He certainly did not want any of the folks whose names were listed there to be on a jury.

When he asked for volunteers to serve on the jury, Maggie Jones, an employee in the dry goods store raised her hand. John Street agreed, but Royal Adams, the lawyer for Berger and Johnson, laughed.

"Women can't serve on a jury," he scoffed.

Judge Jones stared at Adams. "I hope you did a better job preparing your case than this, Mr. Adams. They can and did already last year. Approved. Next."

The jury was picked in fifteen minutes. Most of the names on Royal Adams' list were named in the ledger. They were turned away while John Street accepted most of the volunteers. Once the jury was picked, Judge Jones called for a five-minute break before the start of the trial. He called the lawyers forward and showed both the ledger.

Royal Adams turned purple. "I should have had this last night," he sputtered as he read the names and amounts listed there.

"Your clients should have told you about it. Then you could have asked to see it," Judge Jones replied coldly.

John Street was amazed. It backed up everything his clients had told him. He flipped through looking for the key name they had given him, and he noted it, along with the amounts and the number of entries. He took his seat with a smile on his face.

As the trial began, Royal Adams began to call witnesses, most of whose names were listed in the ledger.

As they came forward to take their oath, Judge Jones showed them the ledger and their name. Nearly all of them decided not to testify, and horses could be heard racing down the street after each of them hurried out of the saloon.

Royal Adams then called Charles Johnson to the stand. The judge handed Adams a piece of paper that showed how much money Johnson had collected from Berger for the use of the rail cars. Adams began to sputter. He tried to release Johnson from the stand, but Street cried foul. The courtroom erupted in chaos and the judge banged his gavel to return order.

A Central Pacific Railway representative was in attendance since one of their top employees was on trial. When he heard about the rail cars, he left to check the train manifests to see if all money was accounted for. Upon his return, the rail representative volunteered to testify. Adams tried to refuse him, but the judge accepted the man as a witness.

Royal Adams stared from Johnson to Berger. He pulled their heads together as he whispered, "You have given me nothing to support your cases. The prosecution is holding all the cards. If you have anything you are holding back, I need to know it *now*."

His talk did no good. Neither man told him anything.

Lance presented the drawings of the brands and explained how they could be made with a cinch ring while Rowdy testified about the cinch ring, the penned cattle, and the four graves.

The ten cowboys who had brought the two hundred head of cattle in from Berger's ranch had appointed a spokesman, and he presented a tally for each altered brand in the herd.

The bank gave an accounting of the money found in Berger's safe. Sheriff Boswell returned early, and the judge ordered him to open Johnson's safe. Sheriff Boswell presented those items to the court.

Then John Street asked for his first defendant to come forward.

The cowboy was known as Chancy Jones. The other two were Vic Miller and Tobe Smith. Chancy told how the three of them had taken the job, how long they had worked for Berger, and the number of gathers they had made. As he talked, Judge Jones made notes and checked the ledger. Finally, John Street asked Chancy Jones if he or either of the other two defendants had anything else to add.

As Chancy's eyes moved around the courtroom, a well-dressed man in the back stood and moved hurriedly toward the door. He tried to get out of the courtroom, but the sheriff blocked the door.

Chancy stated quietly, "This rustling ring is a lot wider than just Cheyenne. The top guy is a cattle buyer. I was out late one night, and I came up on Berger and him talking. He gave Berger orders, and Berger carried them out. His name is Jack Sneld, and he is back there by the door."

Rowdy and Lance both looked toward the back of the room in shock, and Jack pulled a gun. He pointed it at the sheriff, "Get out of the way!" he shouted.

Pandemonium broke out and three men tackled Jack Sneld from behind, smashing him to the floor and removing his gun.

Judge Jones banged on the desk with his gavel and asked if anyone else wanted to testify. When no one responded, the judge set a box on his desk.

The room was quiet as the judge removed items that came from Johnson's safe. Among the money and papers, Judge Jones found a letter from Jack Sneld to Charles Johnson. At the end of the letter, Jack told Johnson to destroy the letter so there would be no evidence of their relationship.

The judge read the letter aloud, and Jack Sneld shouted at Johnson, "You fool! Why did you keep that letter!"

Johnson looked back at Sneld coldly and answered, "Because I didn't trust you. I knew if this operation went down, you would try to hang all of this on Berger and me."

Jack Sneld was not originally on trial, but the judge quickly added his name to the list of defendants.

Judge Jones recessed for forty-five minutes for the jury to decide their verdict. He handed the cash to the quiet man who had guarded the prisoners and said, "Make sure this goes to the bank. Get an accounting and have them put it with the cash from Berger's safe."

"Court will resume at eight-thirty," he ordered as he banged his gavel and stood.

Most of the crowd moved to the bar for drinks. Trials were good for business, especially one as lively as this one had been. The Gold Room even offered half-price drinks during the recess.

Rowdy and Lance were quiet. It shocked them both that Jack was part of the rustling ring. Rowdy especially was surprised. That shock turned to anger. He walked over to Jack and stood staring down at him.

Jack looked up at Rowdy angrily. "Don't give me your high and mighty look. You Rankins always thought you were better than everyone else with your hard lines on right and wrong.

"We may have been best friends at one time, but times change, and people change. You go on home to your pretty little wife. I'm guessing you married her for her money anyway. I don't need your sympathy, and I certainly don't need your friendship."

Rowdy's face went cold at the mention of Beth. As he drew back his fist, Lance grabbed him and jerked him away.

"We are still in court, and you don't want to be found in contempt," Lance whispered loudly. "Let it go. Jack changed long ago, and you can't do anything to bring him back to the friend you once knew."

Rowdy looked back at Jack again before he went to the other side of the room to sit down. His heart hurt. He hadn't made many good friends over the years, and he had just lost one of them. As a knot built in his throat, he thought about Beth. Somehow, just thinking of her pretty face and bright smile made him relax.

He glanced once again at Jack's angry face and tight mouth, and he felt his anger start to fade away. *Cheyenne is my new home. I am surrounded by family I know and trust here.* He was sorry for Jack, but Lance was right—there was nothing Rowdy could do for Jack now.

The jury was back in thirty minutes, and Judge Jones called court back into session. The jurors had chosen J. C. Abney as their foreman, and he held the verdicts in his hand. As Judge Jones called out each name, the foreman was to state guilty or not guilty.

The judge started with Emmett Berger and the response was "Guilty."

"Charles Johnson."

"Guilty."

"Jack Sneld."

"Guilty."

"Chancy Jones, Vic Miller, and Tobe Smith."

"Not Guilty."

The room murmured in surprise as the foreman sat down.

Judge Jones glared at Chancy Jones, Vic Miller, and Tobe Smith. "You boys pack up and head out of Wyoming Territory. There is no place for you here. If you ever step foot in Cheyenne again or in any part of this territory, I am going to forget that you were found not guilty. And in this case, the 'not guilty' verdict certainly doesn't mean you're completely innocent."

As the three cowboys rushed from the courtroom, the judge turned his hard eyes on the leaders of the rustling operation.

"You men are sentenced to hang by the neck at noon today. You may ask for a visit with the pastor of your choice and for your family to be notified. In addition, you may have either breakfast or dinner but not both.

"The cash taken from the two safes will be divided among the ranches whose cattle were stolen." He pointed at Sheriff Boswell. "Take the ledger over to the bank. There are records of cattle numbers in the back of it. The bank accountant and you will decide how the money is dispersed. Court adjourned!"

After he banged the gavel, Judge Jones stood and looked at his watch. *Eight-forty. I have time to grab some breakfast before I catch that train*, he thought with satisfaction.

As he walked out of the Gold Room, he tipped his hat to Maggie Jones. *I'm guessing she pushed for the acquittal of those three cowboys. Hard to tell though. Sometimes the women on these juries are tougher than the men. Well, maybe they will learn from this. If not, I'll see them at another trial, and they won't be so lucky.*

CHAPTER 76

A Good Friend Gone

ROWDY WALKED OVER TO WHERE JACK SNELD WAS being pulled to his feet. He followed as the man was led to jail.

"I'd like to talk to him alone if you don't mind."

Sheriff Boswell left the cell door open and nodded as he left the cell area, closing another door behind him.

Jack was looking down. When he finally looked up at Rowdy, he was surprised at the pain he saw in Rowdy's eyes.

Rowdy cleared his throat and began to speak softly, "Jack, I'd like to notify your family if you don't mind. I believe your folks have the right to know that you won't be coming home." He paused and added, "Your wife too if you have one. Maybe you would like to write them letters. I will make sure they are posted."

Jack looked up, stunned at what Rowdy had just offered. Tears filled his eyes as he shook his head.

"I don't know what to tell my folks and there is no wife. I almost married little Mary Taylor—she was younger than us, so you probably don't remember her. She lived right up the creek.

"Mary caught wind of some of my shady deals. She refused to marry me until I made an honest living."

"I'm sorry for what I said back there. I always admired how you took a hard line on ethics. I always saw the world as gray when it came to right or wrong, but you never waffled on the important things." Jack looked away and pondered softly, "Maybe if you hadn't died in Columbus, you would have kept me on the right track."

Rowdy didn't answer. He could feel the tears in his eyes. Not only had this man been his best friend, but numerous times during the war they had covered each other's back.

When he looked up, Jack's eyes were full of tears.

"Just so you know, Rowdy, I gave the boys strict orders not to touch Lance's cattle."

Rowdy's face tightened, and Jack added with a wry grin, "Yeah, it wasn't just because we were friends—I knew if you Rankins became involved, you wouldn't stop digging until you found answers." Jack's face became somber again.

"I wasn't dishonest in the beginning. I loved buying cattle and working with the ranchers. Once the price of beef started to jump, I just got greedy. I asked myself, why make $.50 per head when I can take it all?" The man paused. "Greed. It took over and it ruined me."

He pulled a picture out of his wallet and handed it to Rowdy.

"Mary's address is on the back. She told me to write her when I was ready to come back." He stared at the tintype for a moment and swallowed a sob that was coming up in his throat.

"If you don't mind letting her know I won't be coming home, I would sure appreciate it." Jack's eyes were full of pain as he stared hard at Rowdy. "I know you won't try to gloss things over but maybe you can tell her I am sorry. Next to you, she is the best person I have ever known. She's a fine woman and I was a fool to leave."

Tears leaked out of Rowdy's eyes, and he reached his hand out to this man who had been like a brother to him most of his life.

"Goodbye, Jack. I will miss our friendship." Rowdy released Jack's hand and stepped away from the cell. He turned quietly and left the jail.

Sheriff Boswell said nothing as Rowdy wiped his eyes before walking out the door. He watched as the man paused briefly before crossing the street to the dry goods store.

Isaac Herman had been at the trial and had watched the exchange between the leader of the rustling gang and Rowdy. He had also watched Rowdy follow the sheriff to the jail. When Rowdy walked into the dry goods store, Isaac handed him several envelopes and some paper. As Rowdy looked at the man in surprise, Isaac smiled.

"Most folks are not all bad, Rowdy. Sometimes you have to dig a little, but oftentimes a little good is there just hoping to get out." He pointed behind the counter at his small office. "You're welcome to use my desk if you want. Not much for privacy but that's kind of hard to find around here anywhere."

Rowdy gave the man a bleak smile and accepted the writing material. Isaac pulled the curtain shut and Rowdy stared at the paper in front of him. He held the picture of the young woman in front of him and cursed softly. Finally, he started to write.

November 16, 1870

Miss Taylor,

I write this letter as a mutual friend awaits his hanging. Jack Sneld was tried and convicted today of cattle theft. He was the leader of a well-organized gang of cattle rustlers operating here in the Wyoming Territory.

Jack was my best friend growing up. We also served together during the war. We lost contact during the battle of Columbus in Georgia, but our paths crossed several months ago here in Cheyenne.

I had no idea Jack was involved in rustling—in fact, I was stunned when it came out during the trial. The Jack I knew was a fun-loving fellow who would do anything for a friend in need, right down to sharing his last dollar. In fact, he did that for me several times during the War for Southern Independence. He also saved

377

my life numerous times at the risk of his own. I'm not sure when Jack went bad, but I know I will miss him.

Jack would like your forgiveness. He told me you were the best thing he ever walked away from. Please know he is sorry. He does have a little time to make things right with the Lord before he dies.

I am sorry to send you this sad letter, but I believe you have the right to know what happened to him. I will leave town today before the hanging as I can't bear to watch it.

Don't worry about telling Jack's folks. I know them well and will send them a letter even though it will break his mother's heart. May God spread his mercy on our friend.

Sincerely, Paul Rankin
Cheyenne, Wyoming Territory

Rowdy quickly penned a letter to Jack's parents before he stood. He thanked Isaac and shook the man's hand.

Isaac watched Rowdy cross the street to the stage office. He murmured under his breath, "Cheyenne sure gained a good citizen when Rowdy moved to town. That young man is one of the finest men I have ever met."

Rowdy handed the station agent the letters and money to post them without speaking. The agent stared for a moment at the name on the second envelope. Martha and Harold Sneld, Macon, Georgia. He nodded at Rowdy and put the letters in the pouch to go out on the stage.

"If you wouldn't mind taking this over to the jail, I think Jack Sneld might like to have it back." Rowdy held out Mary's tintype. His hand shook a little as the station agent took it.

"I'll make sure he gets it," the agent replied quietly.

Rowdy Rankin walked out of the stage station and took a deep breath. His stomach was growling, and he headed to the Ford House. "If Lance hasn't already left town, he will be eating there," he muttered as he took another deep breath and wiped his eyes again.

CHAPTER 77

A Second Chance

LANCE AND HANK WATCHED ROWDY FOLLOW THE sheriff out of the courtroom. Lance pointed down the street and signaled Hank to join him.

"Let's go have some breakfast at the Ford House. Rowdy is going to be tied up for a bit. Besides, I figure I owe you for catching Johnson's sleeve gun. You saved my bacon, so the least I can do is buy you a meal."

Hank grinned. "I was watchin' him 'cause I noticed how he favored that arm. There was an officer in our unit who carried a small sleeve gun. It was against regulations but by the end of that war, we were usin' anything we could to give us an edge. The captain, he showed me how he could get it into action quick-like.

"Johnson wasn't near so smooth as Captain Plant, so I was ready for 'im."

Lance nodded as he thought about what the man had said.

"You were in the same unit as Rowdy?"

Hank nodded. "Sergeant Rankin was a sharpshooter. They moved him around some, but we were both part of the Georgia Light Artillery at the Battle of Columbus." Hank paused and commented softly, "Sarge was hard—there was no give in him at all. He didn't smile much an' he didn't talk to us unless he needed to give an order. We lost so many men. I think maybe he just didn't want to know who we was."

Hank looked out the window as he added, "He was fair though, an' he put himself in harm's way to save the fellows. We all liked an' respected him.

"The Yankees called him One Shot because he was so deadly with his gun. Sergeant Rankin hit what he aimed at." Hank looked at Lance again.

"He's softer now. No way would he have given me a second chance five years ago. He doesn't seem to be wound so tight now as he used to be neither."

"Beth is good for him. She's bright and happy." Lance laughed and added, "In fact, Rowdy met her at his grave. They buried another fellow under Rowdy's name, and Beth met him when he was reading his own tombstone."

Both men laughed. Lance was quiet for a time. Finally, he looked hard at Hank.

"So, what are your plans, Hank? Do you intend to stick around or are you moving on?"

Hank looked down at the table before he met Lance's gaze.

"I'd like to stay on if Rowdy will have me. I always admired him, an' I figure I owe the two of you for givin' me a second chance. I like workin' with horses an' my pop loved mules. I worked an' trained both before the war though I ain't done much of either since then."

Barney came by and Lance ordered their food.

"Rowdy will be joining us in a little bit so you might want to put on another ham," Lance joked.

Barney smiled and hurried back to the kitchen.

Rowdy walked through the door just as the food arrived. He gave Barney a big grin when the smiling owner returned with two plates.

"I have a third on the warmer, Rowdy, just in case you want three," Barney told him with a smile.

Rowdy grinned and it wasn't long before the third plate was placed in front of him.

Joe from the telegraph office came in as they were finishing. When he saw the Rankins, he stopped by their table.

"Telegraph came in for the sheriff a little bit ago, Rowdy. It showed no horses missing with the brands that you gave him. Sheriff Boswell is kind of busy this morning with the hanging and all. He told me to tell you to just keep those two horses with the Kansas brands. Pay the bill at the livery, and they are yours."

Rowdy thanked him and the three men were quiet as Rowdy scraped his third plate.

Samuel greeted the men as they entered the livery. He led out one of the horses with the Kansas brand and handed the reins to Rowdy.

"Looks like you picked up a couple of new mounts. I don't know what the other one looks like, but this is a fine animal.

Rowdy nodded and accepted the reins.

Samuel put his hand on Rowdy's shoulder.

"Sure was sorry to hear about your friend." He squeezed the younger man's shoulder before he turned back into the barn.

Rowdy looked after him without speaking. He quietly led Smoke and the other horse outside. Hank followed with his horse.

Lance grinned at Rowdy.

"Same, I think my father-in-law almost likes you better than me," he said as he bumped his brother.

Rowdy growled and Lance laughed.

Hank dug his toes in the dirt as Rowdy tightened Smoke's cinch. He finally looked over at Hank and asked gruffly, "Well, are you coming?"

Hank grinned and the two men turned their horses west.

Just then, Samuel hollered from the livery door as he waved a paper.

Rowdy rode back and Samuel handed him the sheet he was holding.

"I just received the manifest for your horses, Rowdy. They will be arriving on this morning's train which is due in just a few minutes. I thought you might want to pick them up before you left town."

Rowdy took the paper from Samuel. "I forgot they were coming in." He looked seriously at Samuel and added, "Thanks for catching me. I guess I was a little distracted today."

As the train pulled into the Cheyenne station, Rowdy asked the conductor for the car number on the manifest. The agent offered to walk with him. He put out his hand to Rowdy as he introduced himself.

"I heard you recovered some stolen livestock penned along the tracks between here and Laramie. My name is Howard Cox. I am replacing Charles Johnson."

Rowdy was surprised as he shook the man's hand.

"The railroad sure didn't waste any time putting a new fellow in that position, did they? The name is Rowdy Rankin, and it's good to meet you." He studied Cox a moment and then asked, "Say, what are the chances of loading and unloading livestock along the route between here and Laramie? I'm a sizeable distance from both towns, and it would save me a lot of miles if I could ship and receive there."

Cox thought for a moment. "I don't see a problem with that. You will need to have someone available to load and unload, and the earlier we know you need cars for shipping, the better. If we have several who want to use the pens, we will have all of you gather at the same set of pens. We will only load or offload stock once between the towns each trip."

Cox paused and then added, "Of course, if you are going to ship or receive large numbers, those will need to go through the yards in one of the towns."

Rowdy agreed and thanked him as the two men shook hands again.

CHAPTER 78

Finally Home!

WHEN ROWDY PULLED OPEN THE RAIL DOOR, A spirited thoroughbred, an Arabian, and three Appaloosas moved around in the car. They spun around quickly to face him. The large, black thoroughbred snorted and wheeled back and forth while the others stood more quietly. Rowdy moved forward to clip on their halter ropes. The thoroughbred charged for the open door. Smoke met him with an outstretched neck and bit him hard on his chest. The thoroughbred screamed and backed up, trembling.

Hank was surprised at the dapple horse's reaction.

"I wondered about you, and I was right," he muttered softly to Smoke as he moved around him carefully to help Rowdy. He hooked ropes on the other four horses with no problem and quickly led them out of the car. The thoroughbred was snorting and throwing its head as Rowdy tried to calm it. It was still trembling when he led it out of the car and onto the platform. Hank was already mounted, and Rowdy handed him the rope to the thoroughbred while he took the ropes of the other four horses. Hank had his saddle on the Kansas horse and Patch was trailing behind.

"Patch will follow," Hank told Rowdy. He hates to be left behind."

Rowdy nodded and then pointed at the thoroughbred. "Let's keep that black away from Smoke on the trip home," he commented as he mounted. The two men wheeled their mounts around and headed west. They stopped for water and then rode at a mile-eating lope until the new horses showed a little fatigue. They slowed to a trot and kept that pace for about an hour before they walked to cool them down.

Smoke wasn't tired and was anxious to go, but Rowdy didn't want to get the other horses lathered up. They were in good condition but that didn't necessarily mean they could hold the same pace as the range horses.

Rowdy pulled his coat closer and thought again of Beth. "Good thing she thought to pack us jackets the other day," he muttered wryly to himself.

They turned down the lane to the R4 about two hours later. Rudy, Maribelle, and Beth all ran out to greet Rowdy.

As he wrapped his family in a bear hug, Rowdy raised his eyes to the sky and thanked the Lord for giving him this life. *I'm finally home*, he thought as he kissed Beth and pulled the children in for another hug.

"So did you miss me?" he teased Beth with a drawl as he kissed the top of her head.

She smiled up at him and started to answer but Maribelle interrupted.

"Momma was afraid, but Rudy pertected us," she declared proudly as she beamed at her big brother.

Rudy blushed and Beth explained, "There were some coyotes bothering the chicken coop last night, and Rudy shot one of them. He has a steady hand for a ten-year-old boy."

Beth was smiling proudly at Rudy, and Rowdy turned to look at him with surprise.

"With your old gun?" he asked.

Rudy nodded seriously. "Pa only gave me one bullet at a time, an' I had to come home with somethin'. I learned to be a purty good shot."

Rowdy put his arm around Rudy's shoulders. "Good job, Son," he said softly. "Now how about you help me with these horses."

They led the new horses to the corral, and Rowdy pulled the saddle off Smoke to rub him down. Rudy brought him the currycomb and a rag. Hank did the same with Patch and the Kansas horse he had ridden.

The three of them talked as Rowdy showed Rudy the proper way to cool down a horse.

Rowdy looked up at Rudy as he checked Smoke's shoes. "So, what are you going to call your new horse?"

"I get to keep him?" Rudy asked with big eyes.

"You sure do. He's all yours but he needs a name."

Rudy smiled shyly. "I think I'll call him Kansas since he came from down that way. I tried that name on him while you were gone, and he seemed to like it."

Rowdy nodded and smiled at the serious young man.

"A name is an important thing. It's always good to have a reason for what you choose," he agreed.

Hank had turned old Patch loose in the yard, and Smoke pulled to join him. As Smoke trotted out of the barn, he nickered at Sister and blew a couple of times when she came up to him.

Scout was playing in the kitchen when Rowdy walked through the door. As he began to wash his hands, he raised an eyebrow.

"A dog in the house?" he asked as sat down at the table.

Beth already had the children seated, and Maribelle looked up at him with big, brown eyes. "Scout, he was afraid of the coyotes last night," the little girl explained, "so we let him in the house. Then he slept with me, and I wasn't afraid either."

As she smiled at Rowdy, he felt his heart melt. He looked over her head at Beth, and she laughed softly.

Rowdy grinned. "Well, I guess I can't say no to that, now can I?"

As Maribelle's smile became larger, Rowdy forced himself to look serious.

"Okay, but you bathe him when he's dirty—*before* he gets on a bed—and you are both responsible for that. Not Beth and not me. And no dirty or wet feet in the house."

Both children nodded seriously.

Rowdy looked at Rudy. "How is Waldo?"

"He's doin' better. I check his leg ever' day an' rewrap the rag. I adjust the splint ever' time an' he doesn't seem to be bothered much by it. He's tryin' to put weight on it, so I had to make the splint longer."

Rowdy smiled as he tousled Rudy's hair.

"Good thinking, Rudy. We will look him over after supper."

As Hank stepped into the doorway, Rowdy pointed to an empty seat at the table.

"Wash up, Hank, and then sit down. You are about to eat some of the best food this side of the Mississippi." He grinned at Beth. "You might have to rethink how good the food was at the Rocking R after you taste Beth's cooking," he stated proudly with a wink and a big smile for his wife.

Hank moved quietly to the water basin and washed. As he sat down, Maribelle gave him a big smile.

"Welcome to the R4, Hank!" Beth exclaimed. "We are pleased to have you here, and I'm sure Rowdy will keep you busy."

Hank smiled at her and nodded as he scooted his chair forward.

Beth had a large meal prepared. As everyone joined hands around the dinner table, Rowdy thanked the Lord for his family and for their safety.

Then he stared at the platter of chicken in the middle of the table.

"Fried chicken! It sure is good to be home, Beth!" he exclaimed as he began to eat.

Beth laughed softly. She reached across the table to touch his hand.

"Welcome home, Rowdy," she whispered as she smiled at him, her pretty eyes covering him in love. "Welcome home!"

Made in the USA
Monee, IL
20 November 2024

70698589R00224